THIS edition, issued in 1956, is for
members of The Companion Book
Club, 8 Long Acre, London, W.C.2,
from which address particulars of
membership may be obtained. The
book is published by arrangement
with the original publishers,
William Heinemann Ltd.

GREEN AND PLEASANT LAND

"A blessed companion is a book" —JERROLD

GREEN AND PLEASANT LAND

*

DUDLEY BARKER

THE COMPANION BOOK CLUB
LONDON

Made and Printed in Great Britain
for the Companion Book Club (Odhams Press Ltd.)
by Odhams (Watford) Limited
Watford, Herts
S.956.ZT

PART ONE

1

A MAN in an old battle-blouse, cord trousers and thick boots, with the skin of his face and neck hardened by the weather, mounted the bulldozer and began to push stubbornly at the first sand dune. His name was Michael Callaghan, and he came from Liverpool, where his mother had recently died. Away to his right three other bulldozers, like a squadron in extended order, started to thrust at other dunes. The gulls overhead screamed at the novelty, calling in their comrades from the strip of cobalt sea beyond the dunes where three trawlers sprouted black cotton into the empty spring sky. Callaghan shoved his bulldozer back and forth at the sand, like an ant struggling timelessly with a twig. His ears were listening to the sound of his engine. His thoughts were of the girl he had picked up three nights earlier, and the flavour of beer upon her mouth, and the thickness of her thighs.

From the top of the next sand dune, where Charles Neve was standing with several other bareheaded young men in duffle coats, the whole scene was in view—the bulldozers levelling this long stretch of sand dunes by the sea, teams of men planting the uprights of an overhead bucket-line, others erecting small wooden huts, tentatively swinging mobile grabs, wiring the long perimeter of the site, or driving lorries whose tracks were already tracing in the sand the map of service roads.

For centuries until yesterday, reflected Neve, the dunes had lain emptily there, troubled only by the wind or the waves of a winter gale. From the day that the Norsemen ran their ships aground, until yesterday, nothing had happened there except the occasional bathing frolic of a family picnic party on a summer's afternoon or a couple making love in the twilight. To the people of the countryside the name of the place, Skelstrand, had meant an area of waste land by the sea: to the rest of the world, nothing. But now it would. Ships loading with ore in Spain or Scandinavia would name it as their destination. Men making ploughs, or frying-pans, or armaments, would hunger for its steel. Evil men silently weighing the risks of peace or war would put it into the scale—"now the British have also Skelstrand." And, if the issue were war, this stretch of sand that was to be Skelstrand would be circled upon the bomber pilot's target map.

"We ought to have had some sort of opening ceremony," said Appleton, standing beside him.

Neve laughed. "The mayor, and the band from the Boys' Brigade, and somebody cutting a white ribbon?"

"Good public relations. You technical chaps only worry about things like suitability of site or accessibility of labour. It never occurs to you that somebody owns the land, or somebody has common rights on it, or it pays tithe, or there's an oyster-bed off the coast, or any damn thing. You never think of the locals."

"Don't they want any progress?"

"Surely you know that progress is building the new gas-works where it obstructs the neighbour's view."

"Well, it's nothing to do with the locals," said Neve. "This is bigger than a parish pump. This is the survival of England."

"The locals don't think it's nothing to do with them," said Appleton, jerking his head towards the roadway behind them where, at one end of the new wire, some people from the town were standing and staring at the men and the machines on the sand dunes, as they would have stared at road repairers, or a funeral, or a girl mending stockings in the window of a dry cleaner's shop.

A shooting brake drew up at the roadside, and an elderly man and a girl got out.

"There's the squire and his lovely daughter—Colonel Melmoth of Shard, the place up the road at the back, beyond the cross-roads where the pub and the duck-pond are," said Appleton. "Even the pub's the Melmoth Arms. Local gentry, my boy. He owned the land we're building Skelstrand on."

"Fat lot of good it was to him, I should think," commented Neve.

"May be, but in the end we had to compulsory-purchase it. And did he raise hell! I've written more letters to that man than to my own mother. There's a special shelf for the Melmoth file at the Ministry. Can't say I blame him, privately. He didn't get much of a price."

Neve stared at the man and the girl, who had now left the people by the roadside and were walking slowly towards the sand dune. Walking as though they still owned it, he thought. There was the man, tall, straight back, tweeds, white moustache, stick, as though he had dressed up for the part. The girl too, tweeds, riding hat, slim ankles, stepping over the sand as though she were being photographed at a point-to-point for a fashion magazine.

"What's he done with his bloody spaniel? He ought to have a spaniel, eh?" whispered Appleton.

Colonel Melmoth came up the sand dune without panting, and said at the top, "You've started, I see."

Appleton was busily introducing him to the group. ". . . and this is Charles Neve, one of the engineers. I'm from Power and Industry myself."

"I have had correspondence with your Minister."

"And this is Bob Frame," added Appleton hastily, "architect. Bob, this is Colonel Melmoth. We bought the land from him."

"Stole the land," said Melmoth.

"Show him what we're going to build on it, Bob."

Frame turned slowly round, describing, in his soft, unhurried voice, the mill that would arise. The blast furnaces at this end, starting close behind Gulport's old harbour—a bit ugly, those, he admitted, but what could one do? The rail tracks and the marshalling yards, the overhead carriages, the vast dump for scrap, the tips and travelling grabs.

And then—with a long sweep of his arm—the huge sleek body of the mill itself, bay after bay, slashed with tall windows, a monster brooding silently on the sands beside the sea; and inside it the red-hot steel slabs, slapped and

10

buffeted by mechanical giants, patted into shape as a grocer pats butter, propelled through the rollers at ever increasing speeds, flattening out, racing forward. A hungry monster lying on its bed of sand and concrete, taking tremendous gulps of scrap and ore and coke into its jaws, and emitting from its tail, in a hot ribbon travelling at twenty-five miles per hour, a million tons of sheet steel a year. "Perhaps even more," said Frame, "perhaps even more."

"What colour will it be?" asked the girl suddenly, the first time she had spoken.

"My dear Elizabeth," replied her father, "surely you understand that it will be a nice glaring shade of red brick. Have you never seen a factory?"

Frame stared coolly at him. "Steel and pre-cast concrete," he briefly said. "The colour will be cream."

"That'll look nice," she said, "against the sea."

Neve stopped himself from demanding what in hell it mattered what it looked like. They could paint it bile-green or magenta and it would still be the finest hot-strip mill in the world. They were not trying for a landscape, but for a million tons of sheet steel a year; more, it would be much more, he was sure of that. Six Skelstrands, and they could defy the Russians and tell the Yanks to go to hell. But what would be the use of saying that to this girl? Her England was a water-colour, or a garden party at the vicarage. His was a pithead, a machine shop, a woman in a shawl coughing from her lungs in a damp room, or his father in a dole queue on a bleak November Friday. Skelstrand was his answer to that. Night-classes and engineering text-books, newspaper stuffed into leaking shoes, sweating on a construction gang, thrusting a bridge across a river with the Huns shelling from the Belgian hills—all that was part of his answer, part of his England, that Skelstrand would help make secure. But for her it was just scenery. He listened with contempt to Appleton: ". . . the economy of the country, the export drive, sir, the pressing needs of rearmament. Surely you see it."

"All I see," snapped Melmoth, "is a man on an ill-shaped mechanical horse knocking down the sand dunes over which my father shot, and his father before him, and where as a child I took my first walks with my nurse."

2

THE Town Hall, with its palladian front, faced the Stag across the Market Square of Gulport, in which, on this day, the canopies and trestle tables of the vendors of hardware and vegetables, stockings, paste jewellery, china, day-old chicks and pocket-knives were set up in rows. A pleasing, leisurely hum rose from the stalls. Country people descended from the single-deck green county buses which edged their way into the eastern corner of the square. The cattle market was in the pens near the railway station. A smell of fish gently invaded the square from the direction of the harbour.

In the saloon of the Stag the one topic was that they had started construction of the new steel mill out at Skelstrand. At the end of the bar where the town councillors were gathered—freshly arrived from the council meeting that morning—the conversation was excited. Had they not heard, that morning, something of what the project would mean to the town? A thousand houses needed on the other side of the estuary, just as a start, to hold the key workers who would be there in three years' time. The sewage plant multiplied thrice. The old Army camp taken over as a hostel for construction men. A fly-over bridge to replace the level-crossing. New docks—and part of the fishermen's quay to be sacrificed, there'd be a row about that. And the cost. Phew, that had made them sit up, that had brought it home to them! Most excited of all was Councillor Jimmy Jafet, a bustling, jovial little man, a lover of committees, advocate of a happier and better-planned world; and Labour, of course. In his excitement he was spending far more in the Stag that morning than he usually dared permit himself to do. For how, on his wages from the railway, could he expect to keep up with the plump tradesmen who formed most of the council? Elsie, with her mouth like the snap-fastener of her housekeeping purse, would tell him to keep away from drink. But Jimmy could not do that. It was not so much the taste of the beer, though that he loved, as the need to be one of the company, part of the maleness, the heavy shrewd faces, the thick hands clasping mugs, the voice-noise and the blue smoke against the dark oak walls, and the electric light on the row of bottles against the mirrors. And this morning there was something to celebrate. So Jimmy bought his round, put a match leisurely to his pipe and even listened to the smutty story which was absorbing Joe Wilkinson's attention—Joe with his neck poked eagerly forward, and then the cackle of laughter that wobbled his belly. That was how Joe Wilkinson got his fun: more than he ever did, thought Jimmy, with that thin wife of his, in the stiff bedroom over his ironmonger's shop, and not daring else more than to leer cautiously at the legs of a girl getting off a bus. But the dirtier the story, the more Joe loved it, displaying his manliness in his bubbling laugh.

At the other end of the bar were the newcomers, the Skelstrand lot—youngsters mostly but a few grey hairs, in flannel trousers and duffle coats forming up defensively against the regulars of the local. And the regulars very aware of them, sizing them up sidelong, but ignoring.

But none of that for Jimmy. He pushed his way to them, taking his pipe from his lips. "I'm Councillor Jafet. Everyone calls me Jimmy. You're the Skelstrand people, isn't it? We'll be meeting a lot, sure to. How are you? I hear you've started."

"Yes, we've started," replied one of them, nice-looking young chap, black hair, thick horn-rim glasses. "Glad to know you, Councillor." Appleton doing his usual P.R.O. stuff, thought Charles Neve, ingratiating the natives. He stared silently, holding his glass, at the little man bobbing up and down before them.

"Holy snakes, what a thing, eh? Made 'em sit up, I can tell you. Those chaps over there, they're the councillors—shopkeepers, most of 'em, been running this town for donkey's years, little Tory clique, small-minded. But now we'll get some changes, eh? I'm Labour.

"Planning, eh?" he said happily. "That's the thing.

Where would you get anything like this under capitalism?"

"America," said a tall, thin man, the architect.

"And in a sense, of course," added Appleton, "this is capitalism too. A curious mixture. The steel syndicate put up the plan and a good deal of the cash. They couldn't carry it through without Government backing, Marshall Aid, all sorts of things. So in comes the Ministry and the Corporation. But the steel barons still maintain it's their show, and in a way they're right. They still have a lot of say-so. Gazzard himself is moving down here to live."

"Gazzard?"

"Aye, he's chairman of the syndicate—Sir Russell Gazzard. Self-made chap, you know, millionaire of course, shrewd as they come. He wouldn't get far with Skelstrand without us, but we'd find it a devil of a job without him. It's a compromise, a partnership between public and private enterprise. Not a bad thing, compromise."

"I don't get it," said Jimmy. "What it comes to is—is steel nationalised or isn't it?"

Appleton grinned. "Ah, if only we knew!"

From the other end of the bar Joe Wilkinson called, "You lunching here, Jimmy? They want to know how many."

Jimmy, putting on a bright smile, turned and shook his head. "Got to get back on the job, Joe," he said. Dearly he would have loved to join the Stag lunch that followed every council meeting, gossiping into the afternoon. But four and sixpence and another round of drinks—out of the question. In the world Jimmy wanted, a man who devoted himself to public work would automatically get a lunch in the pub afterwards. He stared unhappily at the dark panelling of the saloon, where the light glowed in upon it from the door. And then he saw the doctor come in.

"Chap there I've got to talk to," he said, turning back to the Skelstrand group, and now cheerful and bright as ever, "but we'll be seeing lots of each other, eh? Sure to. Well, good-bye, and good luck to you. You're doing a great job."

The group nodded good-bye to him, and he gave them

14

the thumbs-up as he turned to push his way across the room.

"Odd little man," said Appleton. "The primitive socialist. But he might well be very useful. What'll you have, same again?"

Jimmy worked his way across to the doctor, nudged his elbow. "Have you been in to see her this morning, Doc?"

Dr. Irons looked down on him, turning his huge body slowly, smiling in recognition. "Hullo there, Jimmy my boy. Yes, I've been in to see her. How's your glass? What is it, bitter?"

Jimmy nodded his thanks, the doctor reaching across to the bar. "What d'you think, Doc?"

"Well, Jimmy," said the doctor, handing him the beer-can with the gentle movements of a big man, "she's not too good, you know."

"You don't think . . . ?"

"It wouldn't hurt her to go away for a spell. She needs the treatment, Jimmy, you know that."

"But she's not happy away," he muttered. "It isn't as if she does any harm, and Elsie looks after her proper. This morning was an accident. It doesn't cure her, does it?"

"No," admitted the doctor softly, "we know it won't cure her. We all know that, Jimmy."

Jimmy nodded sadly. Then, feeling in his pocket, offered the doctor a return beer. But Irons shook his head. "No time to-day, Jimmy. I've got to go out to Shard. I'd ask you to lunch with me, but I'm eating out there."

"Oh, I've got to get to work anyway," replied the other, putting down his beer and brisking his shoulders.

"Sure, Jimmy. No hurry, no hurry."

Councillor Jafet came out of the pub into the spring sunshine. The market was quieter, people gone off to eat. He turned to walk slowly in the direction of the harbour, thinking of his small house and his two sisters—Elsie, the prim, sour one who ran it, worked hard, he admitted, spun his wages out somehow into respectability; and Kathy, the gentle, simple one, who never cried except when they took her away for treatment in a "home." And no harm in her, he defended to himself, never violent, but loving rather,

15

loving all little and helpless things, chickens especially, and sparrows, or frogs. Never did anything worse than wandering out into the streets and taking her clothes off, innocent as a baby, and funny, really, if it weren't so pathetic. He came out from a narrow walled lane on the brightness of the fishermen's quay, and stopped to look at it with pleasure —cobbles, the satisfying slopes of masts and funnels, patches of bright orange paint, the black-tarred timbers of the water-front buildings, trawling-nets spread to dry on tall posts; and, beyond, the blue water running out through the estuary, marker buoys dipping in the race, and the yellow streak of the farther shore. His own town, his own place, and he helped to run it. He walked along the quay, humming.

A bunch of fishermen stopped him as he went. "Hey, Jimmy, what's all this about them wanting some of our quay for the steel works? 'Tain't true, is it? Can't be, eh?"

"There was something about it at council," he admitted. "The new docks go beyond, but seems they'll have to over-lap a bit. You chaps know the tides and the waters."

"If they started to muck us up. . . ."

"Bloody bastards, they can't do that. 'Sbeen fishing 'ere since Gulport was built."

"If they take this quay"—this from Ted Flowers, one of the skippers—"where do we go then, eh?"

"Now, take it easy," said Jimmy, "I'm watching for you, ain't I? You know me. There's got to be progress, and that'll mean changes, can't be helped. But no one's going to suffer, this is going to make us all. You know me, mates; d'you think I'd let you down?"

"You're all right, Jimmy. But some of the other buggers. . . ."

"I'm watching," smiled Jimmy, "I'm watching all right."

He moved on past the end of the dock, along the track over the sand at the edge of the water, till he came to the very point, from which he could look along the coast towards Skelstrand. His heart glowed when he saw, above the distant dunes, the tips of a couple of travelling cranes. Machinery. He could faintly hear the sound of the bull-dozers.

He climbed a dune and picked a spot sheltered from the wind. He felt good. He felt fine. The world was a grand, adventurous place, now being organized upon sound Labour principles.

From the bottom of his jacket pocket he pulled out the thick cheese sandwich which Elsie had cut for him that morning, and, in the lonely sunshine between sand, sea and sky, Councillor Jafet contentedly chewed his lunch.

3

DR. GILBERT IRONS got into his car to drive to Shard. He made his way through the muddle of traffic in the town, waited at the level-crossing, where he lit his pipe, then took the straight road with hills on one hand, dunes and the sea upon the other, the green and the duck-pond and the pub of the hamlet, and at last the tall gates open on to the worn drive, cows and a couple of horses in the park raising their heads at the noise of his car, and Shard itself, long, dark red, tall chimneys, the rooks calling irritably from the elms.

He was, as usual, late, and they were waiting for him in the green sitting-room, the windows open on to the lawn. Melmoth gave him a glass of sherry. He nodded to Elizabeth, and said, "Good morning, Dorothy, hullo, Roger," to the Hentys. Irons had never more than tolerated the parson, though he sang joyfully in his choir every Sunday—singing was always joyful to him, the deep bass notes booming from his frame as from an organ. Dorothy, of course, everybody loved.

"Elizabeth and I went over to Skelstrand this morning," said Melmoth. "Heart-breaking. Men and machines knocking the dunes down, barbed wire, ugliness and noise. It's like an invading army."

"They're all over Gulport too," chuckled Irons. "The Stag was full of them. Nice enough chaps, I thought."

"One of them, an architect, told me what they would have when the thing was finished. An inferno."

"They say it will bring a lot of work into the town," said the Rev. Henty, feebly.

"If only it were an invasion," continued Melmoth, ignoring him, "one could fight that. But this is an invasion of ourselves by ourselves. A self-mutilation, that's what is so horrible. And for what purpose?"

"They tell me the country needs more steel," said Henty, worried.

"But what for? To build puny armaments for a war that must destroy us if we ever embark on it, and which nineteenth-century diplomacy would have arranged to avoid quite privately and without any fuss. To build motor-cars which are killing our children at a rate which no war has ever yet attained. To make tractors which are crumbling the top-soil of our fields into dust, and starving them of horse-manure so that in a generation we shall have ruined the most fertile land in the world. To make refrigerators so that all our food will be stale and tasteless, and cinematograph and television machines to turn us into a nation of passive spectators. And the most curious argument of all is that we need steel to make employment—to keep everybody hard at work making these useless, horrible things, so that they can themselves buy more of them until the whole thing becomes a fiendish sort of roundabout, an hysterical civilization chasing its own tail, like America. Oh, my dear fellow, what this country needs is not more steel, but more quietness."

Irons chuckled. "When you get wound up, Henry, I understand why all the medieval Melmoths went on Crusades."

"Deflate me," said Melmoth, smiling, "I rely on you for that. I rant, don't I? Forgive me. Have another sherry."

"And what do you think of it all, Liz?" asked Irons.

"Don't tell my father," she said, "but this morning I thought it was bringing a marvellous lot of handsome young men into the town."

Mrs. Cushion came to the door and announced lunch. As they went in, Irons pondered that this was what was really being challenged, this graciousness of an old house, a meal served in a panelled room with a few darkening paintings and chairs bought a couple of centuries before, and the

18

dignified figure of Melmoth standing to carve at the side-table where his father and his grandfather had stood. And now it was ended. It had really ended a quarter of a century before, but the shadow of it lingered. Irons, whose childhood had been spent in the Sheffield slums where his irascible father had conducted a busy, heart-breaking, semi-bankrupt practice, had no inborn sense of gentry. But for thirty years he had lived with it, grumbled at its obstinacy in acknowledging change, scorned its superiority, and come to love it. The English squire, pig-headed but gentle, with the parson and the doctor at his table; it had the sadness of some polite old forgotten book that had once expressed its times.

"All the same," he cheerfully expounded, "Liz hit the nail on the head, as usual. The sudden arrival of all those handsome young men in the town—there'll be thousands of them, most of them neither handsome nor young, but all men. It has started already. Have you heard the stories of the labourers they've put into the old camp?"

Henty cleared his throat, warning.

"But that's your department, isn't it, morals?" asked the doctor. "I come in later. I have already stitched three broken heads and set a shoulder."

"A fight?" asked Elizabeth, interested.

"They do practically nothing else, once the drink is in them. A lot of 'em are Irish. They moved the first batch into the old camp yesterday, and by evening they had picked a little pub near-by, in Buckingham Street, the Duke's Head, old Charlie Hyslop runs it. Of course, he'll make a fortune, if his nerve lasts. He was almost in tears this morning. I advised him to get a new till, and hire a couple of chuckers-out."

"If they bring a few of them up before the Bench," said Melmoth from the head of the table, "we shall know what to do with them."

Henty came in with, "These men who have come to build the factory, there will be a good many of them, I suppose. It offers us a great opportunity, you know. Perhaps I could start a mission, or hold some special services."

He looked across at his wife, seeking help. She briefly replied, "There will certainly be plenty to do."

"Sometimes these things that look like disasters," he wandered on, "prove to be the very chance that God offers. But then, a lot of them Irish, you said? Oh, dear, I suppose that means R.C. That makes it very difficult. . . ."

Melmoth leaned forward. He wanted to make his own attitude quite clear. "I am fighting the whole thing."

The Crusader, gloated Irons to himself, the blood showing itself, the Englishness of refusing to see a lost battle, the relish of being right in among the Saracens, hand to hand, horse blowing, sword flailing—admirable, pathetic.

"Wherever there is a chance of legal obstruction, I shall take it. Wherever local feeling rises against it, I shall encourage that feeling. Yes, Gilbert, I can see it in your eye, I'm ranting again. Mrs. Cushion, give the doctor some more pudding."

"But, Henry," said Elizabeth doubtfully—she always called him that, "have you the right to? I know you have been half joking, but seriously. What are you attacking? A development, a lot of people who are doing their best to make the country strong again. And what are you defending? Us—the quiet, comfortable life, the privilege, I don't know how to say it."

"Oh, we're finished, I know that. We're like the dinosaur, we haven't evolved. But even the dinosaur must have put up a struggle before he went under."

She had the same worry about her father, thought Irons, listening, that he had: lest he get gripped by an obsession.

"Let him fight, Liz," he advised, wanting to stop the conversation. "Every man must have a hobby when he gets older. Water-colour sketching or fishing would have been more restful, and cheaper—he'll spend all your patrimony on lawsuits, and you'll finish up a pauper, and have to get a job in the steel mill in the end."

Melmoth smiled. "Oh, we're paupers already. The patrimony went on the new pigsties, and repairs to a few cottages, and a couple of pounds of tobacco. They'll take whatever remains in death duties. We were eaten up long ago, we're just ghosts. But we'll haunt 'em, eh?"

Ghosts in a world after two wars, pondered the doctor to himself, which they had fought and won to their own destruction. He glanced under his eyelids at Elizabeth, sitting where the sunlight from the windows illumined her hair against the dark panelling, and guessed that she was thinking, as he was, of the futile gallantry of men; the gallantry of her brother who had gone cheerfully off in his light-blue uniform to defend this sort of life, and by his own death high up in a bright sky on a May morning had ensured its extinction. If Peter had been here now—but what was the use of such speculation? thought Irons, staring at his plate, upon which he was idly chivvying with his spoon the last piece of pudding.

4

It was Bernard Appleton who first got the news of the fishermen's charter. He was called to the phone while they were at breakfast in Tregonwell, the boarding-house into which the group of them had settled, one of a tall Victorian terrace with an endwise view of the harbour, and a small unkempt garden at the back that led down to the shore of the estuary, so that the sharp breeze that entered the back windows collided with the fish-smell that permeated the front.

Appleton came back from the telephone and sat down opposite Charles Neve. "God," he said, "that's torn it!" There was a veil of worry on his face, which had already looked troubled enough—pale and, behind his thick spectacles, heavy black smudges beneath his eyes. But that was because of his wife. Appleton and his wife were a pitiful sort of joke to them all. He was terrified to let her out of his sight. Laura Appleton was a dark-haired woman with pouting, dissatisfied lips and gibbous breasts. Appleton's nervous obsession was to satisfy her, to exhaust her with love, to concentrate her upon him. Neve had the room adjoining theirs, and he went to sleep to the murmur of Appleton's endeavours, the grunts and the bedcreakings and the low, urgent mutter of his voice.

"Well?" asked Neve across the breakfast table. "What's up?"

"That was a call from Gazzard's office. Trouble. Those fishermen, and the defence committee they've got up, led by that skipper, what's his name, Flowers. They've turned up some old charter nobody knew about, Henry VII or something, giving them that quay in perpetuity—you know, 'to all ye fishermen of our beloved manor of Gulport,' that sort of thing."

"So what? It can be altered, can't it?"

"Of course it can be altered, but, my God, the trouble it'll be. And the time it'll take, and the money. Probably need an Act of Parliament."

"What do they want," asked Neve, "steel or wet cod?"

"Point is, somebody's trying to pull a fast one. Gazzard has the tip that they're going to apply in the High Court for an injunction to restrain."

"Meaning?"

"If they get it, we could be held up for months. Heron is coming down this morning."

"And who is Heron?" asked Neve.

"Gazzard's right-hand man, surely you've heard of him, used to be an M.P., smart fellow, but wants watching. I wish I could talk to the Permanent Secretary."

"Ring him up."

"Don't be a damn fool, it's half-past eight, there won't be anybody in the shop for hours yet. We'd better have a conference."

"You have one," said Neve, folding his napkin, "I've got work to do."

"But what's the use of going on when the whole thing may have to be altered?"

"That's your headache. Anyway, it can't be altered. The docks have to go where they are planned, fishermen or no bloody fishermen. Ten thousand conferences won't alter the tides in that estuary, and you can't slew the mill round, because there isn't room."

As he got his car out, and drove towards Skelstrand, Neve thought of Appleton with contemptuous pity. How could a man tie himself up and deliver himself over to a woman, especially a bitch like that? It was indecent. When Neve needed a woman, he found one, and afterwards dismissed the thing from his mind with distaste; a necessity, but a nuisance. It was mostly when he was idle, and bored. During, for instance, the months of waiting in London, hanging about for this project to begin, he had picked up with a typist in one of the contractors' offices. She had rooms in Bayswater, and he went there intermittently. She was a randy little piece, dark skin, brown eyes, rounded hips, a faint shadow of hair upon her upper lip. At first all was well. They gave each other what they wanted, and that was that. But then she started wanting to introduce him to her friends, and for him to sentimentalize with her, and writing him long letters in a childish hand in which she tried to echo, in trite and deliberately sensual words, the pleasures of their meetings. So he cut off. And luckily Skelstrand then got going, and erased all thought of her from his mind.

As he pulled his car off the road on to the site, he gazed about him with calm delight. It was a fine, clear morning. On the one side rose the gentle blueness of the hills, on the other lay the clean glitter of the sea. And between them, Skelstrand, the job. It did not yet look much. A few huts and lorries, the overhead bucket-line, the drawling bull-dozers, the cranes gently swinging, the rig of the drills probing for water, the gangs of men.

Yet Neve was already beginning to get that wonderful feeling of a machine that starts to function, its joints and wheels gradually fitting together, beginning to turn in a rough harmony. He had to work with coarse material, men who were little more than animals, idle men, cunning and cantankerous men; but construction engineers always had to. His bridge-building company in France had been much the same—throw-outs, roughnecks, drunk and violent any-where near a town; but when they got under fire, sweating and cursing, brutally indifferent, they flung the bridges across. He had a similar problem here. While there was nothing but a stretch of sand dunes to be levelled, with some vague purpose of building some sort of factory, they took little interest in it. Later, when the thing began to shape, when there was something to see, it would be easier.

Strictly, they were not his men at all. The jobs on the site had been let out to sub-contractors, each of whom had put up his own little wooden office, erected his own title-board, and brought his own gang. But Neve had centralized the authority, insisted on one canteen for all, one hostel, one first-aid post. His own office, a portable wooden bungalow, dominated the straggling colony of sheds. Standing at his draughtsman's desk in the window, with the site-map covering the wall behind him, the survey and the plans rolled on bare wooden shelves, the letter-files, telephone, drawing instruments, bottled samples of subsoil work-charts, he had something of the feeling of a captain on his bridge. This was to be his home for three or four years. Now it seemed to stand high up over the flat plain of sand. In the end it would be a tiny, unnoticed outbuilding in the shadow of towering concrete cliffs. But it would always be the heart, the headquarters, the first to go up, the last to be dismantled when, the job done, the machinery for doing it was cleared away.

Cross, his works foreman, came in.

"Well, Bill?" said Neve. Cross and he were on those terms, and had been for years; he had been his sergeant-major, and when the war ended he hung on to him. He was a ponderous, sleepy man with a timid voice, but unusual muscular strength. The incident that Neve best remembered took place one cold morning in Belgium. They had skidded up through the mud, cursing and floundering, behind the shelter of some trees, until they came to the bank of a small river, where the bridge had been blown. They had started to work the Bailey across when the shelling unexpectedly started; the hills beyond were supposed to be clear of Jerry, but evidently they were not. The men scattered, but a near miss overturned a lorry, trapping one of them by the leg; he lay with his head tucked into the mud, and Neve thought at first he was dead. Then Sergeant-Major Cross strolled casually forward, not hurrying himself, ignoring the bursts, got his great paws under the lorry, and gently lifted it for sufficient time for the man to crawl away. Cross carried him back to the ditch behind the trees. Neve recommended him for a Military Medal, but all he got was a Mention.

"Well, Bill?" Neve repeated.

"Not so good, guv," said the foreman, standing there placidly, slowly blinking his eyes. Whatever the weather, Cross always wore a leather waistcoat beneath his old jacket.

"What's up?"

"There's some rumour got about that the job's off."

"Who says so? Off, my foot. They're having some trouble back at the office about the dock-site—local fishermen making a shindy. But what the hell's it got to do with us? Of course the job's not off."

"Wish you'd put that round, guv," said Cross. "They've not shook down yet, and it's unsettled them. And there's a couple of bastards making the most of it."

Uh-huh, thought Neve, here it comes. You begin with a crowd of nameless figures in thick trousers, old shirts, woollen caps, soiled boots, all looking alike, all bunched up together. And then gradually they began to sort out into men with names and stories, characters you could rely on, characters you had to watch, and somewhere in the pile the genuine trouble-makers.

"Who's at the bottom of it, Bill?" he asked.

"His name's Papelian, he's on the foundations, concrete-mixer. He wants to see you; I've got him outside now."

"They made him a shop steward?"

The foreman nodded, blinking his eyes. "'Course," he said.

"Okay, bring him in. What's the trouble, canteen?"

Cross nodded again. "That's the way they always start."

Neve settled himself in a chair for the interview. He could not remember who Papelian was, and even when he came in he did not recollect him. He was a short, stringy man with dark skin, thin lips, angry brown eyes, and a general air of cockiness, assurance.

"Glad to meet you, Papelian," Neve said. "It takes a while to get to know everybody. You from London? On the concrete, aren't you? Well, it's not going badly so far. Now, what can I do for you?"

"I'm here on behalf of the men," the other replied. He spoke briskly, confidently—not insolently, but with the impression that defiance was not far behind. "They've made me a shop steward."

"The foreman tells me you've got some complaints about the canteen."

"That is so," replied Papelian, almost grinning. He knew as well as Neve that this was only sparring, almost a courtesy, serving notice of the tussle to come. He pulled out a piece of paper on which he had solemnly written notes, and read off the complaints, all trivialities: this man's dinner had been served cold, that man's cake was stale, the tea was too weak, why couldn't they have hot soup in the morning? there was no paper in the toilet, and so on. Like schoolboys, thought Neve. But he made a note of each complaint as solemnly as Papelian read it, both of them aware that the thing was a farce. Neve promised to speak to the canteen manager.

"He says he'll have no meetings in the canteen, and no notice-board."

"It's for eating, ain't it?" asked Cross, blinking his eyes slowly, "not politics."

"Who's talking of politics? What the men want is the right to do what they like in their own canteen—if it is their own canteen. That's what we want to know. What is it, the bosses' place or the men's place?"

Neve nodded to Cross to be silent, and said smoothly, "I'll give you a straight answer to that, right at the beginning. It's the men's place, Papelian. I expect reasonable consideration for the canteen manager, no interference with his working arrangements, and no keeping him there until all hours. But, apart from that, the men can hold any meetings they like there, in their own time, and you can put up whatever notices or posters you want. I'll speak to the manager."

"Well, I'm glad to hear that," muttered Papelian. Neve chuckled internally. One round to him.

When he had gone, Neve asked the foreman, "I suppose he's a Commie?"

"He's a bastard."

"Ah well, just so long as I know who and where they are. Watch him, Bill, that's all."

He settled to his letters, looking up every now and then through the window, to keep an eye on the site—as though, he scoffed at himself, there would be any perceptible change from one hour to the next. But he could never cure himself of the habit of gazing at odd moments at the job, gathering it all in with his eyes as though he could get his arms right round it, hold it to him, nurture its progress; just as an ardent gardener will happily contemplate a seedling, imagining in advance the fruit.

He was thus engaged when the door of his office opened, and a head poked round it. An odd head, stout cheeks, red nose, hair shaved like a summer German, a comedian's mask of a head.

"Mr. Neve?" inquired the head.

"That's me."

"Pomeroy," said the head. "Christened Eustace. Who names this child? I name this child. Eustace Pomeroy, and nothing to be done about it."

The head advanced into the room, followed by a long body in tweed jacket and grey trousers, followed in turn by a large Alsatian bitch which minced to the centre of the room and lay down, head on paws, ears pricked, patient, waiting.

"Borough engineer," said Pomeroy. "I thought we'd better meet. No sooner thought than done. When? No time like the present. So into the old car, and out to the site. Presto, here we are."

"Glad to know you. Have a seat."

"Big job here, eh? Big changes to the little town, I'll say. Councillors wag their heads and look solemn. What's to become of the fishermen? How about the holiday visitors? Will all those rough labourers put our daughters in the family way? But then, look at the rateable value. Ha-ha. And the Government puts up the money. Small minds, Mr. Neve, small minds. But you and me, we understand. Progress. Up with the mill and churn out the steel. Up with the houses and double the sewage disposal. Brother engineer, fellowship of the blue print. Shake."

Neve laughed and shook hands.

"Big job for you," continued Pomeroy. "Big job for me too. Housing estates, water supplies, nag, nag, nag with Ministry. And no rise in wages. Same old pay, same old housekeeping worries for Mrs. P. But it's the life, ain't it?"

"Wouldn't have any other."

"Wouldn't mind going abroad, though, eh? Engineering —goes without saying. See a bit of the world. You been abroad much? Ah well, during the war. Job advertised the other day in Uganda, free house, twelve-fifty rising to seventeen-seventy, home leave every third year, black servants by the score, bit hot, though. Roads and buildings."

"Sounds interesting."

"Chap from Birmingham got it," said Pomeroy sadly.

Neve offered to take him round the site. "Not much to see yet, of course," he said. "We're in that slow, dreamy starting period, where nothing shows. You know how it is. Not in our stride yet. We haven't even got any troubles, though that won't be long now. I left the office wallahs this morning worrying their guts out about some damn fishermen's charter that can muck up the new docks, and when I got down here the first Commie showed his hand and had a preliminary go at me."

"Goo' lor!"

Neve laughed. "They'll try anything, of course. A steel-mill, man; imagine how that looks to them. And you can't keep 'em out, because you never know who they all are. Anyway, I'd rather have 'em where I can see 'em."

"Nothing like that in Gulport, so far as I know," mused Pomeroy. "New experience for us, that. Red hand stuff, eh?"

"Leave me to handle them," Neve reassured him. "They can't stop us. We'll have strikes, and go-slows, and scandals stirred up, and probably a bit of sabotage. They'll try everything. But in three to four years' time there'll be the finest hot-strip mill in the world on this stretch of sand, if I have to bust all hell open."

They were standing by the edge of the first stretch of concrete, with the mechanical shovels dipping and rising just beyond, the buckets clanking on the wire overhead, the bulldozers droning in the distance as their echelon advanced. The Alsatian's head was pointed at some gulls, accustomed now to the disturbance, strutting idly over a nearby cleared space, rising now and then to scream at each other. There was no hurry about the scene, just a leisurely pace, gradual, inevitable. But up to schedule, and a bit ahead of it, Neve assured himself.

Then Pomeroy pointed out to him a woman walking towards them across the stretch from the nearest dunes. "Local squire's daughter," he said. "Nice girl, great fun, friend of the wife's. Her old man's a bit sticky. Gentleman, but snappish." Neve looked up. Of course, he recalled, the water-colour girl who had been there with her father on the day the bulldozers started. He was irritated. What the hell was she doing there, walking casually across the place as though it still belonged to the family, with a flop-eared dachshund running from her heels. Not that it mattered, of course. Lots of people walked through. But it irritated him. Damn sauce.

"That's another lot who'd cause trouble if they could," he grunted.

"Who, the Melmoths? No, really?"

"It doesn't matter," he said. "They can't. The old squires. I'd swap one Commie for a dozen of 'em."

Pomeroy looked shocked. "Come on now, be friends," he urged. "Nice people, good sorts. Hi, Elizabeth!" She smiled at him as she came up. "Come and meet the engineer," he called, and then, as she reached them, "This is Mr. Neve, great chap, you'll like him. This is Miss Melmoth, from Shard."

Neve nodded.

"We haven't exactly met," she said, "but we've seen each other. Weren't you here when my father . . . ?"

"I was."

"Yes, I thought you were," she said, disconcerted.

"You ought to know each other," Pomeroy protested. "Tell you what, a party. You coming over Saturday, Elizabeth? Good, that's right, Venetia expecting you. Come along too, eh, Neve? Little house, Bridgnorth Street, few

29

drinks, sausage rolls. Doc Irons'll do the singing. We all do
the washing-up. How about it, eh? Six thirty. No fuss, no
dressing-up. New citizens, Elizabeth, got to entertain 'em.
Good-neighbour policy. I'll round a few more up: Jimmy
Jafet, Skipper Flowers, the town clerk, old George from the
Stag. I don't suppose your dad'd come?"

"I don't suppose he would," replied Elizabeth, smiling.

"Never mind, party all the same. How about it, Neve, you
come, eh?"

"It's very kind of you," said Neve, looking at the girl.
"I'd like to."

"And bring some of the other boys from your outfit,"
urged Pomeroy happily, "real get-together, Gulport old and
new. Saturday, six thirty."

<h2 style="text-align:center">5</h2>

THE arrival of Robert Heron had everything about it to
dismay Appleton. He felt like a juggler, engrossed in a most
intricate manipulation, when somebody smilingly flicks
away three or four of the balls. A neat analogy, he told
himself; he loved a clever phrase, a paradox, an ingenious
clue in *The Times* crossword puzzle, at which he habitually
peered at odd moments during his day.

There was the Ministry, which he formally represented,
which could be thrown into the wildest contradictions by
a parliamentary question, or a chance decision of some
damn-fool committee, or the indigestion of an elderly
Under-Secretary plodding daily back and forth between
his office and Wimbledon. There was the steel syndicate,
with that old fox Gazzard at the head of it and the smooth
Heron to do his dirty work, pretending to co-operate,
mouthing platitudes about the national interest, but merci-
lessly seeking every advantage, palpably hating the Ministry
and all its works, plotting to grab everything that was offered
and to turn it to the advantage of profits, dividends, controlled by the power of money. At Skelstrand itself there
were the contractors and the sub-contractors to be juggled
by Appleton into the common pattern, each pig-headed

bunch fighting for its own interest, and to hell with the rest; and the technicians, men like Charles Neve, with their cold, logical minds working like machines, unable to understand why anything that was necessary should not at once become possible, and brushing aside as trivial all the human relationships and power-struggles which impeded the simple performance of a mechanical operation.

Appleton laughed sadly. Local opinion in Gulport was one of the most erratic balls that he had to manipulate into his juggler's pattern—local politics, local prejudices, local power such as that of the obstinate old squire out at Shard; trivial things that, unless carefully handled, could wreck the whole project.

These were the chief of the many responsibilities which pressed upon Appleton, wearied him, and delighted him. As he frequently told himself, and occasionally others, it was a creditable load for a man not yet quite in his forties. He had always accomplished things at a younger age than his contemporaries—the scholarship to a grammar school, then one to Oxford, the first in Modern Greats, the early selection for responsibility in the Civil Service. Looking forward, he could see the K.C.B. The hope consoled him for the thought that, had he put all that energy and success into industry, he would by now have been a rich man. Though, as a matter of fact, he had found out that Charles Neve, for instance, earned little more than he. But Neve was single, whereas Appleton had Laura.

It had been a war-time marriage. He was in the Ministry of Aircraft Production, and she came in as a temporary clerk. Around her circled always a group of squadron leaders, lieutenant-colonels, commanders, lean and lithe young men in uniform with the ribbons of gallantry on their chests, to whom Appleton mentally crawled, in his black coat, toiling long hours with the bumf on his desk, trembling in the privacy of his flat at the nightly blitz. It gave him a great kick when she smilingly accepted his long-considered invitation to dinner. He took her to a quiet place, very expensive, where uniforms were not prolific. Afterwards she knew of a cellar where they could dance, or rather shuffle in a crowd. She fitted herself to him like a clamp, and when he pressed his hand tentatively against her breast, gazed up at him with a misty smile, her black hair two columns on either side of her pale temples. As they got into the taxi, the all-clear siren sang. Without question or answer he took her to his rooms. Three days later he asked her to marry him. There was no possibility of leave from the Ministry, and their honeymoon was a thing of underground restaurants, night taxis, black-out curtains beyond which the bombs exploded unheeded while he toiled with her upon the bed, waking to the grey all-clear of the morning with his eyes yellowed and his shoulders furrowed with the marks of fingernails. During the day he caught mere glimpses of her at the Ministry, surrounded with the customary circle of lieutenant-commanders, group captains and majors. Ever since, when she was with him, he felt himself to be measured continually against every other man they met; but that was better than to have her out of his sight.

On this morning of Robert Heron's arrival, Appleton took her in the car to the station to meet him. Appleton fidgeted nervously on the platform, nodding to the ticket-collector (who kept on smiling at him), glancing at his wrist-watch, making conversation that he knew to be fatuous and that Laura received with indifference. He was relieved when at last the train arrived and Heron stepped from his carriage, the porter instinctively jumping to take his raw-hide bag. His greeting was affable and brisk towards Appleton, flattering towards Laura. Appleton felt, or thought he felt, that she responded gladly to the man. Yet nothing was said but the banalities of greeting.

At the station entrance Heron stopped and shook hands with the ticket-collector. "Councillor Jafet, isn't it?" he asked. Appleton swore at himself for not having recognized him. That was the sort of thing in which he always failed. and the Herons always succeeded.

"Good heavens," he said, "I never noticed you.'

"Oh, Jimmy's a great old enemy of mine," smiled Heron; "denounced me from every platform in the county, haven't you, Jimmy? And how are your sisters?"

"Fine, fine, Mr. Heron. What brings you here? Not standing for Parliament again?" The little man was beaming with pleasure at being recognized.

"No, no, Jimmy," said Heron, "I'm done with all that now. Business this time, my boy. We're on the same side now. I hear you're a great advocate of the new mill—oh, we hear these things in London, you know." The little man was immensely tickled. "You and I must get together, Jimmy. We've got things to talk about. Can you spare me a lunch?"

"Why yes, Mr. Heron. Bygones be bygones, eh?"

"Funny little chap that," said Heron to Laura when they were in the car. "Little busybody of a fellow, full of cock-eyed ideas, but a useful man on a platform, as I know to my cost. And they like him down here, they listen to him. We'll have him on our side in this."

"You've got a memory," she said.

Smug, self-satisfied oaf, thought Appleton, slick, smooth operator. What was so irritating was that the bastard had in fact remembered the stupid little councillor, whereas he simply had not recognized him.

It was in this mood of anger with himself, which made him the more vulnerable, that Appleton took Heron into the office, and they began the conference on the fishermen business. Half a dozen of the others were there, sitting smoking round the table, at the head of which Heron automatically seated himself.

"Now, gentlemen," he began, "briefly, we are up against a local opposition which has managed to get hold of some ancient charter giving fishermen's rights on the quay in perpetuity—a document which our famous planners seem to have overlooked."

Appleton said nothing. He was waiting his opportunity for a dig, but this was not it.

"The legal position has some curious characteristics," said old Hardcross, the lawyer. He launched into a long, wandering discourse, mumbling on and on, as he always did. Heron listened to him with patience.

"Thank you, Mr. Hardcross," he said, when the other had finished. "I think I can say on behalf of all of us that we are grateful for that explanation of the legal position. Mr. Hardcross has shown us, in the most lucid fashion, exactly where we stand legally."

"It's a highly interesting position," agreed Hardcross, sitting back, gratified.

"But with due respect to your profession, Mr. Hardcross, lawyers take a devil of a long time. Every day is valuable. What we must consider, gentlemen, is how we can proceed, and go ahead, while all the legal formalities are taking place."

"I have been talking to the Permanent Secretary this morning on the phone," said Appleton. "He made it quite clear that we must proceed with the greatest caution. His first reaction was that we ought to hold up the work until we are sure that this legal objection can be overcome."

Heron smiled bitterly. "Well, there we have the Civil Service view. Mr. Appleton counsels delay."

"I do nothing of the sort," replied Appleton tartly, "I report what the Ministry tells me. It's all very fine for you, Heron, you have no one to satisfy except your Board. But we can be held answerable to Parliament. There's a good deal of public money going into this thing."

"There is also a good deal of private money. And we are answerable to shareholders, Mr. Appleton, who are rather more sensitive to loss and delay. We have to look after our money, on our side, there is no bottomless public purse at our disposal."

"Oh come," said Appleton, "let's not talk like a political meeting. We're as anxious to go ahead as you are, you know that. What I am telling you is that we won't countenance anything which the Ministry can't get up and justify in the House. The point is, what can we do inside that limit?"

"Ah, there we come to it. Precisely. And Sir Russell thinks there is a good deal we can do without in the least involving the Minister—who, as you know, is a good friend of his—in anything which he could not countenance.

"After all," he discoursed to the whole table, "we are not really fighting local opinion here, but some small group of people who are trying to block this project. The point is, who are they, and what are they after?"

"The man's name," said Appleton, "is Melmoth—Colonel Henry Melmoth."

"The comic squire who gave us all that trouble over the land?"

"The same."

"Quite unbribable, I suppose?" asked Heron.

"He's a gentleman," replied Appleton, sitting back and feeling better.

"Ah, pity," murmured the other. "Such awkward people. Now, please, I want from all of you any information you can give me about this thing. Put me in the picture, please. I have only just arrived."

Appleton, listening, could perceive the unscrupulous plan shaping in the man's mind. He sighed; such luxuries were denied to a public servant. What Heron had to carry with him was the support of the local traders—the solid, waist-coated shopkeepers, the church and chapel people in their prim houses with television aerials on the roofs and well-built cars in the garages. And, of course, there was only one approach to them—money.

"It seems to me," Heron was saying, "that Gulport does not yet realize the benefit that the mill will bring to the town, the flow of business, the prosperity. There are only a few workers on the site as yet, nothing to make any appreciable difference to the trade of the town. I think we should hasten that process, gentlemen. We need the men in a month or so in any case. Let us bring them in now."

Appleton entered his formal warning. "The Minister's view is that we should hold up the work until the legal issue is decided, not hasten it forward. If we rush up the buildings, and then don't get the quay, we shall have wasted countless thousands of public money."

Heron smiled. "Never fear, Mr. Appleton. Private money is involved too. We shall get the quay all right. We are not growing ground-nuts here."

The risk the man was taking, Appleton pondered. Of course, it was true that to flood the place with labourers, at the rates of pay they would get on the site, would bring a boom to the town. The shops would flourish, the shop-keepers would quickly see the advantages of the project, and Heron would probably win public opinion to his side. When the fishermen held their public protest meeting in the Town Hall three weeks hence, with Melmoth in the chair—and that was the crucial date—a boom in trade would most likely turn the town in favour of the mill.

"But that won't save you," he pointed out. "The basic fact is the legal one—am I not right, Hardcross? These fishermen have got a legal right to that quay, and if they stick by it, public opinion won't help."

"Mr. Appleton is quite right," agreed Heron, smiling again. "The fishermen must be persuaded where their best interests lie. We must hope that they see the light, mustn't we? I think we shall have sound reasons for hoping so."

Appleton was probably the only other man in that room, he thought, who knew just what that meant. Wrap it up how you would, it meant bribery. He sighed again. To have so much money to dispense, and no need to account for it, except privately, in an inner office, to a man who reckoned not costs, but only results! The jungle of big business. Appleton thought with envy that there was something very attractive about it.

6

On the following Monday morning motor-coaches came racing over the hills, packed with men in rows of four, staring ahead, like the gallery, Hippodrome, second house. Most of the newcomers were lodged somehow or other in the town—the single men in the old camp converted into a hostel, the married in rooms wherever they could be found.

Heron laid on more motor-coaches between the Market Square and Skelstrand. Each morning there were long queues of men, nailed boots shifting on the pavement, as the coaches pulled in and sucked them away to work at the site. The centre of the town was loud with shouts, and snarling coach engines, electric horns and the tramp of feet. Then there was quiet, until the children came shrieking through to school—two children to every desk, and the education officer hastily converting a disused parish hall and an old warehouse, and despatching desperate pleas to the county offices for more teachers, more equipment, hundreds of gallons more free milk; every café in the place was impressed to help prepare the school meals.

As the morning settled down, the women came in to shop; women talking in distant accents, with their hair in curlers and shawls around their shoulders, but plenty of money in their old leather handbags. Grocers and butchers shook their telephones and harangued the wholesalers. Bakers stoked up their night-ovens and cast around for more hands. From each direction came the commercial travellers in their little motor-cars, sharpening their pencils and, businesslike, flapping open their black order-books; not bothering about samples. The shopkeepers plunged tremulously, plunged deeper than ever they had thought to do in their lives, and within a few days were writing from their back rooms for more: "Yours of the third inst. to hand, repeat previous order and oblige, delivery at the earliest convenience to your good selves." The goods depot at the railway station was piled with crates. Into the offices of the bank managers filed excited tradesmen, arranging temporary overdrafts. On market day every stall was cleared by three o'clock in the afternoon, and the Stag ran out of beer. Shop windows that had languished for years with the same dusty displays began to blossom with new flowers—fur coats and baby linen, dresses and paste jewellery and television sets. At one time there wasn't a reel of cotton to be had in all Gulport, and the ladies' hair stylist in Little Bridge Street was booked with appointments for two weeks ahead. Councillor Jafet exulted. He took people out to watch the Market Square and the High Street, to remind them that "back in the thirties, two shops in three were closed; and look at 'em now, boy, look at 'em now. Planning, see?"

In the afternoon things quietened down a bit, until the

children came shrieking home from school. Then in the early evening the motor-coaches streamed back from Skelstrand, expelling their loads of men, clothes daubed with soil and cement, shouting to each other, heavy boots caked in sand and clay clumping away up every side street. Men anxious for a wash and a meal, and then out for the evening's fun. Every bar in the place was jammed with men and tobacco smoke and thick voices. The queue for the Odeon stretched way past Woolworth's, the cinema manager out in front, clean white shirt, "two more one-and-nine-pennies, a single at two-and-four," his face sweating. Up and down the High Street, and round the Market Square, sauntered the Gulport girls, prinked, giggling, chattering in high voices; the young men in knots on corners, caps aslant, white-silk-chokered, hands in pockets, whistling. Crowds jostled on the narrow pavements, and the thin electric light in the shop windows glared like Piccadilly, or the gas flares of the saloons of Klondike. Such a bustle and thrust and clatter that the youngsters of Gulport came out to stare, and the old people shuttered their shop windows, made cocoa, and in the back rooms counted out the takings of the day. And, as the lights dimmed, and the odour of fish and chips faded, couples leaned over the parapet of the bridge, staring at the river as it wound mysteriously round the dark bulk of the gasometer; or wandered, arms twined, along the quay and on to the sand path beyond, where the sea came up gently, and the clumps of rough grass muttered in the night breeze.

It was, Appleton grudged, a sweet piece of organization, this boom that Heron created. Appleton re-christened him Bittern, but nobody saw the joke, not even Laura; a neat, cross-wordish sort of joke, Appleton reflected sadly. From the Ministry daily cautions came to him, tortuous misgivings about legal action and the use of public money, instructions to slow down the work—while the work daily accelerated. Out at the site, which he went to see, the steel rods were going in for the first concrete structures, the service roads were rolling out, the brickies were already getting at the beginnings of the furnaces, the tracks of the new marshalling yard were going down, and the foundations of the fly-over bridge. He sought out Heron, protesting. But Heron only smiled, and took responsibility. Fat lot of responsibility he would take, Appleton well knew, if the thing went wrong. But meanwhile everybody except himself was happy. Neve was grimly happy, watching the job take shape. The office was happy with movement and busyness. The townsfolk were delirious as the people and the money rolled in.

One of those who were happy—though he never showed so trite an emotion—was Bert Papelian, concrete-worker and shop steward. These were precisely the conditions that best suited him, gave him something to work on. He and his wife Rosa perfectly understood what was going on, they saw Heron's plan, they discussed it at night, she sitting in a chair by the window with her thin, cropped head held upright in the posture of haughty contempt which was natural to her, and with books and pamphlets scattered on the ledge; he moving up and down the room, brisk, lithe, restless. They were lodged in rooms in Buckingham Street, next the Duke's Head, in which Papelian had already hired from old Charlie Hyslop an upper room for committees.

"It's quite clear," he told his wife, "what the man's after. He brings in the workers, and their money bribes the shop-keepers to stick up for the mill when the question's put. Typical bosses' manœuvre—they get double value for their wages."

"It will work out," she said coldly. "On a Marxian analysis, the capitalists always betray themselves."

He listened to her with respect, as he always did. She was the intellectual, he the worker, the organizer, he knew that. All they shared was the same faith. But he was uneasy about Heron.

"How about the fishermen?" she asked.

He stopped by the window, staring out of it, lighting a cigarette. She took one from him and put it into her ivory holder, drawing the smoke into her thin lungs.

"Slow," he murmured. "They need educating. Blind. I got half a dozen of them to a meeting last night, but they were slow, suspicious."

39

"They'll come round. It is inevitable that they see it in the end."

"This blasted little town of smug bourgeoisie!" he exclaimed. "The men on the site are all right, they come from a good industrial background."

"Is he all right, this skipper who's leading the fishermen, what's his name, Flowers?" she asked.

"Course not. How can he be? He's going the right way at the moment, but that's because it suits him. He'd turn in a flash, if that suited him better, and he'd carry the men with him. Heron knows that."

"Heron has no more time than you have," she pointed out.

"But he has money."

She was looking at him coolly, and he wondered whether she was despising him. He often wondered that. For her, things were a theory. They worked out in the correct way because it was inevitable that they should, it was written. Hers was not a working-class approach. She came to the party from a university, intellectually convinced, but no more. Whereas he, with his background of poverty, of unemployment, of hatred, knew the practical difficulties of the task, knew just how hard it was to foment a strike, for instance, in times of plenty, against the opposition of right-wing trade unionism. She was convinced it was all bound to happen automatically, given the right Marxist approach. He sometimes wondered, irrelevantly, if she had married him only because her theories demanded a working-class partner to her intellectual powers. But if she had, he told himself, she had acted correctly, and his own impulses for a warmer relationship were environmental betrayals of the class struggle which he must rigorously repress. As he did.

She went back, after a pause, to the arrival of the new workers. Was he sure of getting the right men elected into the responsible places?

Here he was on firmer ground. He assured her, baring his teeth in a sort of smile, that she could leave that to him. And then he had to leave her. There was a meeting at the hostel to elect the hostel committee.

It was a fine evening, which pleased him; there would be

fewer at the meeting. That always made things easier. The technique was so simple. Your own people, well disciplined, always turned up to vote. Your opponents were too lazy, too disinterested, to come; or, if they arrived, you talked and argued until, weary, they went away before the question was put. Then you voted your own man in, and ever afterwards had control. He glanced contemptuously at the Duke's Head as he passed. A babble of voices floated from the windows of the bar, with the smell of beer. There they were, so many of them, wasting the evening over pint mugs. And while they did so, he and his few would capture the hostel committee, put Duncan in as the chairman and Mostyn Jones as secretary, and create an instrument which he, Papelian, could use at any time he chose to make trouble, arouse discontent, possibly even up to the level of strike action. The beauty of it was that all the men would feel they had right on their side, he thought, as he turned in at the hostel gates. The place was a disgrace. Fenced in with rusty barbed wire, just as it had been left at the end of the war, it looked like a concentration camp. The wooden huts, hastily erected, had mouldered now and settled into a bed of weeds. Through their open doors showed long rows of iron bedsteads, battered lockers. The concrete floors of the wash-houses were cracked, and everywhere lingered the ineradicable smell of soiled towels, thick socks, grey soapsuds and shag tobacco.

The meeting was in the dining-hut. As he entered, Papelian noted with pleasure that only a couple of dozen men had gathered there, but with annoyance that the Pole was one. He expected some opposition, of course, but the Pole was the man he least wanted. An emigré who had somehow worked his way across Hitler's Europe to fight in Anders' Division, he had chosen not to return to the People's Republic that his country became after the war; probably could not return, Papelian conceded. He had been rich, a landowner or something of the kind, the sort of swine for which the new order had no place except a salt mine. Nobody knew much about him, and none of the men could bother with his name, which was Paul Jablonskowy. They called him Jabby. There were stories that his whole family had been wiped out; those whom the Germans had failed to slay, the Russians had expended as slave labour.

Several of the men turned to greet Papelian, and Duncan casually suggested that he should take the chair; since he did not live in the hostel, he would make an impartial chairman.

"What's he doing here at all, then?" asked the Pole.

"Shop steward. Everyone agree Mr. Papelian takes the chair?"

There were a few vague dissentients, but Papelian ignored them and seated himself, glancing around, sizing them up: his own men not quite the majority, a small bloc which he strongly suspected to have been organized around the Pole, and a few neutrals, men living in the hostel who had just wandered in to the meeting, and upon whom the voting would probably depend. Get it over quickly, he thought. Smiling, he looked around and said briskly, "It's a nice night, and the Duke's has been open a couple of hours. I don't suppose anybody wants to hang about long, so let's get on with it. You all know what we're here for. Conditions in this hostel are unsatisfactory, and we want a men's committee to put them right. Agreed? My suggestion is chairman, secretary, and three members—nothing unwieldy. Agreed? Take the officers first. I'm open to receive nominations for chairman."

One of the men proposed John Duncan, a brother from Clydeside, and those who had known him there knew his record of tireless work on behalf of his mates. He said a few words about that work, organizing ability, energy. The Pole said nothing, but from the other side of the room a man proposed Dan Collins, an Irishman and, Papelian believed, a Catholic. The Pole still said nothing, and nobody else spoke. Papelian saw at once what was happening, and his respect for the Pole increased. He had it organized. He was going to let Duncan slip into the chairmanship, and then fight for the job of secretary, which really counted. It was what he himself would have done if he had been out of the chair.

42

He called for a show of hands, first for Duncan, then for Collins. His own group, the dolts, voted energetically for Duncan, and there were one or two waverers who raised their hands uncertainly, not much caring which man it was. Papelian announced sharply that Collins was elected.

"I made it Duncan," said the Pole from his corner.

"Mr. Jabby doubts my arithmetic," smiled Papelian. "Very well then, put 'em up again. Who wants John Duncan?"

The lead he had given ought to have been enough for his own party, but the fools voted solid again. He and the Pole counted carefully. "Now, Dan Collins?" They counted again. Duncan was in by two hands.

"I was wrong," Papelian conceded with a bitter smile, "John Duncan is the chairman. Nominations for secretary?"

Another of his men at once proposed Mostyn Jones, a doughty fighter for the workers, a man from the valleys of South Wales who knew what was what, and was not intimidated by the bosses. . . .

"Mostyn Jones is proposed," cut in Papelian quickly. "Any other nominations? Very well, then, I . . ."

"Hang on a minute, Mr. Chairman," interrupted the Pole, getting slowly to his feet.

"You're out of order. There is only one nomination, so . . ."

"Oh no, there isn't. What's going on here?" On his feet, he was a tall, thin, grey-haired man with a long face, hard mouth, a scar running across one temple. "Can't you see what's going on?" he addressed the far side of the meeting, where the neutrals were. "We're being railroaded into electing a Communist committee."

"Nonsense," snapped the chairman.

"No, it isn't nonsense. Duncan is a Communist, isn't he? Go on, ask him. And Jones is a Communist, that we all know. And you're one too, aren't you, Mr. Chairman? Local party boss, aren't you?"

Papelian rapped on the table. "All this is out of order," he decreed, "politics have nothing to do with it. We are choosing a social committee to take a hand in running the hostel.

43

I won't have any man cross-questioned about his political views for a thing like this."

"I don't suppose you will," said the Pole, "but I will. This is how it's done, my friends. They slip their own men into the key jobs, pretending it's nothing to do with politics, and before you know where you are, you're being used to bolster up the Communist game. Let's have it out in the open, let's see what we are doing."

Papelian's own men began to shout to sit down. The Pole stood staring at them, unsmiling. But then some of the other men began to shout in opposition. "Let's have some fair play here." "What's the bloody game?"

He rapped on the table and, unable to get silence, shouted against them, "I will not have this uproar. All this is out of order. There is a nomination before the meeting for the post of secretary. . . ."

A stout old man whom Papelian did not know got up and stared at the crowd of them, waiting patiently until he got silence.

"I propose Mr. Jabby as secretary," he said, and ponderously sat down.

"Second that," came a call from somewhere.

"Too late," ruled Papelian, "you had the chance to make your nominations before and now. . . ."

But he was swept back by the clamour that arose. He looked around, and decided swiftly. "If that's the feeling of the meeting, very well. We have two names proposed for secretary, Mostyn Jones and Paul Jablonskowy—to give the chap his full name. Before we go on, are there any other nominations?" he demanded, and waited in sarcastic silence. "Very well, then, a show of hands. Mostyn Jones?"

The hands went up.

"Paul Jablonskowy?"

The other hands went up.

"I make it a tie," Papelian announced, "so as chairman I give my casting vote. . . ."

"Demand a ballot," cried someone from the back.

"I give my casting vote. . . ."

Then there was shouting for the ballot. Papelian, knowing

44

when to give in, conceded it. One of the men began to prepare bits of paper, another fetched a cap to collect the votes.

"And scrutineers, if you please," said Jabby pleasantly.

"If you doubt my word. . . ."

"No, no, I never said so. But we'll have scrutineers."

Papelian watched in grim silence as the men scratched their votes, borrowing pencils, and as the scrutineers, hawk-like, watched the papers going into the hat. The Pole was in by four votes. Papelian had a sharp vision of Rosa, sitting in her chair by the window, listening scornfully when he told her the result. His nostrils were narrowed in anger.

When the meeting was over, he went with a few of them into the Duke's Head, pushing into a corner to take his glass of beer, not saying much, gazing at the men who were crowded into the public bar. This, he reflected moodily, was the part of it that Rosa did not comprehend—that this was the material they had to work with, these clods without any idea higher than a pint, or a horse-race, or a football pool. These were the workers, and how infinitely he despised them. They didn't care, that was the tragedy of it, they didn't care. The rows of muscular arms leaning upon the bar were not raised in the clenched salute of revolution, but merely to grasp beer mugs. The deep voices were in strenuous argument, not about the injustices of the capitalist system, but about the merits of teams in the First Division. The fuddled group in one corner was not chanting joyful proletarian songs, as it would have been in a Communist state; it was singing "Nelly Dean". This was the truth of it, which he scarcely dared to admit to himself, much less to assert to Rosa. It could not be like this, he thought, in other countries. The workers' leaders elsewhere were vigorously supported by a solid, thoughtful, indignant working class. But here he had to make do with beer guzzlers, football enthusiasts, men who were not only indifferent to their wrongs, but actually seemed to enjoy the lives they were living. In all that saloon, he thought despairingly, there was probably not one man upon whom he could count as a staunch ally in his struggle against this

45

damnable mill, that was to produce steel for the armaments of reaction, strength for the imperialists of big business in the fight against the under-privileged.

Yet, although Papelian did not know it, there was one such—one ally, though unconsciously one. His name was Michael Callaghan, from Liverpool, and his job at Skelstrand was to drive a bulldozer. All that day the longing which periodically came upon him had been accumulating in his mind. He had driven his bulldozer against the sand dunes in an automaton state, mechanically handling the engine while a white pattern of moving limbs formed behind his eyes. At the end of the day's work he had returned to the hostel, whistling softly to himself. He had cleaned himself up, changed his clothes, eaten his supper almost without a word to his neighbour, intent on his inner vision. He had sat throughout the evening, solitary in a corner of the bar, slowly drinking beer, until he had taken enough of it to warm his desire.

Now he rose quietly and went into the street, hesitated for a moment, then turned to the left, away from the centre of the town, towards the beginnings of fields and lanes. He walked slowly, doggedly, his eyes searching the road ahead of him in the dusk, his stomach turning over in delicious anticipation. He walked without much purpose, meeting nobody, for some half-hour, glancing sharply this way and that, like a scout on patrol. As he started on a steep hill, a girl on a bicycle overtook him, and dismounted to push her machine up the hill. Callaghan increased his pace, humming quietly to himself. He strode a little faster. The girl was wearing a cotton dress, she had fair hair, and the action of pushing the bicycle caused her to lean to one side, throwing out the curve of her hip. At first she did not notice him, but as he drew closer she must have heard his regular footsteps, for she glanced quickly round, and then ahead again.

As he came up to her, he said, "Evening. Nice night." She looked at him, frowned, but said nothing, and walked quickly on.

"I'll push your bike for you," he offered.

"No, thank you," she said, primly, a bit scared.

Callaghan was silent, but he kept pace, walking beside her. He had stopped humming, and there was a little smile on his lips. The humming seemed to go inside his brain, rising in sound until it was a huge great orchestra of music. The road was deserted. On one side was a high hedge, on the other the flatness of common land, scattered with bushes.

"Here, let me push that bike," he suddenly uttered, going swiftly across to her. He got his hand over her mouth as she started to yell.

7

EUSTACE POMEROY'S house in Bridgnorth Street was not very large, but, like Eustace Pomeroy himself, it seemed to surrender joyously to a party. It opened its front door wide, and gathered into its downstairs rooms far more people than they could comfortably hold, to say nothing of the large table covered with cold meats and fruit salads in the dining-room, the tea-trolley laden with bottles wedged into the hall, and the plates of nuts and chocolates and cheese savouries scattered on every possible ledge, piano-top, occasional table. It switched on all the electric light it had, and played loud music on its gramophone, so that the party seemed to strain at the walls of the house, bulge out of the open windows, and tail off among the cars parked in the road outside. The women's coats were laid in a careful row on the quilt in the spare bedroom. The men's clung as best they could to the pegs in the downstairs lavatory.

The party buzzed, of course, as all Gulport was buzzing, with the story of the rape. It added a little tinge of gratification to the most humdrum life; even Venetia, Pomeroy's plump, placid wife, sparkled noticeably with it as she proffered the jellies and pastries which she had herself made, toiling all day in the kitchen.

"It was a great disappointment to Melmoth," said Dr. Irons, from the corner of the sitting-room entirely filled by his bulk and a pint mug of beer, "that rape is an indictable offence. I never saw a Bench send a man to the Assizes with greater reluctance."

"I suppose they've got the right man?" hazarded Appleton.

"Identification parade," replied Pomeroy, handing round a tray of drinks, "everything slap-up. Girl picked him out at once. That's the villain, little scream, fainted away. Drama."

"Poor child," sighed Venetia.

"Any man would have done for Melmoth," said Irons, "so long as he worked at Skelstrand."

"It's a great pity," worried Appleton. "It'll set the town against us. Most unfair really."

"If you employ gorillas you must expect monkey tricks."

When Jimmy Jafet arrived the whole story had to be gone over again, for Jimmy, as a J.P., had all the drama of the court-room to relate at first hand.

"Terrible for poor old Wilkinson. He was like a man out of his mind. His own daughter. 'Don't let me go out there,' he begged, in the room at the back, 'or I shall do him an injury.' The Colonel was all for letting him take his seat on the Bench as usual, but the clerk wouldn't have it. And of course the clerk was right, it would never have done. And then Daphne herself having to give evidence, poor girl. Just formal, of course, identification. And Joe Wilkinson sat there in the back room, sobbing like a baby. We sent a constable in to keep watch on him. Crying for vengeance, he was. And after, coming round to lead the girl away, his arm round her waist, helping her into the car, all the women watching them. The women came in crowds to stare at the girl, curiosity like. It was a terrible ordeal for her."

"And after all she had been through, poor thing," murmured Venetia.

"Of course," said Robert Heron smoothly, revolving a glass of whisky in his fingers, "it is all very deplorable, but the rape isn't proved yet."

"When the girl arrives home, late at night, terrified?" protested Jimmy. "Clothes torn, her face cut? It's a mercy it wasn't a murder charge we had to hear this morning."

"Girls have been known to get frightened afterwards," murmured Heron, "and scream that they were robbed of what, at the time, they gave."

48

"That'll be his defence, naturally," said Jimmy.

"I suppose the girls of Gulport, or some of them, are not absolutely indifferent to the male, eh, Doctor?"

"We do have a birth rate," agreed Irons, "that does not invariably tally with the marriage register."

"We're all human," said Heron.

Precisely what one would expect of him, thought Appleton, with a glance of agony at his wife. Laura in a red dress, like a dark flower uncurling in the heat of the room. The thought of her and Heron was becoming an obsession with him; he knew it to be an obsession, unreasoning, but like a string tightened around his temples.

"I mean," said Heron, "God knows, I'm not trying to condone rape, of course. But, after all, a man is held innocent until he is proved guilty. You do agree, don't you, Jimmy?"

"Well, naturally," nodded the little councillor, "I'd scarcely be on the Bench if I thought otherwise, would I now? Everything was conducted proper, I think. It looks black against the man, of course. . . ."

"I was in court," replied Heron. "I thought the chairman, what's his name, the old squire fellow—Melmoth, that's it—I thought he was simply vindictive. The case may look very different at the Assizes, with a good defending counsel."

"Whom you will provide, eh?" chuckled Irons.

"Possibly. Sir Russell Gazzard is always very conscious of his responsibility towards his employees."

Appleton laughed. "Come off it, Heron. What you mean is that this business will inflame the town against the mill, and you'll do any damned thing to gloss it over."

"No, no, Mr. Heron is right," interrupted Jimmy Jafet. "Let the man have the best possible defence, that's right. After all, as a magistrate. . . ."

"Thank you, Jimmy. Of course I want Skelstrand to go ahead. That's what I'm here for. But what has that got to do with this crime, if it is a crime? All I said was that we don't know that it was a rape. That's the girl's story, but we don't know whether it's the truth or not. It will be settled at the trial. Only, if I were this man Callaghan, I'd be pretty

49

relieved that I was to be tried by a judge and jury, and not by that vindictive old so-and-so who sits on the local Bench."

"Why do you call him vindictive?" asked Elizabeth. She had not spoken before. She was sitting, with Mrs. Pomeroy, on a settee pushed against the wall, and Charles Neve had been covertly watching her, admiring the cool look of her, the set of her head upon her shoulders like a well-constructed piece of machinery, the stillness of her hands resting upon her lap. Now, realizing that Heron did not know who she was, he had the instinct to jump in to protect her. The old doctor, he noticed, felt the same, but checked himself with a slight smile. Pomeroy got as far as, "Ought to warn you, Elizabeth here. . . ."

But Heron, unlike himself, rushed in. "I call him vindictive because, on the Bench this morning, it was pretty clear he was not concerned with the merits of the case, but exultant at having such a stick to beat Skelstrand with. Everybody knows he's the prime mover of all this agitation against the mill—he hates it because it cuts out the antediluvian squire stuff that his family has fed on for centuries. Well, that's all right. I'm a Tory. I'm not against the squirearchy—lot to be said for it. But it ought to be kept out of a case in which a man's liberty is at stake."

There was a nasty silence, in which Heron glanced swiftly around, wondering. Appleton was mentally squeezing himself with joy; the great Heron, the smooth one! Neve was surprised at the intentness with which he was watching the girl.

Then she said, in a calm, clear voice, "I think you do him a wrong. Everybody knows that he is wholeheartedly opposed to the new mill, and his reasons may or may not be selfish. But my father is too honourable a person to allow private motives to interfere with justice."

"Your father?" exclaimed Heron, moving quickly towards her. "Oh lord, I have put my foot in it! What can I say?"

"It would be better to consider," she replied, gazing at him, "what to stop saying, in public anyway."

"Now, more drinks everybody," hastily cried Pomeroy, diving towards the trolley. "Ven, old thing, give us some music. Phew, hot in here! Open the french doodahs, Ted. Garden a lovesome thing, eh?"

Everybody started to babble. And across the room throbbed the loud, deep, extraordinary sound of Dr. Irons in full-throated chuckle. Neve joined him. In a moment they were all laughing, Heron as loudly as any, gesturing helpless apologies towards Elizabeth. Pomeroy was whispering urgently to Jafet: "Crimbo. Nasty situation. Fur flying, practically. Start something, Jimmy. Stand on your head, give us a song. Keep the old party going, eh? Lummee."

The party started to move about, to mingle, to split up into little groups and conversations. Here in one corner was Appleton talking to Doctor Irons; he took a liking to the immense doctor, and to the sharp remarks that emerged from his owlish face. There in another Jimmy Jafet and Ted Flowers, the fishing skipper, were pinned together.

Charles Neve, standing by himself in one of the rooms, wandering, glass in hand, into another, was bored by the party. He did not like parties, he told himself. A waste of time, and he wondered why he had come. But he really knew why: curiosity about that girl. Curiosity, he considered, rather than mere attraction. She was the sort of person he would normally despise, yet he did not find her despicable. He recognized in her a dignity, a self-confidence, and at the same time a charm, that derived, he supposed, from centuries of being the acknowledged bosses of a small country district, the hereditary monarchs of a village. It was different, quite different from power in a town, a centre of industry, or a capital city. It was so slow and trivial, and yet it seemed to produce a sort of person that could be matched in no other way of life in England, or probably in the world. The squire sort of person. He was surprised to find that he rather admired it. The cool way in which she had stood up to that shocker Heron, put him in his place like an old *grande dame* checking a schoolboy—and he such a fine fellow to his own way of thinking, politician, financier, big shot. So this country girl treats him like a rude child. Neve chuckled at the memory of it.

51

It was hot in the room. Glancing through the french windows, he saw that several of the people were strolling in the dusk of the garden. He stepped out. It was quite a large garden, and well-kept. Venetia, he guessed, was the gardener, an untiring weeder. Then he saw the girl, sitting by herself on one of those swing-seat things, the canopy pushed back.

"Hallo," she said. "Sit down. It's cool out here."

"And quieter," he agreed. "You can barely hear that damn gramophone."

"It's pleasant in the distance."

"That's where all parties should be," he smiled grimly, "well in the distance."

She laughed, nodding. "Why did you come, then?"

"To meet you."

"Well, at least you are direct."

"You asked me, and I told you."

"Do you want me to flatter you in return?"

"It wasn't flattery. I came because you aroused my curiosity."

"Oh, that's a bit better."

"The first time I met you, you asked such a damn silly question about Skelstrand—you asked what colour it was going to be."

"I don't call that a silly question."

"No, that's the point. It's the last question I should ask about a steel mill, and the first that you asked. Hence my curiosity. What sort of person thinks of a mill in that way?"

"Yokel," she suggested.

He shook his head. "I don't suppose you've ever been in Sheffield."

"Never have."

"Then I don't think I can explain it to you. You see, for most of the English, England is something like Sheffield— machinery, and grime, and trams, and a few hard-headed men making a lot of brass, and most of the rest fearing either a war or a slump. And pubs and cinemas on Saturday nights, and working men's clubs. And the kids sharp as needles. And technical schools. And the pits not far off. That's my England."

"An exciting country."

"Far from it. A hard, grinding, cruel country. And a country that is struggling not to go under, and not very likely to win the struggle. God, how we've fought for it all my life. The slump—do you remember that? I suppose not. The men on the dole, my father was one of them, and the kids in clogs, and sometimes without even clogs. Somehow we survived that. Then the war. And those same kids put on Army boots, and went all over the world to fight like devils. To fight for what? For the sort of England they'd grown up in? There must be something to it, mustn't there? Something that doesn't show on the surface."

"And only a war brings it out?"

"In a way, perhaps. When a war starts, at least you think you know what you are fighting, and what you are fighting for. But the war didn't save us, of course. It was ten times worse after. Oh, plenty of work and high wages, and football pools and the dogs. But underneath it all, the hardest fight of the lot—for survival. And we haven't won that. We may not win it. The whole thing may slide down into poverty and despair. The only chance we've got, and it's a grim one, is in building things like Skelstrand. Steel, coal, power—if we get enough of them, we've maybe a sporting chance of pulling through. And you wanted to know what colour it was, and how it would look against the blue of the sea."

"I'm beginning to think," she murmured, "that it was a damn silly question."

"And I'm beginning to realize that it wasn't. It was just a question from another sort of England. The squire and the village, field sports and getting the harvest in, tradition and tweeds. I've always despised that sort of thing, but maybe I was wrong. It produces somebody like you, so there must be something to it, I'm beginning to see that. You're all right. You'll do. You're not even a snob."

"Good heavens, but you are—a machinery snob."

"Admitted. An intolerant, bloody fool of a machinery snob, that's me. You've got me there."

He put his head back and laughed. "It was a fine idea, putting Skelstrand down here, mixing us up. Perhaps we'll

53

learn from each other. Perhaps one day there'll be one England instead of two. Wouldn't it be a funny joke if we all got to like each other?"

"Could we leave Mr. Heron out of it?" she asked plaintively.

"Oh, rather. That's one bond we already have in common."

"Such a very pink face," she murmured.

Through the darkening garden behind them loomed up the large shadow of Dr. Irons, and his mug of beer.

"Well, Liz," he observed. "I see you've started the flirtation."

"I'm not making much headway," she complained.

"Flirtation?" asked Neve.

"She publicly announced her delight that your factory is bringing so many good-looking men into the place. It's a change for these parts."

"Then I've been quite on the wrong tack. I could easily have made a pass at you. Why didn't you say?"

"You talk so much," she replied, "that I didn't have a chance to say anything."

"That's a change for these parts, too," observed the doctor. "What was he talking about?"

"About me, of course. Otherwise I shouldn't have listened so meekly."

"I was explaining how odd it is for a fellow from the industrial slums to run up against the quaint old English squirearchy for the first time."

Irons nodded. "I know. I did that thirty years ago. The superiority of 'em, eh? You get used to it in time."

"But he doesn't think that, Gilbert. He likes us—that's what makes him so surly. It's against his trade union rules."

"It isn't really a joke," said Neve. "I was saying that this country will go down the drain unless we pull off things like Skelstrand. And yet the local people are whipping up an opposition that could even wreck the whole thing—because it spoils the view. Is this a crazy country?"

"Always was, old chap," answered Irons. "The English have fought desperately, throughout history, against every advantage ever offered to them. It has to be forced on them. And of course it always is. There is always a Mr. Heron about."

"How is he forcing it, Gilbert?" asked Elizabeth, puzzled.

"Money, my dear," murmured Irons, "just money."

"Money? How money? Oh, but that's disgusting. It isn't true, is it, Mr. Neve?"

"Of course it's true," he abruptly replied. She irritated him now. He wanted brutally to smash down her little world of sentimentality into which he had drifted on a couple of drinks, a warm spring evening and a woman's voice. "What do you expect? Skelstrand's going to cost eighty millions. It's going to give work to four thousand men. It's going to produce a million and a half tons of sheet steel a year. Do you think we're going to stop that because it mucks up the landscape, or the squire's shooting, or because a girl gets raped?"

"Trivial obstacles," said Irons, "in the path of progress."

"And so anything goes?" she asked, "any dirty means towards the end?"

"Anything," he assented, "absolutely anything."

"The individual doesn't count?"

"Not a button. The prejudices of your father, the livelihood of a few fishermen—frankly, what are they, against a thing like Skelstrand?"

"The greatest good of the greatest number," murmured Irons, who was enjoying himself.

"Would you do the dirty work yourself, if you had to, Mr. Neve?" she inquired.

"That's not my side of it. I'm a technician."

"That's very cosy for you," she said.

Cosy, he thought. That she should speak to him of cosiness! But all he said was, "Ah, well, we shan't agree. Let's go and get another drink."

When they got back into the room, he contrived to break away and leave her with the doctor. He sat down in a corner with his drink, and angrily watched the party. So the individual doesn't count? he mimicked to himself. Bah! How much did the individual count when the fighting was on? How much did they worry about individuals when his father stood in the dole queue? It was not a tea party at the vicarage, but a battle in the streets. Look at them in this room, drinking, laughing, whiling away another evening on the way to death. And the battle was in every one of them, they were all fighting helplessly in its ranks. Heron, the smoothie, with the steel barons' money behind him, wriggling out a career for himself, salting away a private fund that, one day, would give him—what? Appleton, the official, tangling up his days with memoranda and torturing himself over the tart he had married. The clown of a Pomeroy, dreaming of building vast roads and bridges across tropical deserts, and actually laying drain-pipes to a provincial sewage farm. The tall fishing-boat skipper who had sold his mates for a few pounds with which to buy himself a cottage. Elizabeth Melmoth, with the face of a madonna, trying not to admit to herself that all she really needed was to get into bed with a man. The funny little Labour councillor—what was his name?—who simply desired to be important. And he himself, Charles Neve, construction engineer, who found no flavour in anything but work. Ah, that was the only thing that counted, the work. And it did not much matter who did the work. If all in this room were suddenly swept away, what difference would it make to the town, to the mill? Precisely none. The town would go on the same, the mill would be built the same, so what were they bickering about among themselves, these little wasting pieces of flesh? But Skelstrand would be concrete, and would emit steel. He felt bleak and tired, and a little muzzy with drink and the chatter of the room. They were all talking at once, on different notes, loosened by what they had drunk. And all laughing, from Pomeroy's intermittent cackle as he took around his tray of glasses, to the deep roll of the doctor's chuckle. Mixed in with it was the angry voice of Appleton as, his spectacles shining, he started on a quarrel with Heron. Something to do with Laura, and a charge that they had been out into the garden together.

"Don't be silly, Bernard," she said. "You're making a fool of yourself."

"A fool, is it?" replied Appleton, who had certainly drunk too much. "I think you're right, I have been a fool. And I'm getting tired of it. As for you," he swung round on Heron, "I'll trouble you to keep away from my wife."

"My dear fellow," deprecated Heron, trying to quieten him.

"Or take the consequences. And there will be consequences."

"Oh, for God's sake, shut up," murmured Laura. "You're tight."

"So I'm tight. But I'm not too tight to see what's going on."

"Nothing's going on," assured Heron. "Come on, have a drink."

Appleton looked for the moment as though he would knock the proffered glass from the other's hand. But Pomeroy slipped adroitly in and drew him away with a hasty joke. Venetia started talking brightly to Laura. Heron, left awkwardly alone, moved across to Jimmy Jafet where he sat with the trawler skipper, saying brightly: "Well, Jimmy, how's things? We haven't had a proper chance for a get-together. . . ." And the little wave of anger that had arisen subsided into the sea of chatter and laughter.

Charles Neve, a few minutes later, got quietly up, went out to his car, and drove home. Nobody noticed him go. An hour later, as he lay in bed, he heard Appleton's stumbling entry into the next room, and the voices of the two of them, murmuring through the wall, on and on, sometimes rising, sometimes falling; and at last the creaking and labouring of the bed. Disgruntled, Neve pulled the blankets over his ear, trying to sleep. And then there was silence. And he suddenly laughed out loud at the absurdity of emotions.

8

WHEN Ted Flowers discovered this business of the old charter, he had naturally come to Colonel Melmoth. Everybody had always naturally consulted Shard in matters of local importance. And Melmoth had willingly taken it on, this organization of a protest, though he was startled at the

57

warmth it aroused. Almost before he had thought about getting a little committee together, the question dominated the town. That beastly business about poor old Wilkinson's girl, of course, had done it. Melmoth pondered grimly, but with some uneasy satisfaction, that at least it had shown the people the sort of thing that this damnable mill would bring upon them—brutality, fierceness, relentlessness, disrupting a quiet and ordered life. There had, Melmoth admitted to himself, been cases of rape before this, but they had been, as it were, accidental. Some fool of a man had got drunk, some stupid young girl had tempted and then drawn back. But this had about it a symbolism. This was the impact of industrial life, of slums, of urban crime, upon a country community. True, there were some people pretending the thing was of no importance. They were those, of course, who were making money out of the newcomers, the tradespeople. Wilkinson himself, Melmoth wryly reflected, would certainly have been one of them, had it not been his own daughter. It was unfair, they said, to blame the mill project because one of the labourers employed upon it had committed a crime. And some of them murmured a slight doubt as to whether, in fact, there had been a crime; a jury, they hinted, might not think so.

Elizabeth's attitude puzzled her father. She seemed half serious in her feeling that it was wrong to obstruct the mill, somehow unpatriotic and selfish. She kept on telling him that he must see there was another point of view, that the men who were putting up the mill were as truly devoted to the country as he was. There was some blasted engineer named Neve who had got at her—"He's honest, and I think rather a good man, Henry," she said. She had kept on at him until he had actually consented to have the fellow out to lunch at Shard, to exchange points of view, as she put it. Now, in a couple of hours' time, Melmoth was faced with the lunch. He was irritated that the prospect upset him. He had walked out across his fields, in the direction away from Skelstrand, as though he needed to get the feel of them more firmly into his mind, to fortify himself against this fellow from a world of steel and vulgarity.

On his way past the bottom coppice, where it neared the road, he saw a man standing. Blasted impertinence. Standing there quite calmly, as though the place belonged to him. When he got up to the man, he demanded whether he knew he was on private property.

"You're Colonel Melmoth, aren't you?" the man asked.

"I am."

"I've been waiting for you.

Melmoth surveyed him curiously. He was a short, slightly built working man with a keen, rat-like sort of face.

"Waiting for me? What for?"

"This fishermen's quay business," said the man, briskly, as though used to coming straight to the point. "I'm speaking for most of the men working on the site, the biggest union leastways. We don't like it."

"On my own land, and in my own town," said Melmoth coldly, "I am not compelled to pay attention to the views of a trade union. Not yet, anyway. Before the day arrives when I shall be so compelled, I hope to have died peacefully in my bed."

"No, you've got me wrong. What we don't like is the quay being taken away from the fishermen. We're on your side."

"Well, that's a surprise. I must confess I had not thought. . . ."

"The fishermen are workers. We're workers. We stand together. This is a bosses' job, trying to whip the quay off the fishermen. Our men don't like it."

"I find you interesting," said Melmoth. "I don't like it either. It is refreshing to find a sense of justice in a trade union. I am obliged to you for letting me know."

"We're going to do more than that," said the man. "We're going to help."

"You're very kind. In what way?"

"At the meeting. There are lots of ways we can help. We can deal with the rowdies that Heron will bring in. We can manage a bit of rough stuff ourselves, if need be. . . ."

"Now steady on," warned Melmoth. "I appreciate your motives, but there is going to be nothing like that. This will be an ordinary meeting, not a melodrama."

59

The man smiled at him, in a way that made Melmoth uneasy.

"I suppose you know what's going on?" he asked. "You know, for instance, that Flowers has been got at?"

"Got at?"

"Bribed, man, bribed."

"Oh, now come."

"Look," said the man, "have you ever been mixed up in an industrial dispute before? No? I've been in 'em all my life. This isn't country stuff, this is town stuff. You'd better listen."

He started to pace alongside the astonished Melmoth, whose face became angrier and paler. Up and down that field they paced for an hour, the little man talking urgently, crisply; the tall man protesting, but with diminishing conviction.

At the end of the hour the small man turned abruptly towards the gate, saying, "Okay, you can count on us."

"But remember," cautioned Melmoth, "I will not have any disorder. Put that right out of your head. No disorder of any kind, or I shall at once summon the police."

The other man nodded.

"Confine yourself," continued Melmoth, "to putting the resolution from the trade union men on the site. That is understood? Good. And I must say I am extremely obliged to you. I had no idea. . . ."

The other man nodded again, and was gone. Melmoth turned and walked thoughtfully back towards his house. The park gleamed yellow on this young summer day, and the elms were friendly. There was a corner at which, from childhood, he had loved to come upon the view of the house itself, and he stopped there now, gazing at it where it lay with the grace of a sleeping animal, sheltered by the hill. Shard. And was it now to be overtopped by factory chimneys, and hemmed in by crescents of semi-detached houses with chintz curtains and rows of runner beans? He would sooner, he thought, with his own hands burn it down. Then he told himself not to be such a dramatic idiot, and set off across the park to this unavoidable meeting with Liz's engineer.

60

They had arrived when he got there. "Ah, I see she has given you a glass of sherry," said Melmoth, filling his own glass, standing on the hearth-rug with his back to the tall fireplace, caressing his buttock with his hand. Then he was conscious of posing a little, so he went and sat down. "Liz tells me you're an engineer on this steel mill."

"Construction," said Neve. "I move on when the job is finished."

"You're lucky. We have to stay here and put up with it."

"It's a nice place to stay," he replied, glancing round.

"It's old, that's all—old and highly inconvenient to run. But of course, as we've always lived here, we're fond of it. We're what you would call privileged," he could not resist to add.

"I suppose so," smiled Neve. "I'm no great politician, myself. I'm a working engineer."

"He's being modest," said Elizabeth. "I have been finding out about Mr. Neve. He's not only a working engineer, he's rather an important one."

"Who says?"

"Oh, I went down to Skelstrand and found a foreman eating his sandwiches—absolute charmer, in a leather waist-coat. He raved about you. I had no idea you were so grand."

Neve laughed. "That'd be Bill Cross. Don't pay any attention—he's prejudiced. He used to be my sergeant-major, and I got him out of the Army before his release date."

Watching them, Melmoth suddenly had the dreadful notion that Elizabeth had brought this fellow to Shard, not really to talk about the steel mill, but obliquely to show him to her father; that she had some intention of being in love with him.

"Were you building things in the Army too, Mr. Neve?" he inquired, getting up to refill the sherry glasses.

"Yes. Bailey bridges, mostly. Thanks."

"He got a medal for it—the same one as yours, Henry."

"You have been getting at Bill Cross. I shall have to speak to him about discussing my secrets with girls he picks up on the roadside."

"Why are men so stupid about medals? Here are the two of you, each with a Military Cross, and you absolutely can't talk about it, either between yourselves or to anybody else. Do you know that my own father refused to tell me how he won his? I had to get a friend to turn up back numbers of the *Gazette*. And then it was rather disappointing—just said he took a machine-gun post, none of the gory details."

"Elizabeth!" her father protested.

"I'm very glad I haven't got a daughter," said Neve.

"What would the *Gazette* say about yours?" she demanded.

"It says I paid strict attention to my work during office hours."

"There you are, you see," she said with disgust.

"I can only apologize for her," said Melmoth. "Let's go and have lunch. It may shut her up."

He felt better towards this engineer than he had done at first. But the girl would not leave it at that. She deliberately introduced the mill into the conversation, which had been proceeding quite comfortably on trivialities.

"We shan't agree," said Melmoth. "Let's not discuss it."

"But that's what I brought him here for. Henry, you haven't heard the other side's case. Unless you're going to admit that you refuse to see any but your own point of view. . . ."

"Aren't women a pest?" said Neve.

"I know the other side's case. I have had it rammed down my throat by the Ministry that stole my land. The country needs more steel. This is—in the opinion of our planners— a suitable place to make it. All other considerations are therefore swept aside. The State has issued an order. We have only to obey, as meekly as we can."

"Now you," said Elizabeth to Neve.

"What else is there to say? Colonel Melmoth's about right. The only difference is that he thinks it's monstrous, and I think it's okay."

"Would you think so," Melmoth asked, "if this village was your home, or the land belonged to you?"

"But then I shouldn't be me. I should be your kind of

person, not mine. And I expect I should think as you do. I grew up in an industrial slum, in a time when there weren't many jobs going. My dad was on the dole for just over three years. For me, Skelstrand is one of the ways of making sure that doesn't happen again."

"Ah, but is it? Will it work?"

"It'll work."

"No, I don't mean mechanically. Look here, Neve, frankly you seem to me a very sensible and reasonable sort of fellow. Tell me honestly, now, do you think it worth sacrificing personal freedom so that your father, and his equivalents, are not again thrown out of employment?"

"It depends on whose freedom."

"Not only mine. Not only the old-fashioned landowner. It isn't just class warfare. Everybody's freedom is being sacrificed—and to what? That's what alarms me. Who gains? It seems to be some sort of ogre called The State. But who controls that? The bureaucrats, the politicians? In Russia we can see who wins—the successful politicians."

"But what is all this," asked Neve, "about losing freedom? What freedom?"

"I lost the freedom to sell my land or to withold it from sale. Agreed?"

Neve nodded. "Yes. But it was time the ownership of land was overhauled. We haven't got enough of it on this small island to waste it on people's whims."

"Aha, but it doesn't stop there. Next thing you know, the Gulport fishermen lose their freedom to earn their livings as they and their forefathers have done for centuries."

"You can't have the mill without a quay," said Neve, "and the tides in that harbour dictate where the quay has got to be placed. What's the alternative?"

"I'm not saying there is one—except to build your steel mill in an existing steel district."

"No good, I'm afraid. Not enough labour, too many calls on existing facilities. Anyway, you're not so far from steel country here."

"All right. For the sake of argument, I'll accept all that. But the fishermen still lose their ancient freedom. And it won't stop there. The working-class people themselves know that, and are frightened by it."

"Think so? I know a bit more about the working class than you, sir."

"No doubt. But it happens that I had a most extraordinary example of it this very morning. I was accosted in my own fields by one of your men. He had come all the way out from Gulport to see me. He wanted to tell me that the trade unionists on your site agree with me—not on my account, but because they resent seeing the fishermen deprived of their livelihood. Now, what do you think of that?"

"I wouldn't trust him."

"And why not, pray? It seems that some of his mates have moved a resolution, and he had the decency to ask me whether I agreed to its being announced at the public meeting. I think that shows a very praiseworthy spirit."

"What was his name?" asked Neve.

"You're not going to hold this against him? I mean, you wouldn't go and give him the sack or anything?"

Neve laughed. "You're behind the times on labour relations, Colonel."

"I think I'm behind the times on ordinary honesty too. This man said that you people are using bribery, and that when it comes to the meeting, you won't hesitate, if necessary, to use violence."

"Henry, you ought not . . ." protested Elizabeth.

The young man, Melmoth saw, was angry, but trying not to show it.

"I'm an engineer," he said, "I build things. I have nothing to do with the business side of it. But your daughter has already pointed out to me once that that's a cowardly way out for me."

"I didn't say that."

"You meant it. And of course you were quite right. So I won't deny that I know such things may be going on, and I accept that I'm as much responsible as anybody else on the management."

"You amaze me," said Melmoth.

"Why should it? Did you really expect that a project of

64

this size and importance would be set aside because of the opposition of a few fishermen and the squire?"

"I expected justice. You used to be able to count on that in England. It seems that you can't any more."

"Justice!" repeated Neve. "Your sort of justice—squire's justice, boss's justice. Good God, I thought I had got over my adolescent socialism, but it comes back strong when I run into someone like you."

"Please," pleaded Elizabeth.

"No, no. Let him go on. It's fascinating."

"I'm sorry," said Neve, collecting himself, "I forgot for the moment that this was your house. I apologize. And I think I'd better go. Thank you for my lunch."

"It was my fault," insisted Elizabeth. "I shouldn't have done it."

"But your object is accomplished, my dear," her father pointed out. "We have exchanged points of view. You must have expected that we should differ. Mr. Neve, we both got a little hot under the collar; forgive me. And, believe me, I have really enjoyed meeting you. Come again, and we'll keep off politics."

"Fair enough," replied Neve, smiling cautiously. "By the way, what was the name of the man who waylaid you this morning? Just curiosity on my part, I promise."

"An odd name," said Melmoth. "He was a Mr. Papelian." Then he asked, as he saw the other checking a comment on his lips, "Got anything against him?"

"Oh no. He can talk for his union all right. One of the shop stewards. Papelian knows what he's saying."

The older man nodded, and left the room.

"Have I properly offended him?" Neve asked her.

"No, I don't think so. Not really. He often leaves a room abruptly. He's really rather a shy person, and he gets moments when he can't stand people any more—not you, I don't mean, but any people, even his oldest friends. Then he goes and broods in a little room he uses for a den. He'll be out again by supper-time, and quite normal. It has been only since Peter was killed."

"Peter?"

"My brother. He was in the Air Force."

"I'm sorry," murmured Neve.

But he said to himself that he was not sorry, that he did not give a damn for any of the Melmoths, not even the girl. He knew he was unreasonably angry—unreasonable to be angry because a man behaves true to type. Yet there was something about him that attracted Neve's liking. He wished, almost, that he had warned him about Papelian. He ought to have done, instead of letting him drop naïvely into that trap. Oh well, he'd find out soon enough.

He got up to go, and she walked slowly alongside him. The house was empty and quiet. In the hall she paused, leaning against the edge of a table.

"Don't judge him too harshly," she said.

"Of course not. It isn't a question of judging at all. Why should I? It's no business of mine."

"Do you still think there's anything good to be said for the squirearchy?"

He laughed. "Did I say that?"

"Yes. And you said it was a fine idea, putting the steel mill down here, to mix us all up, so that we could learn from each other."

"Is that why you brought me out here today? I've been wondering why."

"Partly. Perhaps it wasn't such a good idea."

He looked at her, against the old oak and dark portraits. "It has its pleasant side," he said. "What were the other reasons for bringing me here?"

"Curiosity," she considered, "to see how you and Henry would react. Although you're so different, you're curiously alike—you felt that, didn't you?"

"Can't say that I did."

"Oh well, it doesn't matter. You are, though. And I think that the rest of the reason was that I wanted to."

"That was a good reason," he said, "I'm glad about that one."

She raised herself from the table and they began strolling again. At the entrance, where the sunlight fell, she leaned against the warm brick, her head pressed upwards, and said,

66

"I don't think you can understand quite what a difference it has meant to us, all you people suddenly here. The chief feature of life in the country is its extraordinary dullness. Only Nature happens, if you see what I mean. Nature, and whist-drives, and the conversation of people who knew you as a baby. At least you have brought us a snatch of life. When you sit there describing the horrors of your boyhood slum, I can't help thinking what a wonderfully lively, exciting place it must have been to grow up in."

"Oh yes, it was wonderful."

"Well, I suppose it wasn't comfortable. But, I suppose because I've always had it, comfort seems such a triviality. At least you have had liveliness, change, variety—the things that I want, or think I want."

"Surely you know what you want," he said.

"No, I don't think I do."

"But it's so evident," he said. He leaned forward and kissed her mouth. She made no attempt to stop him, and no response. He stepped back, a little disconcerted. She gazed at him, neither smiling nor frowning.

"Perhaps that was a mistake too," he said. "If it was, I'm sorry. It's the sort of thing that goes on in the slums. I think I'd better go now."

"Good-bye."

He walked to his car without turning his head. When he looked round, the doorway was empty. He drove out and through the park without looking back again, angry with himself. He had done the sort of thing that they would have expected his sort of person to do. Hell, but why should he care what they thought or expected? He considered for a few minutes whether it were simply because the girl was good-looking—he almost used the word beautiful. But no, he decided, it was not that. Her attraction for him was not particularly sexual—the kiss was rather a taunt, an expression of independence—so much as agreeable. He liked to be with her. Breeding, he thought; there must be something to it. And yet, devil in hell, look at the stock she was bred from; a cantankerous, stupid, self-important old man. Though even the old man, Neve admitted to himself, had something of the

67

same sort of attraction for him that Elizabeth had, something that you could call, if you liked, quality.

"Hey, look out," he said out loud as he drove, "where the hell are you going? Wanting to mix with the quality! This is a fine time of life to find out you're a snob."

Why should he give one blue damn about the squire of a little village who was doing his best to spite the steel project, and was at any rate proving a bloody nuisance? If it had been the little Labour councillor opposing the mill, he would merely have laughed contemptuously at him. If it had been some other moneyed interest, some business opposition, he would have fought, but not admired. But because it was "the squire", because it was gentry, they all automatically made a bow to it, touched a forelock. Even Heron, with the steel-baron money behind him, had crawled to Elizabeth when he discovered who she was. And he himself, Charles Neve, the hard one, the engineer from the slums, whose success was a quittal for what the world had done to his father, had merely to be introduced to the squire and his daughter to bend his knee to them and curry their favour. "Dear God," he said, "what hope is there for England? We're all villagers at heart."

9

As the days went by it became evident that one would see practically everybody at the fishermen's protest meeting. It was the focus of all the disputes in the town.

Neve grew so sick of hearing about it that he half resolved not to go. But when the night came he went.

There was a stream of people across the square, and up the broad stone steps into the Town Hall. Neve pushed his way in, looking for a place somewhere at the back, and then saw that Elizabeth, at one end of a row, was beckoning to him. He hesitated, shrugged, and went to sit beside her.

"Going to be a full house," he said, awkwardly seeking something to say.

"Gulport has never had anything like it. I told you that you people livened us up."

68

He looked around the hall. It was odd how, even in this sort of impromptu crush, people kept in their own groups. The burgesses and their stout wives were mostly on the right-hand side, about half-way back. The fishermen were a weather-beaten splodge on the left. Up in front were the mill people—Appleton glancing anxiously at his wife seated beside him, the suaveness of Heron, who was chatting amicably to his neighbour. At the back of the hall, crowded into the seats and standing against the wall, was the bulk of the townsfolk, the young men calling slyly to the girls, and the girls giggling, and the old men smoking their pipes. Neve was looking for Papelian, and at last saw that he was up in the balcony, sitting in the front row, silent and motionless. So that was where the trouble would come from. He wondered who the thin woman with the troubled face was, sitting beside him. His wife? It seemed odd to think of Papelian with something so comfortable as a wife. Not that she looked particularly comforting. Looking more closely around, Neve saw that men from the site were placed in little groups in the body of the hall, and strung out around the walls, and at the back.

"Your father used to handling meetings?" he asked.

"An old hand."

"This one may get a bit noisy, you know."

"Why should it?"

"Well, I feel a bit guilty about this," he uneasily admitted: "I should have warned your father at the time, but I was het up, and I thought he could damn well find out for himself. That fellow that met him in the fields, Papelian, you remember he spoke of him? Papelian's a Communist, a professional at it. His job is to make as much trouble as he can—I've had a brush or two with him already, and it'll get a lot hotter as the work goes on."

"A Communist?" she asked, "a real live one? Oh, do point him out. I've never seen one before."

"He's in the front row of the balcony, next to a thin, angry-looking woman, near the centre."

"That little man?" she said, craning her neck. "But how disappointing. He looks quite ordinary. He's not even

69

throwing leaflets. I thought they always threw leaflets."

"It may be bricks."

"Don't worry," she said, turning round again, "Henry is frightfully good at dealing with interrupters. He freezes them."

The platform party was now coming in—half a dozen elderly, genteel-looking people, of whom Neve recognized only Colonel Melmoth. They took their chairs behind the table with its green baize cover, its water-bottle and glass, its microphone, and Melmoth, in the centre, gazed benevolently round the hall while the committee-men settled.

The hall fell silent as he stood up to open the meeting. He thanked them for coming—an encouraging sign that the town recognized the importance of the very grave matters they had to discuss. He was not against progress, far from it. But he was strongly opposed to injustice. He hoped never to see the day when an act of flagrant injustice could be committed in this land of theirs, without rousing indignant public opinion.

An elderly man on the platform said, "Hear, hear."

Melmoth went briskly on with the business. He outlined the facts of the dispute about the fishermen's quay, the traditional means of their livelihood, to which they were entitled, not only by custom, but by a centuries-old charter. Now it was proposed, by Government action, to seize this ancient privilege in order to erect some sort of a steel mill—he was not conversant with the technicalities, but he understood it was called a hot-strip rolling mill.

He paused. It was well-known, he continued, that he personally was opposed to the construction of this mill in Gulport. But he begged his audience to remember that this was not the issue that night. They were not opposing the mill. They were concerned simply with the injustice to the fishermen. He was going to ask the meeting to stick firmly to that point.

"He does it rather well, doesn't he?" whispered Elizabeth.

Now there was a little figure up on his feet in the middle of the hall. Councillor Jafet was addressing the meeting, to a few cries of "Good old Jimmy". Councillor Jafet orated warmly, but advised moderation. He thought they knew him pretty well, and he also thought that no one in Gulport who knew his record would accuse him of acting contrary to the interests of the workers. But they must not forget that the fishermen were not the only workers. The mill was a great project, which would bring a lot of work into Gulport—had already brought a wave of prosperity. Injustice to the fishermen Councillor Jafet would fight as strongly as anyone present. But would it not be more sensible, instead of starting court action, to try and get the thing settled fairly and amicably? What he wanted to know was, what would the mill do to compensate the fishermen? He suggested that the chairman should call upon some of the mill management people, who he could see were present, to give the other side of the case.

Melmoth judicially nodded, and looked around the hall. And then Heron was rising slowly to his feet, as though reluctant. He had not intended to intervene. But if the chairman thought, and the meeting thought, as his old friend and political enemy Councillor Jafet had suggested, that it would be helpful to have a word from someone not unconnected with the project of constructing the largest hot-strip rolling mill in the world, a vast and visionary feat of engineering that would bring immense benefits, not only to Gulport itself, but to the whole country....

"Smoothie!" declared Elizabeth with distaste.

Melmoth gravely nodded again, and Heron went mellifluously on. But from the back, and from one side, came first a muttering, and then a few shouts. The respectable people in the body of the hall swivelled curiously. The shouts were coming from men scattered around the fringe, men who were laughing as well as shouting.

"Ah," said Heron, his voice rising to a by-election boom, "I see we have some of the comrades with us to-night."

A burst of laughter. "Chuck it, Heron. Get back to your millionaires."

Melmoth rapped on the table, compelling silence.

"This meeting will be conducted courteously. And I will not have politics brought into it. Is that understood?"

71

"They won't worry me, Mr. Chairman," said Heron, smiling, "I've met 'em before."

"And we've met you before." "And we don't want to meet you again." "Oah, isn't he lovely?"

"I was asked to tell you," continued Heron, his voice voluminous, "what compensation the mill management is prepared to give the fishermen. If you don't want to know, that's all right by me. I'm quite happy to sit down, and listen. I always enjoy listening to the comrades."

Cries from the centre of the hall, to let him speak, give him a hearing, shut up at the back. And from the back a roar of laughter, and a man singing, "Tell us the old, old story."

Heron grinned, and patiently waited. Melmoth made to intervene again, but Heron motioned him down. He waited, and the noise gradually died.

"He knows what he's doing, at least," Elizabeth grudgingly admitted.

"It's his trade," said Neve.

"Now then," said Heron, "this is what the management will do. A new stretch of quay will be built for the fishermen, at no cost to themselves. It will be much more modern than anything they have had in the past. It will put the management to a very great expense. But we shall willingly undertake this expense, provided there is no attempt to involve us in long and complicated legal action."

There was a confused shouting from the back of the hall, equally confused cries for silence from the centre. Neve glanced up at Papelian. He was sitting quite still, staring in front of him. So was the woman at his side.

Melmoth rapped for silence.

"It appears, Mr. Heron," he said, when he could be heard, "that the meeting is dissatisfied with your proposal."

"Ah, but how about the fishermen?" asked Heron, "are they satisfied?"

Neve said to Elizabeth, "Now it comes. Here's the sell-out."

She shook her head. "You're wrong. Henry saw Ted Flowers and had it out with him. It is not true that he has been bribed—that's just a rumour that got spread around."

72

"Ask them now," suggested Heron.

"Very well. I have no objection. I will call upon Mr. Edward Flowers. . . ."

But a huge man at the back of the hall called out imperatively, "Mr. Chairman. . . ."

"Now, wait a minute. Let's have things in proper order, please."

"But, Mr. Chairman," roared the huge man, in a voice to match his girth, "I'm speaking for the men working out on Skelstrand. . . ."

"All in good time. You shall have your turn."

"No, Mr. Chairman," in a voice that even the microphone could not smother. "Before you hear the fishermen, let 'em hear what we've got to say. We don't care if our own jobs are threatened, we're on the side of the fishermen. . . ."

A low cheering started up at the back.

"We stand shoulder to shoulder with them, Mr. Chairman. We're fellow workers. We'll stick up for their rights, same as ours, and to hell with the bosses."

The whole of the back of the hall roared with delight. Melmoth stood there, smiling, holding up his hands, imploring for silence.

And then there came a clear voice from the balcony. "It's a lie. He doesn't speak for the Skelstrand workers. He speaks for the Communist Party."

The whole meeting swivelled again, staring. At the far end of the balcony stood a tall, grey figure, white-faced, a scar slashed across his forehead.

Elizabeth clutched Neve's arm. "Who's that?"

"He's a Pole. Mysterious sort of chap. Bit of a fanatic."

The back was growling now, but the Pole stood defiantly. Melmoth was still standing, so was Heron. Melmoth's face had hardened. He was rapping violently on the table. Suddenly there was complete silence. He said, "This is going to stop. Either we have order at this meeting, or I close it. You will all get the chance to say what you have to say, but not until I tell you. Now then. You, up in the balcony, sit down. And you, Mr. Heron, please sit down."

"But, sir . . ." came from the balcony.

"Sit down," commanded Melmoth.

The Pole bowed jerkily, and sat down. Heron smiled approvingly, and sat down.

The huge man at the back suddenly shouted, "But Mr. Chairman. . . . "

"Hold your noise," ordered Melmoth. He subsided.

Melmoth waited again for complete silence. "In this country we have free speech. That means we listen quietly to what every man has to say. We are now going to hear what the fishermen have to say, and we are going to hear it in silence. I call upon Mr. Edward Flowers, whom you all know —all the townspeople, anyway. For the benefit of the others, let me say that Mr. Flowers is one of the skippers of the fishing fleet, and the fishermen have chosen him as their representative. Now then, Ted, come up on the platform."

Flowers rose from a seat near the front, and climbed the steps to the platform. Melmoth passed the microphone across to him, he cleared his throat, and started on a catalogue of thanks. The fishermen were very grateful to their fellow townsmen for taking up their cause. They were particularly grateful to Colonel Melmoth, who had given up so much of his time and all that. They were grateful, too, to the working people out at Skelstrand. They were strangers in the town, but he thought that, after tonight, the working men of Gulport would feel very warmly towards them. Flowers had a white handkerchief in the breast pocket of his blue serge suit, and he kept on pulling it out and wiping his hands on it.

What they all wanted, continued Flowers, was to see that the fishermen, who had earned their living at Gulport for many centuries, were able to go on making a living. That was the important thing. They had their rights, and they knew what they were. They were all set out in the charter, and they could fight on that charter, and if necessary they would fight.

Somebody started clapping, others joined in, and for a couple of minutes there was applause. Ted Flowers stood there, smiling awkwardly at it, pulling out his handkerchief and wiping his jaw.

"But we're not unreasonable," he went on. "We're not out to injure anybody else. We don't want all you chaps at Skelstrand put out of a job, if it can be helped. All we want is the proper facilities for doing our own job."

He paused, and the hall was silent. Neve saw a puzzled look come into the chairman's face. Elizabeth, beside him, drew in her breath. Neve grinned uncomfortably to himself.

"Just before this meeting started," said Flowers, "we had an offer from the Skelstrand management."

"How much?" shouted a voice from the back. Melmoth rapped on the table, and called, "Silence," his face grim.

"It wasn't an offer of money," said Flowers. "It was an offer of a new quay, and buildings and all that, in compensation for giving up our charter rights to the bit of the old quay that is needed for the steel mill. It seems to us that the right thing to do is to accept that offer, if it's made in good faith."

"It has the Government's backing," interjected Heron, without getting up.

The huge voice of the man at the back suddenly roared, "He's sold you out, Guv."

"Order," rapped Melmoth.

"He's leading you up the garden." "He don't talk for no fishermen." A roar was starting at the back, and spreading forward through the hall. "Stabbed you in the back." "He's no bloody worker." The hubbub was rising, against the blare of Melmoth on the microphone, calling for silence. "Sit down, Squire." "Chuck him out of it."

The big man came pushing towards the front of the hall, a few of his mates gathering behind him.

"Let's have the workers' resolution, Mr. Chairman," he demanded. "He's a stool pigeon for the bosses."

"We'll have no resolution," blared Melmoth, "until I say so."

In the centre of the hall people were shouting, "Order, order," some of them rising in their places. Neve glanced swiftly up at Papelian, and saw that he was leaning forward, nodding. The big man was still moving towards the front of the hall, and more and more were coming behind him, and others down the other side of the hall, not fighting, or angry, but good-humouredly moving forward, steadily.

75

"I'll close the meeting," Melmoth was threatening. "Sit down, the lot of you."

"That's all right, Squire," shouted the big man. "You're okay. We like you, Squire."

"Who's all right?" "Squire's all right." "Boom, boom, boom."

Heron, still in his seat, was smiling quietly. Appleton was up, as though to defend Laura. A few of the women were trying to get out from the middle of the hall, and one of them was screaming. The crowd of men was still moving forward, all very cheerfully. The big man and a few of the leaders were climbing up on to the platform now. Melmoth, his face white with anger, made no movement, but stood glaring at them. Ted Flowers made as if to fight, but a couple of them soothed him down. Some of the platform party began to retreat though the back. The men from the hall were all round Melmoth now, standing there firmly, but not jostling.

The big man got hold of the microphone, which he certainly did not need, and began to boom through it.

"Now, then, mates, we're going to have a little resolution. They tried to sell us out at this meeting, but the workers won't have it, will they?"

There were roars of assent from men all over the hall.

"We'll have a bit of a workers' resolution, mates. Don't get excited. We're just going to have a vote."

He pulled a scrap of paper from his pocket, and began to read, "The workers of Gulport, and the workers on the steel mill site at Skelstrand, condemn the bureaucratic manœuvre to deprive the workers of the fishing fleet of their traditional rights, and declare they will fight for justice for the fishermen by every means in their power."

Above the tumult in the hall his voice asked for a mover and seconder. Somewhere a man shouted, "Move that," and another, "Second that."

"In favour?" demanded the big man.

A confused roar went up.

The big man turned towards Melmoth, grinning. "Carried, Mr. Chairman," he said.

"You're a scoundrel," said Melmoth, "and I have sent for the police."

"Oh, they won't find any disorder here. Listen, mates, no trouble. When the coppers get here, do as you're told, see?"

Then the singing started, difficult to say exactly where. The men on the platform took it up, the big man leading, and in a moment the song was swelling through the hall.

"What are they singing?" asked Elizabeth.

"The Internationale."

"Charles, I'm frightened," she said, taking hold of his sleeve, "I don't think I have ever been frightened like this before. Can you get me out, please?"

"I'll try," he said. He looked at the door, but the first policemen were struggling through, to the good-natured cheers of the men. He shrugged. "Not a chance, not yet. We'll have to wait. Don't worry, there won't be any trouble."

Up on the platform the big man was singing strongly, staring at Melmoth, who stood erect, grim, white-faced. Neve turned to glance up at the balcony. In the front stood Papelian and the woman with him, as erect, as stiff, as expressionless. Elizabeth, by his side, was shivering.

PART TWO

1

THE Gazzard family infiltrated, as it were, into Gulport throughout the summer. After Robert Heron, Sir Russell's personal secretary, came Norman Fogg, Sir Russell's bailiff, to farm Overskel Hall, tearing up meadows that had not known the plough these forty years. And now and then one or other of the actual family darted in and out of Gulport, like swallows making a home. A long black Rolls-Royce fled decorously through the lanes and up the Overskel drive, and that was Sir Russell himself come to inspect his property. That afternoon, the long black Rolls stood augustly in the Market Square while Sir Russell, in some upper room of the headquarters building, conferred briefly but incisively with his lieutenants; and then he was down into the car at a run, a huge fur blanket was whisked over his knees, and he was gone in a puff of cigar smoke and the slightest aroma of petrol fumes from the exhaust. On other occasions there were flashes through the district of two tiny, very fast sports cars, one red, one blue. And they contained, so it was said, the two Gazzard boys; though whether it were George in the red car and Andrew in the blue, or vice versa, even their intimate friends could not, at that speed, have discerned. Then there was the visit of a stately Daimler, rather of the shape favoured by the late Queen Mary. This vehicle carried Lady Gazzard and her daughter Cynthia, together with an interior decorator from London. Lady Gazzard and the interior decorator went through all the rooms of Overskel in a morning and afternoon, Lady Gazzard dictating her requirements for each, and the interior decorator making notes. At the end of the afternoon, in the main drawing-room, one of the maids reported, Lady Gazzard preached the interior decorator a sermon on business integrity and the need for scrupulousness in submitting his estimates. "Absolute honesty," said Lady Gazzard. Then, turning to the housekeeper, who happened to be standing by, she repeated, "Absolute honesty, Simpson, and absolute purity. And Simpson, make a personal friend of God."

By the autumn it was apparent that the Gazzards would soon be in residence. In October several platoons of white-coated painters and decorators, in cloth caps, arrived at Overskel. The furniture came towards the middle of November. Early in December the Gazzards were in. A curious countryside craned its neck to get a dekko at them. And the truth is that the countryside was rather disappointed. It had expected something a little fanciful, a little extravagant in appearance. After all, the man was a millionaire, and ought, at any rate, to have looked flashy. But Sir Russell turned out to be a small, lean man in a well-cut suit.

Lady Gazzard was more rewarding. She was, of course, tall. Her hair, deep golden in colour, was combed back over her prominent brows, and worn in a large bundle on the nape of her neck; her dresses, though costly, were usually knitted; and she had a way of walking across a room dramatically, arm extended forward, like Lady Macbeth.

The Gazzard boys seemed nothing remarkable, however; merely two young men in tweed suits that were no louder than most young men affect. Of Miss Gazzard, the chief impression was that she was fashionably dressed.

The countryside regarded the Gazzards as part of the invasion by the steel mill, foreign, transitory people. But Sir Russell, though he said nothing about it, had different intentions. He meant to be permanent. He had had plenty of houses before, but none gave him such deep satisfaction as Overskel. As he gazed out of its windows, or went pacing into the park to look back on it, he was content. Overskel was a red-brick house, built during the reign of the first George, and comely. But it was not its appearance, so much as its existence, that gratified Sir Russell. He stood, one morning after breakfast, at the window of the room set aside as his study, staring at the elms, and, reflecting on his life, mused that this was what it had been for. His apprenticeship in a machine-shop, his boldness in buying during a depression his first factory, a derelict thing that had made bicycles, the risks he had taken over his first amalgamation of three

81

foundries, the tremulous weeks of financial manipulation during which he had scraped out of a situation that at the very least would have been awkward, the building-up on armaments during the war and the deals in surplus war equipment afterwards—all these had been directed, though he had not at the time realized it, towards Overskel. In this house, with its 230 acres, he would create the home of the Gazzards. Centuries hence, he liked to think, the Gazzard family would be living there; and, by then, a noble family. So great had been his services to industry, and so extensive his contributions to party funds, that he was pretty sure, at the next change of government, of his barony. Baron Gazzard of Overskel in the county of Greenshire—that was his dream. And he had the money to back it. The point was, had he the family with enough tenacity to carry it on? There was the flaw in Sir Russell's imagination, there his possible nightmare. Privately, he was anxious about his children. On Andrew, his elder son, he had lavished Harrow and Cambridge; and the boy was dissipated, regarding money simply as something to waste. Sir Russell grimly reflected that he would have done better to have apprenticed him at fifteen. George, the younger, had been given merely Charterhouse and a training in the firm's London offices, and George had turned out better, more serious, more sober and fonder of Rugby football. But George was not the heir. Cynthia, of course, was simply a girl. Sir Russell considered that his best course was to get Andrew married to some girl of a county family—never mind money, he would supply the money, what he wanted was birth—and then perhaps the fellow would settle to the sort of life that Overskel typified. And the sooner the better. Sir Russell was convinced that his own life would not last very much longer. If it were not his kidneys, which gave him a lot of worry, then he feared for his heart. From the other horrors which can afflict ageing men he usually managed to turn away his thoughts, except after a night of insomnia, when he was convinced of prostate trouble. One of his purposes in settling at Overskel had been to provide himself with food from the home farm which he could ensure to be compost-grown, without any irritating chemical fertilizers, but he found that he could not obtain yoghourt locally and would have to have his regular supplies sent from London. He was also suspicious of the capability of the local doctor, that hulking great fellow who had seemed not so much unimpressed by, as indifferent to, Sir Russell's most obvious symptoms. He could continue, of course, to rely on his Harley Street man for his normal maladies. But if there were a sudden crisis it would have to be this Dr. Irons, and Sir Russell greatly feared his competence. It was all very well Violet's urging him to trust in divine guidance. He had never been able to share her confidence in the instructions which reached her during her quiet time every morning, and which she noted with pencil upon a piece of paper. He had been accustomed to make his own decisions.

Well, he bravely assured himself, the end had to come at some time for everyone. He would go easier if he could first see Andrew settled down with a wife at Overskel, with at least one grandson upon whom Sir Russell could entail the place, and sufficient capital to keep it up. He was interrupted in his reflections by Fogg, the bailiff, waiting to make his usual morning round of the home farm with his employer, a daily ceremony in which Sir Russell delighted. He put on his gumboots, his thick hunting mackintosh, a muffler and his cloth cap, and, taking his stick, joined Fogg in the yard.

"Well, Fogg, how goes it?" he inquired, as they wandered carefully through the Danish piggeries, the hens' battery-houses, the gleaming cleanliness of the milking sheds.

Fogg replied cheerfully that it was going very well. The sows were producing unexceptionable litters. The cows were yielding very profitable quantities of milk. The pullets were coming into lay just at the moment when the packing-station price had risen. All in all, Fogg was happy to give an account of his stewardship. It was Fogg's opinion that, unless they ran into unusually bad luck, the farm would be a paying proposition within a twelvemonth.

At this news Sir Russell's brow grew darker and darker.

"Look you here, Fogg," he said curtly, "I'll thank you to leave the financial side of it to me. Your job is to produce for the house a regular supply of all the food we want. What's left over can go on the market. But don't worry about price."

"The price'll be all right, sir," protested Fogg, injured.

"Leave that to me," insisted Sir Russell. "My object in running this farm, Fogg, is to help the country by producing a bit of extra food. I'm not worried about the price we get for it. And if there is any more equipment you need, don't hesitate to let me know."

"We're all right for tools now," said Fogg.

"Surely you want another tractor, or a grass drier, or something?" replied Sir Russell irritably. "Can't we put some more gear into the milking sheds? Damn it, man, don't stint the place."

He thought contemptuously what a fool the man was. Did he really imagine that, with surtax at its present rate, anybody wanted a farm to pay? A profit would be ruinous. Ah well, he would have another barn put up, and buy a Land Rover, and grow a few flowers for market to get the gardeners' wages on the expenses bill. And there was plenty of nice, costly equipment advertised in the *Farmer and Stockbreeder*, which would give him a happy hour or two ordering. If Fogg imagined, Sir Russell thought with a chuckle, that a man with his financial experience could not run a farm at a profitable loss, he was a bigger fool than he took him for.

2

Heron was in the house when Sir Russell got back from his tour of the farm. He nodded to him, and said, "Look here, Heron, we're having too many labour troubles."

"What can you expect, sir? They're encouraged not to work."

"Then we'll discourage 'em," said Sir Russell, changing his overcoat. "Why, hallo, Violet, I thought you were upstairs."

Lady Gazzard advanced across the hall, nodding to Heron.

"Is it true," she asked, "that the men are going to strike?"

"There's a threat of it."

"Communists?"

"I expect so, my dear. It's supposed to be about a chap who raped a girl."

84

"He was acquitted," interposed Heron.

"Whether he did it or not, he's a damn nuisance."

"You see," Heron explained to her, "we couldn't give him his job back, the feeling in the town was too strong. Now the men say—and you can see their point—that he was tried and found not guilty, so either he gets his job back, or they come out."

"It's the most wonderful opportunity," she declared. "Russell, you must accept guidance. Remember the forgotten factor."

"The forgotten factor?" asked Heron.

"God, Mr. Heron. Russell, I beg of you, meet the men's leader as man to man. Never mind who is right, but what is right."

"Aye, but what is right? Should we give the chap back his job, and have trouble with the town, or fire him and have trouble with the men?"

"I will ask God," she promised.

"You do that," he agreed. "Come on, Heron, we'll get down to the site."

In the car, he said, "Violet's all taken up with this religion. Of course, you have to respect it."

"Lady Gazzard is very sincere, sir."

"Know what she wants me to do? Ask the men's leader to come into my office and say his prayers."

Heron dutifully laughed. "Of course, it's all very idealistic. . . ."

"It's on a cash basis, I don't mind telling you privately. The thousands she has made me contribute to that damned organization. Not that I mind that. After all, you never know. They tell me quite a lot of the Government people are tied up in it. Bread on the waters, eh, Heron? Funny world, ain't it?"

As the car sped towards Skelstrand, Sir Russell jerked his thumb at the chimneys of Shard, just showing above the trees.

"I want to know those people, Heron," he said.

"The Melmoths? The old man is dead set against the mill."

"Oh, the hell with that. He's got his point of view, I dare say. Everybody's entitled to their point of view. I'm coming

85

to live here, and I want to be on good terms with my neigh-bours. The trouble about the mill will pass. Send them an invite to come to Overskel."

"I doubt they'd come, sir."

"They wouldn't? Then I'll go to them. Call on 'em. Don't you leave cards, or something, in the country?"

"You could do that," agreed Heron.

"Well, arrange it for me, there's a good chap. You know about these things. Never had time myself."

Heron mused. "We might do something through the girl."

"Is there a girl?"

"Oh yes, a damn pretty one. Bit of a spitfire."

"Single?"

"Yes, she's single. Gossip is that she's a bit smitten with Charlie Neve."

"What, the engineer? She can't be very choosy. The family is county all right, I suppose?"

"Oh yes, the genuine thing."

"Well, you fix it, Heron," said Sir Russell. "Do it yourself, rather particular. I'm keen on this."

"Very good, sir," said Heron.

As they came round the last bend that opened on to the mill site Sir Russell smiled privately. There was now getting to be something to see, and he liked the view. In his day he had owned many places, but mostly he had bought them. This he would build, his monument. Steel, the guts of the thing. They could keep all their plastics and atomic power and aluminium alloys. Steel and coal were the twin props of England, and always would be. The man who had created Skelstrand was sure of his corner of fame. And it was he, and he alone, who was creating Skelstrand—oh, not the technicalities of it, but the vision. The engineering of it, that was nothing. Any well-trained fool could have done that. It was to have conceived the thing, in all its vastness, and then to have had the ability and the power to finance it; to get together the private interests that would entrust their wealth to him, to entwine them with the governing politicians who could lavish the public millions; and then to set the one faction against the other, to balance them, to poise and counterpoise them, so that the control always remained with him. He gave not a damn for the political argument over steel. They could nationalize it or denationalize or renationalize it, they could pin on to it whatever name they liked; the control would be so surely his that he would be able to hand it down to his son. There again he came up against his one foreboding. Would Andrew be man enough to take hold of the thing from his hands, and preserve it for his own son? It would be bitter if the one flaw in his scheme were to be that he, who had created everything else from his own strength, should have bred a weakling.

But even that nagging premonition could not disturb him as he gazed at the growth of Skelstrand. To the west the stout pillars of the furnaces had already risen high enough to overtop the skyline, and beyond them could be glimpsed the crane-tops and the grabs, swinging gently under the clouds, where the harbour works had begun. Away to the east men were rolling yet farther the broad apron of concrete upon which, in the centre, the first hundred yards of the main buildings were already mast-high—broad, stout, but not yet graceful as they finally would be. Everything was clothed in a chain mail of scaffolding, and everywhere men were working—perched high, sunk low, in this corner or that—and in front of them the lorries turning in and out, the buckets clanking across the overhead lines, the ticking of pumps, intermittent jets of steam, tiny showers of brilliant sparks from the welders, the trundling noise of concrete mixers. And all sandy. He felt as though, by main strength, the huge bulk of Skelstrand was being heaved up from the sands; his strength, as though he were doing it with his own biceps. They could talk to him of the cathedral builders of the middle ages lavishing their craftsmanship on imperishable stone. Where was the cathedral that could begin to compare with this great building of concrete and structural steel? Somebody had once said to him. "Ah, but where's the inspiration?" He snorted. The inspiration was money.

Heron helped him out of the car, and they crossed to the office, where a few were waiting for him. He nodded to them —Neve the engineer, whom he liked, the gaunt architect,

Appleton the civil servant, the old fool of a lawyer whose name he could not remember.

"Well," he said, "what is it? This piddling little business of a strike?"

"The Minister is worried," said Appleton nervously. "He has to answer in the House. A strike now would be most unfortunate—he's having trouble with Transport House as it is. There are a couple of by-elections pending."

"What does he want me to do?" asked Sir Russell cheerfully. "This time, for a change, they're not threatening to strike because of me. I didn't rape the girl."

"Nor did the other chap," suggested Heron. "He was acquitted. You all seem to overlook that."

"The feeling in the town is very strong," said Appleton unhappily. "First that blasted meeting, and now this. We can run into a lot of trouble."

"The feeling among the men is strong too," replied Heron.

Sir Russell perched himself on a stool, and said, good-humouredly, "Look, gentlemen, personally I don't care whether we give this chap his job back or not. Justice isn't my business. All I want is a steel mill."

"But, sir," said Heron, "we have got to decide. Do we give this chap his job back or not?"

"Are you sure they'll strike if we don't?"

"Yes, pretty sure."

Sir Russell was enjoying himself. "What do you say, Neve? They're really your men, you know. I don't know why I worry about the thing, except that I want a mill as fast as I can get it."

"That's what I want too," said Neve.

"Ah, so you're against letting 'em strike. Give the chap his job back, placate the men, and have right on our side as well, I suppose."

Neve shook his head. "I'm giving him no job back, right or wrong."

"That's better. That sounds more like it. You reckon he did do the girl, is that it?"

"I don't give a damn whether he did or he didn't. Nothing to do with me. But if you give in to 'em the first time they threaten a strike, you might as well chuck it. They haven't got a case, they won't get official union support, in a couple of weeks they'll need money for Christmas—it's a natural."

The older man looked at the younger, appraising. There came back to him echoes of his own life. If this were the fellow that county girl had picked on, she knew how to pick. That was the way he would have liked to hear his own son talk. Then he suddenly felt obstinate and angry—angry that it was not his own son talking.

So he smiled, and said, "That's it, then, gentlemen. We'll leave Mr. Neve to handle it, eh? He reckons that, in the long run, we should lose more time by weakness now, and I agree with him."

"But, sir——" protested Appleton.

"You leave the Minister to me, my boy. I'll talk to him. Come on, Heron, I want to get back into the town. Good morning."

In the car, he said to Heron, "Sound fellow, that engineer, eh?"

"Bit of a tough egg," agreed Heron.

"Not very likely to ask the strike committee to come in and say their prayers with him?"

"No, I don't think that's very likely," smiled Heron.

"Then I'd better turn my wife loose on him. Get him up to Overskel at the week-end. And Heron, get those county people to come over too, the girl anyway, and the old man if you can."

"I'll do my best, sir," said Heron dubiously.

At Gulport, Sir Russell brisked into his office, a large room that had been extravagantly furnished for him on the first floor. On his desk was the usual pile of papers; at the door the girl with the usual list of telephone calls. He settled agreeably to them; this was the part of the day that he enjoyed, these were the real problems. While those other fellows were worrying about such trifles as strikes, his mind was occupied with the essential—money. The cost was going to be immense, and even in the estimates there were imponderables. A good deal of the machinery would have to be made in the States, and who knew what, in a year's time, the price of that might

be? It depended on complicated (and expensive) arrangements with Congressional lobbies, to get the bulk of it put
to an armaments dollar account. Luckily the American steel
men were with him, he could count on the international free-
masonry. One of his calls was to Pittsburgh, another to
Cologne. Then he rang up the Minister in London and talked
calculatingly to him for a quarter of an hour. When he put
the phone down, he sighed. The elements of his problems
were so simple. The money that he and his friends could
command was a mere fraction of the eighty-odd millions that
Skelstrand would cost. He had to get the rest in public money,
either from here or from America, and at the same time
retain, by guile, the ultimate control. He grimly remembered
the steel men who had tried it in years past and finally found
themselves forced to go to the banks and the insurance companies sometimes found themselves ousted, and accountants
put in their place. Well, that would not happen to him. He
was profoundly grateful that steel was now so bound up with
politics that the public purse could always be tapped, with
skill, and care. But there would be recurrent moments—
there was one now—when the margin would get so small
that there was danger of losing control. He lit a cigarette,
cupping it inside his fingers, a habit from his workman days
of which he had never rid himself, and gave the girl a Scottish
number to get him.

Before it came through, Heron looked in.

"By the way, sir," he said, "the strike's on. A deputation
called on Neve, and he told them there would be no job for
our lusty friend. So they sent out the call."

"They did, eh? Many come out?"

"Not certain yet. Looks like about seventy per cent."

"Ah well, we can take it easy for a few days. Anybody got
here yet from Transport House?"

"Not yet," grinned Heron.

"Look, have you fixed my week-end party?"

"I rang Miss Melmoth—or rather, I got one of the girls
to, she doesn't like me. She is going to ask her father. I think
they'll come, if only out of curiosity."

"Did you tell her young Neve would be there?"

"No. I thought that. . . ."

"You're probably right. By the way, ring up my wife, will you, and let her know the strike's on. She'll want to get cracking."

The phone rang.

"Your call to Scotland, Sir Russell."

"Righto, Heron, see you later. Hallo, hallo. Gazzard here. . . ."

3

BEFORE the dinner party on the Saturday evening, Sir Russell sent for his elder son.

"We're going to have a change, Andrew," he said. "You're going to do some work."

Andrew nodded. He was a tall young man, taking after his mother, but without her tense expression. "I've no objection. What work?"

"At Skelstrand. You've got to know every inch of that mill, as it is built."

"Start at the bottom, mixing concrete, eh? I warn you, I can't climb ladders—makes me dizzy."

"Don't be an ass," said his father, "you'll start with the construction engineers. I'm putting you under Neve, who's coming here this evening. He's able, and he has come up the hard way, like I did. He didn't go to Cambridge. You can learn a thing or two from him."

The young man nodded again.

"You've got to realize," continued his father, "that when I step out, you must carry on. By then you've got to know what you're doing. After a spell on the site, you'll come into the office with me, and get the hang of the financial side of it. Talking of finance, I suppose you're in debt again."

"Nothing much. A few hundreds."

Sir Russell sighed. "When I was your age, I lived on three pounds a week, and never owed a penny."

"It's not comparable. You weren't a rich man's son. If you'd wanted credit, you couldn't have got it. I can't avoid it. They force it on me—positively won't take cash."

Sir Russell gazed at his son. There was something, he admitted, in what he said.

"All right, Andrew, I'm not kicking. Let Heron have an account of what you owe, and I'll settle."

"Thanks."

"But now we've got to understand each other. You've had your fun, and I don't begrudge it. Now you've got to settle down. I'm getting old. When I go, you'll have a hell of a lot of money, and a hell of a lot of responsibility. You've got to be ready."

The young man grinned. "I could manage the money all right."

"Oh no, you couldn't. You're no more fit to handle the one than the other. I'm going to talk straight. I intend to see Skelstrand built, and, when it is, I shall have the controlling interest. I also intend, but keep this to yourself, to get a barony. It's all fixed for the next change of government. So you'll find yourself with a title, this house, the control of Skelstrand, and a lot of other stuff. At the moment you're not fit to inherit a grocer's shop. So let's have an understanding. I'll give you three years to satisfy me you've got enough sense to handle the business, and to settle down as a man of substance. If you don't satisfy me, I'll turn the lot over to George."

"George is steady enough, all right," agreed Andrew, leaning back, smiling.

"George is a good lad. I shall arrange for him. But you're the eldest, you inherit. And I'm going to see that you're fit for it. Before I go, I want to see you ready to step into this place with a family."

"With a family? Cripes, have I got to get married too?"

"I want a grandson, Andrew."

"Now you've shaken me. Are you fussy about who the girl is? Matter of fact, I know a very sweet girl, lives in Kensington, bit of an actress. . . ."

"Leave her in Kensington. I want you to marry into a county family."

"Perhaps you've chosen the girl," said Andrew humorously.

"Perhaps I have. I want you to take a look at the old

colonel's daughter, from Shard, over the way. It's why I've asked them up this evening."

Andrew got to his feet, protesting. "I say, this is a bit thick, ain't it?"

"In all sensible countries," said his father evenly, "marriages are arranged by parents. It's a much better system."

"No, but look here, I draw the line. Sensible be damned. You're not going to pick my wife for me, I tell you that."

"Of course, I can't force you. But perhaps I can persuade. Your salary at Skelstrand will be £40 a week. If I decide on Elizabeth Melmoth, the day you marry her it will rise to £100 a week, and I shall create a trust fund of £250,000, the income to be yours, the capital falling to your eldest son on his twenty-first birthday."

"But suppose she won't have me," said Andrew, bemused.

"That's up to you."

"And it may be the girl who is coming here this evening? Hell, I shan't be able to look her in the face. Are you going to tell her all this, or her old man?"

"Try," advised his father, "not to be such a bloody fool."

There was a knock at the door, and a maid announced that the guests were arriving.

"Blimey," cried Andrew, making for the sideboard, "I've got to have a stiff 'un."

The large drawing-room of Overskel was of magnificent proportions, and Lady Gazzard had not spared the decorations. The electric lights of the cut-glass chandeliers gleamed brightly upon the oil paintings, of the early nineteenth-century English school, in their rich gilt frames. The logs in the big fireplace, before which was stretched a huge polar-bear rug, competed with the unobtrusive radiators to give an impression of aromatic central heating. The arm-chairs and the sofa, upholstered in *petit point*, were vast and deep; the side-tables had been described by the vendor as choice little pieces, and against the wall between the french windows stood a lacquered cabinet; the china was Minton, the silver Georgian, the curtains of heavy scarlet silk. From the green-houses of Overskel had come the banked-up roses, carnations and chrysanthemums. With an instinctive flair for effect, the two black poodles were gracefully poised upon the white fur rug.

In this setting Lady Gazzard and her daughter Cynthia nervously awaited their guests. Lady Gazzard, that is, was nervous; she felt rather as, in her maiden days as mixed-infant teacher in a London County Council school, she had felt just before the terminal visit of the school inspector. Cynthia, a girl with a face resembling a swarthy fish, and with her hair fashionably cropped and ragged, was accustomed to society, and therefore not nervous, but only bored.

Fortunately Dr. Irons was the first to arrive, in an old dinner jacket which managed to look as though it had a roll collar, and Lady Gazzard was certainly not intimidated by him; she regarded him almost as an employee. And he brought with him the Hentys, who, being professionally religious, were already her dear friends, her accomplices.

"Really, Lady Gazzard," said Roger, "a most generous gift."

"Not my gift, Mr. Henty. I asked for guidance, and I got it. I could feel the pencil vibrating as I took down the message. The words came—give £500 to Mr. Henty for a Mission."

"Ah, yes, of course. Wonderful, wonderful. I have secured a hall to rent."

"Near the hostel?" she eagerly inquired.

"A hundred yards away, only."

"You see," she exclaimed in triumph, "it was meant!"

"Most gratifying," said Roger Henty uneasily, reflecting that he should reproach himself for a feeling of distaste, and uncomfortably aware that he had not experienced direct revelation since his undergraduate days.

"How's your dad?" Dr. Irons was asking Cynthia, gently nudging one of the poodles with his massive foot.

"I never know. He complains, of course. You should know, surely."

"Oh yes," replied the doctor cheerfully, "I know. Apart from his indigestion, he's the healthiest man of seventy I have seen for twenty years. But don't tell him, for heaven's sake. It'd bring on a bad attack."

"Of what?"

"Of fright, Miss Gazzard, of fright. The chronic malady of the rich, fear of death—or is it fear of death duties? Same thing, perhaps. Very lucrative for the profession, anyhow, and luckily we never have to cope with it on National Health."

Sir Russell, followed by Andrew, came hurrying in now to greet the guests. Charles Neve was the next to arrive, and Sir Russell found time to slip him, "How's the strike going?" Said Neve, "To plan." The host grinned and went on to meet Colonel Melmoth and his daughter, who were just being announced.

"Glad you came," he said, "and you, my dear."

He glanced quickly, approvingly at her. Graceful, quiet, those high cheek-bones and almost transparent skin, head delicately, proudly held on a slim neck, quality all right.

"Here, Andrew," he called, "come and look after the prettiest girl in the room. Miss Melmoth, this lout is my son. Teach him a few manners for me. Now, Colonel," he said, linking his arm, "come and have a spot of whisky. Can't touch it myself, unluckily. Blood pressure. I have to drink this tomato juice stuff—get it from California, they reinforce it with vitamins. You can't get it here. The Yanks are ahead of us. Well, chin chin."

"I hear you are starting to farm Overskel," began Melmoth. "It was time. The Bradbys let the place go, mostly, I'm afraid, for lack of money."

"Had they been here long?"

"Oh yes, many, many years. But then there was only the old lady left—the Admiral died, and the boy was in the *Hood*—and the place would have passed to a distant cousin. So she sold, and went to live at Bath."

"It's very sad," said Gazzard, "to hear of an old family like that dying out. It's like a bit of England dying."

He could see that Melmoth was surprised to hear him say that.

"You didn't expect that, did you, Colonel, from the self-made man?" He laughed, then added, "Ah, but I mean it seriously."

95

Melmoth twisted his glass in his fingers. "You know my feelings about this steel mill coming here? I've made no secret of them—I'm against you, with all the energy I possess."

Sir Russell nodded. "I admire you for it. And I'd like you to try to see it my way. There are changes, the country depends on developments. You and I won't agree about the mill, I know that. But out of office hours we're neighbours, and I hope we can be good neighbours."

"Of course," he politely agreed.

"And, Colonel, there was a time when the Melmoths first came to Shard. I like to think that this is the time when the Gazzards first came to Overskel." He laughed again. "Bloody sauce, eh, on my part? But why not say it? I believe in speaking out. I've got the money, Colonel, I've got the place, and I've got two sons."

He looked across the room to where Andrew was talking to Elizabeth. Andrew was clowning, and she was laughing with him.

"Tell you what," he offered, "come and try my little car— she'll do a hundred and ten."

"What an inducement. You haven't, I suppose, got an aeroplane?"

"I'll get one," he said, "I can drive one, you know—learnt at a club. We could get an Auster, and it'd put down on the fields all right. How about that? If I get an Auster, will you come for a ride with me?"

"You get a pony and trap, and I'll think about it."

"Oh lord," he complained, "you're one of those quiet girls, I can see that."

"Just something out of Jane Austen."

"Who's she?"

They all began to move in to dinner. The dining-room of Overskel was of panelled oak, and the furniture came from Heal's. On one wall, at the head of the table, hung a large oil portrait of Sir Russell, illumined by a small white tube of light; on the opposite wall, above Lady Gazzard's chair, hung a portrait of her, similarly lit.

"We haven't got any ancestors," Andrew remarked to

Elizabeth, noticing her eyes straying to the pictures, "so we have to start the family portraits from scratch."

"Isn't it," inquired Elizabeth, "rather disconcerting at breakfast?"

"Oh lord, I don't know, haven't eaten any breakfast for years, dear."

Sir Russell had placed Neve close to himself, and to Colonel Melmoth. Did he know Neve, he asked, engineer at Skelstrand?

"We've met," replied Melmoth.

"You ought to be grateful to this young fellow, Colonel," said Sir Russell. "He's the one who wouldn't give the bull-dozer driver his job back, and brought on the strike. He's on your side—he's trying to delay the mill."

"From what he told me," murmured Melmoth, "I thought he was all for the working classes."

"So are we all, ain't we?" grinned Gazzard. "We just like 'em to work, that's all. Any sign of them breaking yet, Neve?"

"They'll come back when the shoe pinches."

"They'll go back," called Lady Gazzard from the other end of the table, "when God sends them back."

"My wife's a great believer in religion, Colonel," said Gazzard, "she thinks it's the only answer to industrial trouble, and Communists, and all that. She may be right."

"You'll see," she said, "you'll see. It's not a question of who's right, but what's right."

"Lady Gazzard has most generously donated," said the clergyman, "a very large sum to found a Mission up by the hostel. Non-denominational, of course. So many of the workmen are Irish, and that means R.C. I understand the wretched fellow who, er, attacked poor Mr. Wilkinson's daughter is R.C."

"He was acquitted," interposed Heron, "I find I have to keep on saying that."

"Do you like Mr. Heron?" Elizabeth murmured to Andrew.

"He's a stinker."

"You and I have much in common."

"Then you'll come for a ride with me?" he asked eagerly.

"When you have a pony and trap."

Gazzard, picking at the breast of chicken—his diet was chiefly breast of chicken and peaches, smooth things that could not irritate the intestines and so lead to cancer—looked around his table as the conversation swelled generally. This, he thought, was what his work had bought, and not a bad bargain. Having no roots, he had purchased them. You could, after all, buy anything, if you had enough money.

4

WANDERING along Bridge Street, Jimmy Jafet asked himself sadly where was the happiness, the prosperity of the town, of which he had boasted? The lights shone from the shop windows, decorated with cotton-wool and holly leaves, every article tagged "Useful Present" or "Acceptable Gift", but the sauntering crowds that should have been gazing raptly were not there. Everybody was hurrying home, bolting and chaining doors, sitting uneasily in the parlour, going upstairs with misgivings to bed. Every child was met at the school gates by his mother, every girl who went out after dark escorted by her father. It was as though a plague were abroad, and fear racing up the streets like a dog. Jimmy was awed that people whom he had known all his life could act so unreasonably. But there was no arguing with them. It was no use telling them that the men of whom they were afraid were ordinary English working men, people like themselves. The townsfolk regarded the groups of idle workmen, dispiritedly wandering the streets, as though they were the troops of some invading power, and the town in occupation. If any of the Skelstrand men spoke to them, asked for a match, nodded and said good morning, the townspeople muttered and hurried by. Already one or two sporadic quarrels had broken out, sudden spurts of temper, even blows.

For the Skelstrand men, bewildered at first, were getting angry. They had their idleness to exacerbate them. They could attend the strike meetings to air their indignation, but after that there was nothing to do but lounge. They were getting as sullen as the empty scaffoldings at Skelstrand, the idle cranes on the quay. To irritate them still further they had the nagging of their wives, nagging for money now that Christmas was upon them. But there was no money, no strike pay. The unions would not recognize them, and they growled at the unions. The unofficial strike committee, in endless session in the upstairs room at the Duke's Head, issued instructions and exhortations enough, but no money. It had no money. In an industrial town it could have been collected from other works' factory gates, dinner-hour. But this was too far away. A few of the men, swearing, went out to Skelstrand, but the pickets, peaked with cold, turned them back. Not many, in any case, attempted it. The strike had reached the stage of blind obstinacy.

Jimmy Jafet stopped at Joe Wilkinson's shop, and rang the side bell. Mrs. Wilkinson let him in, he following her up the stairs to the living-room, where Joe was sitting by the fire with three or four other men, tradesmen, old friends.

Joe nodded to him, and he joined the circle of men, who took up their talk where they had broken it off. They were planning a citizens' defence league, a wildly foolish organization of townsmen who would escort the women, patrol the lonely reaches of the town at night, armed with sticks. Jimmy had known that this was mooted.

"Don't do it," he pleaded. "You'll stir up worse trouble. You'll put yourselves in the wrong. Leave it to the police."

"The police!" growled Joe. "Did the police protect my girl when that beast got at her?"

"They can't be everywhere."

"Ah," said one of the others, "but we can."

"Do the police hustle that bastard out of the town? Not they."

"How can they?" reasoned Jimmy. "After the acquittal, they have no power to."

"He stays on living here," said Joe, his voice rising, "and my girl has to go away. Is that justice for you?"

"Joe, it's terrible, I know it."

"Do you know it? How much do you know? Do you know," he demanded, "that he put my girl into the family way?"

"Oh, Christ," groaned Jimmy.

"Now, Joe," begged his wife.

"And she had to have an operation? And it was illegal to give it to her. Illegal! My God. Don't talk to me about justice, and police."

"This was a quiet place to live," said Mrs. Wilkinson suddenly. "Now we've got all these filthy men among us. Why should we suffer? Why should they drag them out of the slums, where they belong, and bring them here? We've always been respectable people. Daphne is a good girl, never gave us a moment's worry. And now we're disgraced. That beast was acquitted, and what does that mean? They think she was willing. Oh, I'd like to get my hands on that jury!"

"There's nobody in this town believes it, Mrs. Wilkinson," one of the other men tried to comfort her.

"Oh yes, there is, plenty. I've seen the nods and the winks, and the sly glances. Don't think I don't know. There's plenty jealous enough of us, of the business we've built up by hard work, of Mr. Wilkinson's position in the town— there's plenty only too ready to believe filthy things about us."

"That's over and done with, Mother," said Joe, raising his head. "We've got our cross. But I tell you this, Jimmy— it's not going to happen to any other decent girl. We're going to see to that. You're always standing up for the labouring men. You won't see that they're scum. But so long as they stay in this town, we're going to protect our own. And God help any more of 'em that try it on."

"And that's straight," added one of the other men. "You'd better warn your pals. Next time, they get what's coming to 'em."

Jimmy got away as soon as he could, welcoming the cold sharpness of the deserted streets. In the light from a shop window he pulled the heavy silver watch from his waistcoat pocket, and turned off towards the station. The London train was due, and he'd to meet Bill Whistlecroft from it. There were three or four other men waiting to meet the train, and Jimmy saw that each was carrying a heavy walking-stick. He turned away, sick, and wandered to the end of the platform, not wanting to talk to anybody. This whole business was being worked up in a way that frightened him. The very fact that Whistlecroft himself was coming down was extraordinary; the assistant general secretary. The usual thing was for the union to leave a strike like this to the district organizer, but they were sending Whistlecroft, and he was a big shot. Jimmy, of course, had known him for years, ever since he was a clerk in the district office; and a bit of a firebrand in the early days. A couple of good speeches in the mid-thirties had got him on a trade union deputation to Moscow, and the report they made when they got back was a one-day sensation in the papers. That was a stroke of luck for Bill. It set him on the road. By the time the war came along he was rightly placed for work of national importance. After the war he got several of the plums. He'd been a couple of times to Washington, and once to Unesco at Geneva. He'd written a couple of good, sound reports on the economic situation, and come out strong against Communism in a few speeches. He could get into the House if he wanted to, Jimmy reckoned, but he always scorned that. "Let 'em do the talking, Jimmy," he had once said, "and we boys'll handle the real stuff." In a few years it would be his turn for a knighthood. And a man of this importance, Jimmy reflected as he waited for the train, was coming down to handle this little strike. What went on? Why were they blowing it up to this size? Jimmy shook his head, bewildered.

The train arrived, and Bill Whistlecroft, stepping from a first-class carriage, hailed him jovially. "Hallo there, Jimmy, good to see you, boy." Jimmy, feeling more cheerful already, took his suitcase.

"You're staying at no hotel, Bill," he insisted, "you're coming home with me."

"Sure, sure. I'd like to," said Whistlecroft, with the snug

thought of the guinea a day out-of-town expenses he was entitled to. "But you can't carry that bag, it's too far. Let's get a cab."

When they were in it, and speeding through the deserted streets, he said amiably, "Might as well have a bit of comfort in this weary world, eh, me boy? And how're you keeping, eh?"

"Oh, fine, fine. This strike is worrying, of course."

But he already felt better about it.

"It's come at an awkward moment, that's all," said Whistlecroft. "It just happens that the boys can do without a strike at this moment. Wheels within wheels, you know, Jim."

When they got to his house, he saw that Kathy was peering through the front window, excited at seeing the taxi draw up. He waved to her, and she bobbed her head to him.

"How is she, Jim?" asked Whistlecroft.

"Better, I'm thankful to say. She hasn't had an attack for some time now. Of course, we know she'll never be quite right. It just isn't there. But she's happy."

He took the suitcase and they went into the house, bustling and cheerful. He called to Elsie that they had arrived, and she answered from the kitchen to take him up to the spare room, supper was ready. When they came down she had the table laid, and was carrying in the hotpot in its brown dish. With the oven cloth in one hand, she pushed the hair from her forehead with the other, and greeted the guest without a smile. Jimmy was aware of her drawn, strained face. She worked hard, Elsie, managed the house well, tended Kathy, and he never knew what she was thinking; rarely, he guiltily admitted, even considered it. But in the glow of Bill Whistlecroft's cheerfulness even Elsie warmed a little, and did not protest by more than a grimace when Jimmy brought out a couple of bottles of beer. Kathy was cooing and chattering in her seat at the table; they were not exactly words that she emitted, but sounds of pleasure. "Eat your supper," Elsie told her. Kathy, with a sidelong glance, obeyed. Bill Whistlecroft entertained them throughout the meal with stories of intrigue behind the scenes in London.

After they had eaten, Elsie cleared off the dishes into the scullery, and said she would put Kathy to bed, and go off herself. "Don't you two sit up all night," she said. "You're on early turn to-morrow, Jim."

Kathy protested, shaking her head and fluttering her hands, at being put to bed. "No, no, no, no," she cried. When her sister insisted, she darted towards Bill Whistlecroft, seized his hand, and began to mumble kisses on to it. Bill grinned, awkward, not knowing whether to pull away his hand. Elsie took her, still protesting, from the room.

"She's affectionate," said Bill.

"She's got a lovely nature," said Jimmy, "simple and kind, just like a child. She's like a child to Elsie."

"I wonder Elsie never got herself spliced, and had some of her own."

"Never showed any signs of wanting to. Anyway, we couldn't manage without her."

"It's wonderful," mused Bill, "what women'll do. Sacrifices we men would never dream of making."

"Well, she leads a comfortable enough life here," argued Jimmy. "She don't want for anything."

Then Bill Whistlecroft sneaked up to his room, and brought down a bottle of whisky from his bag, and they settled in front of the range, feet on the fender, to hours of blissful talk. They gossiped politics, all the old friends they had known who were now great men. Bill confided the most delicious scandals. They ranged over the whole world situation, and Bill revealed the inner secrets of the Cabinet, and of the U.S.A. He had a few anecdotes, too, of the Kremlin. And they drank a good deal of the whisky. It was the most enjoyable evening Jimmy Jafet had spent in years. Towards midnight they worked round to the strike, and Jimmy told Bill Whistlecroft all that he knew about it.

"Did this chap Callaghan really rape the girl?" Bill asked, interested.

"How can we be sure? The townsfolk are boiling about

it, but the jury was quite right, between ourselves. There wasn't any evidence to convict on. Her word against his. How can you tell? There were always a few silly young girls hanging round that hostel, just asking for it."

"They will do it," murmured Bill, "bless 'em."

All the same, it was awkward; an awkward issue for the strike to turn on; no obvious right or wrong.

"And what's the strike really about, Jim?" he inquired. "It's not about this, can't be. You and I know well enough that the excuse for a strike is never the real reason, and there always is a real reason. What's getting 'em?"

Jimmy Jafet considered. "It isn't wages, particularly. Conditions aren't bad, though that hostel could do with blowing up. It isn't the Commies, though that's what the management really think. Chap named Papelian who's running the strike committee is a Red all right, regular party member, and he's got the usual gang round him. But it isn't really the Commies. They exploit grievances, but there have to be grievances to exploit, eh?"

Bill Whistlecroft nodded. "Though I wouldn't say it in public, Jim boy."

"So what is at the bottom of it? This sounds far-fetched, Bill, but I reckon it's the town. This isn't an industrial town. It's a country place, and the people are country people. The mill has brought in a lot of money, and they like that all right. But underneath they resent it. There's old Colonel Melmoth, decent fellow, the squire of the place, sounds comic, don't it, these days?—fighting the mill for all he's worth. And instinctively the people back him. This town's living in the wrong century. Of course, the men feel it, though they probably don't understand what it is they're feeling. They're resented, so they resent being resented, if you see what I mean. They're made to feel like foreigners, not welcome. The moment something happens to give them the chance, they sort of hit back, they want to. And of course it's dead easy for Papelian and his lot to exploit that."

Bill Whistlecroft nodded thoughtfully.

"What frightens me," continued Jimmy, "is the townsfolk. I told you about this damn silly defence league they're getting up. It'll lead to trouble, sure as eggs. It only needs some little thing, and it'll blow. They can't see how much the country needs steel, they just don't understand. They go on with their old lives, selling things, buying things. Nothing much touches them, unless it comes right home. And this mill does come right home. It's got me worried, Bill. This strike has got to be settled, quick."

Bill Whistlecroft nodded again. "All in good time," he said.

"How are you going to tackle it? Are you going to get at the strike committee?"

Bill laughed scornfully. "Not much. Wouldn't touch 'em with a barge pole. Never go to them, Jimmy. Wait till they come to you."

Jimmy shook his head doubtfully. "Ah well, you know, I expect."

He made as if to go to bed. Bill Whistlecroft tempted him to one more nightcap. He told him some very funny anecdotes about the United Nations. Then they went to bed.

5

THE centre of the strike was the room over the Duke's Head where the unofficial committee sat beneath the insignia and portraits of the local Buffaloes, and to and from which passed innumerable messengers, though what messages they carried, and between whom, most of the men had not the smallest idea. The committee sat like a siege party waiting for the fortress to fall, but they most of them perfectly well knew that it would not fall. A demand was sent to the management to receive a deputation; the management replied that it recognized only official trade-union channels. When Bill Whistlecroft arrived, a demand went to him to come to meet the committee.

He met the deputation cheerfully in Jimmy Jafet's front parlour. "What committee would this be?" he inquired. "Strike committee? Don't waste my time."

"You come out and see us, Bill, or there'll be trouble."

He laughed. "You get back to your jobs, and I'll come and see you all right. Be there in ten minutes. And I'll start negotiations wth the management. But so long as you stay out, don't come and talk to me. Go and talk to your committee. They'll know what to tell you. They've had their instructions, and you know where they come from."

Bert Papelian, sitting sombre in the tobacco haze of the committee room, pondered the chances, and found them good. He had been reprimanded over that business of the hostel elections, and it still rankled. He had thought to wipe out the stain at the public meeting on the fishermen's charter, but even that had not counted for him. He had been told he was clumsy, the thing had been pushed too far, and he ought instead to have concentrated on organizing the fishermen themselves. But this strike had reinstated him in the party. He had kept it going longer than was anticipated, and it had produced a gratifying number of new members, and new subscriptions to the *Worker*. Even Rosa had accorded him a dry word of praise.

Of course, he had had his moments of crisis. Christmas was the worst. It took something to prolong the strike over Christmas. A lot of the wives had come to a meeting at the hostel gates, and turned threatening. He had kept away from that meeting, but had hastily summoned another. He knew it was hard, he told the men, particularly on the kids. But were they going to throw away their position for the whole year, just to get a Christmas dinner? "I warn you, if you give way now, the bosses have got you where they want you. You won't be able to strike again. And next time it'll be wages." He finished by a remark, almost an aside, "Who's master in your homes? Who's going to tell you what to do—the women?"

When he got back after that meeting, Rosa gave him an encouraging nod. "You did it well," she said.

Then, early in the new year, there was the awkward moment when Callaghan wanted to see him.

He was engrossed at the time, and the name did not ring

a bell. "Callaghan?" he said looking up, "who's he? Oh yes, Callaghan. What does he want?"

"I don't know."

"Tell him I'll be round to see him to-night, after tea."

When he got there, he found Callaghan lying sulkily on his bed, bored. He was going back to Liverpool, he said.

Papelian argued with him. All his mates had come out on his behalf. Was he going to let them down? Was he going to make them look fools in the eyes of the bosses?

Callaghan said he didn't give a damn for all that. He'd an offer of a job in Liverpool, and his sister wanted to see him, and he was off. What he wanted was the train fare.

In the end Papelian, his voice cold, had to threaten him. If he backed out now, he'd get no job in Liverpool, or anywhere else. Papelian assured him that he would personally see to that. He would have his name blacklisted with every shop steward in the union. Callaghan would be lucky if he still, in three months' time, had a union card. And there were one or two other things, Papelian hinted, that might happen to him —painful things.

Callaghan sullenly gave way. When he got back to the committee room, Papelian quietly ordered a couple of men he could trust to keep an eye on him, in case he slipped off. Then he hurried away to a mass meeting at the hostel gates. "If the bosses think they can intimidate us, mates," he assured his audience, "they've got another bloody think coming."

He was considerably helped by the religious lark which Henty, the local parson had started in a tin hut down the road from the Duke's. At first it did not make much difference. The parson opened up his hall rather apologetically, and the nearest he got to interfering in the strike was a pathetic little group singing hymns a few yards off a hostel-gate meeting. "Splinter group from the Salvation Army," mocked one of the speakers, jerking his head towards them.

But suddenly a lot of new people appeared at the Mission. They were mostly young people, the lads in flannel trousers and tweed jackets, bareheaded, bespectacled and voluble, the girls in sweaters and corduroy coats. And they did not confine themselves to singing hymns. They bustled everywhere, buttonholed everybody, and in a remarkably short time seemed to know every man's first name. They made no attempt to interfere with the meetings, but little clumps of them canvassed all the lodgings in which married men lived with their families, breezed their way in, invited the wives to tea parties in the Mission Hall, entered upon long and hearty discussions about God with the men. If their invitation to prayer was awkwardly rejected, they switched without concern to economics. Papelian watched grimly. He had heard of the Buchmanites, but never before encountered them in action. But Rosa shrugged and advised him to let them be. "I knew them at college. They'll do us more good than harm."

The person who, privately, found them most distasteful was Dorothy Henty.

"I may be old-fashioned, Roger," she complained to her husband, "but having a pash on Jesus makes me wriggle."

"We can hardly complain, my dear," he uneasily argued, "at a revival of religious interest among young people, even if the form which it takes does appear somewhat, er, brash."

"Ugh!"

"Besides, Lady Gazzard is frightfully keen on them, and, after all, it is her money we're using. She has gone to great trouble to get them here, and regards it as particularly, er, fortunate, that the strike has taken place during the university vacations, when they are available."

"The vacations are much too long. I always said so."

"What worries me a little," he confessed, "is that they seem to be quite undenominational. But perhaps that is an advantage. They are able to approach the Irish people in a way that is hardly open to me. And there seem to be so many R.C.s here."

Dorothy left it at that, and, at the Mission, threw herself energetically into the job of making the tea. That, at least, she could do with a clear conscience, and it kept her a good deal out of the way of the corduroy young women. She reproached herself afterwards, but she could not help enjoying a crowd of them discussing a visit they had paid to the trade-union organizer who, it seemed, was staying with Jimmy Jafet. He had clearly sent them away with a flea in their ear. Dorothy warmed towards the good solid sense of organized Labour—as rocky and impregnable as the C. of E. itself, she reflected, and quite as respectable, and dogmatic.

The young men and women bustled and chattered, exuding friendliness and prayer. But, curiously enough, the strike went on. Its origins and purposes were by now obscured; it was no longer a strike about anything in particular except that some vague wages-and-conditions demands had somehow been added; it was simply a strike looking around for incidents to aggravate it.

Lady Gazzard herself obligingly provided one. It was not so much that she was impatient of the progress of her shock-troops, but that she could not bear to miss the actual fun. One Wednesday morning she arrived at the Mission Hall, telling the chauffeur to put the car at the back and wait. The Buchmanites welcomed her and revelled in her. A party was about to set out on a round of family visits in the home, and Lady Gazzard, tucking her muffler securely inside her mink, went happily with it. Dorothy Henty, smiling grimly, watched them go.

"It labels us nicely, doesn't it? The mercenaries of religion. The paid strike-breakers. Oh hell," she said, "I'm going home."

As she passed the hostel gates, the inevitable meeting was already in progress. From curiosity she paused to listen, shaking her head at the gaunt youth who urged her to get her *Daily Worker* there and then. There was a somewhat insecure rostrum, upon which a short, wiry man was climbing. And then, in triumph, he started. Were their eyes opened yet? Some of them had been taken in by this religious business that had been pushed on them. Now they could see it for what it was—a clumsy bosses' manœuvre. "Her ladyship herself has come down to talk to you," he jeered. "She wants to say her prayers with you. She wants you all to be good boys, and mind your manners, and go back to work hard for her old man. They might have spared us that, eh, mates? They might have credited us with a bit more intelligence than that?"

His harsh, clipped voice went on and on. Dorothy, smiling, found herself in cordial agreement with him. She was standing at the edge of the crowd next to a tall, thin woman with a tortured face, and her arms full of pamphlets.

"Who is he?" Dorothy casually asked.

"He's the chairman of the strike committee. He is also my husband."

"He talks well."

"At least he does not preach."

Dorothy smiled. "Oh, so you know who I am?"

The other nodded. "Yes, I know you, Mrs. Henty."

"And you think that my husband is pretty contemptible, I suppose, that he is working for the bosses."

"The Church always has, and always will."

"Now, that's not quite fair. Oh, I give you Lady Gazzard. But I'm sorry you deny Roger some sort of sincerity."

"I suppose he's like every parson, a lackey."

"Come now," said Dorothy, "you're just theorizing. After all, what do you know about parsons?"

The thin woman looked at her. "My father was one," she said.

On impulse, Dorothy suggested, "Let's go and get some coffee. I'd like to know you."

But the woman shook her head. "No, thanks. I'm not a prospective convert. You're wasting your time."

"I don't want to convert you," replied Dorothy uncertainly. The woman turned her back, saying something to a youngster standing by her side. Dorothy recognized him as young Bruell, son of the publican of the Melmoth Arms at Shard Green. "Hallo, Tom," she greeted.

"Hallo, Mrs. Henty," he gruffly answered, turning away.

Now what was the matter with him? Everybody seemed to have turned sour on her this morning. She looked more closely at him, and saw marks of distress on his face. What on earth? Then she vaguely remembered that he was supposed to have been sweet on Daphne Wilkinson, had followed her dog-like, puppy-like. And so therefore now, presumably. . . . Her heart filled, not with pity, but irritation—irritation at the idiocy of things, which wounded indiscriminately, hitting without aim, punishing blindly without offence. She wandered off, depressed, and made her way home. She pottered from room to room, dusted, took up some darning, picked up a book, and suddenly sat at her piano and thumped out Ebenezer Elliott's mighty hymn, the one that Roger mildly disliked. All alone, she sang to the walls of the cold vicarage.

> "When wilt thou save the people?
> O God of mercy, when?
> Not kings and lords, but nations;
> Not thrones and crowns, but men!
> Flowers of thy heart, O God, are they;
> Let them not pass like weeks away,
> Their heritage a sunless day,
> God save the people!"

In the silence after, she sat with her hands on her lap, staring at the keyboard. Yes, but which people? Only the poor people, was that it? Mere common sense rejected that. All the people. But they strove the one with the other, factionizing, measuring up their little differences of wealth or education, the one party trying to destroy its opposition, one up and the other down, one down the other up, like quarrelling children—or rather, without even the logic of children. Dorothy Henty sighed, then reproved herself for sentimentality, and went out to the kitchen to blanch a rabbit for the vicar's lunch.

As the days went by, the factions in the town strove with increasing bitterness. The citizens' patrols, armed with heavy walking-sticks, spread out each evening through the streets and up by the dark common, jeered at by the loungers as they passed the Duke's, or stationed themselves by the hostel entrance. Increasingly there were incidents, the nastiest when one of the patrols found a town girl, daughter of a small trader in the Market Square, arm-in-arm with a young fellow from the hostel; and sternly ordered her home.

The man showed fight, two or three others came to help him, and a head was broken before the police arrived. Four of them were up before the Bench next morning. The chairman, Colonel Melmoth, bound them over in the sum of ten pounds each.

"Let me make this quite clear,' he warned. "I do not care who you are, or what the provocation. This Bench is determined that there shall be no violence in this town. If any more cases of this kind come before us, the penalties will be exemplary"

The patrols went on. And the strike went on, senselessly and, it seemed, interminably. But Bill Whistlecroft, sitting in Jimmy's front parlour, was unperturbed.

"Oughtn't you to go and meet this committee, and get the thing settled?" worried Jimmy.

"Not on your life," smiled Bill, "not while it's unofficial. Let 'em get back to work, and I'll handle it. But while they stay out against the union's orders, I'll not move. It wouldn't do, boy, it wouldn't do."

Similarly, Appleton was worrying Gazzard; this time, curiously, with Heron in agreement with him. There was another meeting in Charles Neve's office, looking out at the bleak skeleton of the mill walls, and the lorries and machinery upon which lay a thin covering of snow.

"But, Sir Russell," pleaded Appleton, "the Minister himself is urging a settlement. He is highly embarrassed. Public money is draining away, and he has to account for it in the House. The cause of the dispute is so trifling."

"It's only the pending by-elections that are worrying the Minister," said Heron. "We all know that. All the same, sir, I think Appleton is right. It's time it came to an end."

Gazzard, hunched in a chair, looked round at them quizzically.

"It's not my strike," he told them. "You'd better talk to Mr. Neve. He's the man of iron."

But even Neve, staring through the window, confessed to doubts. Christmas ought to have broken it up, but it did not. Now that Christmas was over, it might straggle for God knew how long. "That fellow Papelian's got a stronger hold on them than I gave him credit for. That's what worries me, sir."

"Okay, then," said Gazzard, "we give the sex maniac his job back?"

"Looks like it," muttered Neve.

"I'm disappointed in you," declared Gazzard. "If it were me, I'd have stuck it out. But it's your strike, young man. You have the say-so."

Neve hesitated. "Give 'em till the end of the week," he said at last. "One more pay day without pay may convince them. If they don't kick in then, I think we've got to settle it."

Sir Russell got up from his chair. "Are we agreed? Seems we are. It'll be a sore disappointment to my wife— she's having such a lovely time."

As they were going out, Neve added, "By the way, it's understood, of course, not a word about this to anyone." Looking hard at Appleton, he insisted, "Not even to the Minister."

"But surely I must, confidentially, report. . . ."

"Not one word," said Gazzard cheerfully. "Not even a memo or a minute. Don't worry, I'll square you with your Minister."

6

THAT was on Wednesday. On Thursday it snowed a little more, and in the dusk of early evening a thin fog drifted over the town. The trains were running late. Jimmy Jafet, shoulders hunched in his overcoat, his punch stuck through the lapel, was stamping up and down by the ticket barrier to warm his feet when, to his surprise, he saw Elsie hurrying into the station without a hat.

"Now then, what's up?"

"Kathy's got out."

"Where to?" he exclaimed.

"I don't know, Jimmy. I can't find her anywhere. It's my fault. I went to lie down for ten minutes, I was that tired, and she was quite all right in her room, with the bolt on. But she must have got out of the window."

Jimmy soothed her. "It'll be all right, old girl. I'll come."

He motioned to one of the porters, and got him to take over. There would not, he said, be much doing. He'd square it with the station master in the morning.

"If one of those chaps has got at her——" Elsie said suddenly, as they hurried down the street.

"No, that's silly. She has got out before—we'll find her."

"But in this fog. We'll have to get help. I'm going to Joe Wilkinson," she decided. "He's got men all over the place. They'll find her."

Jimmy uneasily dissented. "It might cause trouble, Elsie." But impatiently she shook her head and turned down Bridge Street. Jimmy stood irresolute, then unhappily made his way towards his house, telling himself that Kathy would not have wandered far, he would soon find her. Usually she went up towards the common. He came clear of the houses, on to the edge of the open space, cursing the mist, into which he plunged in a random direction, calling her name. It was a place of sullen thorn-bushes and the dripping boughs of bare may trees. His feet were soaking, and he started an ambling run, calling, "Kathy, Ka-a-thy." He checked at a sudden humming, but realized it was an overhead telegraph wire singing to itself in the fog. He stumbled on again, coming to a paling, against which he leaned to recover his breath, and then called, "Kathy, Kathy." After a little he began to panic. He turned back towards the road skirting the common, and there ran into the sound of tramping feet, materializing as a group of men, heavily coated, fists grasping stout sticks. As he came up, he saw they were three or four of Wilkinson's lot.

"Hallo, Jimmy, is that you?" called the leader. "Don't worry, we're bound to find her. There's a couple of hundred turned out to search."

"Unless one of those bastards has got hold of her," muttered another.

"No, no," protested Jimmy. "It's nothing to do with them.

She has wandered off before, you know that. She doesn't go far."

But there were thoughts in his mind at which he shuddered. He cursed himself for not having let her go to the hospital, as the doctor had wanted. No use blaming Elsie, she had so much to do. It was his fault, he groaned to himself.

"We've got our beat up this way," said the leader of the group. "You coming with us?"

Jimmy shook his head. "No, I'll turn back towards town. She'll not have gone that far. Thanks for helping."

They marched on into the fog, and Jimmy hastened back along the road, his eyes on the kerb as guide, stopping now and then to shout her name into the silence. But as he drew nearer the houses, it was no longer silence. At first a little scuffle, and then the sound of feet, and blows, and shouting.

"Dear heavens," cried Jimmy, "it's fighting."

He forced himself into a run.

It had started, he afterwards learned, when one of the patrols, coming up past the Duke's, ran into several of the hostel dwellers just turning into the public for the evening.

"Look out, here's the boy scouts," mocked one of the men.

The leader of the patrol, a young fellow from the gas-works office, went across and faced them.

"There's a girl missing," he said quietly.

"Well, good luck to 'er. Got some boy friend, p'raps."

"It's Jimmy Jafet's sister. She's a bit touched, see. Not quite right in her head. Any decent man'd be sorry for her. If any of you fellows've laid a finger on her. . . ."

"Nark it. What's it got to do with us, mate?"

"It was one of you lot last time, weren't it? But this time we're ready for you. We've had enough. We're going to clean the scum out of this town."

A big man, one of the concrete-workers, menaced him. But one of the others pushed him aside.

"Now look here, son, we don't know nothing about it. If there's a girl missing, you go and look for her. But don't try and come it over us."

"What I said was scum."

The big man hit at him, but he ducked and came round with his stick. The others closed on him, but his own friends came running across the road, one of them blowing on a whistle. At first there was only a dozen of them fighting, but at the noise several more men turned out of the Duke's. The whistle brought up another patrol, at the run, sticks raised. A couple of the Skelstrand men dived back into the Duke's for chairs, from which they tore the legs—old Charlie Hyslop jumping up and down at his door, shouting at them to clear off out of it, they'd cost him his licence. One of the mill lads slipped back to the hostel for more men, and, as they came, somebody started throwing stones and half-bricks from an empty building site. Three or four boys ran back into the town to gather more of the patrols. The reinforcements on either side had scant idea what the fight was about, but somehow a rumour had started that Kathy had been found murdered, and a few of the townsmen were convinced of it. For most of them the reason for the fight did not matter. The long months of resentment at the invasion of their town suddenly boiled up in the men on the one side, and they struck out wildly, not so much at the labourers who happened to oppose them, but at what they represented. For the Skelstrand men it was the vent of their compressed frustration by the strike, the weeks of idleness, of hanging about, the poverty Christmas, the nagging of their wives. And for all of them it was the exhilaration of the fight itself, for the fight's sake. They began to sort themselves out, the individual scuffles resolving into formations, the Skelstrand men on the hostel side, the others on the town. What had started in one place, just outside the Duke's, spread into the surrounding streets. Groups of men on either side, coming at the run through the soft mist, clashed with other groups, and set about each other without pause or question. Three or four men were lying in the roadway, and one or two limping off, hugging hurt arms. The fog drifted whimsically round them all, pierced by the sounds of the struggle, and by a clamour of confused shouts, oaths, growls. A man ran off with blood pouring from his mouth. Two men were locked in a

116

wrestler's grip, panting, at the foot of a street lamp. Jimmy Jafet arrived breathless, calling hoarsely upon them to stop. A stone caught him on the shoulder, and a backhand blow struck him across the face, starting a nosebleed. He moaned in despair, but would not hit back. He huddled himself against a wall, weeping, still calling on them to stop, but nobody heeded him. In the middle of the roadway a huge labourer, coat torn, roaring like an animal, was striking methodically at three men attacking him; they suddenly closed, and he went down with a thud. Two other Skelstrand men ran across and flung themselves upon the heap, grunting, legs flailing. Jimmy groaned, and put his arm across his eyes.

Then the police began to arrive—first a couple of constables, blowing their whistles, rushing into the throng, helmets knocked askew; then a car load, then another, with Tom Jenkins, the Superintendent. Truncheons came out, the police formed up and charged in. And the combatants hesitated, ducked, and broke away, the Skelstrand men fading back towards the hostel, the townsmen melting into the side streets, and running. The police leaped upon the few who remained, chiefly the struggling group in the middle of the road, hauling them up, frog-marching them. And suddenly there was quietness, the road was as quiet as the mist that trailed it.

One of the constables seized Jimmy by the coat collar, and then saw who he was. "Were you in this, Mr. Jafet?" he asked amazed.

"Oh God, I was trying to stop it. They went mad."

"Are you hurt?"

"No, no, it's nothing. I'll be all right."

Tom Jenkins came over. "Did you see much of it? How did it start? What's it all about? Somebody was shouting about a murder. What's happened?"

"Murder? Oh no, there couldn't be."

Not Kathy, he suddenly thought; please, God, not Kathy, he pleaded within himself.

"I was looking for Kathy, Tom," he said. "So were the others, they were helping. She got out. We couldn't find

117

her in the fog. You said a murder?" He took him by the lapels. "Tom, it's not Kathy? You're not trying to tell me it's Kathy."

"No, no, no. So far as I know, there's no murder. As for Kathy—she's home, Jimmy. Didn't you know? She's home."

"Safe?"

"Yes, yes, quite safe—or so they tell me."

Jimmy broke away from him, and began to lumber into a run towards his house. It was an endless distance, but he sang to himself as he struggled along that she was home, she was safe.

He arrived breathless, turned in at his door, thumping it open. In the living-room by the fire, sat Bill Whistlecroft with three other men, drinking beer.

"Bill, is she all right?"

"Safe and sound, Jimmy. Elsie's with her upstairs. She has put her to bed."

Jimmy Jafet stood staring at them. Then he suddenly began to sob. Bill got him into a chair and thrust a glass of whisky into his hand.

"Where was she found?" he asked when he had recovered. "Tell me all about it."

"These fellows found her," said Bill.

Jimmy looked across at them. "You're from Skelstrand, ain't you?"

"Aye," said one of them.

"How did you come to find her? Was she all right?"

"We was up back of the common, taking a walk home, and there she was under some trees."

"By herself?"

"Aye, all by herself." He looked awkward. "She hadn't no clothes on," he said.

"Poor creature," murmured one of the others. "Stark as a baby."

"We covered her up quick as we could."

Bill Whistlecroft said, "She were wrapped up in their macks and scarves, and one fellow's hat, and one'd taken his boots off and put 'em on her. They had to carry her

118

home. Jimmy, do you know your face is messed up with blood?"

Jimmy put his hand to his chin and rustled the dry blood. "There was a fight." He banged his fist on the arm of the chair. "Disgraceful, it was. I'm going straight round to tell Joe Wilkinson. . . ."

"Not to-night, Jimmy, to-morrow," advised Bill.

Elsie came downstairs into the room. To Jimmy's anxious look she replied, "Aye, she's all right. She's quiet now. She'll take no harm. What have you done to yourself?"

"There was a fight. A disgrace, it was. Joe Wilkinson's damn silly nonsense. They even started a story that Kathy had been done in. And all the time these chaps that found her were stripping off their own clothes to keep her warm, and bringing her back safe."

Elsie went across to the three men. "We're ever so grateful."

They mumbled that it was all right, Miss, and rose to leave. Jimmy saw them out, with a pressure of thanks on their shoulders. "Hope the poor creature ain't taken cold," said one.

When he got back to the room, Elsie suddenly burst into tears. Elsie, in tears! He put a comforting arm round her, and she wept that it was her fault, she who had gone to Joe Wilkinson.

"Nay," soothed Jimmy, "we were all distracted. It's ended well."

She dried her eyes, and went for a bowl of warm water to bathe his face.

Next morning the whole town was speaking in shamed whispers, and people avoided looking into each other's eyes. A little crowd gathered by the side entrance to the Town Hall, the court entrance. Inside, Colonel Melmoth sat white-faced on the Bench, listening to the police witnesses. Jimmy Jafet had not taken his magistrate's place; he was a witness, giving his evidence briefly and reluctantly. There were eight men in the dock, five of them from Skelstrand, three from the town. They had pleaded guilty. Anything

119

known? Tom Jenkins said there was nothing known about any of them except one of the Skelstrand men, who had three previous convictions for drunken disorderliness.

Colonel Melmoth consulted with the other magistrates, and with the clerk.

Then he addressed the accused. "We have considered very carefully whether to send you to prison. An outbreak of violence such as occurred last night merits the most exemplary punishment. I want to make it quite clear that this court will not tolerate behaviour of this kind, amounting very nearly to civil riot. We are all aware that the incursion of industrial development into a district which is unaccustomed to it places severe strains upon what was habitually a peaceful community—but it is not for this Bench to offer comments upon that. What this court insists upon, and will enforce with the utmost rigour within its power, is that these strains shall not lead to commotion and disturbance of the peace."

He paused, and surveyed the men in the dock.

"However, we are influenced by the fact that you were not the only persons involved. A very large number of people took part in these disgraceful scenes, and you were merely the unfortunate ones who were caught. It is that consideration, and that alone, which has decided us, with some reluctance, not to send you all to prison on this occasion. But I issue a fair warning. If there is any recurrence of such behaviour brought to the attention of this court, a prison sentence will automatically follow."

He fined each of them twenty pounds, and police costs.

At Jimmy Jafet's house Dr. Irons was saying to Elsie, "Now, don't worry. She's going to be all right. Pneumonia is the only risk, but we can take care of that."

Outside the hostel gates, in a bitter wind, Bert Papelian was orating desperately. Don't give in now, mates, hold on just a day or two longer, we've got them groggy. There were not many interruptions, but the meeting was smaller than usual and, as it proceeded, men shrugged and began turning away, drifting away, moving down towards the centre of the town, where the buses had, remarkably, appeared again, and were filling up, making off to Skelstrand, returning for more.

The really active, cheerful man that morning was Bill Whistlecroft. Up early was Bill, humming happily as he shaved, eating his breakfast with gusto, and taking a taxi out to Skelstrand. He had waited so patiently, and now his time had come.

In the office he faced a circle of them.

"Now the union wants negotiations, Sir Russell," he announced. "I've brought along the points—wages, conditions."

He pushed a paper across the table.

"Why should we negotiate," asked Neve, "when the strike has collapsed? You choose your time badly, don't you?"

"Do I?" smiled Bill Whistlecroft. "Ah, but all that was a lot of unofficial stuff, stirred up by the Commies, we all know that. But this is official. This is different. The men have at last obeyed union instructions and gone back to work, on our promise that we would at once seek negotiations on pay and conditions. Now we want 'em."

"And suppose you don't get 'em?"

"I'm not a man to threaten. All I want is to talk the thing out, over the table, orderly, peaceful."

The argument went doggedly on. Bill Whistlecroft settled comfortably to it. This was better, this was his idea of how to go to work. He could keep this up for hours, for days. He loved it. This was the way to conduct labour relations, cosily over a table, with a girl to bring in cups of tea, not at some draughty corner, on a soapbox.

Hours later, when he came out of the office, he was smiling broadly. One or two of the shop stewards were waiting.

"Aye," he told them, "they'll negotiate. Talks start Monday."

It was a true saying, that, he thought, about an ill wind. When he thought about Papelian, he grinned broadly. His gaze traversed the long Skelstrand site. The concrete mixers, sludgily grinding, were spewing their ochre streams. The dead scaffolding was alive again with crawling figures, with the little firework sparks of the riveters. Across the grey winter sky the buckets trundled on their overhead tracks, and the squat furnaces, part constructed, reared their thick bulk; and beyond them again the crane tops rhythmically swung, lazily, where the quay was being built. For music there were the slow distant stutter of a pile-driver, the staccato of pneumatic drills, the scrunch of scoops, and a metallic clanging, and somewhere a steam whistle. And the scream of gulls circling over the dunes by the edge of the sea.

7

IT was at first distasteful to Charles Neve to have young Gazzard in his office. There was, of course, no help for it, since Sir Russell had commanded it. "Andrew has got to carry this place when my time comes. The success of the whole thing can depend on the way you toughen him to it now."

Neve was tempted to reply that, since he himself was due to move on when the place was built, he didn't give a damn whether Andrew ballsed it up or not. But he shrugged, and asked, "Will he work? The boss's son usually doesn't. If he won't work, I can't make him."

"You just tell me," said Gazzard, "and I'll tan his arse."

So there was Andrew, arriving at the site in his little scarlet sports car; and arriving on time in the morning, his father had evidently seen to that. Of course, there was nothing for him to do—nothing that Neve would trust him to do on his own. But in a week or two he began to tolerate the fellow, and in a month or two even to like him. There was a natural gaiety to him, a frankness, a likeableness. In fact he did not work very hard, that was not to be expected, but he did something, and beneath his laziness Neve soon saw that there was a good brain, an affable intelligence. And he came, which was irresistibly flattering, to look up to Neve.

"My old man tells me," he once said, "that you're the goods. Chap ought to model himself on you, my old man says. He thinks you're the sort of person he used to be, and that you'll grow up like him—and, so help me, he reckons that's a compliment!"

In the spring, which was cold and wet, holding up the construction work badly—but Neve had a week or so in hand on the schedule, even in spite of the strike, so carefully had he nursed his timing—Andrew went down with 'flu.

Neve was surprised, and a little irritated, to discover that during the three weeks he was away he missed him, the office seemed duller, lonelier. When he returned, Neve welcomed him with unaccustomed warmth.

"D'you know what pulled me back from the jaws of death?" inquired Andrew. "Ma did. She said it was the power of prayer that fixed it."

"Seems to have worked."

"All according to plan—except that it back-fired on her. She's now down with the 'flu herself."

One day Andrew said to him, "You doing anything to-night?"

"Nothing in particular."

"Will you come and have a meal with me? I need some advice."

"Of course. Where do you want to go?"

He suggested the Blue Goose. Neve nodded. "But we'll go in my bus," he said, "I'm doing no night driving in that toast-rack of yours."

Neve had heard, of course, of the Blue Goose, but had never been there. It was a roadhouse, on the other side of the hills, where the rich men from the factory district around Stockford to the west were said to bring their girls. It lay well back from the road, dimly floodlit, a fine old house now discreetly decorated with neon, and garnished with a swimming-pool and coloured umbrellas. Inside, it was over-furnished and over-heated—steam-heat plus log fires. The dining-room was all thick carpet, except in one corner where a pianist, fiddler and drummer throbbed softly over a small open square of parquet, upon which three or four couples were dreamily jostling. The head waiter welcomed Andrew, and settled them at a retired table. The food was spiced, the wine mellow.

"Classy, ain't it?" said Andrew.

Over some rather spurious brandy, in too-large bubble-glasses, Neve asked, "Well, what's the trouble?"

"It ain't exactly trouble," said Andrew, "although it might be. It scares me. I've been putting it off. But now the old man is coming down rather strong about it. He says I've got to get cracking."

"About what?"

"You know that Melmoth girl? Of course you do, you met her at our place. I've got to marry her."

"Got to?"

"Oh lord, no, nothing like that. She doesn't even know about it. That's where I want your advice."

"You mean, you want to marry her?" said Neve, relaxing the muscles of his shoulders.

"Confidentially, I'm easy, one way or the other. I never did think marriage an absolutely first-class idea. No, it's my old man, he's keen."

"I'm afraid," said Neve, "that I'm not following you."

"Well, it's like this. My old man has got some nutty idea about founding a dynasty. You know, like Abraham, and all that lark about his seed spreading over the face of the earth. He's a great family man is Pa. His secret ambition—and for heaven's sake keep this under your hat—is for the Gazzards to be a fine old English family, titled and all that. He has arranged for the title when the next lot get into power. I say, there's old Heron over there, and he's got an absolute smasher with him. Who is she?"

Neve glanced round. "That's Appleton's wife."

"Hmm. Bit free and easy, eh?"

"So they say."

"She wants to look out, with friend Heron. He's poison, don't you agree?"

"About this fine old English family . . ." said Neve.

"Ah yes. Of course, it'll take centuries before the Gazzards work their way up to the top of Burke, but we have to make a start, as it were, obviously."

"Obviously. But why Elizabeth Melmoth?"

Andrew, still gazing across the room, murmured, "I don't know. She's just taken the old man's fancy; local county stock, get some breeding in right away, sort of short cut."

"What I don't see," said Neve, "is why you should agree to marry a girl your father picks out for you, just like that."

"Oh, the reason, of course, is money. You see, he's prepared to pay. He's always prepared to pay for anything he really wants."

"There are supposed to be some things money can't buy."

"That's the theory," agreed Andrew, "but the old man says he has yet to come across one."

"What is he prepared to pay for Elizabeth Melmoth?"

"He put it to me quite straight. The day I marry her, he sets up a trust fund of a quarter of a million quid. I get the income, and the capital eventually goes to the dear little offspring of our union."

"Blimey!" said Neve.

"Exactly. Wouldn't you get spliced for that?—provided, of course, that she wasn't absolutely a hunchback. As Pa points out, marriages are arranged on a cash basis in most countries of the world—you know, a wife costs so many cowrie shells, or fat cattle or something. There's nothing original in his idea. And, of course, so long as he lives five years, he avoids death duties. And he will live five years. He always thinks he's dying of half a dozen things, but really he's as strong as an ox."

Neve looked round the room, pondering. A fortune, a quite presentable young man, and a title—most girls would jump at it. Would Elizabeth? He found himself hoping desperately that she would not. Then he lowered his gaze and concluded that, if it were wrapped up nicely, she probably would.

"Now, the point is," Andrew was saying, "how do I catch her? I don't think the passionate sort of stuff would go over very well, do you? I thought, a rather gay sort of campaign, light-hearted and all that, rather jolly, eh? Boy-and-girlish, and not a care in the world. Don't you agree?"

"I think," replied Neve with difficulty, "that you're probably right."

"I'm glad to hear you say that. The old man says I always ought to take your advice. He thinks a lot of you."

Neve drove back in silence. At one point, even Andrew protested. "We didn't actually go between that bus and that lorry, did we? Because it wasn't possible."

"Thought you liked fast driving," said Neve.

The next day was Sunday, and breakfast at Tregonwell was not until nine.

"You doing anything to-day?" Appleton asked Neve. "Laura and I are going to play golf, and Heron wants to try and make up a foursome."

"Sorry," said Neve abstractedly, "I've got a date."

Pomeroy had arranged to pick him up. He wanted to show off his blessed housing estate on the other side of the estuary, and then Venetia would give them some lunch. Neve thought of phoning to put him off, but what was the use? It would be absurd, just because of that girl, to work himself into a temper and sulk.

The whole damn thing was absurd, he told himself angrily. He would have laughed to see it happen to anyone else. Here he was, in the character of a tough egg, thrown into a tumult because somebody else was going to marry a girl in whom he had felt faintly interested. It was no more than that, he insisted. Then just because young Gazzard innocently tells him her marriage is being arranged, he kids himself that he desperately wants her. He railed impatiently at himself. What then, precisely, did he want of her? Marriage? Damn nonsense. That he, Charles Neve, the morose wanderer, should want marriage with anyone. Not likely. He had seen marriage, with his own mother and father; had seen his old man tied, by the having taken a woman to church in his youth, to a miserable house in a town he had come to hate, and to slaving at a mean job which gave him no security, and yet which he dared not leave—except when it left him. That was a trap Neve had long sworn to avoid. Then what did he want of Elizabeth? To go to bed with her? Well, naturally, he supposed. But a woman in bed was a woman in bed, nothing to torment himself over. And the emotion evaporated with the desire.

He got up from the table with a grunt and went to his room. There was a mass of figures for him to work out in readiness for Monday morning. But as he sat at them, he found himself staring listlessly through the window at the waters running blue in the sunlight. He was glad when Pomeroy arrived.

Pomeroy was gaily chattering. With the Alsatian bitch sitting statuesque on the back seat of the car, he drove him through the town, over the bridge, and out to the housing estate on the far bank. Pomeroy was immensely proud of his housing estate, and longing to explain it to a brother engineer.

"We bulldozed the dunes, rolled 'em out flat, see?" he chattered. "Then up pop the houses, presto. Poured concrete, laddie."

When the car stopped, Neve got out and stood surveying the estate, scratching with his toe in the fine sand.

"Remember the guy who built his house on sand?" he joked, "How deep did you put your foundations?"

"Foundations? Rot. There ain't no foundations. Old-fashioned stuff, that. Put down a tray of concrete, pop your house on top, finish."

"Won't they shift about a bit, sink and all that?"

"Sure," said Pomeroy happily. "Sure they'll sink. But they'll sink in one piece, get it? Foundations'd crack em' to pieces. On the Pomeroy platforms, they just settle in a few inches, and all hunkydory. Besides, it's cheap, son. Costing us fifteen hundred quid a family—not bad these days, eh? And quick. Up with the moulds, pour in the concrete—no sand, old boy, positively no sand—rip down the moulds, shove on a roof, slap on plaster.

"One house off the production lines," declared Pomeroy with satisfaction, "every twenty-four hours. Happy homes for happy workers. Get it?"

Neve stood contemplating the houses, smiling. It did not matter how shoddy the houses were, provided each contained a refrigerator and an electric cooker. And yet, damn it, they were better houses than the previous century had built for its workers.

With the Alsatian ranging in front, Pomeroy strolled him along the new little streets. Some of the houses were already occupied, with prams, children and scooters littered at their front doors. In one or two of the gardens men, in shirt-sleeves, were digging, and already lettuces, broad beans, patches of grass and small rows of privet were sprouting. How the devil, inquired Neve, did anything manage to grow on sand?

"We dump one load of soil at each front gate," explained Pomeroy. "Chap has to cart it in, and spread it. They're already joining the local horticultural club, biggest marrows, first prize for carrots, best vase of cut flowers, Class II. Hobbies, old man, great stuff. Pride they take in my houses. None of the old stuff—you know, 'Shift pigeons from bath, Willy, coal's come!' None of that here. Good as any New Town in the country, better even. Makes the heart swell, eh?"

Neve nodded. He understood that it did make the heart swell. In each of these shot-up little houses, a new family, striking down roots into the sand. On each patch where, a year earlier, only the gulls had gathered, a small family drama, love and anger, passion and pain, hopes, fears, birth and death.

"Aren't you going to get two towns?" he asked, "this lot and the old lot? Wouldn't it have been better to mix 'em up a bit? They already hate each other's guts, the new and the old."

"No, no," protested Pomeroy, whistling the dog and turning back towards the car, "that's all finished with last winter. You're behind the times, son. Blood brothers now, all of 'em."

"Really? What did it?"

"Football," declared Pomeroy. "That's what did it, foot-ball. Specially Freddie Jones."

"Who's he?"

"You haven't half been in the ivory tower. Freddie works on the blast furnaces. Couple of months back, Gulport F.C.'s a man short. But there's a footballer up at the works, name of Freddie Jones, says someone; played for the Wolves couple of times. Then get him, says Grigson. Grigson's chairman of the F.C. Will Freddie play? Sure he'll play. Put him at centre-forward. All the town turns out, naturally, so do all the Skelstrand boys. Pretty cool atmosphere in the crowd, they remember the strike. Then the ref whistles. Off goes Freddie, passes out to the right, the inside puts it out to the wing. Down the field. Everybody yells give it to Freddie. Winger puts it across. There's Freddie, cool as they come. Crowd yells shoot. Freddie shoots. Goal. One minute! Crowd goes mad. Worthy citizens thump Skelstrand chaps on the back, Skelstrand chaps embrace worthy citizens. Triumph."

Neve chuckled.

"Seven nil we beat 'em," lyricized Pomeroy, "and Freddie scored five. Since then we've walloped every team within range, and we're top of the local league. First time in living memory, old man."

All the way home in the car, Pomeroy described in detail the games which Gulport had played since Freddie Jones was put at centre-forward.

"By the way," he said, "we won't stop off for a quick one, if you don't mind. Promised Venetia we'd be in good time for lunch. We'll have a glass of sherry at home, eh? Suit you? Oh, and by the way, Venetia's asked Elizabeth Melmoth to eat with us. Okay by you?"

"Sure. Of course."

When they arrived, the two women were waiting for them in the sitting-room.

"Hallo, Mr. Neve," said Venetia. "How nice to see you again."

"Been at the sherry already, I notice," said Pomeroy.

"Well, you didn't think we were going to wait for you?"

"Quite a stranger," said Elizabeth to Neve.

"Well, what with one thing and another. The mill's really going up now, in spite of the weather. Doesn't leave much time for social life."

Pomeroy came round with the decanter, and they sat

gossiping. Venetia remarked that her idea of a minor heaven was the glass of sherry before Sunday lunch, especially with the sun shining; such a pleasant, idle moment in the week. Neve complimented her on the show of tulips in her garden. She smiled benignly on him and Elizabeth, the smile of the instinctive matchmaker in every middle-aged, childless woman.

"Well," she said, reluctantly getting out of the chair, "I'd better go and dish up. Eustace."

"Duty calls," said he, "I make the gravy. Famous for it. They ought to get me on the ads. Eminent engineer reveals gravy secrets. Stir well, no lumps, keep fingers off hot tin, and pop in one spoonful Scrumbo. It's delicious, and so-o-o nutritious. Help yourselves to some more sherry."

"For you?" asked Neve, when they were left alone. She shook her head. He refilled his own glass and settled again.

"You doing anything special this afternoon?" he asked.

"No, nothing particular."

"I need a good walk, how about it? Tell you what, I'll walk you back to Shard."

"It's a long way."

"Too far for you?"

"Oh no, I should enjoy it. It's a lovely afternoon. When we get there, I'll give you some tea."

He nodded, wondering if, by the time they got there, he would have said what he had a mind to say; and, if he had, whether she would still give him some tea.

Pomeroy called out, "It's in," from the hall, and they went to the dining-table, all four aimlessly chatting. The Alsatian stretched herself on the hearth-rug. "How," inquired Elizabeth, "do you make this delicious gravy?"

Neve, rather silent, pondered on the Pomeroys. Here was marriage, ordinary suburban marriage. So what did it amount to? Two small rooms for living in, roast lamb on the table and a bottle of gin in the sideboard cupboard. Long fireside evenings with books and sewing, a small garden to toil in, real things to talk about long ago exhausted, a pink silk bedroom upstairs, with a gas fire and a small array of cosmetics on the dressing-table, and regular, decorous copulation. That was the usual union of souls. And yet, it appeared, happiness; or, at least, content. Where in the world was there anything more solidly content? Perhaps this mediocrity was the true end of human emotions, and the wise ones knew it and accepted it. Perhaps tameness was all.

He suddenly realized that Venetia was speaking to him.

"Some more potatoes?" she was asking. "Eustace, do give Mr. Neve some more lamb."

"Oh, no, thanks, I've had an enormous lunch."

"Have some more gravy, old man," said Pomeroy, "recommend it."

Perhaps, thought Neve, that was the secret of happy marriage—to keep the conversation at about that level. A boyish sort of joke.

It was not difficult for them to get away soon after lunch. Pomeroy protested that he ought to run them in the car, but Venetia, understanding like an accomplice, stoutly agreed that the walk to Shard was a splendid idea, nothing like exercise on a Sunday afternoon. She herself intended gardening. And Pomeroy was easily persuaded. His idea of a Sunday afternoon was a drowse, the lunch rumbling comfortably in his belly. Then, thought Neve, a lazy bestirring to tea, a lounging in an arm-chair, a desultory glass of whisky, the television play, and a yawning to bed. Marriage.

It oppressed his mind so that, as he and Elizabeth began their walk, along the suburban road and over the stile into the field at the end of it, he spoke of it.

"Would you call the Pomeroys happily married?"

"Yes, I think so."

"Odd, isn't it?"

"Why?"

"Oh, I don't know. Such a very dull existence. Could you live that sort of life, and be happy? If that's what it means, do you want to be married?"

She laughed. "No girl thinks her own marriage is going to be like anybody else's."

"But it always is. You think it's always a fraud on the woman? God, that's curious. It seems to me always a trick played on the man. It takes his money. It ties him down to one place, one job he probably loathes, and one woman to whom he probably grows indifferent. Perhaps it's a trick played on them both, a sort of natural conspiracy against the human race."

"Is that why you never married?" she asked, smiling.

"I suppose so. I saw it happen to my old man—all children do. What I can't understand is why anybody who has been a child wants to get married when he grows up. Except, possibly, orphans."

"The tough cynic," she mocked.

They were across the field by now, and climbing beside a wood that ascended a hill. At the top they paused, and gazed across the town spread out below them, the streets of little houses that led down to the harbour, and the estuary beyond, and the wrinkled sea.

"Look at that," he said: "every one of those houses was built because some man and some woman wanted to go to bed together. Every shop and office and factory exists so that the man can work hard enough to feed the woman and her kids. There isn't any other purpose, is there? We all spend our lives, bolstering up this curious business of licensed bedding."

"How about the pubs?"

"They're for the men who can't stand it any longer."

She laughed again, and they walked on.

"Did you ever think of getting married?" he asked.

"Yes, once."

"Why didn't you?"

"He was a bomber pilot. I was a W.A.A.F. at the station. One night he got killed."

"Oh, sorry."

"Don't apologize. It happened to enough women. Why shouldn't we talk about it?"

"Then was that the end?"

"For a long time I thought so," she mused. "Perhaps. I don't know. It could, after all, be a way out."

"From Shard? But would you want to change that for— well, for a Pomeroy sort of life?"

"My dear man, you don't know."

132

"But Shard," he protested, "the squire existence. I thought that was your idea of the way life should be."

"Not any longer, I assure you."

"What's wrong with it?"

"Money," she said, "just money. Shard used to have a thousand acres. Now it has a hundred and fifty. I suppose it's Henry, he's not the sort of person for to-day. We barely keep going. We shouldn't do even that if it were not for the chickens. I keep the chickens, did you know? Oh, those bloody hens!"

Neve thought suddenly how easy it was going to be for Andrew Gazzard. If he but knew, he had only to offer the price and the bargain would be struck. There would be no need for plans of campaign, romantic persuasion, or anything of that kind. Just a plain cash statement. Or would that, after all, do? He looked at her as she walked along beside him. Not really beautiful, but with an air of aloofness, of delicacy, that could not, surely, be entirely fake. He had a feeling that, if he told her the plain truth about what young Gazzard proposed to do, and why, he could kill his chances there and then. He was tempted.

They walked for a long time, talking idly, trivialities. She remarked that, for such a pleasant walk, they ought to have had a dog with them, and that led to a protracted conversation about dogs. Neve had never owned a dog, and that she found remarkable.

Suddenly he came out with, "How about the Gazzards? What does the squirearchy think of them?"

"The squirearchy is quite simply jealous of their cash."

He nodded. "So very much money."

"Nobody has farmed that way, in this part of the world, for generations. Even that bailiff they've got, Fogg, is dazed by it. We dare not make butter because we can't do it for less than seven and six a pound. Sir Russell grumbles at Fogg because, no matter how he tries, he can't make it cost more than twelve shillings."

"You think that's a heavenly way to live? I call it cock-eyed."

"A cock-eyed heaven."

"What do you think of them," he ventured, "as people?"

"I rather like Sir Russell, for all his bounce. The old lady's just a comic, of course, and the daughter a bore, she thinks of nothing except what she can put on her back, and the necessity of mixing with quite the best society. She's hopeless. I haven't seen much of the boys, but the younger one is a bit of a prig. The elder is probably the best of the bunch, he's rather charming."

"Andrew? Yes, he's not so bad. He works with me now, did you know?"

"Is he any good?"

"He would be, without all that money."

"Has he so much, himself?"

Neve considered, wondering whether to plunge. "I believe he comes into a lot when he gets married. You ought to hook him."

"Might at that," she replied.

"Would you? Would you deliberately marry for money?"

She smiled. "Money's awfully nice."

"No, seriously. Suppose it were a question of someone like Andrew Gazzard, or someone like me, let's say. Would you pick him, for the money?"

They were just at the entrance to the drive to Shard. She stopped and looked at him.

"Are you popping the question?"

"No," he said slowly, "I don't think so."

"Then you don't really want an answer, do you?"

"Just for curiosity."

"What do you really think of me? I'm curious too."

He stared at her, getting angry. "Fact is, I don't know what I think of you. I try not to."

She turned towards the gates. "Come on, I'll give you some tea."

But he shook his head. "No, I'll not come in to tea. I can get the bus at the corner, can't I?"

"Your farewells," she murmured, "are always so unexpected."

"Was the last one unexpected?"

"Not entirely. A little too casual, perhaps, a bit too pre-sumptuous."

"But welcome, surely."

"Ill-mannered, though," she said. "Thanks for the walk. Good-bye."

He watched her as she went up the drive, but she did not glance back. He shrugged and turned for the bus stop on the corner. There was a grass bank there on which he sat, having no idea how long he would have to wait for a bus—half an hour, maybe, or even longer, seeing it was Sunday. He got out his pipe, filled it with tobacco, and then found that the stem was choked. He searched for a twig thin enough to probe it, and the twig broke in the stem, and he could not get it out. Neve put the pipe back into his pocket, and began to swear to himself, slowly and without passion, but profoundly and methodically.

8

THROUGHOUT the morning Elizabeth had been worrying about the letter. It had lain beside her father's plate at breakfast—the letter with the Kensington postmark, addressed in her mother's hand. Such a letter arrived about once every six months, and Elizabeth never knew what it contained; a request for money, perhaps. Henry, as always, scarcely glanced at the envelope, but was silent at breakfast. Afterwards he put the letter casually in his pocket and retired to his room. Elizabeth sighed and went about her chores.

It was nearly a year now since she had seen her mother; her next visit to Kensington was almost due. Once a year, for a week, and her mother making such an effort to contrive a success of it. The flat, in an old house behind the High Street, was cleaned out, and there were flowers in the guest-room. Harriet behaved with great care, kept a firm control of herself. They went to suitable restaurants and to theatres—Henry provided the money for that. It was as though, Elizabeth continually felt, she were at home on holiday from boarding-school, being treated before the new term began. They spoke only formally of Henry, and never of the past. Harriet took her on a round of visits to friends, old women like herself, living reminiscent lives in the back rooms of Kensington. Harriet introduced her to her friends, at tea parties in faded rooms but with a large silver teapot still gleaming and nearly-complete sets of delicate china. A few of the friends also had daughters, girls of refinement who worked in Government offices, and one or two of whom occasionally pulled off marriage with a young lieutenant or a clerk. The conversation at the tea parties was of coming-out dances and concerts, of Henley and brothers in Kenya or the Sudan, of the tedium of having to stay in London when everything was shut and the damnable taxation that made this necessary, and of the rapacity, rudeness and idleness of the working class.

Year by year, however, the visits grew fewer. Harriet sometimes spoke bitterly of this old friend or that who had proved a viper. But Elizabeth knew of course that her mother had simply retreated a step or two further into her private alcoholic hell. Though there was never a drink when Elizabeth was there. Indeed, the story of Harriet's drinking was something that Elizabeth knew by repute, but had never personally experienced. When she was a child there were days when Mummy had been unwell the evening before and would keep her room, and Uncle Gilbert, the doctor would come. Once she heard two housemaids giggling—"Proper boozed, and no error. Up there in her nightie, chucking things about." "Go on, really?" "It's the master I'm sorry for." But Elizabeth had been merely puzzled. Then she was sent young to boarding-school, and during her holidays there were few occasions. It was Peter, four years her senior, who had first explained it to her. They had been sent to stay for a week with an elderly cousin at Scarborough, whom they both hated.

"But surely you know why," he said. They were walking, discontented, on the beach. "Harriet's got one of her bouts on."

"Bouts?"

136

"She's got drunk."

And, to her incredulous stare, "She can't help it. Uncle Gilbert told me once. He said it's a real illness, like measles or something, that people just get."

"But what's it like?" she asked in awe, "getting drunk? Peter, not like that man we saw in the street?"

"Yes," he cheerfully replied, "something like that."

Elizabeth said nothing more then, but that night she woke screaming.

Of course, as she grew older, she came to understand and to pity. But not to discuss. They were a reticent family, who did not discuss. When the war started she was still at school. When Peter was killed, she was not brought home. A week later her father came to see her, and they took a long, silent walk in the lanes, during which he contrived not to weep. He told her that her mother had gone to do nursing in a London hospital. She had been a nurse, a V.A.D., in the earlier war.

"Wasn't that how you met?" she asked, white-lipped.

"Yes. I had been wounded on the Somme. Not badly, what in those days we called a Blighty one. Your mother was a nurse at the hospital. We were married during my convalescent leave. She was very handsome, and gay."

That was more than he had ever said to her about her mother.

"I think it is very fine of her," he added, "to return to nursing now. It is her answer to Peter's death. Women have more courage than men."

That was the story, the nursing story, and Elizabeth never knew how true it was. But whether Harriet did or did not become a nurse for a while, she never returned to Shard. There was no actual break, it was tacit. Henry said at first that she had gone to do war work in a hospital; when the war was over, and she did not return, nobody dare to inquire. Elizabeth came back from her own war service in the W.A.A.F., and quietly took on the housekeeping at Shard.

One evening after dinner Henry asked her to come to his room, the small room, isolated from the rest, which was strewn with his books and papers, and in which no one ever disturbed him. A photograph of Harriet stood on the desk.

"You're adult now, Elizabeth," he began, "and you must be wondering about this house, and your mother and myself. Or rather, I suppose, you know."

She nodded.

"It was not by my wish that she left," he said, "I want you to know that. There were always difficulties, and I suppose you are aware of those too. I am not blaming her. The thing is pathological. It took me a long while, but I understood that at last. We all have our miseries."

"You need not talk about it if you don't want to," she ventured.

"No, you have a right to know. It makes demands on you that you may not always care to accept. I think we should have managed, and she would still be here, if Peter had not been killed. That finished her. She could no longer see much point in struggling. Do you understand? She had you, of course, but she never had seen a great deal of you. Peter was her anchor. When that parted, she preferred to drift. I was never of much consequence to her, Elizabeth."

He was sitting upright in his chair, not moving. Elizabeth did not dare to speak.

"When she went away," he said, "we both knew that she would not return, though we made some sort of pretence. I see to it, of course, that she is adequately provided for. There is no point in discussing this, there is nothing to discuss. But you ought to know, because you have your own life to consider. Here you are looking after me, tied to a failing property."

"Is it so bad?"

"Fairly bad. What it amounts to is that we can just about hang on here during my lifetime, but after one more dose of death duties there will not be much left."

"It doesn't matter, that side of it," she said.

"But it does. This is almost the end of the Melmoths at Shard. We have outlived our times. It doesn't matter for me, but you ought to be seeking a new future."

She shrugged. "I should get a job?"

"You should get a husband."

"That won't happen."

"Why not? You mean that there is someone, and some barrier?"

"He was killed," she said, "over Berlin."

"Oh, I'm sorry." Then, after a pause, "It seems I am not much of a parent, not to have known anything about that."

"Nobody knew. We were not engaged. I didn't even sleep with him, though I think that he wanted me to. It was something I could have done for him, before he was killed. Since I did not, I feel that I belong to him. So I shall stay here with you."

"Nothing binds you," he said.

But she felt like a novice taking vows.

And for long afterwards she felt that. Her life was decided. It became a constant battle of housekeeping, a battle for Shard. They farmed, in a muddled way. The hens, which she took on herself, were the mainstay. For pigs, that might have handsomely paid, they had insufficient food allocation. She cut the household staff to herself, Mrs. Cushion and a woman daily from the village; three men were all she could afford outside. And they just made do.

Then, in this sedate arrangement for existing, came Skelstrand, and she, as it were, awoke again.

9

On the morning that her mother's letter arrived, Elizabeth went out into the yard to look for Benson to talk about feeding stuffs, and could not find him. Over in one of the fields, she supposed, and turned in that direction. It was a sparkling day, a day to invite living. It had been such a day, it came to her, on which Bill had casually met her on the concrete track that led to the dispersal, and said, "I'm on a twenty-four-hour stand-down. How about a drive into the country?"

They went in his rattling old sports car along the flat roads to Boston. They stared at the Stump, gazed idly over the bridge, ate lunch at the inn in the square, and over coffee in the upstairs room, when an old man with a snuffling head cold had crept away and left them to themselves, he told her conversationally that he was in love with her. They sat there for an hour, holding hands. Then he gently said that he must drive her back to the airfield. What he wanted, of course, was for her to say that, since he was stood down for twenty-four hours, and although she had no overnight pass. . . . But she did not. When they got back, there was a flap on, an urgent call for a strike at Brest. He hurried away to the briefing, and she took her seat in the operations room. Before he went out to his aircraft with the bunch of young men in their flying gear, he looked across the green-lit operations room and smiled at her, confidently. She smiled and nodded.

In the early morning hours, when the returning bombers began to make radio communication, one by one, there was nothing from him. She was tortured by the thought that if, in that upstairs room at the inn, she had consented, he would not have been flying that night. And then, late, there was contact from his aircraft, and it hobbled home with a torn wing and a wounded gunner. She had remained in the operations room, and saw him come in before he saw her; his helmet swinging in his hand, his smooth face tired but serene. When he caught sight of her, he smiled again, and she managed to get out of the room without weeping, knowing that night after night this would happen, and that they were doomed.

Elizabeth found herself standing motionless in the fields behind Shard, not seeing the sunlight on the hedges, but the cold moon on an operations hut, and remembering the smell of the coffee urn, and the sharpness of frost. She shook herself from it and went searching for Benson, but he was not there. At last she turned back towards the house, and found him in the yard. "Ah, Benson," she said, "about the feed. . . ."

"We're three hunnerweight short, Miss," he began, and they went into a long discussion.

It was interrupted by the trot of hooves briskly approaching, and the scrunch of wheels.

"What in the name . . .?" asked Benson, looking up.

Through the gate from the drive a pony and trap frisked smartly into the yard, Andrew Gazzard standing up in it, holding the reins, flourishing a long whip. With comical effort he brought the pony to a stop beside her, and grinned.

"Damn sight more difficult to handle one horse-power than thirty," he announced.

Elizabeth laughed. He had dressed for the part perfectly —a suit of Edwardian cut, narrow trousers, high lapels flaunting a rose, tall white collar, suède gloves and grey bowler.

"What's this in aid of?" she asked.

"Of you, naturally. You're coming to lunch. You promised. No stinking little motor-car, says you, but a pony and trap. Okay, pony and trap it is, and all the trimmings. Whoa there. Hey!"

Benson, grinning, went to the pony's head and quietened it. "I was even rasher than I thought," said Elizabeth. "At least you can drive a car."

"Now, come on," he pleaded. "I've been to a lot of trouble. It earns a lunch."

She hesitated, but then cheerfully agreed. "All right, I'll get a coat and tell Cushion."

"If you've got a crash helmet," he shouted after her, "I should bring it."

When she got back, Benson had manœuvred the equipage into the outward direction. Elizabeth held up her hand, and Andrew leaned down and hauled her aboard.

"Better sit down and hold tight. All right there in front, let her go."

He cracked the whip, the pony plunged and clattered, then shot away with a jerk that seated the driver and dislodged his hat.

"Oh, but your bowler," she cried.

"No time for that. Once you start, you can't. . . . Whoops!"

They successfully grazed the gate-post and were out on the drive. Andrew, his hair blowing, fixed the whip in its holder, and turned to smile at her, slackening the reins.

"Better leave it to the horse," he cheerfully shouted, "and the power of prayer."

As they spanked down the drive, the ironshod wheels crunching the gravel, Elizabeth felt the sunshine, the fun of the thing, the amusement of the young idiot beside her, and she laughed with pleasure. They came out of the main gates and headed towards Overskel. The day, for her, was sparkling again, the trees dappled that sped by them, the cornfields lush. One or two villagers looked up smiling when they passed, and a dog ran beside them for a little way, barking at the pony, until Andrew cracked his whip.

When they reached Overskel, a groom stood waiting to receive the pony. Andrew jumped down and helped her from the trap, squeezing her hand as an Edwardian gallant should, and putting his arm around her to lead her into the house, where the family were gathered in the big drawing-room, the windows open on to the terrace, and drinks on a side-table. It was all, she thought, so beautifully rich, so comfortably secure. Even Cynthia Gazzard seemed a pleasant girl, and towards the old man, who took both her hands in greeting, Elizabeth felt warmly.

"Andrew been playing the fool with that get-up and that horse and cart?" he asked. "Don't pay any attention to him, he's a born fool. What'll you drink, my dear?"

"It's nice fooling. Gin and something, please. Oh, anything. French."

"When I was young," said Lady Gazzard dreamily, advancing with outstretched hand, "ponies were just going out and motor-cars coming in. Absurd, unwieldy things. Those were better days."

"Nonsense," argued her husband. "What's wrong with these days, eh? Forward, that's the way to look. Stirring days, great days, days of science and adventure. What d'you say, Elizabeth? Nobody's going to call you Miss Melmoth, we're friends now, eh?"

"All these wars," declared Lady Gazzard, "are a judgment on us."

"There've always been wars, and troubles, and the weak going to the wall. All you need is guts."

"And money," smiled Elizabeth.

142

He looked at her assessingly. "There's always money to be had, if you go the right way about it."

At lunch, as they chattered, Elizabeth tried to reason in her mind why this offer was being made to her; for the offer, of course, was obvious enough. Even Cynthia was trying to be amiable. Every now and then she got that appraising look from Sir Russell, the sort of wary, proffering look that, she imagined, he adopted when a business deal was being mooted. They were showing themselves off to her, displaying their affluence. All this, the old man seemed to say, you can have if you'll take Andrew. There was no other meaning she could put to it and at first it irritated her, as though she were being offered a price, like a tart. But then she looked at Andrew and the irritation was allayed. He was not posing. He was his usual cheerful idiot, but behind it he was anxious, which touched her.

But why? she kept asking herself. She would have thought that Sir Russell would demand money from his son's marriage, a lot of money; and he would shrewdly know almost exactly the financial state of Shard. It suddenly came to her that perhaps Andrew was really in love with her, or imagined that he was, and had compelled the family against their wishes to do this for him. She had dim perceptions of a series of family rows, the mother wailing, the father threatening, but at last giving way when the boy stubbornly persisted. She looked quickly at him, he smiled back at her, and it seemed to her then that this was what truly had happened. She was astonished at the flutter into which this put her. When she said something to Andrew, something trivial, there was a gentleness in her voice to which he seemed happily to respond. Elizabeth was suddenly unsure of herself, afraid of some chance remark that might reveal her. She was glad when, after a decent interval of conversation with the coffee, the family wandered off one by one, as though to a plan.

"Why don't we take a trip to Town to do a day's shopping?" asked Cynthia with an effort. "That would be really fun. I go up once or twice a week, and you really must."

"I'm going to hold you to that," Elizabeth formally promised.

"It has been so nice," murmured Lady Gazzard, drifting. "But I must go and lie down now, dear."

"My wife," explained Sir Russell when she had gone, "is very keen on religion."

"So I have heard."

"It's a great comfort to her. She always does a little praying after meals."

Elizabeth awkwardly did not know what to say. But the old man grinned broadly, "What I do after meals is take a bismuth powder. It's a prescription a man in Holland made up for me years ago, when I had a shocking attack. You suffer from indigestion at all? No? Oh well, you're young, of course."

He got up.

"And I must go back to the office," he said, "somebody in this family has to do some work. See if you can put some ambition into this boy, Elizabeth."

She smiled and murmured it was nothing to do with her.

"Could be," he said abruptly.

From the door he said, "Tell your father I hope we shall see more of him. I like your father. Maybe we don't see eye to eye on everything, but it's a free country. And, after all, we're neighbours."

A moment later he popped his head back around the door. "And don't let that fool of a son of mine drive you around any more in that horse and cart. Too damn dangerous."

Then she was alone with Andrew.

"Sorry about my family," he said.

"It was a little marked."

"It's the old man," he explained. "Always tends to rush things. That's his business training. He is used to saying what he wants, and getting it right away. They don't half hop when he gives an order. You should see 'em."

"Is he giving an order now?"

"Oh, good lord, no," protested Andrew hastily. "Far from it. This is my idea, you know."

Elizabeth laughed. "You're an odd boy."

"I'm twenty-four. Quite an experienced chap, really. I suppose I ought to own up about all that. Would you like the confessions?"

"Oh, no, thank you."

"Pity, they're quite interesting."

She waited for a little, looking at him. He was handsome, she reflected, and, in his Edwardian suit, amusing. Life with him would be entertaining enough, but whether she could ever be persuaded to take him seriously. . . .

As though in answer to her, he said, "I know I play the clown, but as a matter of fact I rather mean all this."

"Just what?"

"Surely you can see that I'm popping the question."

"That's fairly clear. But a girl likes to hear it, you know."

"Oh lord," said Andrew, getting up hastily, "I ought to do the thing properly, specially in this rig."

He carefully knelt in front of her, taking one of her hands in his, and declaiming, "Miss Melmoth, unworthy as I am of your consideration, may I plead that a true devotion, and a passion, no matter how unworthy. . . ."

Suddenly angry, Elizabeth pulled her hand away. He stared at her for a moment, and then he was on the seat beside her, his arm round her shoulders, his face, serious, close to hers.

"Matter of fact, I'm in love with you, and I want like hell for you to marry me. Any chance?"

"I don't know. I truly don't know."

"Then it's not an absolute turn-down?"

"No," she replied uncertainly, "perhaps not.'

He kissed her on the mouth, embracing her with skill. Elizabeth was aware of her body instinctively responding to him, and her thoughts, confused, yielding, swept into the pleasure, surprisingly fierce, of the caress, the animal reaction. She clung to him, gripping her fingers into his arms, her eyes closed, the muscles of her neck taut. And then the moment passed, and she held him away, turning aside her face, pleading with him. At once he obeyed, and they

145

sat silently together, neither looking at the other, but his one hand still clutching hers.

"I think you had better take me home now, Andrew," she said, as steadily as she could.

"Okay. But you haven't really answered."

"Not now. I can't answer now. Oh, this is too absurd. We have scarcely talked more than half a dozen times. I think you're rather a dangerous young man."

"But it was all on the level, honest," he protested. "Absolutely fair and square. I want you to marry me."

She disengaged her hand, pushing back her hair, and said, "Those confessions should be more interesting than I thought."

But he shook his head, and would not return to the bantering manner. "Elizabeth, I'm dead serious. There's not much to me as a person. There are other things, of course, plenty of cash and all that. All that side of it's all right. The old man's for it."

"Why?" she asked.

"Oh, he likes you, and he's a bit of a snob. Anyway, that's all right. But it's what you think of me."

She said, judiciously, "You seem to be more complicated than I had suspected."

She got up. He stood in front of her and gently took her hands in his.

"I haven't made all that much of a fool of myself?"

"Not entirely."

"And I have got a chance? You'll think about it?"

She promised, laughing, that indeed she would think about it.

"Do I have to wait long?"

"Oh, Andrew, I don't know. You're rather endearing."

She kissed him, quickly and lightly, and escaped before he could embrace her again.

"Now, please," she said, "take me home."

"Not that damn pony and trap again?"

"No, all right, the car."

PART THREE

1

THE few people who thought at all about Tom Bruell thought of him in varying ways. His father, William Bruell, publican of the Melmoth Arms at Shard Green, did not notice much of a change in him. A widower with six children, a public-house to manage, and an absorption in racing pigeons cannot be expected to comprehend the problems of a son who has left home. Tom was the one who had turned out a bit of a scholar, the clever one, the boy who had done so well at Gulport Grammar that the head had seriously thought of putting him up for a university grant. But nothing came of it, and at seventeen Tom settled into a clerk's post in the Insurance in Bridge Street. Even this put his father in some awe. He accepted, as fitting, Tom's national service as a clerk in the R.A.S.C. Though to Bill Bruell, an old infantryman of the local levy who had been next to Colonel Melmoth the day he was wounded on the Somme, a cushy sort of base job did not seem much like soldiering. But Tom, he conceded, had brains. When he returned from the Army to the Insurance, he was accepted among the sons and daughters of the wealthy of Gulport, the councillors, the big tradesfolk. He mixed with the belles of the dramatic society, the bloods of the tennis club. It was a known thing, which his father could only approve, that he and Daphne Wilkinson might some day make a do of it. And everybody averred that Joe Wilkinson, who had this only child, was worth £20,000 if a penny, laid out in shop property and ground rents all over the district. When the blow came about Daphne, Bill Bruell was not only shocked, but disappointed. Supposedly, that was all over. But it did not occur to him that it had greatly changed the outlook of his son, whom, in any case, he saw only at occasional week-ends.

To Joe Wilkinson, Tom was an irritant, a reminder. The old man had grown increasingly eccentric since his daughter had gone away from the town. He brooded in his shop among the iron ware and the drums of paraffin oil, and took unpredictable exception to certain customers whom he would not serve, but from whom he walked away, muttering to himself. Mrs. Wilkinson was usually in the shop now, very abrupt and prim, ready to step forward on these occasions to perform the business, snapping her lips as methodically as she snapped shut the drawer of the cash register. Joe rarely attended Council meetings, and never the magistrates' court. Neither he nor his wife Florence ever went out at night, and their existence was conducted almost entirely in the shop or in the living quarters above it. Tom Bruell felt it a duty to continue to visit them. He would be there for supper, after which he and the old man would sit either side of the fireplace, each dreaming in his own way of Daphne. It was like dwelling in an empty house. How often, before, Tom had arrived to take the girl out to a rehearsal of the society's autumn play. And she had come laughing down the stairs, and kissed her father good-night, and gone off with the young fellow. He had not much approved of him in those days, had in truth been jealous of him. But now when, after an hour or so, Tom made to go, Joe found some excuse for retaining him. He had not noticed any change in Tom himself; indeed, he scarcely saw him at all as a person, but only as a ghost.

Florence Wilkinson, however, took a far more practical view of Tom Bruell. Among the wives of the town she had always been held high. At chapel or at Women's Institute, at civic function or private tea party, Florence Wilkinson had been deferred to. Now, by a cruel swipe for which in her heart she could blame no one but God, all this had been taken from her. But, unlike her husband, she did not despair of regaining it. For the first few weeks she had indeed despaired, but gradually she saw a small hope, and the hope was Tom Bruell.

In earlier days she had somewhat despised him.

"You can do better than that stick-in-the-mud," she used sometimes to say to Daphne.

Daphne, laughing, used to reply that there was time enough, nothing was settled between them.

"What he's after is your father's money," Mrs. Wilkinson

used primly to warn. "He'll never have much of his own."

But now she saw salvation in him. In a year or two, she secretly planned, when memories had faded, if Tom should marry Daphne they might brave it out, settle in a little house on the outskirts of the town. Then something could be salvaged. So she kept up the contact with Tom, held him in reserve. It never occurred to her that he might refuse.

The person who really understood what had happened to Tom Bruell was, curiously, a newcomer to the town, Rosa Papelian. She first saw him in the magistrates' court on the day when the labourer was charged with raping the girl. Rosa went to the hearing, early enough to get a place in the public gallery, because she had understood at once that here was one of those opportunities, those natural clashes of a class society, that might be used to advantage.

It was while the girl in the witness-box was pitifully whimpering that Rosa noticed the pallor of the youth sitting on one of the public benches close by. The other women spectators, engrossed in the evidence, paid no attention to him, but Rosa leaned over and murmured, "Are you all right?"

He turned towards her a face so numb with agony that even she pitied. She thought at first that he had not understood her, but suddenly his eyes became sensible again, and he muttered, "Yes, I'm all right, thanks."

When the short hearing was ended she looked for him in the street. He was dragging slowly off towards the harbour. She overtook him and spoke to him. "You look rotten. Come and have a cup of coffee."

He followed her, like a somnambulist, into a small café and sat staring at the cup placed before him.

"Don't think I'm interfering," she tried, "but you knew that girl?"

He nodded.

"If I could get my hands on him," he broke out with sudden intensity, "I'd gladly swing."

Rosa shook her head impatiently. "That's nonsense. It's also nonsense to think, as you probably have, of doing yourself in. It isn't a question of individuals, but of sweeping away all the rottenness and making a new decent society, in which such things would be unthinkable. Oh, you turn your head away. You're probably right. You wouldn't have the courage, probably, to give your whole life to it."

"To what?" he asked listlessly.

It was not a promising start. Rosa almost shrugged it off. Yet because the lad touched her—and not many did—she persevered with him. To her surprise, it was rewarding. He responded to her frigid offer of friendship. He came occasionally, and then more frequently, to sit out an evening in her rooms, listening solemnly to the talk, rarely saying much himself, nursing his silent thoughts in a way that she found uncomfortably pathetic.

Her husband was simply puzzled by him. "What do you waste time with him for?" Papelian once asked.

"I've a feeling he'll be useful. He's filled with loathing of the system he grew up in. Anyway, let him be. He does no harm."

She was irritably aware that Bert suspected her interest to be personal. But it was not so, she told herself, searching her emotions. If anything, it was that unlikely feeling, pity. A self-indulgence, she knew, but she angrily put the thought from her, and the lad stayed.

To Tom himself Rosa Papelian was a haven. His chief distress, which perhaps nobody understood, was loneliness. When Daphne had been there, each evening of the week he had a regular commitment; a party to the cinema, a rehearsal of the drama society, a gathering in the house of one friend or another during the winter months, long evenings at the tennis club in summer. But all this he had abandoned when Daphne went away. He hadn't, he told himself, the heart. He wanted to leave his lodgings in the town and go wherever she went, but Daphne herself forbade him. He wrote her a letter, which he afterwards understood to have been adolescent and ill-timed, begging her to marry him.

He waited weeks for the reply. When it came, it said she would never marry any man, and that devil had given her a baby, what did he think of that? and she was going to have an operation to get rid of it; and if they found out they'd send her to prison; and she didn't care, or want to see him or anybody else ever again, and she hoped she would die of the operation.

Tom carried the letter burning in his pocket, brooding all day. He was desperate by evening when he went to see Rosa. She was sitting, as usual, in her high-backed chair at the window, with pamphlets and books strewn on the ledge beside her.

She looked at him in silence and then said, "Well, what is it?"

He hesitated, thrust the letter at her, and sat down, staring at the floor. When Rosa had read the letter she gazed over at him with a hard face. "Well?"

"What am I to do?"

"Do you want to go to her?"

"She won't see me." He looked up defiantly. "Oh, all right, I admit it. I'm afraid to go to her. I don't think I could marry her now. And it's none of her fault. I hate myself."

Then the gaunt-faced woman, pressing her head rigidly against the chair-back in the fading light from the window, began to talk. What was he to do? That depended on his courage. Had he the courage to put all these personal emotions out of his life and dedicate himself to the task of creating a better society? Could he be single of purpose, accepting a discipline as severe and self-excluding as the monastic discipline of old? Because, if he had the strength, there was work to do, real work, work for all his lifetime. It would run counter to all his accepted ideas. It would demand of him unquestioning obedience and devotion, a surrender to the wisdom of authority. Her voice went on and on. He listened, snake-fascinated.

At the end she handed him back his letter. Slowly he tore it into small pieces which he dropped to the floor.

As the months went by the pain of the thought of Daphne eased and he took great comfort from the evenings that he spent in the Papelians' room, Rosa in her chair, Bert coming in from some meeting, some political chore, pacing up and down the room while he spoke of it, glancing quickly now and then at his expressionless wife. At first the man was wary

152

of talking freely when Tom was there, but soon he came to disregard him. Tom knew, of course, that Papelian thought poorly of him, taking him to be a mere weakling, an unimportant casualty of the struggle of society. But Tom cared nothing for what Papelian thought. It was when the man was away, and Rosa began to talk to him in her quiet monotonous voice, speaking as though she were uttering her dreams, that he had his reward. Not that he fully accepted, or even properly understood, her doctrines. In the day-to-day business of life assurance, of drawing up endowment policies for weekly premiums to yield a capital sum with bonuses added thirty-five years hence, the idea of a revolution seemed absurd and unreal. At a game of tennis on the hard courts of the recreation ground, or at a rehearsal for the forthcoming production of *The Yeomen*, or while watching a football match of a Saturday afternoon, class warfare seemed an improbability. But he was sufficiently impressed by Rosa's lectures to be able, when the Skelstrand strike broke out, to sympathize with the men, even though their aim was the reinstatement of Callaghan.

He was so puzzled to find himself doing this that he took it up with Rosa. "I ought to be on the other side. When I think of that beast, even now. . . ."

"It's not a personal thing," she replied. "Surely you see that. It's a question of principle, having nothing to do with private emotions."

Tom nodded uncertainly, still puzzled. But when Papelian came in, grey with fatigue, Tom found he could listen to his account of progress without bitterness or hate.

"Is he safe?" Papelian uneasily asked his wife after Tom had gone. "After all, it was his girl."

Rosa sat staring out of the window, considering. At last she said, "Yes, he's all right. He has forgotten the girl. Or rather, she has become a symbol for him, a symbol of the brutality of society towards innocence."

Papelian lit another cigarette, inhaling deeply. "Well, you know best." But he was not convinced.

And yet Rosa knew she was right. He was a lad who needed to believe in something. Once it had been this girl, probably no better than any other girl. Now gradually, Rosa thought, she was substituting her own faith in his mind. One day he would have absorbed it completely, and then he would be useful. Rosa shrugged, irritated with herself that this did not seem a satisfactory ending. She damned herself for sentimentality, for being pleased that he had recovered a sort of happiness, a kind of serenity.

2

TOM had not written to Daphne after the letter he had destroyed. From time to time he had news of her from her mother. She had settled down in Birmingham, as a telephonist in one of the hotels. She was living in a girls' hostel. Always she was promising to come back to Gulport on holiday, but she never came. There was this excuse or that: one of the girls had invited her home for the week-end, with another she was to spend a fortnight in Devon. She sent snapshots of herself, which Mrs. Wilkinson showed to Tom. He agreed falteringly that she looked very well, that she was putting on weight, that her hair was pretty. But still he did not write to her, nor she to him. And when he was told, one day at the office, that he was to take a journey to the company's head office at Birmingham, his stomach turned, old hopes and desires fluttered behind his eyes, but he did not tell Mrs. Wilkinson, or ask her for Daphne's new address. Nor did he say anything about it to Rosa Papelian.

All the way in the train he was in a tumult. From his corner seat he stared through the dirty windows at the drab approaches to the city, snatching at the glimpses of what streets could be seen from the railway. At the station he humped his suitcase and went to the small hotel that had been chosen for him. He could not prevent himself, as he walked, glancing at every distant figure of a young woman, half convinced that she might be Daphne. At first he had been sure that he would instantly recognize her walk, even when she was too far distant for him to discern the features. But after several gasps of mistaken recognition he grew uncertain, until he imagined that he would no longer know her even face to face. He could not picture what she looked like, except as a few badly-printed snapshots.

He was three days in Birmingham. During the office hours he was busy and engrossed, but each evening, after tea, he began an aimless tour of the central streets of the city, around the shabby cathedral, hoping at first to meet her, and then glumly despairing that he did not. Towards the women who smiled at him he turned indifferent glances. Somewhere in this collection of houses that was termed a city, she existed. And yet he could not meet her. He found himself willing her to appear in the street before him, and making absurd little promises to God if she should; he would give up smoking for a week, that kind of thing. He kept walking about the city in a kind of desperation, turning occasionally into a pub for a glass of beer, or into a café for coffee and a sandwich, until as the city quietened he had to give up and return to his hotel, where the night-porter nodded good-night from the hutch as he climbed the stairs to sleeplessness in a shabby room.

On the third night he reproached himself for stupidity and went to a cinema, sitting alone in the darkness in which other couples were huddled into motionless embraces, girl's head on man's shoulder. He came out at nine-thirty, intending to go straight back to the hotel, but the sense of his aloneness forced him to a perambulation of just a few streets, just a last little walk, before he should give up all hope of seeing her. He walked aimlessly for a quarter of an hour, and then thought he would get a beer and a sandwich. Close by was a big flashy pub. The saloon bar was noisy and crowded. He pushed his way through to order his beer, glanced along the bar, and there was Daphne. She was seated on a stool with her back towards him, talking to another girl, but Tom had never a moment's doubt that it was she. What a fool he had been to think that he might not recognize her.

He thrust his way between the people, came up behind her and exclaimed, "Daphne."

She turned with a fixed smile on her lips, hesitated for a

moment of recognition, and then said casually, "Why, it's Tom. What are *you* doing here?"

"Business," he replied. "Hoped I might run into you."

He could not stop staring apprehensively at her, and she lowered her gaze, introducing him to the other girl, "Mary, this is Tom, old boy-friend of mine."

"You don't say?" murmured the other girl. A distasteful sort of girl, Tom thought, thick paint, dyed hair, coarse mouth.

He bought them drinks. Two gins and tonic, and a beer for himself. "Well, fancy running into you like this," was all he could find to say.

"It's a small world," remarked the other girl, dutifully.

"Certainly a coincidence," Tom nervously agreed. He was glad when, after a few minutes, the other girl gave them a lidded glance and wandered away. "You'll have lots to talk about," she said.

Rid of her, Tom smiled happily at Daphne. "So good to see you again," he tried.

"Is it?"

"Of course it is."

He could look at her with more leisure now. She had changed, grown older of course, more worldly-looking. She wore a dark suit, a lace blouse, a thick cloth coat. Her feet, cocked on the rail below the bar, were in high-heeled black slippers.

"Well, how are you getting on?" he cheerfully inquired.

"Oh, I get by."

"Daphne," he urged, "don't be angry with me. I know I didn't write, but you seemed to want me not to."

"What does it matter? The past's past. Are you going to buy me another drink?"

"Of course," he hastily assented.

"Have to hurry. It's near closing."

He struggled to attract the attention of the barmaid, who was working with sour-faced concentration on the last orders. When she had got her gin, Daphne said, "Well, cheerio," swallowed it, descended from the stool and smoothed down her skirt.

"May I see you home?" Tom asked.

"Why not?"

He gulped at his beer and followed her out. Daphne took him to the bus stop and told him the fare. They sat on top and she asked for a cigarette.

"I'm so happy I have met you again," he said, smiling at her. When he put his arm through hers and held her hand, she did not object. Tom, looking at her on the seat beside him, was suddenly wildly happy, and the bus was travelling through enchanted streets.

They got off where she directed, at a dim corner, and she led him, arm-in-arm, up a side street of tall houses and blank shops on the pavement edge. Neither of them said much. She stopped at a door lacking paint, an electric light shining feebly through the transom. He glanced up and down the empty street and asked, "May I kiss you good-night?"

"Don't you want to come in?"

"I thought," he said, startled, "you lived in a hostel."

She laughed. "They're not strict." She felt in her handbag for the door-key. He followed her into the hallway of the house and, when the door was closed, put his arm around her.

"No, wait," she said, motioning towards the stairs.

On the third floor another key was required from her handbag to unlock the door of her room. She went in first and switched on the light. He followed and closed the door. He stood for a moment looking at her and at the room. It was a quite comfortably appointed room—table and chairs, a large Victorian wardrobe, flower pictures on the walls, a gas fire, a divan bed in one corner on to which she flung her coat, a vase of flowers. "So this is where you live," he uncertainly remarked.

She pulled the curtains to and stooped to light the fire. As she stood up, he stepped forward and took her into his arms. She raised her face, almost indifferently, parting her lips as he kissed her. Tom clung to her, the room spinning dizzily behind his eyelids. All the infinity of their separation, all the misery, vanished in the embrace.

She freed herself from him and whistled comically.

"Daphne," he muttered, moving towards her again, but

157

she held his hands and said, "Come and sit down." He sat beside her on the divan.

"We two never really knew each other, did we?" she said.

"It was my fault. I should never have stayed away from you. I've been such a fool. I have never stopped loving you."

"Don't be so serious about it. Life's too short."

She kicked off her shoes and drew her legs on to the divan beneath her. "What's the use?" she asked. "Enjoy life, that's the thing."

"But, Daphne, I mean it."

"Forget it," she said.

"All my life . . . ." he began, but she put her arms around him and stopped him with a kiss. His thoughts went wildly tumbling. She sank back on the divan, and he beside her. With one hand she groped for the switch and doused the light. He was aware only of her face, lips parted in a smile, eyes looking up at him from the orange shadows of the gas-fire glow. "Aren't you going to get undressed?" she murmured.

"But, darling . . ." he uncertainly began.

"Don't you want to?"

3

In the train next morning Tom sat huddled in a corner of an empty carriage, staring through the window without seeing. The exultation had long passed. He saw only the room in which he had gathered up his clothes from the floor, and had tried, as he put them on, not to look at the girl beneath the covers of the bed.

He had essayed an agonized apology, but she had merely told him, sleepily, not to be a fool. "What on earth does it matter?"

"You can't go on like this," he suddenly burst out, going over to her. "Daphne, you must marry me, and we'll go away, anywhere, you like, but you must marry me."

"That I won't," she answered from the depths of the pillow.

"But, darling," he pleaded, kneeling beside the bed, "what are you doing with your life?"

158

"It's my life."

He seized her shoulder and pulled her round to face him. "What are you doing with it?" he repeated sternly. "I've got to know. They told me you had a job as a telephonist."

"So I have. What did you think, that I was on the streets?"

"Oh, no!" he protested.

"Don't get excited. I'm not. I just like having a good time."

"Do you call this sort of thing having a good time?"

She smiled slowly. "Don't you?"

Tom got up and walked away to the window. "Only if you're in love," he said.

She stretched herself and yawned. "What's it got to do with love?"

"But, Daphne," he pleaded, turning towards her, "that's terrible."

She sat up, the sheet falling from her shoulders, her eyes angry. "Don't preach at me, Tom, will you?"

"Dear God," he groaned.

"Look here, Tom, I like you. Come and see me as often as you want. If you want to sleep with me, that's all right. But you're not going to tell me what I do and what I don't do."

"Do you think," he asked, "that I'd share you with other men?"

"But you have, haven't you?" she pointed out. She pushed back the bed-covers and stood lazily up, smiling at him. "Do you mean you wouldn't again?"

He stared at her with mounting anger. "You're disgusting," he suddenly shouted. He raised his arm and struck her across the face, so that she staggered back against the bed. Without pausing, he turned and fled from the room, down the stairs, out into the greyness of the streets.

Seated in the train that rumbled away from the city, Tom lived that scene in agony over and over again. He saw the yellowness of her naked body, the smile on her lips; felt again the desire for her, and the loathing, and the wild impulse to hit out at her and run to the end of the earth. He sat groaning in the train, telling himself that all women were a rottenness,

159

and all men too, all human kind; and with disgust he rated himself among the lowest.

That night he went to the Papelians'. He had not wanted to, but he felt impelled. Papelian, who was just going out, nodded briefly to him. Rosa, in her window chair, greeted him with, "Hallo. Haven't seen you for some time. What have you been up to?"

"Been away on a business trip," he replied, sitting down opposite to her.

"You look glum. Wasn't it a success?"

"I went to Birmingham," he reluctantly admitted.

"Oh." She gave a quick glance at him and immediately understood. "You met the girl?"

He nodded. And then, angry with himself, he began to weep. Rosa waited in silence. "I'm sorry," he muttered. She made no reply. Soon, she knew, he would tell it all. As he did. The story welled out of him, the bitterness, the shame, the self-loathing and the hatred.

"We're like animals, and all the rest is a fake. Well, isn't it?"

"A bit sweeping," murmured Rosa.

"Oh no, it isn't. Take this town. I know this town, and I can tell you. Have you ever walked up on the common on a summer evening? The boys call it the monkey parade. Any man can go up there any evening, pick up a girl and take her behind the bushes. Not tarts. The ordinary girls of the town. You can believe me."

"I don't doubt you," said Rosa dryly.

"And it isn't just the low-class girls, either. I've lived all my life in this town, and I know it. All the social events, what do you think they're for? Go out past the harbour on to the shore after any dance at the town hall, and you'll see. It isn't to act in the plays that the girls join the dramatic society, but to pick up with boys who can borrow their fathers' cars and drive them out on to the moors at night. And married women too, ogling and leering. This is supposed to be a respectable little town, but you don't know the half of what goes on, I tell you. Behind all the drawn curtains of the respectable little houses, at this very moment when we

160

are talking. . . . It's rotten. Rottenness, rottenness!"

"Aren't you being a bit smug?"

"Oh, I'm like the rest. I made fine words to myself when everybody was whispering and sneering about her. I would stick to her in spite of it all. I kept on saying to myself that she had been soiled, but it was not her fault, and I would never let her down. And then I hadn't the guts. I pretended I was loyal, and the only reason I didn't follow her and marry her was that she told me to keep away. But really I seized on the excuse. I admit it now. I was terrified she would hold me to my promise. And at the same time I longed to go to bed with her. The disgusting thing is that I wanted her all the more, just because she was mixed up in that horrible affair. I began to think I was going mad."

He put his face down on his hands and fell silent. Rosa said nothing.

"I can't help it," he burst out. "It's the strongest thing in me. After all this time, I walked the streets of Birmingham looking for her, craving for her. And when I found her I just wanted the physical thing with her. And afterwards I was disgusted with myself, and with her."

"Will you see her again?" she asked after a silence.

"I don't know. Oh, I don't know! I want to, like hell. And I despise myself for wanting to. I hate life."

"It's not life that should be hated," she said quickly, "but the way we live it."

When Papelian got back later, he found her alone.

"Well?" she asked.

Papelian shook his head. He was worried. He lit a cigarette and began to pace the room. "The bastards are winning," he said. "All I get at the meetings is indifference, except from the party members of course, but that's no use. Look at the mill now, Rosa. The bays are going up, the furnaces are nearly ready. I heard today they've got the first lot of machinery into Liverpool from the States. Our boys among the dockers tried to hold up the handling of it, but they failed. In about eighteen months the blasted thing will be making steel."

"There are methods you haven't yet tried," she murmured.

He checked and looked at her. "Such as?"

She merely gazed back at him.

"The party wouldn't countenance it," he said.

"Of course not. But the party might not be sorry if it happened without their knowledge. It's a risk of course."

"I don't so much mind that," he protested, "but I have to think of how much use I could be somewhere active. Is it worth a stretch in gaol?"

"You don't have to do it yourself."

"Then who?"

"I think," she said, gazing out of the window, "that you have neglected the obvious material ready to your hand. After all, it's all in the books. There's Melmoth, isn't there?"

"But could he be persuaded?" Papelian doubted.

"Inevitably, if we do it right."

Papelian lit another cigarette.

"And then," she continued evenly, "you overlook young Tom Bruell."

Papelian stared. "That little runt? What can he do?"

"I have told you several times that he could be useful. He has reached the stage of such a hatred of society that he is desperate to hit back."

"What puts him in this state?" asked Papelian suspiciously.

"Never mind. Take my word for it. He has the makings of a fanatic."

While her husband pondered this, Rosa sat motionless and silent. Behind her eyes she was cursing herself for submitting to that despicable little bourgeois emotion, jealousy.

4

If Sir Russell Gazzard could have heard Papelian's estimate of how soon Skelstrand would be making steel he would have laughed wryly. At times he would almost have said, "Eighteen months? Eighteen years, more like." He regarded with amused curiosity the local attempts to hinder the building of the mill. A few strike-fomenters, an irate squire—bah, what could they do? The real obstructions were in London, in

New York, in Washington. The real difficulty was, as always, money. Sir Russell had run into the one trouble that, in the past, had always defeated steel-mill pioneers, and that he had felt certain he would himself avoid. He was short of finance. He had miscalculated; not in terms of the sums required (though costs had risen more steeply than he, or anyone else, had expected), but in terms of politics. He had counted on easy access to the Treasury, but the fluctuations of Britain's fortunes, the situations that newspapers ignorantly labelled "crises of payments", had produced such panic among the politicians that even the planners had drawn in their horns. And he had counted upon the irrational fears of the Americans to stimulate their generosity towards any project of armament construction, but had failed accurately to forecast the lobbying manoeuvres of certain pressure groups determined to divert this flow of generosity into domestic pockets. Sir Russell sighed as he travelled in his first-class carriage to London. There were some weary, tortuous passages ahead of him. To pass the journey, he engaged Heron in a long discussion of chances, pulling out paper after paper from the thick brief-case on the seat beside him.

Heron was the only man even partly in Gazzard's confidence about the financial crisis that had arisen, and the latter sometimes wondered if he were wise to trust him with so much knowledge. Heron was sharp enough to see that it might amount to the collapse of the whole Skelstrand project, or at best the admission of outside finance that might demand ultimate control. If Heron saw that coming, he would certainly swap loyalties in good time.

"If the Minister is going to tighten up on us," said Heron innocently, "we could always go to the insurance companies."

"With their own accountant on the board?" replied Gazzard. "No, thank you. The point is, the Minister must be persuaded. Now then, Heron, that's your department. What are the politics of it? How much have you gathered from that chap Appleton? You're thick enough there, aren't you?"

Heron dismissed Appleton with a sneer. "He's only a post

office and half the time he doesn't understand the information he does get."

"He's too busy looking after that handsome wife of his, eh?" smiled Gazzard.

"Handsome, certainly," said Heron smoothly, "and a bit much for friend Appleton, they say."

He went on to discuss the politics of the Ministry, the pressure from the Left against further expenditure on armaments, the pressure from the unions to safeguard employment, the pressure from the Right for economy, and so on. While he was talking, his employer was thinking, Ah, that's where I've got you, my good fellow. The handsome Mrs. Appleton. Try any tricks on me, and I'll see what I can do with that little scandal.

Heron, as he talked, was wondering how much old Gazzard knew about Laura Appleton. Too much, probably. He began to choose his words carefully. The truth was that Appleton, whose fussiness and neuroticisms he despised, was by no means the fool, in the matter of the mill, that he had described. He was there as the Minister's watchdog and Heron had no doubt that the information that went back to the Minister, in Appleton's formal and meticulous minutes, was shrewd enough.

"Of course, sir," he ventured, "it won't do to underestimate the Minister himself. I dare say he has a pretty fair idea of what goes."

"I never," replied Gazzard dryly, "underestimate anybody who has the power to give me the money I want."

So Heron was covering himself, thought Gazzard, amused, perfectly aware of the other's motives. Gazzard certainly did not underestimate young Appleton. Once or twice he had thought of offering him a change into his own employ. The man had a brain for detail and a perceptive intelligence that had not quite been ossified by official training. If Gazzard had come across him when he had first left college, he could have made something extremely useful of him. Even now, he thought, it was not too late. But there was that wife over whom he was perpetually worrying—and not without cause, Gazzard grinned to himself. He keenly enjoyed watching the sexual difficulties of other men; they gave him a zest.

He reluctantly turned his thoughts to the negotiations he was about to conduct, scarcely listening to Heron's discourse, all of which he knew, and which left out of account the two or three really important facts that only Gazzard himself knew.

He needed another ten million pounds; eight would probably see him through, but ten for safety. The Treasury, with the Budget not, after all, so far off, would oppose as a matter of routine. The Minister, who had certain troubles of his own within the Cabinet of which Gazzard was shrewdly aware, would make a play of opposition, but would then yield, and had already assembled sufficient private support from certain of his colleagues, particularly those with trade-union connections, to be fairly sure of swinging the decision his way. And there was a climate of dissension within the Cabinet on the whole rearmament question, quite plainly indicated by what had recently happened in the House, to give the Minister the support he required. He could produce, Gazzard was sure, the necessary money.

But the Minister was no man's fool. He would impose conditions that Gazzard could not accept. In short, he would want a variation of ultimate control of Skelstrand that would deprive Gazzard of much that he was determined to have. Gazzard had no means, at home, of countering these demands that would certainly be made. Without the money, Skelstrand would run to a halt, and the Minister perfectly well knew it. Gazzard's only alternative, here at home, was to turn to the City; but there he had already exhausted his friends, and was left with only some opponents whose demands would be even less sufferable than those of the Ministry. And the Minister was equally aware of that. Gazzard very well knew that he was in the grip of a nutcracker. It was a situation he thoroughly enjoyed, the only commercial enjoyment still left to him, an adult reminder of the boyish thrills of last-across-the-road; to twist out of a seemingly impossible situation by a move of sheer impudence, smirking at those who thought that, at last, they had got him. The pleasure of these manoeuvres was marred only by the acute inflammation of his duodenal ulcer that invariably followed, and plagued him for weeks.

For escape from his present dilemma he had already planned his impudent move. It was to be made in Washington. His friends there, the usual sources of political power that would ensure delivery to him, at the expense of the American taxpayers, of the machinery he needed to equip his mill, had turned sour on him. America was in one of its periodic moods of self-importance in which it preferred to keep its money at home; and the steel men were naturally using this mood to enrich themselves rather than their allies overseas.

But away in the Far West a new and independent group of financiers, led by a man whose private fortune was solidly based upon a chain of gambling establishments and brothels, was looking for a chance of fighting the older powers in the lobbies of Washington. Gazzard proposed that opportunity. He had already the private guarantee of all the finance he needed, provided he would allow the supplying of Skelstrand to become a pawn when the rearmament game in Washington was joined. He knew it was a huge risk, if the new man should lose. But Gazzard was prepared to gamble. Indeed, he had no choice. At the moment when the Minister and the City were about to close on him, he would withdraw and rely on his new reinforcement from America. If it came up, then the Minister would have to capitulate, and Gazzard would get his ten millions and retain control. If it did not, then, so far as he was concerned, he well knew that Skelstrand was doomed; he would have to regard that as the signal for his retirement to an inactive last few years on his farm.

Sometimes, when he considered the inconvenience of his prostate gland, he almost hoped that he would lose his gamble and be forced into inaction. But then he blew out his cheeks and swore to himself that he would not lose. He hated losing.

He had an uneasy presentiment that the Minister knew something of the American card up his sleeve. If he did, of course—and provided he did not know too much—that might well be turned to gain. If the Minister suspected that he had a hidden reserve he might be more willing to accommodate him, to yield to his plans. It depended on just how much the Minister knew, or whether he did not know but was guessing; and that depended on where he had got his information from.

Gazzard had a hunch about that. He had a feeling, nothing more, that it was Appleton who had worried the thing out, partly from one or two hints in the Gulport office, partly by guesswork, and had warned the Minister. If that were so, then young Appleton was shrewder than even Gazzard had allowed, and he would bribe him without fail into his employ.

5

BACK at Gulport, Bernard Appleton's nervous mind was obsessed with almost the same line of thought, and he showed it by an increasing tetchiness of manner.

"What the hell's the matter with you?" demanded Charles Neve, as the man wandered up and down his office, fiddling with his spectacles. "Sit down, for God's sake."

"Don't you see? The whole thing is in the balance. Why do you think the old buzzard has gone up to see the Minister?"

"I neither know nor care."

"You know what the costs are looking like. Surely you know that, unless something is done, we can't go on. The whole thing may be stopped."

Neve gazed through his window at Skelstrand. The huge scaffolding-smothered bays soared now high above him and stretched out of sight in both directions. The cliff face that so long ago he had envisaged was now there. The major length of the bays was already roofed, the structure of the furnaces was up, and on what had been empty dunes the bulk of the monster shut out all thought of the sea.

"You can't stop that," he growled. "Nothing could, now."

"Oh, can't you!" replied Appleton, pacing again. "They wouldn't of course say so. It would be a postponement, a measure of economy in the national crisis. They would be very sweet and reasonable about it, but this week-end Skelstrand could die."

"Stuff!" said Neve.

Appleton shrugged. Neve's brusqueness came, he realized, from his disappointment over the Melmoth girl. In the past few months it had become clear that she and Andrew Gazzard intended a match of it. A question of money, obviously; at Overskel there was so blatantly much, and at Shard so patently little.

And it was hellish difficult to prevent such private obsessions from interfering with one's work, as Appleton well knew. But it could be done. He assured himself that in fact he had done it. The running misery of Laura, the knowledge which he tried to shut from his mind that she and Heron were engaged in some sort of an affair, did not, he prided himself, hamper his absorption in the job he had to do. He did not dare even challenge her about it, for fear that she would confirm it, turning upon him her slow gaze of contempt and asking what he proposed to do. For he proposed to do nothing. He was terrified of action. Even at those times when the thought of them seemed to swell intolerably in his brain, as though it were being inflated like a child's balloon, and he could feel the blood straining at his wrists and temples, so that he had to lie down on a couch or a bed, close his eyes and remain silent to avoid blacking out, he was intelligent enough to know that to lose her physically would be worse yet than this.

He forced his thoughts back to the present Skelstrand difficulties. At the Ministry they were calculating with quiet pleasure that the unexpected rise in costs, coinciding with an unfavourable atmosphere in Washington, would force the old man to relinquish the elements of his control over the whole project and at last put the Minister into a position to dictate. Appleton's cautious warnings had been politely ignored. One thing, at any rate, he was sure of: that the whole project was at stake. And there, he thought, sat idiots like Neve gazing at the mere physical progress of the building and declaring that nothing could stop it now—as

168

though the concrete and the steel girders were alive and could continue to grow of their own accord. What nonsense. This thing did not depend upon technical powers. It would thrive or perish as the result of a struggle for control, for profits, for money. Though there was something, he conceded, in Neve's theory that it would be difficult to reverse a process which had wrought such changes in the district in which it had been set to operate. He imagined, if the building were stopped, the howl of protest that would go up from the town that, not long ago, had protested against its being started.

And yet it was not really so inconsistent. It was no longer the same town. No Gulport tradesman who had been content with his five or six pounds profit a week, but was now assured of double or treble that sum. People who had been accustomed to bicycles were now buying motor-cars. Site values had enormously increased. A shop well placed in Bridge Street, not far from Woolworth's, had changed hands only a week or two back at around £30,000, where previously it could scarcely have fetched more than eight thousand. An acquaintance of Appleton's, a partner in the local estate agent's business, had privately assured him there were half a dozen property-owners in Gulport whose personal fortunes could now be valued at well above £100,000, without their having done anything to earn this increment except hang on to what they already possessed. One problem that this posed was that of rates. The yield of a penny rate was still little more than it had been before the mill began, and was ludicrously too little for the value concerned. There would have to be a new rating valuation, but the mere proposition of it would cause an uproar.

Besides these superficial differences there were changes in outlook, in what might be called the Gulport way of life. Nobody thought and acted as previously. The placid life-stream of a country town had been swollen, agitated and muddied. There was now a restlessness, a dissatisfaction. And people whose settled lives had been disturbed reacted in unexpected ways. The most extreme example, of course, was old Councillor Wilkinson, upon whom the building of the mill had played a double trick. It had made him a wealthy man (he was certainly one of the half-dozen whose property value now ran into six figures), and deprived him of his daughter. The Shylock situation, mused Appleton. Old Wilkinson had at first withdrawn from life into a sullen moroseness, and now, so the current scandal went, had been discovered trying to interfere with little girls. The thing had been hushed up, there had been some payment to the parents, but Florence Wilkinson was now compelled to watch him continually, and must always fear the unguarded moment in which he might escape her surveillance and fetch up the private horror into public scandal. Appleton felt for the woman. His own obsession was similar. He could endure the torture of Laura's infidelity so long as it remained private. But if ever it became blatantly public so that he were forced into action—into divorce, say, or even into overt separation—he feared that the torment would overwhelm him. Sometimes he had to go into an empty room, lock the door, and allow himself to rage unchecked; and after a while he would then be able to emerge, white-faced, to continue his normal life and business.

The only person he could think of who, to outward appearance, was unchanged by the transformation of the town was the little bouncing councillor, Jimmy Jafet. His faith and vision seemed to be merely confirmed and strengthened.

But Jimmy, if it had been put to him, would not have agreed. Jimmy was one of the unfortunates with a fixed income in an expanding society. In a sleepy country town his pittance from the railway had sufficed. But with growing prosperity Gulport began to assess a man's value by his power to spend money. Where, before, a group of worthies in a saloon bar would tactfully have arranged the rounds so that it rarely became Councillor Jafet's turn, now they would leave silences, awkward periods of waiting, until Jimmy said, "Same again, Maisie, please," and counted out his seven or eight shillings on the bar.

There had been earlier times of running into debt in which Jimmy had turned to Colonel Melmoth, but he did not like to do so now. Instead he looked desperately around the growing town for opportunity, and found it with a builder named Sam Halstead. This man had been at school with Jimmy Jafet, and always in the same class—Jimmy at the head of the class, Sam at the foot. When, at fourteen years of age, they both left school, Jimmy entered the safe occupation of the railway and devoted himself to the social revolution, whereas Sam became a builder's labourer and planned his own advancement. In the late 'twenties he was on the dole. In the early 'thirties he was speculating in building lots and running up houses at £450 each. With the outbreak of war he got contracts for aerodrome construction, sent his son to boarding-school, bought a Daimler and stacked black-market hams and bottles of whisky in his garage. The outbreak of peace was a sad moment for Sam Halstead. Gone were the glorious days of cost-plus. He did some building for the council, but there was so little in it that he could scarcely afford to take his lubberly son into the business. Of Skelstrand he had at first great hopes, but the big national contractors had moved in, and there was little for Sam Halstead. But with the freeing of building restrictions and the abolition of development charges he had seen daylight once more. He prowled round the outskirts of the town, testing land values. All he now needed was a little private information as to the direction in which the town would first develop. So he took his old school-friend, Jimmy Jafet, out to lunch.

"But council decisions are confidential," protested Jimmy, "until they are published in the minutes."

"Course they are, Jim, course they are. I don't want you to do nothing wrong. This ain't nothing to do with the council. You're a knowledgeable man, a clever chap, always was. What I want is your advice."

"I couldn't tell you anything I had learned as a councillor."

"Course not, Jim. I wouldn't play that game, not if you begged me to, which I knows you wouldn't. It's your brains I want, Jim. There ain't no man knows more about land values in this town than you. All right, then, I offers you a job as the firm's adviser on land values. All confidential. Give me the benefit of your opinion, Jim boy, and you won't lose by it."

And Jimmy Jafet was later uneasily aware of the new Halstead building estate, which happened to lie just in the direction the new main road would take, close to where the new bus route would run. He had drawn his fee, as adviser, in a hundred one-pound notes.

"Little side-line like this," said Halstead, "you won't want to bother the income-tax blokes."

A few more pieces of advice had followed since, and Jimmy's worry was then what to do with the money. His first bundle of notes he put in a cardboard box under his bed, until one morning a cold fear took him and he had to run home from the station to make sure Kathy had not inadvertently come across them and innocently distributed them along the street. He dared not put them in his Post Office savings account, for the women in the post office knew, of course, his exact circumstances. He played desperately with the idea of announcing that his football pools had come up, or that an imaginary aunt in a distant part of the country had died and left him a nest egg. But Elsie would instantly have detected either of those falsities.

At last he diffidently took his problem to Sam Halstead. Sam considered, and made one or two nefarious suggestions which Jimmy slowly rejected.

"Well, look here then, why don't you invest it in the building estate?"

"Could I do that?"

"Course you could. I wouldn't offer everybody, but it's all right for you, Jim, as an old friend. You put in your capital, and it'll show you ten per cent, easy—maybe more. And the money'll always be there any time you want it."

"It can be quite, sort of, private, can it? I don't have to register anything anywhere?"

"Private as you like, Jim. We won't have no signing nothing between old pals."

So Jimmy thankfully handed back his £350 to Sam Halstead.

"Now you got a stake in them houses, Jim," said he.

A few weeks later Jimmy was pressed for a little cash. He sought out Sam Halstead.

"Hallo," said Sam, "want another slice of investment?"

"No, not exactly. I suppose we haven't made any profit yet?"

"Give us a chance, mate."

"Well, I wonder if I could just get about twenty quid back, Sam."

The other protested. "You can't have it yet, Jim. It's all gone in bricks and mortar like. You got to wait a bit."

"You did say the money was always there, any time I wanted it."

"And so it is. But you got to be reasonable. I can't rush capital in and out of the thing every few days."

Jimmy did see that. He stood there hesitant.

"Are you hard up for a bit of ready?"

Jimmy unhappily nodded.

"Well, I tell you what, I can let you have a personal loan, fiver say, if that's any good."

"It's better than nothing."

Sam gave him five one-pound notes. "Better sign for that," he suggested. "Personal loans is different, of course. Better keep that ship-shape."

So Jimmy signed a piece of paper. Later on he signed two or three more. At first he felt a little uneasy about it. But, after all, it was in a sense his own money. He found it very convenient to be able to get a few pounds from Sam Halstead now and again. He was spared the awful problem of how to invest his nest egg. There it was, tucked away into the building estate, earning him a cosy ten per cent and literally as safe as houses.

Sometimes, on spare afternoons, Jimmy took the new bus route to the outskirts of the town and got off on the corner by the building site. It stood on the brow of a hill. Looking back, he could see all Gulport stretched beneath him, and, beyond the river, the huge yellow bulk of Skelstrand. A developing place, Jimmy warmly thought, assured of a great and prosperous future. And he, Jimmy Jafet, had a stake in it. He turned to wander lovingly among the half-built houses, touching planks and stacks of bricks, and fancying that this part of it or that was actually his, bought with his own money, the foundation of what might one day become a tidy little sum. Not a fortune, Jimmy Jafet wanted no part of a fortune. Not for him the wiles of capitalism. But there was no harm in a modest little ten per cent every so often—no harm at all that Jimmy could see.

6

HENRY MELMOTH frequently sat for long periods now in his own small room, with the photograph of Harriet on the desk, and a photograph of his son—though nobody knew of it —in the drawer. He sat in his chair with his back straight and his eyes staring uneasily at the wall, as though he were trying to recover, by quietness, from a physical shock. It was not Elizabeth's marriage, in itself, that distressed him, but his own behaviour on account of it.

He slowly repeated in his memory, time and again, the things he had said and done since she first came to tell him that she was to be married. He should have contrived to seem happy. There was nothing reasonably to be said against the match. The boy's family was immensely wealthy, and the father, it appeared, would settle a large sum on him on his marrying. Elizabeth would remain in the same neighbourhood, so that he would not even be deprived of her company.

What he said to her was, "Why in God's name did you have to pick him?"

"I didn't, Henry. He picked me. It was all most conventional."

"I remember you spoke of a loyalty to a man who was killed."

She stared at him. "I did not expect you to say that."

"No." There was a pause. "And I am ashamed of myself for saying it. Forgive me, Elizabeth. But you must see that, for me, it is something of a last straw. I have watched my land being taken away from me. I have seen all the things that I most detest thrust on this one corner of the country that was peculiarly mine, by inheritance, by long custom—oh, I know it's foolish. But then I have had to tolerate the man who is the prime mover of the thing settle as though by right as my neighbour, in a house in which my oldest friend had lived. His son and my son were killed in the war that enriched this man and impoverished us. And now you want to marry into the family."

She waited without speaking.

"Bluntly, are you marrying him for his money?"

"No," she said slowly, "I don't think so. I can't help but be aware of it."

"Then you are in love with him?"

"I don't know. I'm trying to be honest with you. He is attractive, and amusing, and—kindly."

"But you are not in love with him."

"No, I am not."

"You are not painting a pretty picture."

She sat down in the chair beside her, looking at her hands. He remained standing by the window.

"Are there," she asked, "so many pretty pictures in the world?"

"I had hoped for one for you."

"Look at it brutally," she said: "I am twenty-six. You yourself have told me that I can expect nothing of Shard. I am offered marriage by a man whom, at any rate, I like, and with more money than most people dream of."

"And is that all?"

"No, it isn't all, but I'm not sure that I can express the rest. It is the change that has happened to us since the whole town was changed. Henry, I'm trying to be honest about it, even though it distresses you. I had gone to sleep here, with a sentimental dream about a man who was killed. And suddenly there was a new life, a violent, active sort of life. It has taken hold of all of us. The labourers and the machines, the vastness of the building, the sense of riches and excitement—I'm not saying it well."

"The vulgarity, the craziness of a doomed civilization, the reversal of values. . . ."

175

"But just that," she cried, "the reversal of values, old values. Why should the new way be worse than the old?"

Many times, in his memory, Melmoth saw her at that moment, rejecting him, pushing him into the sort of loneliness which, he now saw, she had herself suffered. At first it had been Harriet for whom he had lived; and then after the terrible years had quelled that, Peter. With Harriet he had been patient beyond reason. He could recall, with great pain, the sensitive, sparkling girl he had married, the pride with which he had introduced her into the life of Shard, the delicacy with which he had treated her. And then the shock, gradually numbed by repetition, of the animal she became when she was drunk. It was then that she wanted to go to bed with him; and when, repelled, he could not, she became a screaming harridan, hair loosened, half naked, jeering obscenely at him; and he, grim but patient, trying to quieten her. "Don't be so bloody righteous," she once screamed at him. But he had not been, he could not find the fault in himself. Once, even, he had taken it up with Irons, and Gilbert had reassured him. "No, Henry, it's not you. It's something deep down in her life, in her childhood perhaps, like a flaw in the wool that shows itself in the cloth."

So he had gradually turned to Peter, and in him found unspoken comfort. The boy grew, in appearance, very like his mother, and with all her earlier frankness and gaiety. He was one of those who find life good. When, his schooling done, he returned to Shard he brought cheerfulness and peace to the house. And his presence eased Harriet of her cravings. Months passed in which she never touched a drink. She was changing into a rational woman of middle age, interested once more in the life of her house and her family. Henry began to find a new understanding, a new contact with her. And then Peter was killed. For that, at any rate, Melmoth acquitted himself of blame. Against the bestialities of greed and "progress" which had led inevitably to the war his whole life had been a protest. He had publicly advocated a diplomatic understanding, and been dubbed fascist, and pro-German. The accusation grimly amused him. Henry

Melmoth pro-German! He had merely clung to the old, rejected decencies, the neglect of which gave the demagogue his opportunity. He saw about him, on Peter's death, the tumbling of everything that could matter. It was not, by then, important to him that Harriet left. He saw her go with pity, but without regret. There remained to him, as he thought, only a few last years of seclusion in which, if God were merciful, he might be left until his death.

Into this came Elizabeth, like an unexpected gift. From all the past she had been virtually excluded—kept away, so far as possible, on the pretext of shielding her from unhappiness; but really, as he now saw, because she had counted for little with any of them, except possibly with Peter. But when she came back to Shard, quietly and with self-effacement taking a place there, Melmoth gradually understood that at last his life was to be happy, the sunset to be rich and warm.

Then even she failed him. She revealed herself as quite a different person from his imagination of her. The quietness which he had thought happiness she bluntly declared mere tedium. She betrayed a sexual hunger, a vulgarness, a febrile desire to become part of the coarseness of the world, so strong that she would contract a loveless marriage in order to enjoy it. And he was powerless. Sometimes, when he sat in thought, it seemed he would not be able to endure. No emotion showed on his face, but in his mind his hatred of Skelstrand, his despair at Elizabeth, his revulsion against humanity and his terror of loneliness whirled faster and faster until they fused into a single white-hot rage that, it seemed, would sear his reason. Melmoth was appalled at the severity with which this hatred shook him, and made frequent resolutions to conquer it. He set himself deliberately to tasks that were distasteful—to welcome, for instance, young Gazzard into his home. Elizabeth fearfully brought him, nervous for the interview; but Andrew himself not, so far as Melmoth could perceive, in the least nervous, casual rather, as though he were doing them both a particular favour.

"We thought," he remarked, "to fix the wedding fairly soon. As my old man says, no point in waiting now it's all settled."

"There are, perhaps, some things to discuss with me before it can be regarded as quite settled."

"To discuss? Oh, you don't have to bother about can-you-support-my-daughter and all that stuff. That's in the bag."

Melmoth regarded him stiffly. "I had in mind your own qualities, rather than your family's wealth."

"Oh lord, if it depends on my qualities I'm a goner. Admit that straight away." Andrew laughed easily. "Everybody knows what a poor fish I am. Can't understand why Liz don't see it. But she says she'll have me, you know. So that's more or less that, eh?"

"Are you in love with Elizabeth?"

"Oh yes, rather. Madly. I say, isn't this rather embarrassing?"

"He's not a bad sort, Henry," Elizabeth nervously broke in, "I think I can put up with him."

Melmoth watched the cheerful grin that the young man gave her. He wanted to burst out in rage at his impertinence, but restrained himself. Carefully, carefully! After a few more sentences he rose abruptly and went to his own room, where he sat stiffly in his chair and grieved at the anger that seized him. When at last he came out Andrew had gone.

"I'm sorry, Elizabeth."

"It's all right," she said serenely, "I know it's rotten for you."

There was the inevitable dinner party he had to give for the whole Gazzard family. This, of course, he contrived to carry through in an armour of correctness, though he found old Gazzard nearly intolerable. From his first remark—"Nice old place you've got here"—he patronized.

After dinner he took him to his room, offering him a whisky. Gazzard waved it aside. "Daren't touch it. Poison to me. No, go on, you have one. Don't let me stop you."

They sat in opposite chairs, contemplating each other.

"Cards on the table, eh?" said Gazzard, "that's the only way."

But he meant only his cards. He was not interested in what Melmoth had to say; but simply in telling him with what

178

munificence he had endowed the young couple, as he called them.

"They won't exactly want, eh?" he remarked with satisfaction.

"Are you asking for a marriage settlement with Elizabeth?"

"Of course not. Didn't I just tell you? They won't lack cash."

"I cannot, of course," continued Melmoth, "hope to match the sort of sums of which you have been speaking. I am arranging, however, to settle eight thousand pounds on her on her wedding day, and I am proposing that you should contribute a like amount."

He could see that Gazzard was puzzled. "But why? What for? Liz can have eight thousand from me, that's all right. But what's the idea? Andrew will have all the money they'll need."

"My consent to the wedding depends on this settlement," said Melmoth, "I do not care to see my daughter a dependant in your household."

"And you think Andrew might run out on her, eh? Well, I suppose he might, I admit he's got some poor qualities. You're right, Colonel, to think of that. I agree. But look, you don't have to put in the eight thousand. I'll make it sixteen, or twenty if you like. It's plain foolish to cripple yourself on a point of pride."

"I prefer the arrangement I suggested."

"Now come, man," urged Gazzard. "Where are you going to get the eight thousand, without raising a mortgage or some damn thing?"

"We won't discuss it further," said Melmoth.

"What are you going to do with Shard?" asked Gazzard curiously. "You won't want to go on living in this great house all by yourself."

"Mrs. Cushion will look after me."

"D'you know what I'd do in your place? I'd sell. I'd shift my quarters to the cottage down by the gate, keep the farm, and sell the house itself."

Melmoth laughed shortly. "And who do you think would buy? Can you imagine anyone buying a white elephant of

179

this size? We don't get wealthy industrialists moving into the district every day."

"I admit I got Overskel cheap. But the market is changing, you know, with the mill going up and all the development of the place. You might have a very good thing here."

This man would sell it, Melmoth pondered, and for a good price. Yes, he probably would. To sell at a good price was his trade.

"There have been Melmoths at Shard for a long time," he replied, "I'm the last. I am aware that, after me, it disintegrates. But I think I can manage to stay here until I die."

"I admire you for it. There's something fine in an old family in an old house. But these things are changing, Colonel. For the worse, I dare say, but changing. We have to admit it. You know, I believe you could make a pretty good thing out of this, if we thought it out. Set you up without worries for the rest of your life, and a nice bit to leave Liz when you're gone."

"You are very kind," said Melmoth stiffly.

"I tell you what, if you want to sell Shard, I'll buy."

"You? What for? You already have a house. You mean for Elizabeth? Oh, I don't think she would like to live here while I were still living."

"Not for Elizabeth. Young people won't take on a big commitment like this. No, I'll buy for Skelstrand."

Melmoth put down his glass in astonishment. "For Skelstrand?"

"Aye. When she's built, and production starts, we're going to need just such a place as this to put the managerial trainees. Come, think it over. I'd give you a good price, better than you'd hope to get elsewhere. With a company buying you can afford to splash a bit—tax dodges and all that. And the place'd be properly kept up."

Melmoth shook his head.

"We wouldn't want the farm," urged the other, "just the house and a bit of garden. Probably run to twenty or thirty thousand pounds, and you'd be living comfortably in the cottage with all the land."

"There's no point in discussing it, and it's time we went back to the others."

"All right. But think it over, Colonel, and you'll see the idea's a sound one. If you change your mind, let me know."

Of the rest of the evening Melmoth remembered nothing. Rage was burning at his temples and behind his eyes.

As the weeks went by, his moods of hatred increased in frequency until, in the intervals between them, he feared for himself. He thought of going to Irons, but quailed. Besides, he argued, it was only the strain of these times; once the wedding was over, he would quieten. And he began to long for the wedding day as desperately as he dreaded it.

When it came, he got through it in the steely trance in which a man submits himself to the hazards of a battle. Of that day he afterwards recalled only disconnected fragments. That it rained in the morning, and then cleared. The argument between two female cousins over the colour of a hat. Elizabeth, of course, coming down the stairs of Shard in her wedding dress, and he waiting at the foot to lead her to the car. That Roger Henty had a head-cold and nasally intoned the service, and that one of the saints in the east window of the little church at Shard Green was leering; and the sudden recollection that he had noticed that years ago when he had been a choirboy.

Harriet came to the wedding. Elizabeth had not told him until the evening before. "I wrote to her, Henry, and she wanted to come. Forgive me."

After a pause, he said, "Of course. You were quite right."

Harriet arrived late that night; Benson drove down to the station to fetch her. She was perfectly calm and gave Henry a little kiss on the cheek, saying, "You're greyer, you know."

She looked smaller than he had thought her, and her face ravaged as though by illness. But the pity he felt was impersonal. He said, "You don't change, Harriet." And she smiled like a complimented girl. He saw little of her that night, but went to his room, turning over his files of business papers, wryly reading his will, and the latest letter from his solicitor, pointing out the precariousness of his affairs. He shrugged, and stared at the wall.

At any rate, he could assure himself, no one would have known it from the display at the wedding reception. Overskel itself could not have been more lavish. At one moment he walked aside and turned to look at the marquee on the lawn, the old house in all its gracefulness behind it, the sunshine on the trees, the crowd of babbling guests, the busyness of the hired servants. He pondered that this was the last of the many Melmoth weddings that would be celebrated at Shard. A weariness came to him, and he thought that perhaps it was as well that the long story was ended; it had grown tedious. Gazzard came over to him, looking more distasteful than ever in his morning suit, a pearl pin in his grey tie.

"Well," he said cheerfully, "you've given us a great do."

Melmoth nodded, and turned away. He could not at that moment speak to the man. But later he suffered a long rambling discourse from Lady Gazzard, in a trailing mauve dress and her fingers stiff with diamonds. When he got away, he found himself standing by Harriet. "By God," said Harriet, "that woman's a shocker. I don't envy Liz her mother-in-law. What people are these, Henry?"

He smiled. "Rich people."

"Oh, I can see that. Poor Henry."

He felt a ghost of sympathy for her. "Let me get you some champagne," he said.

"No. I'm not touching anything. I won't disgrace you to-day. Liz looks lovely, doesn't she? And I rather approve of Andrew."

"Do you?"

"Yes, she could make something of him. He's the only one of the bunch who looks honest."

"Tell me, Harriet," he said, "are you all right? You don't want to change things?"

"No. I'm all right. Is the wedding making you feel sentimental? I shouldn't, Henry. It doesn't suit us."

When the absurd speeches and foolery were over, he went into the hall of the house, and Elizabeth came downstairs and kissed him. "Thank you, darling," she said.

Melmoth could say nothing. She went through the door into the sunlight where the car and the confetti and the laughter were waiting. Melmoth turned and hid himself in his room.

Harriet caught the evening train back to London. Mrs. Cushion wept.

Hours later, when the house was silent and dark, Melmoth stalked despairingly through it, like the ghost of an ancestor.

7

THE first hint of sabotage was during that autumn, when a gantry girder was being moved into the slabbing mill and a steel hawser gave. One man fled not quite quickly enough and his foot was severed from his leg; as though some powerful animal had given a swift flip with its paw and then resumed its stance of lazy indifference.

"He didn't have time to scream," said Bill Cross, reporting to Neve, "I nearly copped it meself. Six paces nearer and it'd have been me."

"Accident?"

"Could've been. Or someone could've messed about with that cable."

"Which do you think?"

"Messed about, most like. What surprises me is that this is the first. We haven't had any yet, but it's bound to come, stands to reason."

"Well, it won't be difficult to find out. But keep your mouth shut, Bill. Give it out as accident."

The foreman nodded. " 'Course."

Andrew Gazzard came into the office, pale. "I say, this is a bit of a thing."

"Is the chap all right?"

"They've got him to hospital. Seems he'll live."

Neve nodded to Cross, who went out.

"It was so quick," said Andrew. "One minute the chap's all right, next he's a cripple for life. Makes you think." He stared through the office window at the walls of Skelstrand. "Do you reckon it's worth it, Charles?"

"Nothing big ever gets done without costing lives."

"Suppose it had been me? That's what I keep thinking."

"It might be. Some day you die. On every big construction job half a dozen lives go. Just as in every pit, every year, somebody gets killed. And every day there's the slaughter on the roads."

"Nobody makes any fuss about that," said Andrew, "and somehow that's different."

"There won't be any fuss about this. Paragraph in the local paper, that's all. We don't really think life is important. We only kid ourselves."

"You're a gloomy beggar. It's important to me."

"Rot. You'll eat as good a dinner to-night as if this had never happened. By to-morrow you'll have forgotten all about it."

The young man shuddered. "I'm going to get a drink. Coming?"

"No, thanks. Too busy."

When he had gone, Neve reflected angrily that he was scared of death only because he had so much to lose. A fortune, Elizabeth, a zest in living. And yet Neve, who had none of these things, would be just as unwilling to die. The stupidity, he thought, with which we cling to our microscopic personalities.

Inspection showed that it had been no accident. There were marks of acid on the cable. Neve pondered about it for a while, and then went to see Gazzard in the town office.

"Well, how's that boy of mine doing?"

"He's all right."

"Settling down better since he got married?"

"He'll do."

"It's a great thing," said Gazzard mischievously, "having a wife and a home."

Neve, ignoring that, said, "That business of the gantry girder wasn't an accident. The cable had been tampered with."

"Mm. Who knows?"

"Only me and my foreman, and the fellow I got to examine the cable."

"Trustworthy?"

"Yes, we shan't talk."

"Well, it was bound to come, wasn't it?"

"Of course."

"Any idea who?"

Neve shook his head. "Don't suppose we'll ever know. The point is, now it has started, it will go on."

"Do you want me to get some private detectives in or something?"

"No, not yet anyway. I can handle it unless it gets very big."

"How big can it get?"

"Oh, I don't see it amounting to much. You can't set that sort of construction on fire. The machinery's too heavy to wreck. All we'll get is pin-pricks. But I thought you ought to know."

Gazzard sat back in his chair, smiling, nodding his head. "You can handle it all right. I'm sure you can. I've got a very high opinion of you."

"Thanks," said Neve, getting up to go.

Gazzard sat quietly thinking for a few minutes. Sabotage. Some crazy workman with a grievance against the world making his puny protest. Gazzard smiled again. The midget with his handful of sand or steel filings to drop surreptitiously into a machine. He'd no chance at all against a thing like Skelstrand. You could not fight that with physical weapons. There was always a dour Charles Neve to block your way. You fought Skelstrand with brain, and with money. And even then, he reflected with satisfaction, you probably lost. Because then you were fighting him, Gazzard, and you had something real to reckon with.

He buzzed for his girl and told her to ask Mr. Appleton to step in, if he could spare a moment. Appleton, when he arrived, looked uneasy at the summons. Gazzard, waving him genially into an arm-chair, said, "Well, my Americans are beginning to look like turning up trumps."

He watched the thoughts on the young man's face—surprise, caution, hesitance at deciding how much he ought to pretend to know. Not much good, thought Gazzard, as a negotiator.

"All right," he said, "this is between ourselves. I am assuming that you know what I'm talking about?"

"Yes, sir, I think I do. Personally, I hope you pull it off."

"Why?"

"If you don't, I think they will stop construction."

"With all this committed?"

Appleton sighed. "It wouldn't be for the first time."

Gazzard waited for a while and then asked, "How did you find out what I'm up to?"

Appleton spread his hands modestly. "It seemed a fair guess."

"You know it isn't settled yet?"

"I think it will be."

"Yes," agreed Gazzard, "I think so too."

Or perhaps, he continued to himself, he only hoped so. It could yet go wrong. He considered uneasily whether he ought to make a quick trip to Washington. But no, that would be revealing too much.

"What have you got ahead of you?" he asked suddenly. "Another thirty years in the service, a maximum screw of—what? eighteen hundred, and then a few years of retirement on half pay."

"That would be rather a bald outline."

"Would you like to chuck it and work for me?"

That, he chuckled to himself, shook him. What a flutter of nerves!

"I'll give you two thousand now, and an inside look at a few transactions to which you can help yourself. There won't be any pension."

"Good lord!" said Appleton.

"You've got a first-class brain, did you know that? And you're wasting it. You could make a pile if you applied yourself to it, instead of sticking to security. What do you want security for anyway? There's only yourself and your wife, no kids."

"I'd have to think it over."

"Okay, I'll give you a couple of days. If you think it over any longer with that complicated mind of yours, you'll tie yourself in knots. Just to make it worse, remember that the

186

American thing might still fail. Then I should clear out of Skelstrand and you'd be out of a job. I should have no compunction about you. What I'm offering you is a chance, with all the risks thrown in."

"It's frightfully kind of you," said Appleton.

"I shouldn't offer if I didn't think it would pay me."

As Appleton reached the door, Gazzard added, "Oh, by the way, if the idea of working with Heron bothers you, it needn't. I've fired him."

Appleton stared. "Fired him?"

"Yep. Same as I'd fire you if you ceased to be useful to me."

"But what did he do?"

Gazzard grinned. "He made a mistake. He thought the time had arrived to swap loyalties—and it hadn't. Not quite."

"I see what you mean about security."

"Oh, he has feathered his nest all right. He'd had five years to do it. He won't starve. You might not get so long."

When Appleton had closed the door behind him he stood for a moment in the corridor, feeling a dizziness that threatened to overwhelm him. But he pulled himself together and managed to walk out of the building, without returning to his own office. He kept on repeating to himself that he must tell Laura. As he walked, ignoring the people in the street, a jubilation seized him. It was something when a man of Gazzard's calibre recognized his worth. He could allow himself a moment of triumph. But supposing the old man's gamble, of the size of which Appleton had a pretty shrewd idea, did not come off.

With a shudder he wrapped the thought of his present security around him. Was he to throw away that cloak? To hazard, in a mood of vainglory, an assurance of safety that he could certainly never regain? He stopped in the street to consider it, and then, realizing that people were looking at him, and suddenly conscious that he was muttering, walked on.

And then Laura? Would she, at this news, regard him with new respect? He had, after all, beaten Mr. Bloody Heron at his own game. It was perhaps the most delicious flavour of the whole thing. But then, might not Laura rather take the opposite view, reproachful that he should be ready to risk her own security as well as his on a gamble? He could imagine her telling him that he was a fool to be lured by such an obvious trap; that old Gazzard merely wanted to remove an awkward customer who happened to have found out too much about what he was doing; that he would hire him and, once he was out of the Ministry's pay, contemptuously fire him. And was that, Appleton suddenly considered, what the man was really after? It could be, it easily could be. Was he just falling for a ruse?

He stopped again, tremulous, and looked around. He was out on the headland, past the town. Away to his left rose the broad back of Skelstrand, yellow in the sunshine. In a sense it was as much his creation as anyone's. It would not be there at all without the patient, endless work of minuting and tactful steering which had been his contribution. The organization of society had become so complex that the essential man was the link, the connection. It is, he reflected, the age of the liaison officer.

He turned about and walked briskly back towards the town, suddenly aware that he was hungry. He would take Laura out to lunch. It instantly occurred to him that she might already be out—out, perhaps, with Heron. And this possibility seemed so absurdly disastrous that he almost ran.

But she was not out. She was sitting in the front room of the boarding-house with an illustrated magazine on her lap, which she was not reading. There was a moment before she noticed he was there, in which he was freshly astonished to see how lovely she was.

"Hallo," she said, "what's up? You feeling ill?"

"No. I've come to take you out to lunch. Rather special. I have some news for you."

"Oh? What?"

"Tell you at lunch."

There was a small restaurant in Bridge Street where the food was indifferent, but it was quiet. At the Stag there would have been too many people from the office.

"Darling," he said, when they had started their meal,

188

"Gazzard wants me to leave the service and work for him.

"Why?"

"Well, it's all rather complicated. A financial thing that the old man was up to, and I tumbled to it, and he realized that I had. He was rather complimentary about it. Bit of a feather ir ɔne's cap, really."

"I'm glad."

He felt deflated. "He's offering me a couple of thousand a year," he casually added. "It'll make quite a difference, even with the tax. You'll be able to have one or two things you've wanted."

"You make it very difficult."

"Difficult? I don't see. . . ."

"It's no use pretending," she said. "You must have known this was coming. I'm going to leave you, Bernard."

"You're what?"

"I'm going away with Bob Heron. It's better now that I've said it. I suppose you know that he's leaving Gazzard?"

Appleton, trying to shut out reality, clung to this point. "I know he has been fired."

"Is that what Gazzard says? He hasn't really. He was offered a big job in Canada, and he's taking it."

"Fired," insisted Appleton angrily. "Chucked out on his ear."

"Well, it doesn't matter."

He stared beseechingly at her. "But things will be different now, Laura. I shall have more money, perhaps a lot more money."

"I'm sorry, Bernard. But, of course, it isn't that. Bob and I are in love with each other. I really am very sorry."

"When?" he asked dully.

"I was going to tell you in a week's time. But of course I'll go at once now. I'll pack this afternoon."

"Oh, you don't have to do that," he protested. "Give me my chance, Laura. Stay at any rate the week." He was aware that she was despising him. "Oh, damn," he groaned.

"Listen," she said quietly, "I have tried. I have not been unfaithful to you."

"Do you think I believe that?"

189

"Believe what you like. I haven't. You have always thought of me as going to bed with other men. It isn't true. I have tried to make our marriage work, but you have always been suspecting, and—oh well, you know. You have never trusted me."

"Always," he protested, "always."

"No. But it doesn't matter."

"I can't go on without you, Laura. I can't."

"Yes, you can," she said, getting up. "You don't really love me, you know. You love being a martyr."

He walked beside her back to the boarding-house, pleading. "Stay at least for this week. Give me a chance to prove. . . ." But she shook her head.

In their room he began to sob. She took down a suitcase, packing it. He knelt on the floor, clasping her knees.

"This is ridiculous," she said. "For heaven's sake get up."

He wept and clung to her. "Don't go, my darling, don't go."

She stumbled, trying to free herself, and fell on to the bed. He scrambled on to her, suddenly crazy, tearing at her dress. Silently she fought him, knocking off his spectacles, twisting her face away from his. And then, exhausted, she gave way. Afterwards he rolled from her, dazed and moaning. She lay quite still on the bed.

"I'm sorry, Laura," he pleaded, "I was mad."

She made no reply. Suddenly she jumped from the bed and fled from the room.

"Laura, Laura," he called after her. He crawled around the floor, searching myopically for his spectacles, and crying, "Laura. Come back, Laura."

8

When old Gazzard fell ill, nobody at first believed it. He had complained for some days—but then, he always complained. He fussed about going to London to see his Harley Street man, but took instead to his bed, and his wife sent for Dr. Irons.

Andrew came home that evening and told Elizabeth that,

this time, there really did seem to be something wrong with the old man's innards.

"I'll talk to Gilbert," she offered, going to the phone.

And Gilbert Irons confirmed it. "He wants to get half the medical profession down to see him, and, of course, I agreed. Between you and me, Liz, he's not too good."

"You don't mean it's really serious?"

"It could be, my dear. But no need for alarm just yet."

She went back into the room and told Andrew, "Well, he is ill. But no cause for alarm, Gilbert says."

In her thoughts she found herself calculating chances. Suppose he were to die. Presumably the bulk of his money would go to Andrew, but he had never said so. He might have left it to his wife for her lifetime, and then to the children. And how about Skelstrand? It would continue, of course, but would they lose control of it if the old man went? Would Andrew be able to hold the power and the riches? Then she felt ashamed of such thoughts and went across to kiss Andrew on the cheek.

"Don't worry," she said. "He'll be all right."

But even as she said it there came to her an alarm. It was only a few months since, on their marriage, Andrew's father had settled money on them. Wasn't there some law that a gift made less than five years before a person's death remained part of his estate, and subject to death duties? If they had to pay on that, and if he had left the rest to Lady Gazzard for her lifetime, they would be impoverished. Elizabeth went to pour out the glass of sherry which Andrew liked to sip before dinner, and got herself a gin.

"Oughtn't you to go and see your father tonight?"

"I've asked Charles to come in after dinner."

"Oh, I can look after him."

"Perhaps I ought to slip up there for an hour. But Charles and I had a lot of business to talk."

It was remarkable, she reflected, that Andrew should say that. Six months ago he would not have dreamed of business as an after-dinner subject; and yet now it did not seem odd. She regarded him over the edge of her glass, assessing how much he had changed, and how little she knew of him, or had tried to know. They were as strange to each other as two people encountering by chance in a railway carriage. The comparison came to her like one of those repetitions of something that had happened before, and she suddenly remembered that this had been precisely her thought when, after the wedding, they got into the compartment he had reserved on the London train. She felt then that they just happened to be travelling together, and by no means could she force herself to the realization that this was the man she had just married. He acted, too, with the politeness of a stranger. He made conversation, and little jokes. When, at the ancient hotel at which the family stayed in London, they at last found themselves alone in their room, and it was necessary to go to bed, it was he who seemed embarrassed. He went out into the sitting-room while she undressed, and when he returned, sat on the edge of the bed and said, "Liz, I'm nervous as hell. Rummy, ain't it?"

"Why are you nervous?"

"Good lord, it's not me virgin innocence—but this marriage lark! Solemn, and all that. Liz, you don't repent, do you?"

"No," she said slowly, "I don't think I do, Andrew."

It was a question that she had never clearly answered, perhaps because she was afraid to consider it dispassionately, or perhaps because of the fascination of the luxury into which she was introduced. She became greedy for it—for the obsequiousness of being pampered into an air liner, for the limousine that was everywhere available, the most expensive shop that was always visited, the gift of jewellery, the bowing hotel manager. And Andrew always there, always amusing, confident of himself after that first moment of diffidence. And always, to her, a stranger. She was too absorbed in the new game of being a princess to consider what was happening to him. But of herself she thought a great deal, watching herself change with the impersonal curiosity with which she might have studied the unfolding of a bud, or the ageing of a kitten. She felt herself awakening. At every exertion of wealth she craved a further essay of it, the appetite increasing with the meal. And it was not only in the desire for luxury that she expanded, but in the physical senses. She was startled at the intensity with which she desired fulfilment and Andrew seemed to her only the medium, and not, in himself, the object. She found herself deliberately coquetting at other men whom they met, quite openly, laughing sidelong at Andrew; and he laughing delightedly, proud of the desirability of the woman who was his, stimulated by the glances she evoked. They were both a little drunk with sensation. And she a little frustrated, always a little disappointed that the end never quite equalled the anticipation. On their way home, after a month, from their honeymoon, he said to her, "Quite a time we had, eh?"

"Lovely."

"Happy?"

"Of course."

But not happy, she reflected. Excited, pleased, but not happy. There lacked perhaps, she thought, anything to look forward to. And yet there were things—the new house for example, a mile across the fields from Overskel, and the pleasures of settling to it. Down Mill was an old farmhouse which Gazzard did up for them as a wedding gift. Elizabeth had always known it as a gloomy place behind trees, where a farmer had once murdered a servant girl and buried her body in the copse. But the London firm that had decorated Overskel was turned on to the farm house, and now it was what everyone described as a little gem—white walls and old beams, Sussex tiles, bright colours, a rose garden, and a kitchen like an advertisement in an American magazine. When she came to the house it was not at all like coming home; for a long while she felt as though she were still in one of the hotels of her honeymoon, the airline tickets were tucked into the rack on the desk, and soon it would be time to pack.

Nor was it like coming home when she met people. The Gazzards treated her as though she were somebody else, nothing to do with her previous history, but a new member of their world. The old lady wandered mystically and seemed to regard her as something of a nuisance. The daughter accepted her casually, and Andrew's brother she seldom saw.

Only Gazzard himself genuinely welcomed her. "Had a good time, eh? Andrew to your liking? You've changed, haven't you?"

"Have I? How?"

"Woman of the world now, not a little country girl any longer."

"Is it an improvement?" she asked, amused.

"Sure. Always an improvement to enjoy life. Get the most out of it you can. Take my word for it, it don't last long. Andrew treating you all right?"

"He doesn't beat me."

"You tell me if you've got any complaints. Most sensible thing Andrew ever did, marrying you. I'll see that he behaves. And now, what about a family?"

"Not just yet."

"Well, don't wait too long. I want a grandson."

"You give your orders, don't you?"

"Always have, my girl. If you get into the habit of giving orders, other people get into the habit of obeying them. That's the whole secret of success."

The first meeting with her own father she found much more difficult. He greeted her gravely and politely, as though she had betrayed him. She had a sense of the sadness of him, alone in that echoing house.

"Darling," she ventured after a while, "why do you stay here? I know the tradition and so on, but is it worth it?"

"Are you joining in the plot?"

"Plot? What plot?"

"Gazzard has already offered to buy Shard as a sort of school for his mill-hands, and suggests I should go and live comfortably in the lodge, like a pensioner."

"It's the first I've heard of it. But, honestly, Henry, is it such a bad idea?"

He gave her a sombre stare. "I'll move into the lodge if you and your husband will take over Shard."

"But, darling, what for? It's too big. It's a house from the past."

"I, you see, live in the past. I am a protest against the

present. You go to your life with the new people, and leave me in the past."

He rose abruptly and went from the room. Elizabeth, worried, sought out Mrs. Cushion. "How is my father? Is he all right, Mrs. Cushion? He seems to me to have changed, even in this short time."

"He's getting old, Miss."

"Yes, but there's something odd."

The woman laid down the linen she was folding and said, "He doesn't sleep, Miss Elizabeth. He's up all night, wandering about the house. I crept out once to see, and there he was pacing to and fro and talking to himself. And then he suddenly picked up a vase and dropped it on the floor."

"Do you mean he is going off his head?"

"Oh no, Miss. He's lonely, and things haven't gone his way."

"You're not frightened to be here, Mrs. Cushion?"

"'Course I'm not."

"I don't know what we should do without you."

"Never mind, Miss. It'll turn out all right." Elizabeth wished she could think so. Later she went to see Gilbert Irons, to tell him her worries. He nodded. Yes, he knew about the insomnia, the wanderings.

"Gilbert, is there anything we can do? Have I behaved very badly towards him?"

"No, my dear. You have a life too. The best thing is to lead it. Probably in time you will have a family, and that might help. I think Henry would be reconciled with a grandson."

"It is remarkable," she wryly said, "how anxious everybody is for me to breed."

"Who else? Andrew?"

"Good lord, no. I should think that is the last thing he wants. But his father has practically ordered me to have a son."

Gilbert laughed. "Old men nearing death hanker for any sort of immortality."

She thought about that sometimes, and again on this evening when news came of old Gazzard's illness. If he were to

195

die now, he would be cheated of that. And suppose he had willed his money to her children if she had any; and she had not; and the money would then go irrevocably elsewhere. She could see a situation in which, ironically, his marriage might deprive Andrew of much of the fortune he expected. And yet she could not blame herself. They had used no contraceptives. A child simply had not arrived, and that was that.

After dinner Andrew reluctantly put on his coat to drive to Overskel. Tell Charles, he said, that he would not be away long. Elizabeth nodded. Into the pattern of her evening came the strand of which she had been vaguely aware, that she was to be alone for a time with Charles Neve, which had not happened since she was married. He was often at the house, for Andrew regarded him with immense respect, almost affection. It was Charles says this, and Charles says that, and always Charles to be consulted on any problem that arose. It troubled Elizabeth how much Andrew depended on him. She had pointed out that Andrew must eventually take on the responsibility of Skelstrand, and that, in any case, once the mill was built Charles would no longer be there; his job done, he would move on. To which Andrew had replied that that would never do. He would find some post to keep him at Skelstrand, couldn't possibly get along without the man who built the place, and taught him all he knew. At that Elizabeth had felt a little premonition, not altogether unpleasant.

"Give my love to your father," she said as Andrew left, "and don't worry, he'll be all right."

She went back to the sitting-room, set out some drinks, touched up her face at the mirror and was curiously expectant of Charles by the time he arrived. She told him of Gazzard's illness, and that Andrew would be back later. He said the usual regrets and for a while they talked meaninglessly.

"Tell me something," she suddenly asked. "If Sir Russell should die, would Andrew be able to manage?"

"Skelstrand, you mean? I suppose so. Is the old man that ill?"

"I'm not sure. He might be. After all, he is an old man, it's bound to happen soon."

"Then Andrew inherits, eh? Well, you needn't worry. He'll probably sell out. You could struggle along on the proceeds."

"But he won't do that, Charles. And I don't want him to. It would make him into nothing. If the old man dies, he will need a friend. He will need you."

"I'm a construction man. I can't help him."

"He thinks you can. He thinks more of you than of anybody—even than of his father, I believe. He will ask you to stay with him."

"Not a chance."

"If it's money, you could have what you want."

"It isn't money."

"Then what?"

"Oh, I don't think I should care for it. I don't settle easily."

"You'll have to settle some day."

"Not here."

"But why not?"

"Surely," he said, "you know why not."

"That," she replied, "is absurd."

"Absurd, is it? To keep on meeting you, to have the run of your house, always to be second man? No, thanks. I've got about another year here, and I can stand it that long. But not for keeps."

"I'm sorry, Charles."

"Oh, you made your choice, and I can't blame you. The price was high."

"That wasn't a very pleasant thing to say."

"I'm not a very pleasant person on this subject. I behaved too damn well."

"I didn't notice."

"Look here, would you have married Andrew if it hadn't been for the money? You as good as told me so, that afternoon we walked to Shard, and I was on the point of asking you. Don't pretend you didn't know that."

"But you didn't ask."

"And what would you have said if I had?"

She made no reply.

"I was very tempted to spill all the beans that afternoon,"

197

he went on, as though driven, "I could have told you then that old Gazzard was pushing Andrew into it, but I didn't. And there was so much money that probably you'd have taken him anyway."

Elizabeth, saving up her anger, asked quietly, "What does all that mean, about Andrew's father?"

"Surely you know all about it now. You know, don't you, that it was Gazzard who told Andrew to marry you, and the money he was prepared to put up if he did? Oh God, didn't you know? Then I have torn it."

"Tell me exactly."

"No, no. Forget it."

"I insist that you tell me."

"No. Ask Andrew, if you want to."

"Charles, I can't ask Andrew. If I did, and it were true, we couldn't go on together."

"Then don't ask him," he brutally advised. "If it's a question of saving face. . . ."

He got up as though to leave, but at that moment Andrew returned. Elizabeth noted that he smiled with relief when he saw Charles.

"How is your father?" she automatically asked.

"Not too good, old girl, I'm afraid. He looks beaten. He wants to see you."

"I'll go to-morrow," she promised.

She watched the two men talking together, the younger one slight, nervously affable, boyishly trusting; and the elder powerful, of slumbering energy, almost morose. That had been her choice. And was it true that she had chosen for money? She felt humiliated, and at the same time defiant. Why not for money? After all, who didn't? She had a momentary picture of her father, struggling for lack of it; and of old Gazzard, reigning over his world because of it. Now perhaps he was going to die and his money would not help him. But that was not the point. Even after his death his power lived in his money. All right, so he had bought her with it for Andrew. And he would hold her with it after his death. It would come to Andrew—it must, she argued—and she would see that he made good use of it; she had enough strength and will-power for that. She would mould him and his money, as his father had planned, giving up her life to it. But not, perhaps, entirely, she thought, looking at Charles.

Next morning Elizabeth walked across the fields to Overskel. The leaves were turning and the first gentle frosts were in the air, a forecast of death, like the old man she was going to see. He lay in his bed, drawn up where he could look through the tall window on to the park. His eyes were still bright, and he grinned feebly when he saw her, stretching out a hand towards her.

"That's better. You're the first nice thing that's happened to me."

"How are you feeling?" she asked, sitting by his bed.

"None the better for that fool of a doctor. He will insist. . . ."

"Gilbert's no fool."

Gazzard eyed her warily. "Have you been talking to him?"

She nodded.

"What does he say? Come along, I want to know."

"He says you're ill all right, it's your liver. But you've got the constitution of a man of forty, and you'll be up again in a month."

The old man closed his eyes. Then he asked, "Is that straight, Liz?"

"Cross my heart."

He suddenly said, "It's cancer, you know."

"I asked him that. It is not cancer. He wouldn't lie to me."

She watched him as he lay there, his eyes still closed. He has had a life, this man, she thought—rough, unscrupulous, often dishonest, but vivid, worth living.

He opened his eyes and smiled at her. "You're more to me than any of the others, did you know that? You're the sort I always wanted, and never got. It's next best that you married Andrew."

"It was your idea, wasn't it, not his?"

Gazzard nodded. "I thought you'd guess that. I was right, wasn't I?"

"Perhaps. Why did you pick on me?"

"Instinct, mostly. You'll find out, when you get old, that you worry most about what you'll leave behind. I had a fear that Andrew would lose in a few years everything I had made in a lifetime. Skelstrand specially. That's my masterpiece, Liz. That's the empire. Do you think he can hold it?"

"He's growing up."

"Thanks to you if he is—you and that chap Neve. He's a good fellow, the right sort. If Andrew can keep you two with him, he'll hold. And Appleton too, you'll need him for a while. There are still things to be settled, things that could still go wrong. . . ."

His voice trailed off.

"Appleton has it all in hand," he said.

"You know," she asked coolly, "that Charles Neve wanted to marry me?"

"Yes, of course I know. Did you want him?"

"That's what I've never been able to decide."

"You did better to take Andrew. Neve's too strong a person. You'd never have stuck together. The way it is, you can hold Neve here, and both of you can make Andrew."

"The odd thing is that you assume we will. Why should we? What should make us do all that for him?"

The old man stirred in his bed. "It isn't just for him. It's much bigger. All through the ages great families have been built up, and have lasted for centuries. They're the people who have really counted in the world. They have shaped the world. It doesn't matter what sort of politics go on, it's the powerful families who have the say. Look at this country. Look at this town if you like. Your own family has ruled this place for generations. Now it's played out. Look at the States. What sort of country would that be if it hadn't been for a few powerful families directing it, really governing it, from father to son? Look at Russia. They have a revolution and throw all the old families out. But within a few years there's a new lot in the saddle, hanging on as securely as the old ever did. And now I've started one here. Why do you think I worked for Skelstrand? I didn't need any more money. But it puts the Gazzards in the saddle, Liz. When that mill is rolling, there's a great source of wealth and power, and the family that controls it will have the say-so."

He paused and fumbled for a handkerchief. She found it by his pillow and wiped his lips.

"Hadn't you better take it easy?"

"No, I'm all right. I want you to understand this. My fear was that I should build up Skelstrand, and then leave no family strong enough to hold it. You don't know how I've worried about Andrew. I gave him the best—school, college, all the money he wanted—and he turned out weak. That was his mother in him. Now you've done a lot with him, you and Neve down at the works, he's a good chap. I begin to hope Andrew will make a do of it. He will if you stick behind him when I'm gone. It'll be worth it, Liz, not only for the money, but for the building up of something. Take my word for it. I've learned. I know."

Elizabeth waited a moment, and then said, "You spoke of money. I'm going to be frank, too. Have you left it so that it comes to Andrew?"

Gazzard chuckled. "You're my sort. I'd have asked that. Don't worry, girl. When I go, the others get looked after—Violet, and George and Cynthia. And there's a bit for Charlie Neve if he stays. And some for Appleton, because you'll need him. But the real money goes to Andrew."

He grinned.

"The only one who doesn't get any is you. Now you have it straight. You get yours by sticking to Andrew. Unless you have a son. Then it's different. You going to give me a grandson, Liz? I want him badly."

"No luck yet," she answered, smiling.

"Ah well, there's time. Think you ought to see a doctor or something?"

Before she could reply a nurse came into the room with a tray. Gazzard exploded at her, "Get that stuff out of here!"

"Now, now, Sir Russell, you just do as you're told. We must be regular with our physic."

Elizabeth laughed at him and stood up to go. His eyes followed her to the door. Then he winked at her, and shifted to swear at the nurse.

9

NEWS of Gazzard's illness spread uneasily, and with swift exaggeration. It was widely accepted that he was on his death-bed.

Appleton, stepping nervously up and down Neve's office, talked of disaster. "Couldn't have come at a worse moment. If the old man goes, the thing collapses."

And so, thought Neve dispassionately, do you. Since the man's wife had left him he had been an object of pitying curiosity to Neve. Outwardly he seemed calmer than he had ever been. He made his change of employment, moved into Gazzard's inmost confidence, took up the new work with an aloof, energetic efficiency. But with odd lapses. Sometimes he would sit motionless in a dream, his face grey; or he would mutter swiftly below his breath like a man repeating a prayer. Then suddenly he would return to normality, as if unaware that there had been any pause.

"I tell you I know," pursued Appleton. "The whole finance of the thing is in the balance, and has been for months. I couldn't start to explain it, but take my word for it. The job has been kept in existence by the old man's craftiness. I never saw such an intricate game, absolutely fascinating, a revelation. But if his hand is taken away—disaster!"

"There's Andrew."

"Oh, please don't talk like a fool."

"Well," said Neve, yawning, "it's no business of mine. Funny thing, when I started on this job I was full of high-flown ideas about it. Part of the salvation of England, a great increase of the nation's strength, and me proud to be associated with it—that sort of thing. Now I'm bored by it. We've been stuck here too long, Bernard."

"If Sir Russell dies, we won't be stuck here much longer. They've got cold feet in Whitehall at the cost of the thing."

"You can't abandon a project of this size now."

"Can't you? My dear chap, you don't know. They wouldn't abandon it, just like that. They'd cut down on it, postpone it, let it drift."

"Well, the old man's not dead yet," said Neve cheerfully. "Have you been up there?"

"Of course. It's absolute chaos. Nurses everywhere, the old girl fussing about the place in a dressing-gown saying she's been guided that it's all right, and Sir Russell himself quite changed, quite changed I assure you. He simply wouldn't talk to me. He is lying there in his bed, looking out of the window, and giving them all hell. And yet he must know. Between you and me, he is far deeper committed in Skelstrand at the moment than he ever intended to be. He has put in very large personal guarantees, just to tide over, meaning to withdraw very quickly. And now this. If it goes wrong now, Charles— but for heaven's sake keep this under your hat—the Gazzard family have had it too."

When Appleton had gone, Neve stared out of his office window at Skelstrand, pondering over that last confidence. He had a wild, irrational hope that the old man would die, the fortune tumble, and Elizabeth find herself cheated of the spoils she had bought. Then he shook himself, told himself not to be childish, and returned to his own problems, which were sufficient occupation. He rang to ask if Cross, the foreman, were outside, and bade him come in. "Well, Bill?"

"Yes, they've been at it again. No bloody doubt about it. Here's what we found in the gearbox of the hoist."

He extended his paw, with half a dozen chewed-up steel screws lying on the palm. Neve contemplated them.

"What does that make?" he asked. "Five goes, isn't it?"

"Aye, but no great damage done yet."

"I suppose we shall have to bring in the police in the end."

Bill Cross sniffed majestically. "What can they do that we can't?"

"Not much, probably. But if something really serious should happen, at least it would be their responsibility."

"I've got a few chaps watching on the quiet," offered Cross.

"Have they seen anything at all?"

"Not a sausage."

Neve pondered. This, of course, was the most difficult enemy to fight. It was so easy. The unwatched moment when a switch could be thrown the wrong way, a handful of filings dropped in the wrong place, a few ounces of acid poured where it could corrode unseen—and the rest left to chance. And where, in the vastness of this ant-hill, would you look for the one insect intent on casual mischief? Besides, there was sure to be more than one. One, perhaps, directing the operation, and half a dozen, probably unknown to each other, to carry it out.

"How about friend Papelian?" he asked.

"Shouldn't think he'd do it himself."

"No, of course not. But we know the ones who work with him, don't we?"

"That's what we've been looking for. But, streuth, you can't watch 'em all the time."

Neve sighed. "True enough. It's going to have to be the police, Bill, I'm afraid. Let's give it another week, and if they try any more of it. . . .'

"They can't do any real damage," said Cross. "Not this sort of place. Fire wouldn't touch it."

"That's right enough," Neve agreed. His mind roamed from one end of Skelstrand to the other, from the furnaces and the melting shops, through the slabbing mill, past the roughing shed, the shears, the finishing shed, to the run-out. He saw the whole great welded structure, slashed with windows, massive with girders, tough, durable, impregnable. Still unfinished. Still a hollow shell that was beginning to be littered with ponderous machines. What could a few stealthy saboteurs do to such a vastness? He laughed. "Ah well, let 'em come. They can't do much anyway. Just keep on watching, Bill. And, of course, keep your mouth shut. If it gets around too much we'll have the whole outfit edgy."

"They're beginning to be, at that," said Cross, going out.

And there was, along the vista of the construction, a stirring of doubt, of suspicion; a gingerly testing of machinery before putting reliance on it; an uneasy mutter that might be the gravest danger of all.

Bert Papelian knew it. To some extent he counted on it, but only as a by-product, an extra dividend. He shook his head impatiently when Rosa spoke of psychological war. It helped, he admitted, but it was not enough.

The news of Gazzard's illness came like a signal to him; the first account was that the old man was already dead. But even when that was learned to be false, Papelian sensed opportunity.

"Now or never," he declared to Rosa, he pacing their room in the lamplight, she sitting erect and silent in her chair.

"Reason it out," he applied. "The thing's in the balance. One good scare. . . ."

"You can't destroy it now," she said.

"We never could. But we might delay it by a year. Think what that would mean, Rosa."

She needed no such injunction. The thought of Skelstrand lay in her brain like a cancer. To her gaunt mind the mill was symbol of all the ugly barriers that were being built between mankind and happiness—no, not happiness, that was a trite, unworthy aspiration. Between mankind and fulfilment. She saw the bridge of history stretching forwards in the direction of a civilization without wars and dissensions, without degrading privilege and the rancour of class. It seemed to her so near, so almost attainable. And against this idea the powers of tyranny were being massively marshalled to frustrate, perhaps for centuries, this gleaming hope of suffering humanity. The tyranny of religious myths, the tyranny of wealth poured out into ceaseless propaganda. Above all, the tyranny of military strength, nourishing itself on deliberately-aroused nationalisms, and arming itself with the weapons of utter destruction. All of which led back to steel, and to such as Skelstrand. On that sandy foreshore she saw being forged new and heavy manacles with which to chain up the spirit of humankind. If she could be instrumental in delaying its construction she would feel herself historically justified. She saw herself as a sort of inverted Corday, attacking this potential drinker of blood. But with what dagger? What instruments had she? This husband, this routine agitator lacking imagination, and, she suspected, overmuch courage; commanding the questionable allegiance of half a dozen dissatisfied scoundrels. And the bewildered, angry boy, Tom Bruell, turned to her service by an accident of lust, and yet in whom she placed a curiously strong confidence—instinctive, she realized, rather than well founded in reason. She dared not too closely examine the source of that confidence, for it lay in her own emotions that she did not wish to acknowledge.

"Now or never, Rosa," Papelian repeated, "I'm sure of it. They're on edge, and with Gazzard likely to die. . . ."

"You've not accomplished much so far."

"Ah, but so far we have been secret, and they have naturally had the sense not to talk about it. How many people, do you think, know that anything has happened at all? But it's starting to get round. There's a growing feeling of uneasiness, no doubt of that. Fred was telling me last night that the men installing the machines are going slow, insisting on a test of everything before they touch it. And we're beginning to get Neve worried. There are hints that he's thinking of calling in the police."

"And if he does?"

"So much the better for us. They couldn't keep that quiet. That would turn suspicions into certainty all right. And then, one really effective stroke."

He stopped pacing and faced her.

"Rosa, I do believe that one effective stroke could do it."

"There's a chance, no more. And if they tumbled to it before it happened, and prevented it, you'd have the reverse effect. Remember that."

"All you're saying is that it's risky. Well, of course it is, I know that. I wish it wasn't that young fool we had to rely on. When I think of the chances—but I don't like to think of them, it looks too crazy. A sex-starved adolescent and a mad old man. Aren't we asking too much? Is there a hope in hell it can come off?"

"What's the alternative?"

"That's just it. There isn't one," he muttered, resuming his walk.

"Have you heard from Tom?" she asked.

"Not since last night. Mac went out there to see him. He said then it was nearly fixed. Hell, I don't know. We could be blundering into disaster. Wish I could feel as confident as you in that boy."

"I tell you, he's conditioned to it," she murmured, staring through the window. And conditioned, she mused, he was. Conditioned by her own persistence, evening after evening, quietly on. She shrugged aside her own distaste for what she was doing. That was personal, an emotion which she despised. Her role was to be not a person but a force.

10

IN the room in which he had slept as a child, Tom Bruell sat waiting for the noise below to cease. The room overlooked the side of the Melmoth Arms, the shaft of electric light from the door of the public lying, a yellow oblong, across the dusk of the yard, illumining the stable at the far side, with the elms behind it and the clear dark sky above. The murmur from the bar, where his father stood dignified in shirt-sleeves, was the sound that, echoing back through memory, had night after night, those years ago, soothed him to sleep. To him it was a gentle, childhood noise. There was never tumult here, except occasionally, of a Saturday night, a song or two, an accentuated laughter. Strangers rarely came. Tom was aware, as he had always been, of the peacefulness of it, the permanence. This refuge, while his father lived—and it was inconceivable that that ponderous man should ever die—was always there for him.

But the balm no longer soothed. His father, he understood, realized that, but asked no questions. Tom had come home for his annual fortnight's holiday, and Tom was always welcome. If he were troubled and unhappy, that was his own affair. Bill Bruell believed in leaving people alone. If Tom wanted to open up to him, well and good. He would listen gravely, probably without tendering advice. To old Bruell's thinking, life worked itself out a day at a time, and each man had a right to his own problems. Tom found it comforting merely to be with his father. But he had no wish to discuss with him the preoccupation of his thoughts.

He looked at the tiny glow of his wrist-watch—he was sitting without a light in his room. It was ten minutes to ten.

The bar would soon close, the house soon quieten, and then, in say half an hour, he would go. He was expected at eleven and he knew precisely what he was to do. Rosa had schooled him. He did not question the thing that was to be done, nor his own part in it. He merely accepted it as his task, his minute share in the huge plan which, night after night, she had unfolded to him. To her, he realized, it was a positive thing, the steady construction of a new system. But to that he paid small heed. Perhaps one day there would arise a new sort of civilization for which her voice monotonously pleaded. He did not know. Did not know even whether it were a civilization in which he could rejoice. What he craved was not the creation of a new system, but the destruction of the old. That he accepted from her. Skelstrand was her symbol, and it became his. Confusedly in his mind it was part of the agony of the court-room with Daphne weeping in the witness box, part of the alley of despair at the end of which he could see only his own suicide, and of the glow of the girl's pale limbs from which he had fled in horror into the sordid morning of the streets, shrieking inside himself to destroy.

From downstairs he heard the summons of the telephone-bell, and then his father calling, "Tom. It's for you."

He went down, nodding to his father, and picked up the instrument in the small corridor behind the bar, cluttered with hanging coats, scarves, a crate of empty bottles. "Hallo."

"That you, Tom?" came Papelian's voice faintly from the other end. "Ah, good. All okay?"

"I think so. I'll start in half an hour."

"Now, listen. It's all right here. All fixed. Just stick to what we said. Is the old man all right?"

"Yes, I think so. I saw him last night. He has gone a bit mad, obviously. But he seems all right."

"Well, if anything goes wrong, just give us the signal and get back to the pub and keep quiet. Got it?"

"Yes."

The phone clicked into vacancy and Tom turned to go back upstairs. His father was calling time in the bar, switching off some of the lights as the customers slowly dispersed.

He came to the door, solid and stately in his shirt-sleeves, his thick moustache black in the dimness. "You off to bed now, Tom?"

"Yes, Dad. Think I'll turn in," said Tom, turning to the stairs. He sat down again in the window-chair of his darkened room, watching the customers going off down the road. Then the downstairs light went out, leaving the yard mysterious. He waited for the sound of his father's feet ascending the stairs, the closing of a door, the silence in which, in some distant field, a cow was bellowing for the calf that had been taken from her. Give it another quarter of an hour, he thought, looking at his watch.

At the end of that period he raised his window and stepped across the sill on to the roof of an out-house. The familiar route of his boyhood. His feet and hands perfectly remembered the way down that they had taken so often, years ago, to join the village boys in their midnight orchard raids, the tremulously sweet adventures of a child.

Once on the ground he left the yard by the back gate and made across the fields towards Shard. The moon, in its third quarter, was just rising, and there were small grey clouds drifting across the sky.

"Is the old man all right?" Papelian had asked, and Tom had confidently assented. But really he knew he was incalculable, and Tom could not understand why he was lending himself to this at all. When Rosa had first suggested that Colonel Melmoth could be persuaded to help, Tom had stared at her.

"You must be crazy," he said to Rosa.

"No, it is he who is crazy." She gave him a long analysis of the inevitability of the dispossessed landowners joining forces with the workers in a revolt against capitalist exploitation. Tom listened patiently, but it made no sense to him. Perhaps it was all right in theory, but when applied to an actual person, to Colonel Melmoth, it became ludicrous.

"You'll see," said Rosa. "You try him, and you'll see." And she had schooled him carefully in what he should say.

On the first day of his holiday he went up to Shard on the pretext of paying his respects. The Colonel was touched by the courtesy and kept him talking mostly of his memories of Shard when he was a boy, and the awe in which he had held it.

Melmoth grunted. "You find it different now, eh?"

"It's sort of—lonelier," hesitated Tom.

"It's a ghost, inhabited by a ghost. That's me, Tom. I ought to have packed up years ago. My world has gone. It must stand aside to make way for factories and mechanics and wealthy men." He raised his fist and suddenly struck the side of his chair. "The mechanics I can tolerate, but the rogues who have accumulated riches by manipulating them I hate. A strong word, Tom, hate. But I mean the whole strength of it—hate, hate, hate."

Tom was silent. Melmoth stared angrily at him. Then he controlled himself and continued in a calmer voice, "But you will not agree with me. You are young, with your life ahead of you, and a career to make. What is anathema to me must be progress to you."

Tom shook his head. "I do agree with you. I hate quite as strongly as you do, for good reason."

"Reason?"

"I had hoped to marry Daphne Wilkinson."

Melmoth looked puzzled for a moment, and then, remembering, passed his hand across his eyes. "There is nothing that is not defiled, no person in all this place who has not been injured. In the town, rapacity where there was once contentment, ugliness of mind where there was once peace. In my own family, Tom, the defilement is present. My daughter chose to marry for mere riches—nothing more, I swear to you there was nothing more. Every value has been debased, every decency. You have experienced it cruelly in your own hopes, I in mine. And we are only two. Knock on any door in any street of the town and you will find a person who has been coarsened by nothing but the intrusion of this damnable mill. The devil is among us, Tom. What was once a happy place. . . ."

His voice drifted off into a dream. For a few minutes he was by himself. Then, recalling his company, he gazed sadly at the younger man.

"What I find so bitter is that I, whose responsibility it should be, am helpless. Or perhaps too weak. For centuries it has been for Shard to guide the destinies of this place. Looking back, Tom, as I frequently do, I cannot see that my forebears gravely failed in that duty. But I have failed. I fought, my dear chap, I struggled. But it was not enough. I wander sometimes up and down this house at night, tormented by the knowledge that it was my job to avert this degradation, and I was beaten. Too weak, too weak. . . ."

Suddenly, glaring, he struck the arm of his chair again and fiercely declared, "If I could wipe Skelstrand off the face of the dunes, and all the people in it, I would do it, Tom, by God, I swear I would do it."

Tom thought to break it to him then, but hesitated. It was not until after his third visit, to which Melmoth eagerly pressed him, that he dared to return to the subject. He led towards it by speaking of Sir Russell Gazzard's illness, of rumours that Skelstrand was in truth in the balance, and of the disquiet of the construction men at the series of accidents that had occurred.

"Accidents?"

"They are believed not to be accidents," said Tom diffidently. "There are thought to be men deliberately. . . ."

Melmoth stared at him. "Deliberate sabotage, you mean? Ah, but that is not the way, that cannot be the way."

"Why not, when every other way has failed? You yourself spoke the other day of wiping out Skelstrand."

The old man shook his head, muttering. "But that is precisely it. You cannot wipe out Skelstrand by a few trifling acts of mischief."

"Suppose," ventured Tom, "that it could be done psychologically. Suppose the whole project were, as I said, in the balance. The finances are rocky. Gazzard is ill and may die. The Government is uneasy about the increasing costs against a background of economic crisis. It wouldn't take much to tip the balance. Suppose there were some rather sensational piece of wrecking that brought the construction men out in revolt?"

"Well?"

"Some people," said Tom, "think that a combination of all those things might frighten the Government into postponing the project for a while, on the excuse of economy at a time of crisis. And if once it were postponed—well, what a victory that would be!"

Melmoth, still staring at him, asked with deliberation, "Are you trying to tell me that something of the kind is actually being planned?"

"I am inviting you to help in it," said Tom recklessly.

"No. No. I will not hear another word. I refuse to know anything about it. And if you take my advice you'll free yourself from any contact you may have with such madness."

He rose abruptly and left the room. Tom waited a while, not knowing whether he were expected to stay. Then, as there was no sign of the Colonel, he left the house and wandered home. So that was that. When Papelian phoned he would simply have to report that it was no go.

But the phone message came that night not from Papelian, but from Colonel Melmoth.

"He phoned through," Tom's father told him. "Wants you to go up there to-morrow."

"Ah. You said I would?"

"Course I did. Seems he's taken quite a fancy to you, Tom. Fine man, the Colonel. We'll not see his like in these parts. It'd have been different if Mr. Peter'd lived."

When Tom went to Shard next day, Melmoth took him into his own room, and asked without preliminary, "What do you want me to do?"

"There's some stuff we want stored. We need somewhere near Skelstrand where a few crates can be left and nobody will pry."

"Crates of what?"

"I don't know. Not very large, I'm told. A stable loft or something would do."

"How would they come?"

"They'd be brought here one night. And another night, later on, they'd be taken away again."

"Is that all?"

"That's all I know."

212

Melmoth sat in silence, his face immobile. At last he asked, "Would the night after next do?"

Tom nodded.

"I can send Mrs. Cushion away. She wants to visit her niece."

"I'll go and arrange it," said Tom.

And now, as he walked across the dark fields towards Shard, it was arranged. Even now it seemed a fantasy, an extension of some imaginative adventure of childhood, a boy's game. But he remembered the look on Melmoth's face as he had asked whether the night after next would do—grim, strained, unquestionably a little mad. Tom stopped in the field, suddenly asking himself what insanity he was committing. Then into his mind came another recollection of Melmoth's face, the magistrate's face of gravity up there on the Bench, and the staleness of the crowded court-room, and Daphne whispering from the panelled box. His thoughts fused, and he went on across the field.

Shard was dark and silent, the trees muttering. He kept off the gravel and made his way along a grass border towards the door. When he touched it, it moved slowly open. He stepped inside and paused, trying to accustom his eyes to the darkness of the hall. Then his arm was touched and he jumped nervously round. Beside him he could make out the tall figure of Melmoth, in a hunting mackintosh. The older man nudged him and, without a word, led him through the back quarters of the house, in darkness. The ludicrousness of it, with nobody else there, came to Tom. He wanted to laugh. But Melmoth hissed angrily at him and led him on.

By the gate to the courtyard they stood and waited, still without speaking. The trees murmured. And then there was another sound, the distant hum of a car engine drawing nearer. Tom peered across the park and at last saw the lights, side-lights only, making their way along the road, pausing at the lodge gates, turning into the drive. He winked his torch twice in that direction and the car came on. As it drew nearer Melmoth waved it into the courtyard, and he and Tom closed the gates behind it.

It was an old, shabby shooting brake, from which two men whom Tom did not know descended.

"Where?" asked one of them.

Melmoth pointed to one of the stable lofts, against which a ladder had been placed. The man nodded, and he and the other opened the back of the brake, lifting out three long, narrow boxes which appeared to be heavy. The men took the first box and struggled up the ladder with it. Melmoth followed, and they all disappeared into the loft. They came down again twice for the other boxes, blowing and sweating at the weight, and one muttering under his breath. When all three were stowed, the two men came down the ladder and watched Melmoth secure a padlock on the door of the loft, and then himself descend.

"Do we have the key?" one of them asked.

"No, I'll keep that."

The other man began to demur, but Melmoth glared at him, and the first man shrugged and said, "Okay." Then they took down the ladder and carried it into the stable.

When they came out again they got into the car and swung it round in the yard. Tom opened the gates and they drove away, the dim red tail-light vanishing down the drive. Tom looked round, but Melmoth had gone. He went out of the yard, quietly shutting the gates behind him, and turned homewards across the fields, feeling flat and unsatisfied that that was all there was to it, as though a firework that had promised display had merely fizzled.

PART FOUR

1

SEVERE frosts came in the early months of that winter, in November even a sneeze of snow. But the weather could no longer worry Charles Neve, leaning on the drawing-board in his office which by mid-afternoon now needed electric light, for the window stared closely at the massy wall of Skelstrand. The main structure was up, and weather could not touch him. His office, that had seemed the bridge of a ship surveying the open sea, was now like a small snug cabin deep amidships, electric fire glowing, tobacco smoke lazily drifting, and stacked all around him the records and mementoes of the work that closed his view. Once, just before Christmas, he pulled down his three progress diaries and calculated exactly how long, two years, seven months and fifteen days, since he had first come to this office, fresh with new-swept ideas.

He had over Christmas and into the New Year to consider whether to take the offer that Andrew Gazzard had now explicitly made, to stay on, settle, reap. Perhaps once in a man's life came such an opportunity. Here on offer were riches, power, a lifelong comfort and ease. The thing would not, of course, be simple. The financial battle that had been going on for months, and of which Neve knew the outlines, was by no means won, as Bernard Appleton frequently reminded him. But Neve did not fear that. Appleton, for all his jeremiads, was subtle enough to continue the plan that the old man had commenced; was already, in fact, winning a preliminary victory of his own. All day, and often into the night, Appleton sat in his office nervously conducting his campaign.

The point was, should Neve take Andrew's offer? Did he really want to drop his true work and take a rich sinecure which had come, not as the result of his labour, but by chance? Two years, seven months and fifteen days ago he would have despised the idea. He was a construction man, he built things. From one job he moved to the next. He could look back on his work and be satisfied that it was useful, that he had contributed more than most to his country's struggle for existence.

But he was getting older, perhaps too old for toughness. There was also, of course, Elizabeth. Neve was grimly aware that she was part of the offer—not Andrew's offer, of course, but hers. Perhaps the whole thing was hers. Here again he looked back over his two years, seven months and fifteen days, the exact time for which he had known her. The girl who had wanted to know what colour Skelstrand would be against the sea. The woman who had seemed to him the sort of honourable person whom he might marry, and who had taken Andrew Gazzard for his money; and who had recently started to look at himself with contemplative, greedy eyes. And again why not? he angrily asked himself. Why in hell not? They had virtually said as much to each other a few evenings before, when he had gone to Down Mill for dinner, and Andrew had phoned to say he was tied up with an accountant; would Elizabeth please give Charles some drinks and postpone the meal for half an hour?

"Curious," said Neve, when she came back into the room with the message, "that you should marry the playboy and find yourself with the man of action as husband."

"Not so curious," she answered, smiling. "People develop. You never know about the seed until the plant shows."

"You, for instance?"

"Oh yes, me, certainly. Though can one really see oneself?"

"I can see you," he said.

"More clearly than you could before?"

"Much."

"Pretty sight?"

"Now, what on earth do you expect me to say?"

She sat down, facing him across the fireside, in the glow of the logs, pausing, as though considering.

"I went to see my father-in-law the other day," she said slowly. "There he was, an old man, dying in a bed pulled up by the great window of his room. I found myself envying him. I felt quite sure at that moment that what I want is what he has had."

"Money? Power?" asked Neve, surprised.

"No, not essentially. Though those are the necessary means. I had the feeling, sitting by his bed, that there was a person who had taken whatever he desired, and to the devil with the consequences. I began to wonder, if it were I lying in that bed, what sort of a verdict I should be passing on my own life. Rather empty, a thing of stifled ambitions and petty little repressions—and not much fun. That was the point. The old man had had an immense amount of sheer fun."

Neve said nothing for a minute or so. Then, "And do you now intend to remedy that while there is time?"

She smiled coolly across at him.

"Oh yes," she said. "That is what I intend.'

Andrew came in soon afterwards, making his apologies, warm in his greeting, as he always was to Neve, though it might be only a few hours since they had met.

2

NEVE was broken from this recollection by Cross, the foreman, entering his office to say that Jabby wanted to speak to him.

"Who?"

"Jabby—the foreign bloke."

"Oh yes. What does he want?"

"Dunno, he won't tell me."

"Send him in, then."

When the Pole came in, Neve nodded him to a chair. He had always been a little curious about this fellow, though he had seen little of him. He made one, Neve reflected, feel the triviality of one's personal problems. Here was a man who no longer had any. His whole former life had been expunged—family, friends, surroundings, country, no longer existed, and all that remained was to work, friendless in exile, at a labourer's task.

"Well," said Neve, "what can I do for you?"

He offered him a cigarette, which the Pole smilingly took.

"I have come to warn you," he began.

"About what?"

"I am not sure. I cannot discover all I wish. But I think there is enough that you must know."

Neve waited patiently.

"There has been some sabotage, is it not so?" the other asked.

"There have been some accidents."

"As you want. We will say accidents. Soon there will be a big accident."

"Oh, there will, will there?" said Neve, leaning back in his chair. "What are you going on?"

"There has been some high explosive moved into this district. I do not know exactly where, and I am not sure who. But somewhere it is, that I know."

"How do you know?"

"I cannot quite tell you all. There was a conversation overheard, there was a car seen by a man I know, who was a quarryman, who understands the sort of boxes in the back of it. And, if you remember, there was a theft two months ago of some high explosive from a train near Liverpool."

"Was there? I don't remember."

"It was briefly in the newspapers," said Jabby.

Neve, drawing on his cigarette, considered. What were the chances that, having read the item in the newspaper, this man's nervous imagination supplied the rest? Pretty high, of course. And Neve had no inclination to chase wild geese. On the other hand, there had been small attempts at sabotage, and the thing was not impossible.

"Is that all you know?" he asked.

Jabby nodded.

"Well, thanks very much," said Neve. "You were quite right, of course, to tell me. Naturally, you won't say a word to anyone else."

Jabby nodded again, but made no move to go.

"Is there anything else?" asked Neve.

"What are you going to do? The police?"

"Could be," said Neve, noncommittal.

"It would be better to stop them," said Jabby, "without the police. They cannot destroy Skelstrand, but they could frighten the men."

"I shall have to judge for myself what to do."

"Let me help you, please," the Pole asked suddenly, "I am not a fool. I could help."

Neve hesitated. "Tell me first, why are you here? Not here in this office, but here at Skelstrand at all, working at this sort of job."

"For me, here is as well as anywhere. And here there will be steel."

"Is that so important to you?"

"My friend," said the Pole, "you have not seen it happen as I have. When I am young, there is a civilized Europe. There is a respect for human life, and there is dignity. Now, over so much of the land, is barbarism. But this is not the end. There is more yet to be fought. Perhaps the fight cannot be won. But that depends on England. Not America, or France, or any other nation, but England, my friend. The only grace left is here. I tell you, I a foreigner tell you, and I have seen. You all in this country mock yourselves, and say you are slack and lazy, and things are not as they were. But for one such as I there is only one lamp still burning, and it is England. When the time comes—and it will come—England will need every inch of strength. In special you will need steel. That is why I am here."

Neve busied himself stubbing out his cigarette, embarrassed. "And how, in this other business, do you think you could help?"

"You are watching, is it not so? There is something for which it is necessary to watch? Not accidents?"

"Yes, there is something."

"I too could watch, and perhaps in different places. Do you think you know who it is? Will you not tell me how far you know?"

"We do not know anything. I suppose the easy answer is to say that we suspect the comrades."

The Pole shook his head. "No. The easy answer is not the

right one. They would try many things to delay—strikes, go slow, fomenting unrest—but not sabotage. Not crimes."

"But, my dear chap," said Neve, "if not them, who?"

"There is some fanatic, some half-mad person, who would do anything."

"Any idea who?"

"Yes," said the Pole slowly, "some idea. But I cannot tell, not yet. Let me watch. I too have friends. But if I watch I want that you believe me. And if I come and say, I want that you are ready to strike. Yes?"

At that moment the door opened and Andrew Gazzard came in. The Pole rose from his chair. Neve nodded to him, and he went silently from the room.

"Hallo, what did he want?" asked Andrew.

"He had some idea he can help us get hold of the chaps who are having a go at sabotage."

"Oh, that," said Andrew indifferently. "Well, that doesn't amount to much. If only that were all our troubles."

"Things not too good?"

"Charles, I simply don't know. I wish I did. Appleton seems to think it's going all right now, or better anyway. I feel as though I'm struggling in the deep end."

"By what I hear, you're doing all right."

"I feel so incapable, so inexperienced. If only the old man were just that little bit better, so that I could take it to him and get his lead. But I can't. He lies there, only half alive, and every day I discover how much more there is at stake, how deeply he has committed himself and us. He made a gambler's throw, Charles, and fell ill before the result. And now it's left to poor old me."

He turned quickly up and down towards the window. Neve, from his chair, laughed and encouraged. "You shouldn't have been born so rich."

"Upon my word, I wish I hadn't been."

"Well, that's easily fixed. Bungle this, and you won't be rich any more."

Andrew giggled. "And what about your precious project for steel? England needs us, and all that stuff."

"Oh, Skelstrand won't stop if the Gazzards lose it," replied

Neve comfortably. "Much more satisfactory really if the nation completely owned it."

"It wouldn't offer you such a good job."

"I'm not sure that I want it anyway."

"Oh, come now, Charles," pleaded Andrew, "for Pete's sake don't you ditch me. If you do, I swear I'll chuck it."

"Not you. You've got your old man in you. It's wonderful the way it's coming out, now that you've got the show to look after yourself."

Andrew mocked a groan. "You ask Bernard Appleton, he don't think so. Pushes me around worse than my old nanny did. Just given me orders to go with him to London this Friday and act the big financier. I suppose I'll have to go. You know, Charles, once they get the cigars out, and the brandy, and settle down like a comic drawing in *Punch*, I feel such a bloody fool."

"You'll be all right. After all, you've got Appleton. He's the chap you ought to stick to, you know, Andrew, not me. I don't understand why you can't see it."

Andrew protested with his hands. "That bundle of chicken's nerves? Every time I'm with him for long I'm so scared he's going to bust out crying I don't know where to look. What's he going to do, by the way, about that wife of his, divorce her?"

"I wouldn't dare ask."

"Rummy, ain't it, how an obvious tart like that can muck up a brainy chap like Appleton? I should think our old friend Heron's getting a bit sick of it, out on the Canadian prairies. All right for a quickie at Brighton, but not much cop in a log cabin, if you ask me. Ah well, one man's horse-flesh, eh? Coming up home for a noggin to-night?"

"All right, I'd like to."

"Good-oh. I'm going to turn Liz on to you. Someone's got to make you stay on and help us. I'll tell her to vamp you into it while I'm away over the week-end."

"You do that," said Neve steadily, "I'd enjoy it."

When the other had gone, Neve sat staring at his desk. That sort of uneasy feeling, he reflected, was what you might call conscience, if the word meant anything. But what was it, except a sentimental sort of nonsense? It ignored all the facts. And the facts were that Andrew had bought his wife, not even at his own desire, but on his father's orders. So why now trump up some high moral issue? The truth was that he could not even feel it as a moral issue. And, even if he could, was there anything that any of them could do about it? Probably not. It seemed as though, once something started, it went inexorably on, whatever the people involved thought about it, driven from outside. Events followed events, unaffected by arguments.

And this had certainly started. Both he and Elizabeth knew that. Started—and would continue. He felt as though he were standing back, watching it with detached curiosity, an observer. That evening, when he drove to Down Mill for a drink with them, neither he nor Elizabeth said anything in particular to each other, but each knew that the other felt it. On the Saturday night he went to dinner with her, as Andrew had insisted. "Course you must have him to dinner, Liz. I've told you, you've got to vamp him into staying on." And then, to Neve, "How in hell can the girl do her stuff on you if you won't come and see her?"

They had all laughed at the time. But on the Saturday, when the meal was over, and he and Elizabeth sat with cups of coffee before the fire, he went deliberately back to what Andrew had said. "Isn't it time we had this out?" he asked.

"I suppose you could say that it is a question of timing."

"You always seem to say something that I don't expect you to say."

"Well, but, my dear, what could be better than this timing? It's melodramatically right. Husband away, husband's best friend to dinner. It happens all the time in the books. It's a well-known situation."

"And how does it end?"

"Oh, in disaster, always."

"Shall we leave it at that, Elizabeth? A joke, and nothing more."

"Is it anything more?"

"You know damn well it is," he said.

"How should I know? You never said so."

"Then I'll say so now. I never fell in love in my life, and never intended to. Then you came up on to a sandhill and asked a damn silly question, and you've been an irritation to me ever since. You know perfectly well that I was on the edge of asking you to marry me when you chose Andrew and the cash. I don't blame you. In your place I'd have done the same."

"It sounds silly," she said, "but at the time I really didn't know about that. I knew, of course, that there was cash, as you put it. But I had the motives the wrong way round. I thought that the family were taking me because Andrew was determined to marry me. It was only a few weeks ago that I had it out with the old man."

"What did he say?" asked Neve curiously.

"Oh, roughly, that he usually got what he wanted."

Neve leaned back and laughed. "Scruples of conscience sound so pompous, don't they, when you measure them against him."

"At any rate," she murmured, "he knows that we live in the jungle, and no pretences."

"Do you think it matters," he casually asked, "to fall away from one's own standards?"

"The question is, does anything matter?"

"Ah, but it has practical results," he pointed out.

"For instance?"

"All right, let me put it plainly. Here's the choice in front of me. Not right now, but in say a year's time when Skelstrand is built, and the job I came here to do is done. I can either move on, taking up the next job somewhere else, living at about my usual level, never expecting much more than I am getting now. Or I can take the opportunity that Andrew offers me to stay on here practically in charge of this thing, and make my pile, and be easy. One doesn't usually get that sort of offer more than once."

Elizabeth was gazing from her deep chair, not at him, but at the heat of the logs on the fire.

"And the complication," she murmured, "is me."

"Of course. You stand in the way. I have been in love

with you for two years, Elizabeth. That is the first time I have said it properly, even to myself."

And even now, he immediately asked himself, was it true? If he went to bed with her, would that not end it?

"We're in an awkward spot, aren't we?" she said, still not looking at him.

"We?"

"Yes, I think so. No, stay where you are. This had better be just talk."

He shrugged, and leaned back again in his chair. "What else is there to say?"

"We have alternatives, surely."

"First alternative. I keep out of your way as much as I can while Skelstrand is still building, and when the job's done, I move on."

Elizabeth shook her head. "That would be cowardly of you. It leaves me knowing, all my life, that I cheated you of your chance of success."

"Then what's your alternative?"

"You stay on with Andrew, and we behave ourselves like sensible people, like friends."

"It wouldn't work."

Elizabeth suddenly rose and came across to him. "Charles, why not? We're not children."

"You know damn well why not. I want you."

She looked at him gravely. "And I you, my dear. But we have—responsibilities. We must put up with things as they are."

Her voice was pleading. He reached out and took her hand.

"So what," he asked, "becomes of old Gazzard's philosophy?"

She let go his hand and turned to stand by the fireplace, still looking at him. "It is so easy to say things, all bravely and cynically. But when it becomes real. . . ."

Neve got up and went slowly over to her, holding both her hands in his, smiling gently down at her. "I know. My alternative wins. I leave."

"Oh, Charles," she said. Her hands were gripping his. "Oh, Charles, no!"

Then they were together, her mouth searching up for his, his hand against the smoothness of her shoulder. That was it, he found himself thinking, the inevitability. Holding her close to him, and gazing down at her closed eyes, he found himself thinking that things that start, finish.

3

As they returned in the train from London, Andrew Gazzard listened with embarrassment to Appleton's praises.

"Do you really think we did all right?" he asked, fending off.

"I don't see how they can get out of their promises now," said Appleton, considering. "Your father couldn't have done better, if you ask me."

He began a long explanation, to which Andrew half listened sleepily. The Skelstrand problem so clearly absorbed the man, fascinated him, occupied all his thoughts.

"You know, Bernard, you ought to take a holiday," Andrew suggested, "get away from it for a bit. Go fishing or something."

Appleton blinked. "Oh no, I don't want a holiday. No, thanks."

Poor devil, thought Andrew, turning his gaze out of the window. They were running through the flat middle countryside of England, fields, copses, little hills, roads that converged and diverged with lorries trundling along them, a canal, willows, a sleepy factory with a tall chimney, a row of red-brick houses and a baker's van. He regarded this scenery with gladness, because it was leading him back to Skelstrand. "Cripes," he thought, surprised at himself, "am I getting that much tangled up in the place?" And he knew that he was. He understood with a sense of wonder that it was for Skelstrand that he was glad to be travelling away from London, and not for his home, his personal life, Elizabeth.

Elizabeth. There was that remark that his sister had made, quite deliberately, when she came up to London during his visit. It kept on coming back at him, as Cynthia had of course

226

intended it should; her motives were fairly clear. It was when she and George had met for drinks in his sitting-room at the hotel; there they were, brothers and sister, and he had thought to himself what strangers they were to each other, the three of them who as children had been so close, sharing games and secret plots and imaginations. Now Cynthia, though she lived at Overskel just across the fields from him, was a strange woman whom he scarcely ever thought about, obsessed with her desire for clothes, her longings to be in London, her boredoms. He did not even know, he thought, whether she had some man with whom she was in love. As for George, sober old George, he was tucked away in the tiny London office of the firm, with his small flat in Kensington, and what he made of his life Andrew had not the slightest notion.

They came in for drinks before dinner. It was the one evening on which he had no business engagement, and he had sent Appleton off to a cinema, or to see some old friends, or get tight in a pub or something. The strain needed easing. He himself had felt rather sentimental at the thought of having his brother and sister in, the three of them together, family. He tried to talk cosily of family things, but George, who came first, kept on steering back to only one of them, the family money. In the London office, of course, George got a fair insight into what was going on, and he needed reassuring.

"Can't think what came over father," he insisted, staring into his glass, "to take all that risk. Do you realize he has put practically everything into it?"

"Oh, there'll be the odd crust," said Andrew. "Anyway, it looks like turning out all right now. Keep your fingers crossed."

George frowned, worried. "Wish I had your confidence. Do you feel you've got a real grasp of it? After all, you're new to it."

"Of course not. Don't understand the half of it, me boy. Always was a bit of an ass at figures. But there's the worthy Appleton. He knows. And even that prophet of woe is cheering up a bit."

George hesitated, and then ventured, "Are you sure you're quite wise to put so much faith in that chap?"

"The old man thinks the world of him."

"Ah, but father took him on when his illness was already coming on. Frankly, I think his judgment was failing even before he took to his bed. How was he when you left, by the way?"

"Not so good," said Andrew quietly.

"We've got to face it, you know, Andrew. He can't last long. And when he does go, you'll be taking a hell of a risk leaving everything in the hands of this chap Appleton."

"I don't know who else."

"Well, there is me," said George. "Frankly, I think you overlook me."

"Oh no, come, George."

"I want to put this bluntly. I can see a position, when father dies, of you—rather inexperienced, let's face it— getting properly into the hands of this chap Appleton, and getting twisted, Andrew. After all, what does he care about us?"

Andrew had a swift memory of driving through Gulport a few nights before, seeing a light in the office, stopping to investigate, and finding Appleton, after midnight, looking up with blinking eyes from the papers at which he was still working. He wondered what George did with his midnights.

"Frankly," continued George, "I think you ought to con- sider selling out of Skelstrand while the going's good. You don't want, any more than I do, to spend your life slogging away at a bloody mill, and perhaps going down the drain, when we can take the cash, invest it in gilts, and be secure."

Andrew was surprised at how angry he felt.

But the conversation was broken by Cynthia's arrival. She came drifting in, reminding him for a moment of the way their mother moved, murmuring a tired apology for being late, but everything was such a rush, and he must forgive her but she would have to tear off again in a few minutes to a dinner date. He got her a drink and asked how everything was at home; she had followed some days after his departure for London.

"Oh, all right," she said, "except for a bit of talk going on."

George butted in, shifting the subject. They went on stiffly about this and that, quite strangers, pondered Andrew. She talked of clothes and horses, and George of people they knew in London, and theatres, and a party he had been to. Then after a time George looked at his watch and left. Cynthia took another drink, idly declaring that she too must go. But she did not. Andrew was aware that she was staying to say something to him, and he was getting so bored with the evening that he gave her the chance.

"What was that you were saying about a bit of talk going on at home?"

"Talk? Oh yes. Nothing important."

"Come on, Cynthia, out with it."

"Well, really, it's scarcely worth repeating. Just small-town talk."

"About Elizabeth?" he asked casually. It was obvious that it must be about Elizabeth.

"Some sort of gossip that she's enjoying herself with that man at the mill, what's his name? Neve. I don't suppose there is anything in it."

"I'm quite sure there isn't," said Andrew.

"You know how people talk."

When he had got rid of her he made a bitter mouth and stubbed out his cigarette. The pair of them, his brother and sister, moving vindictively but clumsily into position for the grapple when the old man should die. "Tasteful, ain't it?" he said out loud to himself. The motives were so obvious; to get the money out of his hands lest he should drop it, and to remove the two men who might sway him into going on, taking the risk, doing the job for the sake of the job. Appleton and Charlie Neve. He was suddenly angry. That Cynthia should have dared to poison him against Neve, the one man he completely respected, his friend. That George, that slug of a George, should have supposed himself more capable of handling this delicate, intricate affair than Appleton, who devoted to it all his nervous subtlety. Then it began to come to Andrew that there was something else he ought to be angry about, and with a feeling of guilt he realized that it was the slur on Elizabeth. Ah, but that was too obviously absurd. Of her integrity of spirit he had no doubt. No, it was to separate him from the two men that his dear kindred had made their palpable moves, and it was at that that he should be angry. Yet he felt that his real anger lay behind, as something more essential to him, and he dimly understood that it was because the attempt was finally directed at divorcing him from Skelstrand itself; and that this was his vital interest. He had a hunger to hurry back, merely to look at it, to recapture the feeling of accomplishment in it.

Of this hunger he reminded himself as he travelled back in the train with Appleton. It assailed him again, and increased with each approaching landmark. There was a period of a few minutes when the train ran out from between the hills and presented a view across the estuary where the mill stood. Andrew, with an apologetic grin at Appleton, shifted to the corner seat and put his nose to the window like a schoolboy approaching the seaside. The waters of the estuary were grey-blue in the pale winter sunshine, and beyond them the cream-coloured walls of Skelstrand dominated the coast, the furnaces like stout sentries at the near end where the cranes swung lazily over the quays of the new harbour and a couple of steamers with orange funnels discharging scrap; and then the sleek body of the mill itself, impassive, satisfying just by being there.

"She looks all right, don't she?" he said to Appleton.

And Appleton, glancing up from his inner thoughts of statistics set out neatly on foolscap sheets, said, "Looks all right? Oh yes, the mill. Ah, looks all right. Sure."

When they got to the station and into the waiting car, he told Appleton he would drop him off at the office. "I'm going out to Skelstrand," he said. It was market day, so that the car with difficulty got through the square. Andrew did not mind. He sat surveying the bustle of stalls, buses, people, with a warm feeling that he was home. Several of the people he knew, people from the office, and he smiled and nodded at them. This was just the size, he thought, for a town to live in. And now it had vigour and muscles, which meant it had prosperity; and always would have, so long as Skelstrand was running, and people needed steel. The women buying at the market stalls wore good thick overcoats, and were filling their baskets with goods for which they paid from stout leather purses. There was a press at the entrance to Woolworth's, and another round the Stag, including a small group supporting a little man who had lunched too well—he was, Andrew saw with surprise, the little Labour councillor, Jimmy Jafet. Farther out, where the fly-over bridge looped in modern fashion above the now disused level-crossing of the railway, he looked back across the roofs to the hill up which the new housing estate grew like a creeper on a wall, every domestic chimney emitting its foliage of smoke; and, away to the right, the mountain of scrap which had been accumulating for six months or more, and to replenish which would be a continual worry once the furnaces began to consume; while ahead the new road, flanked with freshly-painted advertisement hoardings, rushed like a white river towards the tall wrought-iron entrance gates to the mill. The commissionaire saluted him and he told the driver to pull up by the gatehouse, where he got out and looked with gratification at the busyness of the scene, lorries turning in and out over the huge concrete foreway, squads of workmen moving in multiple directions, sign-posts, a three-ton lorry laden with carboys of acid, a trailer bearing a brightly green-painted transformer, and the distant clangour of a trip-hammer.

"Happen to know where Mr. Neve is?" he asked.

"He was here a minute ago, sir," replied the commissionaire, "I think he went into the first bay. Boy! Run over and see if Mr. Neve's there, and tell him Mr. Andrew wants him."

At that "Mr. Andrew", like the old-retainer stuff, he suddenly thought of his father and, guilty, went into the gate office to telephone Dr. Irons. Much the same. A few words about temperatures, a hint at the possibility of a blood transfusion, a hastily arranged appointment for that evening to discuss it.

When he came out of the office, Charles Neve was waiting for him. He greeted him with pleasure. "Let's talk, Charles. And let's walk down the middle. I want to have a look at the place."

"Miss it so much in just a few days?"

Andrew laughed. "Shocking, ain't it? But as a matter of fact I did."

They turned across the foreway in the direction of the melting shops.

"Successful trip?" asked Neve.

"Appleton thinks so. Of course, I was lost in all that talk—just did what he told me."

"You're coming on, aren't you?" said Neve, looking at him curiously. "I never thought, when your father first pushed you on to me, that you'd take it seriously. But you have. You're nearly ready to run this place."

"If you'll stay and help, me boy."

"Oh, as to that. . . ."

They stepped across the rail-tracks which were now laid for the ingot trains and entered the main building of the mill, where the winter light through the high windows mixed palely with the yellow electric bulbs festooned high up on cables. Men were working everywhere, in the nearly-constructed furnaces, in the soaking pits, on the platforms high up, on the vast crane in the roof. Skelstrand was no longer a shell, but a nearly-completed organism. From this western end Andrew let his eye run down the length of the mill, brick and steel and concrete, into the dimness of distance. And all the way down the centre the machinery was there, men fiddling with it at every point, and the echoing clangour of steel on steel, like the sound of a giant railway station. Step in step with Neve he began to walk down the length of the mill, Neve pointing out to him the things that were being done. Here at the centre of it, with the mill around him, and beyond that the town now dependent on it, the several thousand personal lives and family stories that hung to some extent upon his actions, Andrew felt a sense of panic. This was what George would sell and re-invest in gilts. And here by his side was the dependable man against whom Cynthia would try her dirty little hints and intrigues, to separate him from him. He glanced warmly at Charles, with an impulse to put his arm around his shoulders and assure him of his friendship.

232

As they came towards the site of the roughing stands there was a group of men putting down more concrete in a side bay. Neve, with a little jerk of his head, said, "See that fellow over by the mixer, the little chap with the blue shirt?"

Andrew nodded.

"That's friend Papelian."

"Goo' lor'," said Andrew. "Do you know, I've never actually seen him before. He don't look so fierce."

"It'd be nice to know what he was up to."

"Is he up to anything? You mean that sabotage story? What's happened about that, Charles? You're not taking it seriously, are you?"

"I just don't know. There have, as you know, been piddling little attempts, amounting to nothing. But Jabby, the Pole, sticks to his story that there's going to be a big one."

Andrew waved his arm towards the ceiling of the vast building, and towards the massive machines being foundation-bolted into the concrete. "How could anything touch that?" he asked.

Neve replied by jerking his thumb at the nearest group of workmen. "True. But almost anything could touch them. Somebody has been deliberately spreading nerviness."

They turned out through a side door and went into Neve's office. Andrew perched himself on a stool, and Neve leaned on the drawing desk.

"Jabby insists," said Neve, "that there are enough of these stolen explosives in this district, somewhere hidden, to make a real dent. Yesterday he came to me and said it'll happen within the next week."

Andrew sucked his thumb. "Do you believe him? How does he know?"

"He's not a fool, and he has some sort of private contacts down into the political stuff among the men. On the other hand, he's damn nearly crazy with bias against anything that smells of even a whiff of Reds. I don't know, Andrew. I just don't know."

"Anything we can do about it?"

"I'm putting on a private watch at night—couple of chaps

I can rely on, and Bill Cross my foreman, and Jabby, who insists, and myself. We take spells."

"I'd like to join you."

"If you want to, but it's damn dull. Better wait till we've got something a bit more to go on. I'll let you know if there's anything doing."

Andrew nodded. "Well, I must get back into town, and I suppose I'd better show up at home, eh? Liz been doing her stuff with you all right while I've been away?"

All that Neve replied was a joking, "Oh, sure." But as he drove back into the town Andrew kept fancying that there was some implication in the intonation of it. But this, he told himself angrily, was only his imagination poisoned, as she had intended it should be, by the thing that Cynthia had said. It was a shock to realize how one remark could make a whole relationship shabby.

4

THE week passed during which, according to the Pole, an attempt at sabotage was to be made; and nothing happened. Andrew laughed, and put the thing out of his mind.

Besides, it needed no melodrama to add to his anxieties. The humdrum ones were sufficient. There was his father, who still lay in his illness, still protracted. The specialists from London hummed and said nothing much, but Gilbert Irons told him frankly that it was remarkable the old man was still alive, the vitality still there.

"Can we hope?" asked Andrew.

"The truth is, no doctor knows the answer to that one. By medical standards, no. But by medical standards he ought to be dead already. And, so far as I can see, he's not quite as bad now as he was a month ago. I should hope, but in moderation."

Andrew went frequently to Overskel, but it was little use taking this news to his mother. Lady Gazzard now lived in a dressing-gown and a mist of prayers. When she could be brought to talk to him, it was usually about the early days of her married life, and the ambitions she had then entertained for her family. Andrew was sorry for her, but not because she was his mother. He was puzzled to find that there was nothing emotional in that relationship any more, and he wondered whether there ever had been. For his father, when he went up into the bedroom to see him, he had much more feeling. Andrew sat for a long time in a chair by the window, gazing at the old man who lay half-sleeping in the bed, thinking that this was the man who gave him life, and who was likely soon to die, leaving him, Andrew felt, woefully lonely, and with ponderous burdens. It was Christmas Eve, and for no particular reason that seemed to make the moment sadder than ever. Then the old man woke and was for a few minutes quite lively in his mind. He said, strangely, nothing about Skelstrand or business, but talked only of Elizabeth. "Trust her, son," he said, "trust her."

"Oh, rather," Andrew awkwardly replied.

"When I'm gone, she's the one to listen to."

"Come off it," Andrew tried, "you'll be up and about, right as rain, in no time now. The doc says so."

From the bed the old man grinned at him, one of his former wicked grins. "Be a shock for you all, wouldn't it, if I should?"

Then the vitality seemed to go out of him and he dozed away again, so quietly that Andrew had a moment of fear until he moved a little, and grunted. He sat on for another half-hour or so as the light faded from the sick-room, thinking of Elizabeth. Could it be true that she was having an affair with Charles? It could be, for all he knew. He knew so little of her, man and wife though they were. And had he, he asked himself, any right to quarrel with her if it were true? He had not married her because he was in love with her, but because he had been told to, bribed to. Perhaps she had known that from the start, and felt therefore no particular obligation to him.

After a time he stood up and crossed quietly to the bedside. His father lay with his head to one side on the pillow, uneasily sleeping. Andrew walked softly from the room, gently closing the door, and down the stairs and out of the house without speaking to anybody. He set out on the footpath to his home, suddenly seized with the intention of bringing this thing to an end, and asking Elizabeth straight out whether it were true or not. But by the time he had crossed the two fields, and could see the lights of Down Mill through the trees, the decision had gone out of him. When he got in, Elizabeth was waiting dinner for him. He looked at the set table, the pleasant room with a log fire burning, his wife sitting opposite him. And suddenly he told himself what a fool he would be to mar all this. Even if it were true—and he did not believe it, but even supposing it were—then let it be.

"Seeing as it's Christmas Eve," he said jovially, "how about let's get the car out and go down to the Stag for a little something? We could ring Charles, and Pomeroy and his wife, and Gilbert if you like. Have a bit of a party, eh? There's too much gloom about the place."

Elizabeth nodded. "All right, I'd like to."

"You nip up and powder your nose, and I'll do the phoning. Okay?"

When she came down again, wrapped in her fur coat, he told her that everything was arranged. In the car, as they turned out of the gate on to the road into town, he squeezed her knee and grinned, "Nothing like a bit of whoopee to do the heart good, old thing."

Elizabeth smiled at him and said, "You're rather charming, you know, Andrew."

He pressed jubilantly on the accelerator and they sped along the road, Elizabeth warning him to look out, he was going far too fast; and Andrew putting back his head and laughing. They must have been doing nearly sixty round the bend just before the gates of Shard when Elizabeth screamed, Andrew jammed on his brakes and the car went looping across the road, he clinging over the wheel to try to avoid a shooting brake which suddenly appeared in front of them, travelling in the same direction. He thought for a second that the car would overturn, but just managed to right it as he pulled across the rear of the other vehicle, catching bumper and wing, then wrenching free. He got the car to a halt on the grass verge on the wrong side of the road, with one forewheel dipping over the ditch. "Phew!" said Andrew.

The shooting brake, though the glancing blow had slewed it, pulled straight again and drove on.

He took out his cigarette-case. "Have one? We need it."

Elizabeth, the cigarette in her mouth, bent towards his hands cupped round his lighter. She said nothing.

"Okay, I admit it," he agreed, "I was going too fast. Sorry. But, honest, I didn't see him until I was absolutely on top of him. God knows where he came from—there's a straight bit back there, and I saw no lights. Materialized from nowhere. Unless," he added jokingly, "he was one of your father's friends, coming out of those gates."

He put the car into reverse and gingerly eased it back; the grass verge was very muddy, and for a moment he thought the wheels would spin, but they just managed to grip. When he had the car on the macadam again, he got out and walked to the front, inspecting damage.

"It's all right," he said, getting in again, "only the wing. Nothing much."

"Andrew," she said, "you don't think that car really did come out from Shard?"

"Well, it could have done. I'm damned if I know. I was going too fast, I admit it."

"No, but seriously. Henry's all alone up there, except for Mrs. Cushion. And there have been robberies in the county. . . ."

"If you're worried, Liz, we'll go up and see."

"Oh no," she said, "it's too damned silly. He just didn't have much of a rear light, and we didn't see it, that's all. Come on, let's get to the pub. I could do with a drink."

So Andrew started the car and drove, much more carefully, to the Market Square. Pomeroy and Venetia were already waiting for them in the Stag, and had to be told all about the near accident. Soon Gilbert Irons came in, and the story had to be done again. Gilbert clucked reprovingly.

"You're a fine one to lecture," said Pomeroy. "Worst driver in the town, as everybody knows."

"Thirty-five years," replied Gilbert with satisfaction, "and not a smudge on me licence."

"By the way," asked Elizabeth, "where's Charles? You did ring him, didn't you, Andrew?"

"Sure. He ought to be here by now. But he'll be along. Probably breaking off a date with a girl friend."

As he said it, he thought he saw a quick glance between Pomeroy and his wife. But then he told himself to stop being an ass, imagining things that weren't there, and he turned to the bar to get another round. Then there were Merry Christmases to be wished, and joking and laughter, and friends in the bar to nod to, and Venetia and Elizabeth chattering away of this gossip and that. Still no Charles. Half an hour later Gilbert commented on his absence, and Andrew said he'd give him a proper ticking-off in the morning; but he could not help wondering what had happened to delay him. On the phone, he had promised to set out straight away. But after another ten minutes Charles came into the bar, arriving unexpectedly behind them, and being greeted with a chorus of derisory questions.

"Sorry," he apologized, "I got tied up. Well, as a matter of fact it was business."

"Delayed at the office," crowed Pomeroy. "That's not too good a one, old boy."

"Well, now you are here," said Andrew, "you've got some drinking to make up. Dorothy, treble whisky for Mr. Neve."

They went on chattering, and Andrew, standing back a little, found himself watching Charles and Elizabeth. They were not paying much attention to each other. But then, perhaps that was just it; they were not paying enough attention to each other, deliberately. He was caught, shamefaced, in this thought by Charles himself glancing round at him, and then stepping quietly over.

"Listen, Andrew, just after you rang, Jabby turned up. He insists that it's to-night. That's where I've been, out at Skelstrand."

"Cripes," said Andrew, "do you reckon there's anything in it?"

Neve turned to lean on the bar, so that they seemed merely

in casual talk with each other, but out of hearing of the others.

"I don't know. Nothing's happening out there so far. But it wouldn't be a bad night for it, you know—Christmas Eve, everybody a bit sozzled, nobody much about."

"What have you done?"

"I've got Bill Cross, and Jabby himself, and a couple of men I can trust, on the prowl up there. I've had the night-watchmen specially picked for more than a week now, and I sent the man on the main gate home. Told him we had a rush electrical job to do, so we'd take on his shift. He went easy enough—got his son home from the Army for Christmas."

"You going back?"

"Aye."

"I'll come too."

"How can you," asked Neve, "without letting them know there's something up?" He glanced over at the party.

"I'll tell Liz," he said, remembering his father that afternoon.

"You two secret drinkers?" Gilbert called across.

"Just slipping a couple in while you weren't looking," said Andrew cheerfully, moving back.

Venetia, luckily, was worried about the bird which she intended to stuff that night, ready for the morning, and the party made to break up. When they got out to the cars he let the others drive away, full of merry wishes, and then told Elizabeth that he wanted her to drive back alone. "There may be some trouble up at the mill, and I'm going up there with Charles."

"This sabotage thing you've been worrying about?" she asked.

"There's some scare about it."

"Can I come?"

"'Fraid not, old girl."

"Charles," she said, "is this dangerous?"

He answered, from the darkness of his turned-up coat collar, "We'll probably get lumbago, that's about all. It's a phoney, I'm sure. But we have to go, in case."

"Take care of him, Charles, won't you?" she asked. Then she let in the clutch and moved off.

5

ANDREW got into Neve's car and they followed her as far as the road junction, watching that she turned off for home. Then Neve turned away to the right, along the white new road to Skelstrand. Andrew found himself reading the advertisement hoardings in the light of the headlamps.

When they got to Skelstrand gates Neve shut off his lights. A man came over and, when he saw who it was, opened one gate sufficiently to let the car in, then securely locked it.

"Anything doing?" asked Neve.

"Not a thing, sir."

"Where's Mr. Cross?"

"He told me to tell you he'd be working his way back along the main fence."

"Come on, then," said Neve.

He and Andrew got out of the car and began walking along the outer service road, eastwards. Neve put a heavy torch in his hand, but said not to use it unless he had to. They went on in silence, the heavy wire fence on their left, the massive wall of the mill on their right, and every now and then outbuildings, stationary locomotives, parked lorries or piles of boxes, in the darkness behind which it was possible to imagine anything.

"Nobody could get through this fence," whispered Andrew.

"You can cut wire."

A pause as they walked. "But even if they did, could they get into the mill itself?"

"It's open at the far end, but I've got a man posted there."

Suddenly Neve checked him with a hand laid lightly on his arm. In the shadow behind a wall was a deeper shadow. Andrew gripped his torch. But Neve, after a moment, went on. It was the foreman, Cross, incredibly silent for his bulk.

"Well, Bill?"

"Not a break in the wire anywhere, and nobody's tried. I've been all along."

"It's a phoney," said Neve. "Where's master Jabby? Time we talked to him again."

"We fixed a meeting place in that builder's hut at the far end."

"Okay." And they went on.

As they came round the far end of the mill, another shadow materialized.

"Anything happened?" asked Neve.

"Not a thing, sir."

"Are the others in the hut?"

"Jabby's in there, and a couple of the others."

Neve nodded, and led the way. It was cramped with the six of them inside the hut. A hurricane lantern stood on the floor, the window thickly covered to shade even its meagre light.

"Well, Jabby," said Neve, "so what?"

The Pole shook his head and muttered, "It is to-night. That I know."

Andrew stared at him with curiosity. A tall thin figure in a huge coat, from which his head rose like a scrawny turkey's. He knew, of course, that the others by now disbelieved him. But the look of him impressed Andrew. He had a stance of authority, of a man suddenly resuming the position of command which he had once habitually occupied, but had long since abandoned. The others might think it a delusion, but this fanatic was sure.

"Does it make sense?" asked Neve. "The wire is sound. The place is always guarded. Anybody who wanted to break in would know that. The only possible plan would have been to cut the wire previously, in some out-of-the-way place, and patch it temporarily so that it could be torn aside in a few minutes. But they haven't done it, Jabby. The wire is sound."

The Pole listened in silence, head sunk in thought. Then suddenly he raised his eyes, snapped his lean fingers.

"Stupid fool that I am," he whispered. "The sea!"

They all stood quiet for a moment, pondering.

"Well, Bill," asked Neve, "what do you think?"

"Might be," replied the foreman. "There's five miles of

241

shore, and six of us. That's a mile each, and one of us can have a kip. It's bloody silly, guv."

"The sea," repeated Jabby, "that must be the way."

"If he's right," ventured Andrew diffidently, "I suppose they'd be making for this end of the mill. To get in, I mean. So if it was my party I'd try and land this end."

Neve said, "You want to try it?"

"Anyway, it would be a bit of fun."

"It'd be bloody cold," said Bill Cross.

Neve turned out the lantern and they left the hut.

"Single file," he instructed. "No use spreading out, we'd only lose touch. You lead, Bill. Keep a fix on that star."

They set off, Cross in front, Jabby behind him, then the two men who to Andrew were nameless, then Andrew himself and Neve in the rear. For a time Andrew kept his eyes on the middle of the man's back in front of him, but he stumbled once or twice over roots and roughnesses in the ground. Neve caught his elbow to steady him, and whispered, "Better watch your feet, I'll steer."

So he walked cautiously on, watching his feet as they followed one another across the rough earth, that gave way to rising and falling sand dunes, and grass tufts. Then he collided with the man in front, grunted, and realized they had stopped. Neve stepped swiftly to the head of the line, Andrew following him. Cross was standing there, listening. They all listened. From the distance, where the shore lay, there was a sound of something being dragged. And then a light thud, as something fell.

"Cripes," murmured Andrew.

Neve motioned them all together. "I'll lead now," he instructed in a whisper. "Quietly does it, as far as we can. When I put my torch on, run for them. Got it?"

There was a murmur of assent.

"Where's Jabby?" asked Andrew softly.

Neve glanced round, and began quietly to swear. The Pole had vanished.

"Bloody fool. See if we can catch up with him. If anybody gets to him, hold him back. Andrew, you'd better keep out of this."

"Not much."

There was no time to argue. Neve moved them forward as fast as he could. But before they could reach the next sand dune there was the sound of a man running and screaming out foreign words.

"Come on," shouted Neve. No use in concealment now. They all ran, up and over the dunes. Andrew, panting, was dimly aware of shouts and hubbub ahead. He tripped. By the time he had picked himself up and got there, he found them standing around a few long boxes that lay just inside the water mark. From the darkness beyond came the stutter of an outboard engine.

"Five of the swine," growled Cross. "If that bloody Pole hadn't...."

"Where is he?" asked Neve, alarmed.

They found him lying a few yards beyond the boxes, the blood seeping from his forehead where he had been struck by a bar.

Bill Cross dropped down and lifted him gently.

"He's alive, guv, but pretty bad."

One man ran off to get a car as close as he could. The others stripped coats, formed a stretcher and began to carry him in.

"The bloody fool," muttered Cross, tenderly.

"One of you stay and guard those boxes," ordered Neve, "I'll send a lorry."

Andrew, walking beside the man on the stretcher, saw his eyes open and his mouth twist. He bent down, and got the words, painfully uttered. "It is not matter. Put me in hospital, but do not say. Say accident."

Andrew held his hand and walked beside him. When they at last stopped, he was aware of a darker darkness ahead, almost pressing down on him. He looked up and saw that it was the great wall of the mill.

6

EARLY on Christmas morning Andrew went to see Tom Jenkins, the Police Superintendent, a man of great dignity and pliability, who received him with deference. Some accident, he understood, there had been at Skelstrand during the night, and greatly he appreciated Mr. Gazzard's trouble in reporting to him personally.

"Look here," said Andrew, "I'm going to tell you straight what happened." And he did. "But we don't want any hint of it to get out, Superintendent. That was their object, to make a noise of the thing. I don't want to play their game. And there's no harm done, except to poor Jabby."

Jenkins, fiddling with a pencil, looked grave. "And suppose he should die, Mr. Gazzard?"

"Why, then, of course, it's different. I rang the hospital this morning, and they thought he would be all right. What I am suggesting is that you should make your inquiries behind the scenes."

Tom Jenkins nodded. "You can rely on me, Mr. Gazzard, to handle this matter personally, myself." And then he added, with finger raised, "And it suddenly comes to me. Yes, where's that report I had this morning?" He turned to a pile of papers on his desk, searching. "There was a car, in the early hours, coming from the harbour area, going too fast for one of my constables to stop it. Now, if these fellows put round in their boat somewhere into the harbour, where they'd left the car, and then drove off in it. . . . Ah, here we are, here's the report. Yes, hum, so-so, so-so, yes, shooting brake, very muddy, travelling over fifty miles per hour, unable to stop same, unable to read number-plate as no rear light. Ah."

Andrew, feeling afraid and sick, muttered, "Not much to go on, then."

"If there was a boat that was left, there'd be that to go on, Mr. Gazzard. But leave it to me, sir, leave it to me. Absolute discretion, I promise you."

Thanking him, Andrew was shown out. He drove slowly homewards through the quiet streets of Christmas morning. As he came to the gates of Shard he almost turned in; but decided against it at that moment, and went on home. A shooting brake, with no rear light.

Later in the day he and Elizabeth did go to Shard, to make a Christmas call on her father. He received them in the drawing-room, coldly polite, and they went through the ceremony of exchanging gifts, pretending it was a gay thing to do. Elizabeth tried to persuade him to come back to lunch with them, but he would not; Mrs. Cushion had prepared for him, and he could not disappoint her. It was stiff, but quite normal and ordinary.

The rest of the day dragged on, and in the evening they had to endure a family dinner party at Overskel. George had come down from London, and Cynthia of course was there, but Lady Gazzard, in spite of having her three children round her table, was tearful because her husband, on Christmas Day, still lay in bed upstairs. Andrew, in desperation, drank more than he normally would. Cynthia and Elizabeth seemed able to chatter quite affably together—which vaguely irritated Andrew, remembering what his sister had hinted— and his fate was to listen to George's pompous, slow-spoken comments on politics and the opera season; cripes, what a bore old George had become! After dinner Andrew managed to get away upstairs to see his father, who was awake and, seemingly, better than of late. Andrew talked and the old man listened, putting in a word now and then. Suddenly Andrew noticed Gazzard's face smiling with pleasure and, looking over his shoulder across the dimly-lit room, saw that Elizabeth had come in. She kissed the old man and took a seat by his bedside, Andrew standing back a little and watching them together. He felt now a moment of restfulness, almost of happiness, better than he had felt all day, watching his wife and his father so friendly with each other, so in tune, in peacefulness like a family. After a while, when they left the old man, Andrew was in more comfortable mood, putting his arm through hers and squeezing her hand; but she did not respond. He took her home soon after, silent in the car. When he came in from the garage she was sitting by the fireside, with whisky and a siphon on a tray beside his chair.

"Have a nightcap," she said. "I want to talk about something."

He poured the drinks and then settled, comfortably sipping. "Well?"

"When you went to London, you did fix things all right, didn't you? I mean, it worked out? I know the whole thing was in the balance, and that your father had staked more than he ought. Is it all right now, Andrew? Could you get out of it and leave the old man with his money safe?"

"Appleton says so, duckie. I suppose it's all right. It could still be tricky, but it should go along now."

"Then let's get out."

"Get out? You mean leave Skelstrand?"

"Leave the whole place. It's beginning to frighten me. We have enough money, haven't we? Let's go and lead useless lives somewhere."

"What's this all in aid of, Liz? What gives?"

"I began thinking about it last night, when I was waiting for you and wondering what was happening. I suddenly realized how we are all being caught up in this huge mechanical thing, and being changed, and altered into different people. Not only you and I, but everybody who has anything to do with it, everybody in the town if you like. Little Jimmy Jafet, for instance. Did you hear about him?"

"Nothing special."

"He has got himself mixed up with some speculative builder who corrupted him, and then cheated him out of his money, and now threatens to expose him unless he finds a hundred pounds or some such sum."

"How do you know this?"

"He went to see Henry, who has helped him before. But he could get no sense out of him, so he came to see me. This was when you were in London. It was so pathetic. Little Jimmy who was all starry and brave new world, and can now be bought for a few pounds."

"Send him to see me," said Andrew.

She nodded. "I told him to. But it wasn't so much him as Henry himself. I went to talk to him, and I think he is going over the edge. Andrew, it's pitiful. He meant something here once, something rather worth while. And now he's an old man with an obsession. He hates me now because I married you, and you are Skelstrand. I'm scared he'll do something crazy."

246

"Such as?"

"I don't know. I have a feeling of evil all round me. We're caught up in this thing that breeds hatred and corruption. So much hatred that now a man has been nearly killed over it. Andrew, we must get clear."

He considered, and suddenly made up his mind. "I wasn't going to tell you this yet, but I think I ought. The probability is that the men who had a go at Skelstrand last night were travelling in a shooting brake without a rear light."

"A shooting brake? Like the one that . . . ? Oh, Andrew, you don't mean. . . ."

"I've been asking myself that question all day. Did it come out of Shard?"

She got up and turned towards the fireplace. "Oh God!" she said.

"Now, come on, old thing, it's probably all imagination."

Elizabeth shook her head. "My dread is that he has gone mad."

"That's drawing it a bit steep."

"Mad from hatred. From the moment he started hating Skelstrand I feared the obsession. Gilbert Irons knew it too. We were both afraid that some day the obsession would swamp him. Everything that happened made it worse, by giving him more to hate. When your family came here, he hated you. When I married you, he hated me. He thought our marriage was a betrayal. As it was, Andrew. It was."

"A betrayal of what?" asked Andrew, quietly.

"Of ourselves, of values. You were not in love with me. You married me because your father offered you money to."

"Who told you?"

"I heard. And then I challenged your father with it. He was quite frank; from his own point of view, quite logical."

"It's true, of course, or it was then. Did you know it at the time?" he asked.

She shook her head.

"Then why did you marry me, Liz? Where was your betrayal?"

"For money, I suppose. It was obvious that you had a lot. And I have always wanted money."

247

"Aren't we saying things that we shan't be able to unsay?"

"We had better say them, Andrew. This is why I am asking you to give up Skelstrand, to go away, to get clear of the whole thing. Then we might have a chance."

"A chance?"

She turned to face him. "Charles and I are in love with each other. I think we were before I married you, but I didn't know then. Not for sure."

He sat looking at her, his face immovable.

"I thought I could keep our marriage, Andrew, and have Charles too. I persuaded him of it. There was to be Skelstrand, and you getting the money out of it. And Charles was to take your offer to stay on, and privately we would be lovers. Now you know."

"I already knew."

"Did you? I wondered. I thought that perhaps you did, and it didn't matter to you. You had your bargain, the money. It could have worked out."

"Yes, it could have worked out," he agreed in a low voice. "And now it can't?"

"No, Andrew, it can't. A man was nearly killed last night. And I suddenly understood how rotten the whole thing has made us all. If we stay on, it will destroy Charles, and perhaps you. That is why I beg you to get away from it. Let's go away, Andrew, get clear of the whole damnable thing, and then perhaps we shall be able to see more sensibly."

He got up and put the fireguard in front of the embers of the grate, as though by this ordinary action before going to bed he wanted to make the scene normal and customary.

"But, Liz," he said quietly, "should we settle anything by running away? The funny thing is, you know, that I want to stay, because it's my job. I want to get that mill working, and keep it working. I just feel like doing that job. If I left it now, I should never do anything useful again. And after a time you wouldn't think much of me."

"Does that matter to you, Andrew?" she asked.

"Yes," he said, "it does rather. I haven't much of a claim on you, I know that. It's true that I married you because the old man put up money. And I was just a bit of a clown. Still am, really. If you left me and went to Charles, I couldn't blame either of you, I haven't the right, when you come to look at it. But I couldn't stick it if you despised me—or if Charles did either. I respect him. And as a matter of fact I'm in love with you. Awkward, ain't it?"

He tried to grin cheerfully. But she began to weep.

"Oh lord," he said, "don't let's decide anything now. Let's think it over, old girl. Probably work out in the end, somehow or other. We can't chuck it in five minutes anyway, lots of things would have to be arranged."

7

WHEN work re-started on the mill a couple of days later he still had the problem with him, unresolved. To throw it in on Liz's implied promise to go away with him and make something fresh of their marriage; or to stay on to see Skelstrand up and let the personal things work out as they might. But once he got back to work other decisions and events came pressing on him so hard that he had little time for pondering.

There was Superintendent Jenkins with what he had so far discovered. "Ah yes, Mr. Gazzard, there was a boat, pinched from one of the fishing quays and returned unharmed. And we have got the shooting brake—abandoned, thirty miles from here, near a big railway station. It is one that had been stolen in Leeds six months ago, and never found since. Nasty knock it had had on the back."

"And the men?" asked Andrew.

The Superintendent shrugged in despair. "What have we got to go on? I think some of them were local—that is my guess—and some came from London, say, or Glasgow. I am trying to do this very quietly, Mr. Gazzard, as you know. We police sometimes move slowly, but in the end we usually get results. But slowly, Mr. Gazzard, for reasons which you appreciate. And in this case we have plenty of time. No need to rush, or cause a fuss.

"Of course," he added, "if the Pole should die it would become a different matter."

If the Pole should die. But Jabby was not, thank God, going to die. Andrew went several times to the hospital, and the reports were good. At last Jabby, still desperately weak, was allowed to talk to him.

"Did you recognize any of them, Jabby?"

He shook his head.

"Was Papelian there?"

Jabby smiled in faint derision. "It is not he who would take the risk."

Then there was a sudden visit from Jimmy Jafet, about whom Andrew had forgotten. When his name was sent up to the office, Andrew asked, "Who? Oh yes, Councillor Jafet. Show him in."

He came in like a cringe, it was pathetic. Andrew greeted him warmly, and said, "Now look here, Jimmy, my wife has told me that you have trouble. What's up?"

And out it all came—Halstead, the old school friend, whom he had obliged with a little technical advice on housing sites.

"As a councillor?" asked Andrew.

"Yes, Mr. Gazzard, damn it, as a councillor," burst out Jimmy in despair. "I admit it to myself now, though at the time I pretended that it was not so. I am ashamed. And I dare not take my punishment. I have resigned from the Bench, but I can't face making a confession."

He was, thought Andrew, taking his punishment all right, the wretched little man.

"It is my sister," he said, "I could not stand her to know that I have been dishonest. I could not."

"But none of this is to do with me, surely," protested Andrew quietly. "What do you want of me?"

"I want help, Mr. Gazzard. For I have been more than a knave. I have been a fool. When I took money from him, I did not know where to put it without letting it be known that I had it. So he said I could re-invest it in the housing estate. So I did. I gave it back to him."

"Oh dear," murmured Andrew.

"But it is worse. When I wanted money, I signed notes to him. Not for very much—or not for very much at a time. But then he said there was interest, exorbitant interest. And the total was greater than the sum I had invested, by more than one hundred pounds. He is pressing me, and I cannot pay him."

"Why don't you tell him to go to hell?"

"Then it would all come out, and my sister would know. As it is, I fear she will know anyway. Halstead says if I cannot pay he must sell me up. Oh my dear heavens!"

"Jimmy, I'm sorry about this. But why do you think I should help you?"

"To avoid a scandal in the town, Mr. Gazzard. I am not asking for a gift, but only a loan, except that I cannot pay interest from my wages on the railway. Where else should I turn? If this had happened to me in the old days I would have gone to Colonel Melmoth. I did go to him. But he is not the rich man any more. Shard used to govern Gulport. Now it is Skelstrand that does. That is you."

"No," dissented Andrew, "that is my father. My father wouldn't lend you a hundred pounds."

Jimmy Jafet sat twiddling his hat. "Your father's days are finished, Mr. Gazzard. He was a capitalist, a self-made man, and all honour to him for it, though I do not agree with the system that allowed it. But that is changed. You are not a capitalist. You control Skelstrand as a partner of the Government, on trust. You hold this wealth as much in trust for the town and its people as Colonel Melmoth used to hold his land. You have a part to play here, and so have I. There are many things I have done for this town. I have been useful to my fellow-men. Now, unless you help me, my usefulness will come to an end. It is my own fault, but which of any of us has not at some time been a fool, if not a knave? On my past record, I have some claim to be helped."

"Jimmy," said Andrew after a pause, "I will not lend you the money direct. But send this builder to me, and I will pay what is necessary—I think we shall do it cheaper that way. Then you will pay me back a pound a month—can you manage that? Good.

"And, Jimmy," he added, as after protestations of gratitude the little man was leaving his office, "don't do it again. I shan't help you next time."

For days afterwards Andrew's thoughts returned to what Jimmy Jafet had said. He remembered it every time he wanted to consider Elizabeth's plea that he should sell out of Skelstrand and leave. It was an uncomfortable argument that he could not counter. Responsibility. When he felt the weight of it, he groaned. But it was there. Would it mean that because of this responsibility for which he had not asked, he must lose his wife? It might, he acknowledged. He would have to have the thing out with Charles, there would be no help for that. But he kept on putting it off. And in any case he had other things to talk to Charles about. For early in the New Year Superintendent Jenkins came to him again with a little more proof, a little more discovery. Somebody had seen the boat put out, late on the night in question, with five men in it; four strangers, but one local man he could recognize, a young fellow named Tom Bruell who worked in an insurance office and was well known to associate with the Communists, particularly with Bert Papelian. The Superintendent thought he had enough to pull Bruell in for questioning, but he was not going to act precipitately, seeing how delicate the matter was. And, he added, the young fellow came of a respected local family—son of the publican at Shard Green, a fine old chap, great sorrow it would be to him.

When he had got rid of the policeman, Andrew drove out to Skelstrand to find Charles Neve, to tell him all he knew, and the one thing he suspected and feared.

"Melmoth?" asked Neve. "It's not possible."

"Think not?"

"No," replied Neve after a pause. "I don't think not."

Suddenly he was blazing angry. "The bloody old fool! Mr. bloody squire, pretending to be God."

"I'm going out to challenge him with it," said Andrew. "Will you come?"

Neve hesitated, then nodded. They drove out in silence to Shard. Mrs. Cushion, who opened the door, said nervously that the Colonel was in his study. Andrew replied that they would go to him there. They found him sitting upright in his chair, staring at his desk, on which stood the photograph of his son. He looked up when Andrew and Neve entered, but did not seem to be surprised.

"Something pretty serious has happened," began Andrew. "On Christmas Eve there was an attempt to sabotage Skel-strand with explosives. It didn't come off, but one man was seriously hurt, nearly killed. The police have been inquiring quietly, and they are beginning to find out something about it. What they don't yet know is where the explosives, which had been stolen, were stored locally until the attempt was made."

"In my stables," said Melmoth, without emotion.

Andrew sat down in the chair facing him. Neve continued to stand by the door, staring sulkily at the old man.

"Well, I don't know what to say," said Andrew, adding irritably, "At any rate, don't go round admitting it."

"I have nothing of which to be ashamed, and nothing to fear."

"Oh, nuts! Suppose the police find out."

"If," said Melmoth with dignity, "Tom Jenkins requires any information from me, he has only to ask for an appointment. I think my record of public service, particularly on the Bench, is sufficient guarantee that I acted with the interest of the community at heart."

Andrew peered at him with a sudden suspicion that he had gone completely off his rocker.

"Who were the others?" asked Neve quietly from the door, but Melmoth ignored him.

"We know about Tom Bruell," said Andrew.

"They set down here an abomination," said Melmoth, still in a calm voice, "which it was my duty to destroy. I am Colonel Henry Melmoth, of Shard."

Neve said, without stepping forward, "A man was nearly killed. It might have been murder."

And Melmoth, staring at the photograph on his desk, replied, "Men have died before this."

"Look, Henry," Andrew began to plead, "this is devilish

serious, you must see that. There may be a criminal charge. I shall do my best to hush it up. But you must tell me, just me, who the others were. I must prevent it happening again."

"You? I should tell you? I loathe you." But suddenly he leered, got up from his chair and poked Andrew in the ribs. "I tell you what, my boy, you must come to dinner. And bring your wife, my boy, bring your wife, eh?"

Neve moved quickly, laying his hand gently on the old man's arm. "Come on, sir, sit down. Sit down, now."

Andrew, horrified, watched the old man glare at him, then suddenly nod and drop back into the chair, crumpled, head lowered. He put one hand on his desk, staring at it, moving the fingers. Neve, keeping an arm on his shoulder, muttered backwards to Andrew to get Doc Irons, ring up for him. Andrew, hastening to the phone in the hall, found himself shuddering. When he had started the doctor on his way he saw Mrs. Cushion standing quietly by the door, and he asked her to make some tea.

"I think he's very ill, Mrs. Cushion."

"Shouldn't we get Miss Elizabeth here, sir?"

"No, no. Not yet. Dr. Irons is coming."

She went away to make tea.

Back in Melmoth's study he found Charles sitting comfortably by his side, listening to him; and the old man babbling, no other word for it. What he said had no particular meaning for Andrew, jumbled phrases, with Elizabeth's name here and there, and occasionally Harriet's. Andrew waited in agony, standing by the door. It was to tell Liz that he feared. But at last Dr. Irons arrived, massive, ponderous, restful. Melmoth rose with a smile to greet him.

"Ah, Gilbert, have a glass of sherry."

"Love one, Henry, love one," he replied, "but let's have a look at this arm of yours now."

Obediently the old man took off his coat and let him roll back the shirt-sleeve, revealing the thin forearm into which Irons neatly injected a sedative. "And now, old fellow, you're going to lie down. Come along, I'll help you to bed."

He shook his head at Andrew's proffered aid. The two of

them were left to stare at each other until the doctor came down again.

"Nursing home," he said, "that's the only thing for it. He'll be all right now. Never was one for violence." He busied himself at the phone. "And, Andrew, you'd better go and break this to Liz. I don't want her here. Tell her he's going to be all right, but it'll take time. Hallo, hallo. Dr. Irons here. Put me through to the matron please. . . ."

"I'll drive you back," said Neve, touching Andrew on the shoulder and leading him to the door.

"Thanks, Charles. You're a good chap. I can rely on you."

"Oh, for God's sake," muttered Neve.

He drove him to Down Mill. "You tell Elizabeth yourself," he said. "It might be important in other ways."

Andrew nodded. Neve watched him turn abruptly and enter the house. Then he put his car into gear and got quickly out of the drive and on the road to Skelstrand. He tried not to think of human relationships. He was fed up with human relationships. He swore at himself for having fancied that he was in love with Elizabeth; that he could contemplate an indulgent life as her lover, scarcely troubling to hide the fact from Andrew, lazing out his days and drawing rich wages, like a ponce. It was suddenly amazing to him that he could be so softened by a woman. That was the sort of thing that happened only to tense idiots like Appleton. What was this woman that she could alter his life?—an intonation of voice that suddenly went husky, a trivial passion, a staring of breasts and a movement of limbs in a bed, a second-rate ecstasy and then indifference. He told himself that he had only one aim, to finish the job at Skelstrand and see the ribbon of hot steel rolling, and then to get out and on to something new.

As though to drive the point home, Skelstrand came into his view as he pulled the car round a bend in the road. The long cream building, stretching in perspective towards the squat outlines of the furnaces, and the distantly-seen derricks of the quay. As he swung his car in through the main gate, checking with the gate-keeper, he felt an impulse to do something to emphasize the reality of his mood, and at once he knew what it was that he had to do.

He went into his office and sent for Cross.

"Bill," he said, "get hold of Papelian and send him here."

The foreman, unconcerned, turned and went out. Neve waited, sitting motionless at his desk.

Papelian came in, bristling, suspicious, the little dark man ready to fight, expecting some controversy which perhaps he could turn to his account.

"I'm giving myself the pleasure," said Neve, "of doing this personally. You're out. You can collect a week's money from the pay office, and then scram."

"Me?" asked Papelian, flabbergasted, not quite as yet comprehending.

"Yes, you. And no reason given."

"You can't do that. It's victimization. You fire me, and I'll bring the whole lot out. You want to watch you're not too bloody clever. Fire the chairman of the shop stewards' committee? How do you think that'll sound?"

"I don't give a damn how it sounds. And, talking of being too clever, you might think a bit hard before you start something you might want to stop. I'll tell you one thing, Papelian. I've just been up to Shard."

"So what?"

"Nothing. That's all. Unless you'd like to know where I'm going next. I'm going down-town to have a talk with the Police Superintendent."

Papelian scoffed. "Do you think any of that frightens me? You may think you know a lot, but there are some things I reckon you don't know. Would you say young Gazzard wants his father-in-law mixed up in anything?"

"I wouldn't say anything like that. To you, I wouldn't say anything more at all. Get out."

"Not me."

But Neve, watching his eyes, saw a shadow of fear in them.

"If you're not off this mill in half an hour," he said deliberately, "I'll have the company police throw you off. And you can do whatever you bloody well like. Sue me, if you want. Call a strike, if you dare. I've put up with you for more than two years, but now it's over. Now, if you want a fight, you can have it, Papelian. Get it? And if you want to check your ground, go and ask a young fellow named Tom Bruell."

Papelian stared at him, then swung round and went out, saying nothing more.

Bill Cross, thumbs in the pockets of his leather waistcoat, sucked his teeth contemplatively. "I enjoyed that, Guv," he said. "Will he make trouble?"

"Could be, Bill. I rather hope so. Just at the moment I could do with somebody's head to knock in."

"Ah," said Cross. "Know how you feel. Feel the same way meself, sometimes."

8

CERTAINLY Bert Papelian, swinging on to the bus into Gulport, uneasy at its unaccustomed emptiness, brooded making trouble. He was not bitter or angry at his own dismissal, that was part of the fight, and had happened often enough before. All that mattered was how it could be used. He was not much of a theorist, he left that to Rosa. He could come out with Marx as readily as the next man, but privately he rarely thought of the coming revolution and the workers' State. He cared little for the victory; what he enjoyed was the struggle. That he, Bert Papelian, by his own tactics, could direct three thousand men, swing them into action, rouse them with his sharp speech, get his own back on the bastards who hated him—that was the thing. His instinct now was to convene the shop stewards' committee, put his case—victimization for union activities, a clear case. They'd follow him all right. Restitution, or they'd call all the men out. He pictured himself, with almost orgastic pleasure, leading the delegation back to Neve, spitting quiet ultimatory words at him. He wondered if it would be possible to get that lout of a foreman in somehow, to hear the fun.

But first he had better talk to Rosa.

He found her at home, lying on the rug before the gas fire, reading a book. She glanced up. "Hallo?"

"Neve fired me. Out, like that."

She sat up. "Why?"

"No reason given," he said.

"Tell me every word he said. Don't miss anything."

Papelian told her. Then he added, "I'm convening the shop stewards to-night. We'll have the whole bloody lot out in the morning."

She got up and leaned on the table. "He mentioned Tom, you say?"

"Sure. Threatened me with him."

"They must know more than we thought."

"So what? They've got nothing on us."

"Suppose Tom should talk?" she asked.

"Let him talk. What can he prove? Nothing, Rosa. I've taken bloody good care of that. He can talk himself into gaol, and old Melmoth too. But not us, girl, not us. Nor any of the others. He doesn't even know their names."

"The charge would be conspiracy," she mused. "There are long sentences for that."

"Bah!" he uneasily replied. "They can't touch us. Maybe they can get him, but that's his look-out."

"That wretched boy," she murmured.

"Look, Rosa, what is this? I told you from the first that the thing was dangerous and I didn't like it. You were the one who pushed it. I only agreed when it was clear that I was not personally mixed up in it. 'Try young Bruell, he's your instrument'—you said that. I'm not frightened of a sentence for myself. But I'm too valuable to the party to be wasted in prison. There aren't so many of us who can handle industrial action. I can. As for young Tom, he's no more good to us anyway. He's cracked up."

"You are not to call the men out," she suddenly ordered.

"What? Not call 'em out? What'm I to do, then? Just take my cards, say nothing, and slink off? You must be nuts. It's a chance from the gods."

"If you don't call a strike," she argued, "they'll probably hush the thing up because of Melmoth. If you do, you force their hand. Then they'll get Tom."

"Well, I can't help that."

258

"If you take action," she said slowly, "I shall leave you. If they charge Tom, I shall got to the police and lay information against you."

Papelian stared at her. "But why, Rosa, why?"

"I have my reasons."

"Have you fallen for this kid, or something?"

"Yes," she said, "yes. You may as well know—he doesn't. He won't, either. But I won't have him gaoled. Not even if it costs us a strike. Oh, I know—I'm betraying the party. Do you think I don't know? And care? I've argued myself daft. But it doesn't make any difference."

"I ought to beat the daylights out of you," threatened Papelian, moving towards her.

She stared coolly at him. "Go away now. I don't want to talk any more."

Slowly he lowered his raised arm, hesitated, then turned. At the door he defied her with, "I'm going to see the committee, to-night." But she did not answer him. She had said all she had to say. She moved across to her customary chair, sank into it and gazed through the window. So the police had got that far, they had got as far as Tom. Neve must be very sure of his case to fire Papelian, but she did not care about that. Nor, for that matter, she knew, did he. She wondered briefly whether he cared about knowing that she was in love with Tom. In love with Tom—she repeated it to herself as though admitting it for the first time, tenderly. Papelian, she imagined, would not greatly worry about that. There had never been much between them except a common devotion to an idea; or rather, her devotion to it, and his revengeful usefulness in carrying it into practice. But love she had despised, and love-making, to call it so, had been routine. Of all the nights on which they had copulated—his tentative caress of her breasts which she had to restrain herself to endure, the sudden heave of his body on to hers, the brief struggle during which he grunted, and then his sleepy exhaustion and her sleepless indifference—she could remember none as distinctive or worth the treasuring. To lose that was not, for either of them, to lose very much.

But it was not that at all that she felt for Tom. Perhaps it was merely pity. She admitted that that might be so. Certainly there was pity in it. When he had come there after the night of the Skelstrand attempt, the fear in his eyes had moved her. Papelian, she had thought, was a fool to have insisted on his actually going with the others; he did it only to embroil him irretrievably in the thing. Yet it was the very move that could betray them all—had, as it turned out, seemingly betrayed them. For if the police faced Tom with it, he would certainly give way and talk. He was bursting with the confession that he longed to make. His pitiful face, his nervous dismay, almost made it for him to any casual observer. As the weeks went by, he degenerated to the point of being perpetually on the edge of tears. Almost, she thought, he would now welcome arrest and punishment. But she was determined for him against it. As she sat motionless in her chair, the image of an escape formed in her mind; a break with Papelian, and she and Tom to go away together, to lose themselves in the crowded quarter of some big city, in a back room high up, with drab curtains to shut out the world.

As she sat there she saw through the window, to her surprise, that Tom himself was coming down the street, hurrying, evasive. The unexpectedness of it, at that time of day, made it seem as though he were only a shadow invading the phantasy of her thoughts. But when he came through the door he was physical enough in his terror.

"There was a policeman asking for me at my digs," he burst out. "He only just missed me. Rosa, they must know."

"Come here, Tom," she said. He ran across the room and clung to her, sobbing, slipping slowly down her body, on to his knees. She held his face against her breasts, warmed and stirred by the contact, and laid her fingers on his neck. "Yes, Tom, I'm afraid they know—or, at least, suspect."

"Oh God, what shall I do? What shall I do?"

"Stay quiet," she murmured, "and don't fear. You are safe with me."

He accepted that as a child would. The feverishness of his body permeated to hers. The top button of her blouse had slipped and his lips lay against her skin. She was acutely conscious of his right arm that, the hand clutching at her waist, was pressed into the hollow of her thigh as she sat.

"I will take you away, Tom," she whispered. "We will go away together."

"Away where?" he mumbled.

"It doesn't matter. To some city where we can lose ourselves." She understood, from his indifference, that he was not really listening, had not properly understood. "They will not look very hard for you, and I will see that they do not find you."

"Oh, Rosa, you are so kind to me."

For what seemed a long while they stayed quiet in the embrace. The warmth of it kindled her. Her thoughts began to run confused, unclear. She began slowly to ease herself from the chair, more closely towards him. The fingers which she had laid on his neck she edged forward to his cheek, to the corner of his mouth, under his chin. Then suddenly she raised his face to hers, at the same time slipping her body from the chair so that they knelt together on the floor. Without a cry she pressed her mouth to his, thrusting her tongue between his teeth, pushing her belly against his, so that they swayed and toppled slowly. She wrenched open her blouse, beginning to gasp his name, forcing her body at him on the floor. He began an automatic response, but his face was stupid with surprise, uncomprehending.

"Tom!" she cried.

She felt again for his mouth with hers. But suddenly he heaved himself up, swept her back with his arm so that she sprawled across the room.

"No, no!" he shouted, getting on to his knees. His eyes were filled with dismay.

"Tom," she begged, dragging herself towards him. "We need each other."

He sprang back from her clutching hand, got to his feet, and ran shuddering from the room. And she collapsed on the floor, her face pressed against her arm, her clothes awry, her outspread fingers spasmodically grasping. And she began to howl softly, like a mutilated thing.

After a little while she stopped, rose from the floor and sat in her chair by the window. She tried to consider what

261

Tom was likely to do now. Go to the police, make a confession that would involve them all? She did not much care. But she felt that he would not do that, he would be too frightened. Not that it would make much difference. Before long the police would find him. She wondered idly whether Papelian knew of this yet, and, if so, whether he would bolt. But that she doubted. He was, at any rate, prepared to fight and take risks for his beliefs. "Which I am not," she moaned to herself, "which I am not."

How long she sat there she did not know, nor did she notice, as usual, what went on in the street before her window. So she was startled by a tap on the door of her room, and by the entrance of a woman whom at first she did not recognize, and then saw to be Mrs. Henty, the parson's wife.

"May I come in?" she asked. Then, lacking reply, she crossed the room and sat on the window-ledge. The two women looked at each other. "This afternoon young Tom Bruell came to my house. He used to belong to my husband's church, and it was really Roger he was looking for. But Roger is away for a couple of days, so I had to do."

"Well?"

"He was in rather a state, and he broke down and—told me all about it."

"What did he want? Money?"

"Yes," said Dorothy, "and I'm afraid I was rather foolish about it. I gave him some. Just a pound or two. He said he had to get away, and I thought that, until we had sorted everything out a bit, it would be better if he did. He said that if he could get to Birmingham, he had a friend there who would help him."

Rosa was silent for a while. Then she said, "Do you know who the friend in Birmingham is? I thought not. It's the girl who got into trouble, the ironmonger's daughter, the girl he once thought he was going to marry."

"Oh dear," murmured Dorothy.

"She has become a sort of prostitute there. Tom went with her once, and the degradation of it nearly drove him out of his senses. If he goes back to her, she will destroy him."

Dorothy gestured helplessly.

"It does not matter," Rosa pursued. "We are all being destroyed. It was inevitable from the moment that this thing started."

"This thing?"

"The mill, the project to make steel to bolster up a system of rottenness, to strengthen people like the Gazzards, a weapon in the international fight against the working class. . . . But you know all this, and in any case I have no right to say it, having betrayed it."

"It isn't true," said Dorothy. "I can see your point of view, of course, but it isn't so. This is my town, I know it intimately. I could show you a hundred ways in which it has brought new life, new hopes, new ambitions, even happiness. It seems to me just part of the general human struggle to go on living, building things, making mistakes but meaning well—the way we all pass our time until we die."

"I no longer care," replied Rosa. "I am indifferent. I found out to-day that I no longer believe the things I have always believed. I am nothing, since I have lost faith. But you wouldn't know about that."

"It's my special subject."

"Yours?"

"For years. Not suddenly, but gradually." She smiled wryly. "It's particularly difficult, being married to a priest. As you are, in a way, aren't you? But I found I could keep it to myself. You and I meet half-way, you know. And after a time I found that I could get along with a sort of instinctive belief in human beings themselves, a feeling that on the whole they weren't bad, and that there is more kindness about than we have a right to expect. Kindness, that's the heart of it."

They fell silent and they looked at each other. Then Dorothy said, "You know, what we two lost women need most of all at this moment is a cup of tea."

Rosa, hesitated, then got out of her chair, almost smiling. "I'll put the kettle on," she said.

9

WHEN Andrew came into the house to tell her of her father's illness, Elizabeth was writing in her diary. She had started in a moment of idleness to keep this personal diary, and found in it a confessional. Years after, no doubt, she would glance at the sentence broken off in the middle, and recall that it was at that moment that Andrew came in and told her that Henry, as he tried gently to put it, had "had some sort of breakdown".

She wanted to go and see him at once, but it was days before Gilbert would let her. He explained that he was keeping him more than half doped—the induced rest which he believed all medicine fundamentally to be.

"And afterwards, Gilbert?" she asked.

"Well, my dear, if he were a young man there would be all sorts of things I should suggest trying. But, Liz, he is an old man. He is not insane, you know, and never will be. But he will ramble a bit. He will need looking after, that's all. Old age, Liz—call it that."

When at last she could go to the nursing home to see him, she found him gentle, happy, apparently quite normal, except that he did not talk about recent things. When she kissed him good-bye, touching the woollen dressing-gown he was wearing, and aware of the faintly antiseptic odour of illness, he smiled so peaceably at her that when she had left the room she began to cry. Andrew, waiting for her with the car, took her home to tea.

"Tremendous news to-day," he announced cheerfully, seeking for cheerful things to say.

"Yes?"

"We made some steel. Not much, just a drop or two, you know. Getting our hands in. We've got the machines set up, from the slabbing mill right down to the run-out table. And now we've got to start 'em up gently, work 'em in. It'll take time, of course, adjusting and all that. And we need a bit of material to play about with, so we made our first steel. The technical boys are rather pleased about it."

"And you too," she smiled.

"Well, you know, Liz, it is rather a thing. All that effort, and all that money—and at last a teeny-weeny little result. Gratifying, if you see what I mean."

She held his face in her hands and kissed him. "I do see."

264

"Reminds me of when I was a kid, I built a radio set. Got the plans out of the *Boys' Own*. Fiddled with it for weeks, burned a hole in the carpet with a soldering iron, all that sort of thing. And then the moment came to plug it in and turn it on—and a voice came out of it. We had lots of radios, great big ones that cost the old man heaven knows how much. But none was like the set I built. Got a great kick out of it."

Sitting beside him on the sofa, with the fire flickering and the tea beside her on a tray, she suddenly felt secure and comfortable enough to talk about themselves; not a word had they said to each other about that since the night when she spoke of being in love with Charles. It was as though they had tacitly agreed on a truce, but the truce was now over.

"You're not going to leave Skelstrand, are you, Andrew?"

"No, old thing, I'm afraid I'm not."

"So then we have to make up our minds about us."

"I suppose so. But there's no hurry, is there? I mean, it's not so bad as it is."

"That's because I haven't seen Charles. We agreed to keep out of each other's way for a bit. But it doesn't solve anything."

Andrew humbly agreed that no, he supposed it didn't.

"A long while ago, when I first met Charles, he said it would be an interesting experiment to mix up the different sorts of England—the industrial sort, and the village sort, and the little town sort. He thought we should all be the better for it and work out a kind of brave new democracy. He saw Skelstrand as a saviour of us all. But what a lot of nonsense it was. It seems to me now as though it was an evil thing to do, Andrew, to disturb old ways of life. Ever since the mill started to build, we have all lowered our standards. It's Henry who drives it home to me. He was such an honourable person, and he stood for something real. And he gradually slipped and slipped away, not stopping at a crime, until I saw him to-day as a half-crazed old simpleton."

She paused, but he said nothing.

265

"And then Charles," she went on, "that hard, tough person who believed in what he was doing, and that it was something worth doing—to build new sources of power that would give men work, and the country strength. He doesn't believe it any more. Or, if he does, he no longer lives up to it. He was prepared to take comfort and ease instead, to work alongside you, and sleep with me. He accepted without protest what two or three years ago would have horrified him.

"And then I myself—I need to talk honestly to you, Andrew. I craved money, and you were a way to get it. I'm not really in love with you, or with Charles either. I once fell in love with a man who died, and for years I was faithful to that. I was going to be so always. And then there was you and money, and afterwards there was Charles, and it all seemed so easy, and to hell with right and wrong. But to-day, when I saw Henry, I saw what was happening to me. And I can't take it, Andrew. If we could go away together, I have a feeling it might work out. But to-day you made steel. I can see what it means to you, and that you are right. Andrew, I wish I were a better person for you. You are the only one who hasn't lowered his standards."

"Perhaps because I didn't have any to lower," he murmured.

"That's not true. I respect you very much."

"Oh, come off it now," he urged, embarrassed.

"What am I going to do?" she asked, despairing.

"Do you want a divorce, Liz?"

"I don't know," she cried, "that's the hell of it."

This conversation went over and over in his mind for days. He could see no answer to it. He thought of having it out with Charles, in a friendly way, but dismissed the notion at last; there was no solution by that. And gradually the problem receded a little into the background, against which so much was happening. There was Skelstrand. From the moment of the first trial run of the machines it seemed to progress at a sharper pace. It had sloughed its scaffolding like an athlete stripping for a race. It came to life. Inside the huge body was the crimson flare of the furnaces in the melting shop, the trundling roar of the overhead ladles from the nozzles of which, now and again, the molten steel vomited into the ingot moulds. And down the vista of the building the glowing metal passed to the first tentative embraces of the slabbing mill, of the great shears, and gradually into a lengthening ribbon along the table. It was, thought Andrew, when he and Charles came in now and again to watch it, a spectacle in two mediums, sight and sound, at the same time a painting and a symphony. For the eyes there was the grey-blue interior lit by daylight through the window bays that seemed dim compared with the dazzling streaks around the edges of the furnace doors, and then the sudden flood of scarlet as the doors were raised and the imprisoned heat burst out; as though for a moment an edge of the sun itself had dipped into the building, tolerable only through dark goggles. The men at the furnaces were swarthy pygmies, sweat-rags gripped between their teeth. And through bay after bay the crimson light moved and shifted as the sample ingot, urged by the buggies, gripped by the rollers, crept at increasing speed and in lengthening dimension along the central line of machinery. For the ears there was the grumble of rollers, the trundle of the roof-slung cranes, clang of metal, growl of furnace, all set against a background of echo from the distant walls.

The spectacle and the noise seized Andrew with a deep excitement, felt but inexpressible. This was achievement. Nothing would equal these tests and trials. There would be the opening day to come—the pomp of that was already being arranged. Afterwards there would be the steady succession of working days on which Skelstrand would roll out, for ever it seemed, its interminable product, engulfing the scrap and the ore and emitting the coils of rolled steel. But that, he knew, would by then be routine to him, not to be compared to these first essays, these moments of bliss in which the huge machine was first started up and was found to work. He understood very well Charles's reply to his remark that at last the thing was beginning.

"For me, it is ending."

"Yes, I see what you mean. The only thing that matters is

to construct something, to build. And the only people who matter are the makers."

"I suppose I do sound a bit pompous, if you put it that way."

"No, Charles, you're right. At the last it's the technicians who count. They decide what sort of a civilization we are going to have."

"Don't see why you should put all the blame on us," joked Neve.

But in Andrew's mind the thought remained. First the inventors, then the technicians; a nation depended entirely on them, in war or peace. Some men fiddled with radar, or made a turbine jet work, or found a new drug, and the nation won a war, or prospered. Others gathered the fruit—the salesmen, the financiers, the artisans. But without the technicians, nothing.

During this last stage of Skelstrand, there was the accumulating anxiety of the police inquiries, slow but seemingly inevitable. Tom Jenkins came now and then to see him in the Gulport office, to keep him in the picture, as he put it. And Andrew was uneasily aware that the picture which the Superintendent was gradually piecing together was going to be complete and awkwardly true. The moment was bound to come when it would include Shard and Melmoth. Indeed, Andrew wondered whether Jenkins did not already know, or guess at, this part of it, was holding back through embarrassment, but in the end would no longer be able to conceal it.

"This young fellow Bruell, now," continued Jenkins, "we've got tabs on him again, and I've half a mind to pull him in, Mr. Gazzard."

"Ah, you've found him, have you?" asked Andrew, seeking something noncommittal to say.

"We have that, sir. He's in Birmingham, rather on his uppers, got himself some sort of job as porter in a cheap hotel. What do you make of that, eh, Mr. Gazzard? Suspicious, that. Young fellow with a good position in an insurance office runs off and takes a menial job. And there's another funny thing. He has linked up with a girl there, girl with not too good a reputation. And who do you think she is, eh? Old Joe Wilkinson's daughter, the one who got into trouble with that labourer from Skelstrand, couple of years ago."

"Oh cripes," was all Andrew could think of to say.

"Yes, funny how it all links up, eh, sir? There's no doubt in my mind he was one of the party. And of course he was thick as thieves with that Communist chap you fired, Papelian, and his wife—she's a strange woman, that. More of the brains of the outfit than he was, if you ask me."

"Are they still in the town, the Papelians?" asked Andrew.

"She is, sir. Mrs. Henty, the vicar's wife, has befriended her, spends a lot of time with her. It's goodhearted of her, but I'm not sure it's wise, and I've a mind to drop a hint to the vicar. As for Papelian, he has gone. We don't rightly know for the moment just where, but there's some report he's up in Newcastle, lying low. If you ask me, I don't think he was one of the party, and we'd have a job to pin much on him, more's the pity.

"No, our chap is young Bruell," the Superintendent went confidently on. "He's the key. And I've a mind to slip across to Birmingham one day soon and have a talk with the young fellow."

Andrew wanted to urge him to do no such thing, but thought it would sound odd, so said nothing.

And then, a week or two later, there was Tom Jenkins again, asking for a quarter of an hour's very private talk, if Mr. Gazzard could spare the time, but rather urgent it was.

Andrew settled him in the chair on the other side of his desk, and Jenkins, looking grave and awkward, started fumbling with a few notes he had on a piece of paper.

"Well, Mr. Gazzard," he began, clearing his throat, "I've been over to Birmingham and had a word with young Bruell. And a most surprising allegation he makes. You're not going to fancy this much, Mr. Gazzard."

"Go on," said Andrew desperately.

"Well, this young chap, he swears that the explosives were stored at Shard, and that Colonel Melmoth knew all about it. It seems a lot of damn nonsense, and I told him so. But he sticks to his story. It's a pity that the Colonel had this illness, and can't come right out and deny it. I'd be easier, I tell you frankly, sir, if he could."

"Well, he is much better than he was," said Andrew, "though certainly not in a fit condition to be worried about a thing like this. Hadn't we better let things lie for a while, Mr. Jenkins, until we can have a word or two with the Colonel?"

"I'm inclined to think so," agreed Jenkins, "but it can't go on for long, sir. Once inquiries have started, they must proceed, if you see what I mean."

"Quite, quite. All the same, it won't hurt to wait a bit, will it? I think that would be best. I'd be grateful if you'd move very cautiously."

"You can rely on that, Mr. Gazzard. I'm attending to this matter personally, you know."

When the Superintendent had gone, Andrew pondered how much longer he could stave off the thing. Not much, probably. He sighed. It could no longer have any repercussions on Skelstrand, the work had gone too far for that, the job was practically finished. As Charles had said, once you've built it, there's nothing can stop it for half a century at least. Frightening to think of, sometimes. Who could say what might happen in the next fifty years, what forces might not gain control of the country? And yet, whoever they were, this monster which he and Charles and a few others had built would go on pouring out steel, a source of strength uninterrupted.

To such moods the best antidote was the remarkable spring weather that broke forth that year. It glowed and shone over the wakening countryside. Everything was vigorous, everything seemed newly strong. Even old Sir Russell, who had lingered far past Dr. Irons's expectations, began to stir a little more vigorously as the new sunshine fell through the large window-panes on to his bed. One day he cursed his nurse, which he had neglected to do since before Christmas. The next day she found him out of bed, just managing to support himself on his feet by grasping heavily at the bedclothes. With a cry of, "Oh, Sir Russell!"

she ran to get him back into bed. But he gasped, "Get me into the chair, you old cow." And would not be denied.

They phoned in haste, of course, for Dr. Irons. When he arrived, he found Gazzard still sitting defiantly in his chair in the sunny window. "I'm better, you scoundrel," he declared.

"Looks like it," agreed Gilbert, "but if you want to stay that way you'd better get back to bed."

Gazzard gestured impatiently with his hand. "I was ill, and now I'm better, in spite of all you could do, eh? That's all there is to it. You tell these stupid women that to-morrow I want my trousers."

The remarkable thing was that, when Gilbert persuaded him back to bed, and gave him a quick examination as he lay there exhausted, he was quite extraordinarily better.

"Well, Doctor?" he whispered, with a little grin.

"One day they'll have to take you out and shoot you. Yes, you are better, though I'd have laid a hundred to one against it. If you show a bit of sense and do what I tell you, we'll have you out and about again in a month."

To Lady Gazzard, hovering at the foot of the stairs, he nodded his reassurance. "He really has made a sudden and quite astonishing recovery."

"Would you say a miracle, Dr. Irons?"

"You could call it so, if you like. I reckon to see an average of ten miracles a year."

"A miracle, I assure you. An answer to prayer."

He smiled kindly at her. He was perhaps the only one who had a soft spot for the prattling old woman; a sympathy for all people who seek to escape from the daily harshness of the world in harmless delusion. "Don't think that lets you out of paying my fee. I have a specially high rate for miracles."

"You are the Earthly Instrument," she assured him, floating happily away to telephone Andrew.

He, naturally, came rushing up to the house, though when he got there his father had fallen into a sleep, and so he could not see him. To his mother he listened tolerantly as she wove a triumphant dance in slow motion through the

271

rooms of the house. Of course it was wonderful. Well, certainly, there was no telling the power of prayer. "And has he really recovered?" he asked, scarcely able to credit it.

"Oh yes, the doctor said so," remarked his sister Cynthia, who was passing through the room. And she added, with a laugh, "Upset your apple-cart, hasn't it?"

He reddened at the injustice of that. But was it unjust? He told himself with what relief he looked forward to passing over to his father the unsolved problems that beset him. Yet did he not also feel a disappointment at having to step down from the job which, it seemed to him, he had not done too badly, all in all? He dearly wanted to hear his father say that he had done it all right; but he much doubted if he ever would.

10

To Sir Russell's annoyance, the doctor was right about the month it would take to get him on his feet; he expected to be back at work within a week.

"You're a bloody old fool, Doc. If I'm better, I'm better."

"Well, let's try," said Gilbert. "You get out of bed and walk over to me."

Gazzard gave him a hard look, then stubbornly tried. But it was no good. Gilbert had to catch him at the second step.

"So now, you old bastard," said Gilbert, "do as I say."

Gazzard grinned feebly at him from the pillow. "You win. But as soon as I'm strong enough I'll give you hell."

From that moment they liked each other, and Gilbert had control. He nursed the old man back from weakness to cheerfulness, from cheerfulness to querulousness.

"Look here, Doctor," Gazzard burst out as he came into the room—Gazzard then sitting in an arm-chair for two hours a day, "what the devil are you going to do about my indigestion?"

"We're winning through. We've got your indigestion back. Give me a week and you'll have cystitis. The day your heart begins to worry you again, you can go to the office."

"What a rogue you are," said Gazzard with satisfaction.

Gradually he gathered about him the news and the people of his life. He had a longer cord put to his bedside telephone so that he could use it in his window chair. And the first man he summoned was Appleton. Gazzard sat hunched in his chair while Appleton told him everything that had happened about Skelstrand. At the end he said, "Not bad."

"It wasn't me, you know," insisted Appleton nervously, "it was your son."

"He wouldn't have got far without you."

"He handled it as well as you could have, Sir Russell," declared Appleton; and then, getting bolder, "he did it better than you could have done, sir. I'm telling you, and I was on the inside of it all. He made rings round 'em."

Gazzard frowned, as though angry. "Nonsense. I know the boy better than you. If there's any strength there, it's his wife. She's shrewd."

"Oh, as to that . . ." began Appleton, and then hesitated.

"What do you mean by that? Come on, spit it out."

"I don't mean anything at all. No, really, it's no concern of mine." And from that he would not be budged.

Gazzard said nothing more then, and took no action. He needed to know more. He said nothing about it, either, when next Andrew came to see him; Andrew anxious and worried because Jenkins the Police Superintendent was pressing closer and closer, almost insisting that he must soon question Colonel Melmoth.

"And the old man had the guts to try to blow Skelstrand up?" asked Gazzard with a chuckle, when he had heard the story.

"Not exactly, Father. But he was far enough in it to land a lot of trouble. And I can't hold Jenkins off much longer, because the old chap really is getting better. He's not very bright—Gilbert doubts whether he'll ever be quite all there again—but he knows what goes on round him. It's Liz I worry about. She's very fond of him."

"Ring through to George in London," said Gazzard after a pause, "and tell him to send Plumstead up to see me."

273

Plumstead was the solicitor Gazzard used when the affair was, as he put it, particularly confidential.

The one person he did not at first ask to see was Elizabeth. She wondered about that, but said nothing. She told herself that she did not in the least care, but she knew very well that she was hurt that he had not asked for her; she had felt herself to have a special place in his thoughts. Not to have him ask for her gave her a sudden feeling of loneliness. For from Henry, whom she visited in the nursing home every day, she was quite cut off. He smiled pathetically at her when she arrived, and he knew who she was. But he had nothing to say to her. He seemed to be lost in a dream, quite happily. And yet, she sometimes thought, Henry could be her escape. She would take him away to some small seaside town, engage rooms, tend him patiently until he died; and after that she did not allow herself to think. That would to some extent assuage her loneliness, to look after him as though he were a child.

Otherwise she did not know what she would do. Go away with Charles? She had seen him only twice since her father's breakdown, and each time he had grimly asked her to. Grimly, that was the word. He had reverted to his first manner.

"I was a fool to think of staying here," he said. "It's not my trade. I make things, not run them."

"Where are you going?"

"I'm not quite sure yet. Out of England. Africa, probably. There's a big construction project in Northern Rhodesia, and I think I can get it, if I go for it. Would you come?"

She flattened out her hands in despair. "Would it be any good? I don't think so, my dear. It sounds all right—cut away from everything here, and all the people we know. Start fresh. But you'd find me an encumbrance. And I. . . ."

"And you?"

"I'd want more of you than you'd give."

"Don't make it a definite no," he suddenly pleaded, urgently. "Take a little time. I need you so much that I despise myself."

But she held off his hands. "And Andrew?" she asked.

"It wouldn't really hurt him, would it? I'd hate to do that. He's all right, Andrew."

"He knows about us."

"Then why in hell has he said nothing to me? Liz, it can't mean anything to him, surely, or he'd have said something."

"You don't understand him. He feels that, because he got me with money, he has no rights."

"Well, has he?"

"Nobody has rights," she burst out. "I long to shout at the whole world to leave me alone."

But afterwards she still did not know whether she would go away with Charles. She drove over to the nursing home again to see her father, and, in his quiet presence, felt calmer.

Then came the summons to old Gazzard. It was a fine morning of summer. He had left his bedroom and, wrapped in a rug, with a cap pulled comically too low on his head, was sitting on the terrace outside the house. She took a deck-chair in front of him and looked at him with an ironical smile. "Well, old man?" she said.

Gazzard laughed. "I should have sent for you before. You do me more good than any of them."

"Why didn't you?"

"Several reasons. One was that I had something to fix first."

"And you've fixed it."

"Yup. The police won't bother your father. I had a quiet word with my Minister, and he had a little chat with his pal the Home Secretary. Case closed."

He grinned. "Pleased?"

"Yes, in a way. Not that it really matters. What could they have done to him now? And it's a bit irritating, the way you behave like God."

"Oh, there's my side of the bargain to come yet. I want Shard, as I told him long ago, for a trainees' college. He can keep the lodge. That old housekeeper'll look after him, won't she? Why doesn't your mother come back?"

"She's an alcoholic."

"So? The way we men suffer. Melmoth's wife's an alcoholic. Mine's got religious frenzy. What's wrong with Andrew's wife?"

"She's a nymphomaniac, I hear."

"Ah, I heard that too. But to get back to Shard. You'll have to do it, your father's in no state for business. I've had my lawyer up here. On the doctor's certificate, you can get power of attorney. Then you sell me Shard. I'll give thirty thousand quid for it, and I'm not haggling. I'll invest the money myself for your father, to show him a safe ten per cent. More than enough for his needs. And when he dies you'll have a decent little income, in case you decide to leave Andrew."

"And if I refuse all this?"

"Nothing. I'm making no threats. But why should you refuse? Have you got anything better to suggest?"

She thought for a moment of the lodging-house in a seaside town in which she had pictured her father and herself; and then of some township in central Africa, and a bungalow where she kicked her heels all day, waiting for Charles to come back from the hydro-electric works at the falls. "No, I can't think offhand of anything better."

"Good, then that's settled. And now I want to talk about Andrew."

"You know all about it, it seems. Did he tell you?"

"Not a word. I just inquired. This isn't a big town."

"You seem to have got around since you got better. By the way, I should have said how glad I am that you are better."

"I'm not."

"But your illness. . . ."

"Oh, that. I was going to get over that anyway, with or without that damn fool doctor. What I mean is my duodenal. That idiot Irons says I haven't got one. As I said to him, I've spent hundreds of pounds in Harley Street *proving* that I have a duodenal ulcer. And this country quack has the impertinence to tell me. . . ."

Elizabeth leaned back her head and laughed aloud. The laughter suddenly eased her tension. Gazzard glared angrily for a moment, then chuckled too. "It's a pity," he said, "that you're going to leave Andrew. You're my sort of person. I get so much fun out of you."

"Who says I'm going to leave him?"

"I do, Liz. It was me who said you were to marry him, remember? And I made a mistake. You're a great girl, but not suited to him."

Elizabeth flared up. "Why do you always run Andrew down? He's fine. You ought to be damn proud of such a son. In spite of all you did to try and spoil him, and in spite of all your jealousy of him, he turned out all right. When you were ill, he ran Skelstrand better than you ever did. Ask anyone who knows. And he did it without being a mean, warped old man. I think more highly of Andrew than anybody I've ever known."

"And so do I, Liz," he answered, smiling gently. "You've got me wrong. I want you to leave him, not for your sake, but for his. I know he's all right. I've been inquiring, and I've found out. He's more than I ever hoped of him. I wouldn't tell him, but I'm as proud as hell. I want something better for him than a wife who goes off with other men."

She shrugged. "Only one thing you've left out of account. He's in love with me."

"Is he?" asked Gazzard, seemingly astonished. "Um, that is awkward."

"And I've a damned good mind to stay with him, just to spite you."

She half-smiled as she said it, and Gazzard laughed, smacking his fist down on the rug. "You ought to have been born early enough to have married me, Liz. What a hell of a time we'd have had."

There were sounds of nurses coming, and Elizabeth got up to go. Gazzard caught her hand and pulled her towards him. "Here, Liz, before you go, tell me one thing. Did you actually hop into bed with Neve?"

"Yes," she said.

"And was it worth it? What was he like, eh?"

She could not help winking at him. "You're a filthy-minded old person," she said, "and, if you must know, it was very satisfactory."

277

He sat back in his chair, cackling with appreciative laughter.

11

THE day on which the hot-strip rolling mill at Skelstrand was to be officially opened was fixed for the first Saturday of September. A royal Duke had promised to perform the ceremony.

The mill had, of course, made several trial runs some weeks earlier. On each occasion this vast machine, with its six thousand attendants, had stirred lazily from sleep, taken deep draughts of ore and scrap, and smoothly emitted, at a speed of more than twenty miles per hour, a ribbon of sheet steel, in neat coils. It was a good machine, and had proved the worth of its ninety millions. Well built. But the official pretence was that those rehearsals had never happened, and that the success or failure of Skelstrand depended on that central moment when the royal Duke would solemnly press the master button that started it into operation.

The preparations for the great day were, of course, lavish. In the town they were left in the hands of a sub-committee, of which the chairman was Councillor Jafet—no longer a railwayman, but warden of the new Skelstrand trainees' college which had been opened at Shard; a job that young Mr. Andrew Gazzard had got for him. Nobody was more ebullient then than Jimmy Jafet, his troubles all forgotten, his belief in the virtues of planning reinforced by the advantages it had brought to him. For Elsie no longer slaved in the grim little Gulport house, but in the warden's flat carved out of the rear quarters of Shard, with trees to look upon. And Kathy was happier there, with country things around her, and no children to jeer her down the street. So the decorations which Jimmy supervised in the streets of Gulport were also something of a personal celebration, and he gave his soul to them. There was bunting at the station entrance, and all up Bridge Street. There was a crimson dais on the platform of arrival, where the local regiment's band would play; and white-painted railings to hold back the crowds outside, where the Duke would inspect the guard of honour of the Boy Scouts. There were loyal messages everywhere, and flags in all the windows, and a red carpet running across the Market Square up the steps of the Town Hall.

"We'll make it a good do," declared Jimmy Jafet, "for Skelstrand deserves well of Gulport."

And he was right. Nobody but would have to admit that, because of the steel works, the town was vastly bigger, more important, more vivid, prosperous. Of course, there were drawbacks. A lot of drinking, a bigger police force to cope with the outbreak of juvenile crime, a string of prostitutes patrolling regularly along the river bank each night and, as Gilbert Irons could testify, an alarming jump in the venereal disease rate. But there was a new modern sewage farm, the streets had been widened and repaved, a penny rate yielded five times as much as formerly, a large dance hall and cinema had been built in the direction of the new town across the river, and the shops flourished.

At Skelstrand itself the arrangements for opening day were in the hands of Bernard Appleton. It was felt that a man who had been a civil servant must know about such things. Bernard at first had tried to dodge this chore; had, indeed, tried to leave Skelstrand altogether, some months earlier, soon after Sir Russell Gazzard had recovered from his illness. The establishment of the mill was now assured, Appleton had nervously told him, and he was no longer necessary. He wanted to leave.

"To go where?" asked Gazzard.

"Oh, I don't know. Haven't decided yet."

"Now look here, Appleton, for a clever man, you're a bloody fool. We both know why you want to get out, don't we? You're still allowing yourself to get worked up because your wife ran off with that scoundrel Heron. But it's done, man. It's finished. Accept it, or you'll go daft. Now listen to me."

And then Gazzard let him into his secret. Once Skelstrand was opened, he was going to retire from the chairmanship and managing directorship in favour of his son. "He has proved himself, Appleton—and a good deal of it was due to your help. I know it. I'm going to reconstitute the board. You can have a directorship. What do you say?"

Appleton wavered and hesitated. It was very good of Sir Russell, very good and generous. Could he have a couple of days to think it over? No, he could not. He would make up his bloody mind there and then.

With trepidation Appleton accepted. And once he had done so he seemed to change as though he had passed a climacteric. He changed in manner, bought himself a lonely house on the outskirts of the town, hired an elderly man and his wife to look after him, began to form a library, and to collect jade. He changed, too, in appearance. He aged, and in ageing acquired a distinction. He became very dignified, and was always addressed with respect, partly because he was also becoming soundly wealthy. He took up, as an exercise, horseriding.

In his hands the preparations for opening day at Skelstrand were both expensive and in impeccable taste.

During the few weeks before opening day Andrew Gazzard was engrossed in the final adjustments to the mill. His time was always with engineers and technicians. He shifted his office from the block in the town, and took temporary quarters out at Skelstrand, from which he rarely emerged in time for dinner.

But in the last week of all he had little to do. It was all done. One evening when he came home he said to Elizabeth, with a little sigh, "Well, it's finished. It's as good as we can make it."

Throughout dinner he seemed nervous, on the point of saying something, but not quite coming to it. They sat with the french windows open, for there was a heat wave, and afterwards they moved on to deck-chairs in the garden while the woman cleared the meal away. She brought them some coffee out, and Andrew fetched brandy. "A sort of celebration," he apologized.

They lit cigarettes, and gazed quietly at the evening sky beyond the trees. The bats began to dart.

"Charles left this morning," he said suddenly.

"Yes, I know. He phoned me to say good-bye."

"I never hated him. Never felt I had the right to, Liz. But I thought at one time that you would be going with him."

"He asked me to. At one time I thought I would."

"Why didn't you?"

"I don't know. I simply don't know, Andrew."

He got up to take off his jacket. "Mind? It's so hot to-night. You look wonderfully cool in that frock thing."

"Like it?" she asked.

"Liz," he said, after a pause, "if you'd like me to cut away from all this, and the two of us go off somewhere, I'm willing."

She said nothing at first, staring into the darkening night. Down the drive she could see the rear light of the woman's bicycle as she went home to her cottage and her husband's supper. He was a cowman. Elizabeth wondered what sort of a life they had, shut away together in the lonely cottage, as she and Andrew were now shut for the night in the house.

"How about Skelstrand?" she asked.

"Well, now the old man's better, there's no particular need for me. No, Liz, I'm lying to you. It's because I'm frightened. He told me this morning that next week he wants to retire, and hand the whole thing over to me. That's what I'm frightened of. You'd be my excuse for ducking it."

It was now, she understood, that he was really lying. She was touched that he should offer, for her, to sacrifice his self-respect. She stood up and held out her hands towards him. "Andrew," she said, "come here."

He jumped from his chair, then hesitated in front of her. She put her arms round him, feeling his shoulders beneath the thinness of his shirt, and held up her mouth to him. "I don't think it matters very much whether we go away or not," she whispered. "Let's go to bed."

Afterwards, when he lay sleeping naked beside her, she studied with gentle curiosity his face on the pillow, in the little light that still seeped through the window from the sky, recalling the urgency with which he had loved her, eyes closed, lips apart. The hands grasping at her breasts, the thrust of his body, the cries that broke from him; and afterwards the shuddering, and the words of foolish love whispered into her ear. She had tried to respond, feeling at least a deep pity for him, a compassionate affection, but she knew that on her side it was pretence, and always would be. Yet perhaps even from pretence something worth while could be contrived.

When she woke in the morning he was gone. But he came in soon, bringing her breakfast on a tray, making a joke of finding her still naked, touching her skin as he put a wrap round her shoulders, and she gently pushing him away. He sat on the end of her bed, smoking a cigarette while she drank her tea.

"Andrew," she said, "you're not giving up Skelstrand. And you're not really frightened of it."

"This morning," he replied with mock drama, "I fear nothing."

"No, don't be an ass. I'm serious about this. I've done you a lot of hurt, but I won't do that."

He put out his cigarette, dropped on his knees beside the bed, and put an arm round her. "Do you mean that you think we can make a go of it?"

"I don't know, my dear. But I think we can try. With a person as good as you, I'd be a fool not to."

He made to kiss her.

"Now look out," she cried, "you'll spill the tea. Behave yourself. And go right down to the office and tell your father you accept. And give him a message from me. Tell him that satisfaction isn't everything."

"Just what does that mean?"

"Never you mind. Just tell him."

When, later that morning, Andrew did tell him, old Gazzard chuckled. He was very merry these days.

"Andrew, my boy," he said, "you're stuck with that woman. We'll all have to put up with it."

"Matter of fact," said Andrew, "I like it that way."

"Well, every man's a fool about something, and you're not doing badly in business. And now, for heaven's sake, stop chattering and get Appleton in. I've just seen the menu for the opening lunch, and it's ghastly. If His Royal Highness

282

don't have dyspepsia after that lot, he's got the stomach of a bull."

Appleton came hurrying in, and the preparations for the great event entered another day of confusion, orders, counter-orders, hope and despair.

Yet, when the day actually arrived, all the doubters took credit for how well everything went.

It was, to start with, a day of magnificent weather. The sun got up in brisk, business-like manner and the sea shone with a high-gloss blue. The train carrying the Duke arrived on time (a little too early, if anything, for the regimental band, which was still adjusting its instruments, but nevertheless rendered a sepulchral National Anthem). The Duke was even more handsome and charming than the women in the crowd had expected. Not a single Boy Scout fainted. Jimmy Jafet, escorting His Highness, was in a Socialist's seventh heaven. The route to the Town Hall (for light refreshments, and, at Jimmy's insistence, to give the Duke a discreet opportunity of relieving himself) was adorned every inch with bunting, and packed on either side with the townspeople. In local opinion, quite as good, if not a little better, than London for the Coronation. So was the route from the Town Hall out to the gates of Skelstrand. Lines of well-scrubbed school-children, frenziedly waving flags. Lines of excited women. Lines of workmen, in Sunday best, ostensibly a bit patroniz-ing, but secretly thrilled. This was one of *their* Dukes, coming to open the mill they had built with *their* hands. From one point at the back of the crowd watched Rosa Papelian, stand-ing with Dorothy Henty, who had been so kind to her, let her live in a room at the vicarage while she recovered from the trap into which she had fallen. It was on Rosa's lips to scorn all this parade and nonsense, and yet she hesitated. Hesitated in the face of such obvious happiness of people. "What is all this?" she asked Dorothy. "Why do they do it? Why do they cheer the things that are fighting to keep them under?"

"I'm afraid," replied Dorothy, "that it's just England, and there's nothing any of us can do about it, except take it as it is. And, if you ask me, it's not bad."

283

England, mused Rosa. Even within herself she could feel a warmth which she despised, and yet could not gainsay. What was she to do? Two days earlier she had had a letter from Papelian. He had got work on a big new trading estate outside Liverpool, and he wrote to her to come, there were opportunities again. Papelian was excited by these opportunities. But would she go? At that moment she doubted it.

When the processional cars reached the gates of Skelstrand, the Duke was greeted by everybody of importance, headed by Sir Russell and Lady Gazzard, the Lord Lieutenant and his lady, the county councillors—everybody. The Duke was graciously impressed with the size of the mill. "And such a wonderful effect," he added, "that cream colour against the sea." Elizabeth Gazzard, at that remark, felt her soul flying backwards to a sand dune. She looked with determination at Andrew standing beside her, felt for his hand, and gave it a comfortable little press.

The furnaces were fully fired, the smoke streaming in the wind from their chimneys. Into the mill, packed with the ranks of the workmen, the Duke was led in procession. He did everything with immense good-nature and calm. He put on goggles and peered into a furnace. He spotted with unerring eye the crane driver who was wearing the Distinguished Flying Medal, and said exactly the right thing to the widow of a county councillor. There were, of course, speeches to be made, and made they were. The Duke's speech was a model of good humour, good taste, and good sense. He made at least four remarks about industry, steel and the export trade which would assure a leading place in the next morning's newspapers. He ate a hearty lunch and congratulated Sir Russell on the wine.

After lunch he moved to a decorated platform, and with ceremony pressed the master button. Over the ceiling lumbered the 300-ton crane, emptying its ladle with scarlet magnificence into the ingot moulds. There was a shout, a cheer. The Duke turned and shook Sir Russell warmly by the hand. One of the county councillors' wives, complaining of the heat but really overstrained emotionally, fainted.

The process had been carefully prearranged along the

whole huge length of the mill, and now the ducal party moved slowly towards the ingot-stripper bay and the soaking pits. The fantastic drama of steel, with its glowing reds and purple shadows, flickered and played all about them. The Duke passed the time with the necessary inquiries about the sick bay and the workmen's canteen.

While this panoply was being conducted inside Skelstrand, the only outward sign of it was the belch of smoke that clung to the top of the furnaces and drifted inland across the blue sky like a banner. It could be seen from Gulport, as it would now always be seen, a signal of prosperity, work and good things. It could be seen from Shard, as it would now always be seen, a symbol of the order that had changed.

Colonel Melmoth, indeed, strolling quietly, leaning on his stick, along the terrace in front of Shard, was at that moment gazing over the tree-tops towards the black smear on the blue sky. He had walked up after lunch from the lodge where Mrs. Cushion looked after him, as he often did, to talk desultorily to the young men who were living now in the house that had been his. The young men, tolerant, were somewhat fond of the half-daft old gaffer who came slowly across the park to pass a few grave, gentle words with them. Nice old boy, they said, no harm in him; and his daughter, young Mr. Gazzard's wife, was certainly a smasher. On this day most of the young men were at Skelstrand, watching the great happenings. But a couple of them, convalescing after an illness, were sitting outside the house, smoking their large new pipes.

Colonel Melmoth gravely saluted them, and they found him a chair, in which he sat stiffly upright, leaning his stick against the arm. "Don't let me interrupt what you were talking about," he said.

They were talking about the opening of the mill. Melmoth was not quite clear just what this was; things were not always quite clear to him now. But the young men were evidently enthusiastic. This was something that, so it seemed to them, was of great advantage for their country. They emphasized that nowhere in Europe, and probably nowhere in the world, not even in the United States, was there quite so modern or so vast an undertaking of this kind under a single roof. They spoke to each other of the technicalities of it, as all young men will. He was reminded of an occasion, some years earlier, when he had listened in silence to technicalities being discussed, with just such enthusiasm, by some other young men sitting in deck-chairs in the open air on a lovely day. One of them, he faintly recalled, was his son Peter, to whom he was paying a visit. The young men were discussing the technicalities of aeroplanes—a discussion interrupted by a sudden alarm which called them springing from their deck-chairs into the sky, which was darkening with shell-bursts. Colonel Melmoth remembered that on that occasion, without a sense of shame, he had covered his eyes with his hands, and wept.

From these recollections he was returned by one of the young men at Shard drawing his attention to the black smoke in the sky.

"That's it," he said, "that's Skelstrand. An achievement, eh, sir?"

Colonel Melmoth nodded. An achievement, he agreed—though with just what he was agreeing he was not quite clear. But an achievement, no doubt, if these young men said so. He let them talk on. The sun was warm on him, and the world seemed free from pain. In these latter, rather muddled days he found himself welcoming the sound of young men's voices once more at Shard. They seemed to give the place a purpose. Now and then he even imagined, momentarily of course, that one of the voices was Peter's. Now and then, by a trick of the light, coming round a corner he almost felt that he saw Peter himself. It always turned out, of course, to be one of these young men, who treated him so courteously that they gave him a kind of happiness—though he was too tired to try to discover about what he was happy. A sense of the way that things went on, continuously, perhaps. But it did not matter. The sun was warm.

By that time, inside Skelstrand a few miles away, the Duke and his party had arrived almost at the end process. The Duke had seen the ingots slabbed and weighed and sheared and trimmed. He had seen them rolled out into a long ribbon of red-hot metal, passing at increasing speed to the finishing stands, through the flying shears, on to the run-out table. The Duke's private interest in hot-strip rolling had waned, but his public alertness was as fresh as ever. And then came the steel, running swift into the coilers. The Duke turned once more to congratulate Sir Russell.

Sir Russell grinned at him. "It's running now, sir. We started this on sand dunes, and now we've got what we wanted. Long after all of us here are dead, it'll be running yet."

The Duke, privately dubious of the taste of this remark, smiled politely.

From behind him Andrew Gazzard was staring fixedly at the running sheet of steel. Elizabeth glanced at him and saw the fascination. She slipped her arm into his, and he looked down, then nodded his head towards the machines.

"Worth doing, eh, Liz?"

"Yes," she said, "worth doing."